Regency

LORDS & LADIES
COLLECTION

Two Glittering Regency
Love Affairs

Rake's Reward
by Joanna Maitland

&

The Unknown Wife
by Mary Brendan

The Regency

LORDS & LADIES

COLLECTION

The Regency

LORDS & LADIES
COLLECTION

*Joanna Maitland &
Mary Brendan*

*M&B™ and M&B™ with the Rose Device
are trademarks of the publisher.
Harlequin Mills & Boon Limited, Eton House,
18-24 Paradise Road, Richmond, Surrey TW9 1SR*

First published in Great Britain in 2003 and 2003

THE REGENCY LORDS & LADIES COLLECTION
© Harlequin Books S.A. 2008

The publisher acknowledges the copyright holders of the individual works as follows:

Rake's Reward © Joanna Maitland 2003
The Unknown Wife © Mary Brendan 2003

ISBN: 978 0 263 86706 0

052-1208

*Printed and bound in Spain
by Litografía Rosés S.A., Barcelona*

Rake's Reward
by
Joanna Maitland

Joanna Maitland was born and educated in Scotland, though she spent most of her adult life in England or abroad. She has been a systems analyst, an accountant, a civil servant, and a director of a charity. Now that her two children have left home, she and her husband have moved from Hampshire to the Welsh Marches, where she is revelling in the more rugged country and the wealth of medieval locations. When she is not writing or climbing through ruined castles, she devotes her time to trying to tame her new house and garden, both of which are determined to resist any suggestion of order.

Rake's Reward features characters you will have already met in *Marrying the Major.*

Readers are invited to enjoy Joanna's website at www.joannamaitland.com

Chapter One

'I have been waiting too many years for this, Hugo. Nothing you can say will make one whit of difference.' Kit Stratton spoke with quiet certainty, smiling calmly across at his elder brother as if they were discussing the turn of a cravat, or a new blend of snuff. He lounged back in his chair, with one immaculately booted leg thrown carelessly over the arm, and watched his brother. It might have been Kit, rather than Hugo, who was the owner of this comfortable, book-lined study.

Sir Hugo Stratton ceased his angry pacing and stood looking down at his brother in obvious exasperation. 'For God's sake, Kit, you must be out of your mind,' Hugo said bitterly. 'Stratton Magna has been in the family for generations, yet you would risk losing it to that old harridan on the turn of a card. You cannot intend to go on with this senseless charade. Besides, it all happened years ago. Cannot you let it lie?'

'No.' Kit shook his head decisively. 'You forget what she did to me...to us. She acted out of pure malice, Hugo, and I swore then that I would have my revenge on her one day. I mean to do it now.'

'And it matters nothing to you that you could lose the family estate in the process? By God, I wish—'

'You wish, now, that you hadn't persuaded John to leave it to me in the first place, don't you, Hugo?'

Hugo coloured a little. 'John will be turning in his grave,' he said. He sounded very near to losing his temper. 'And I...' He gave a snort of disgust. 'What a fool I was. I was the one who persuaded John to leave Stratton Magna to you, instead of to me. I was the one who said that you needed land of your own in England, so that you would stop playing the rake in Vienna. I was the one who thought you would—'

'Settle down and raise a brood of hopeful children?' finished Kit sardonically, rising to refill his glass. 'Never. Unlike you, I have no turn for the infantry, so I am more than content to leave the getting of Stratton heirs to you. You know very well that I have no intention of being caught in parson's mousetrap. Much too close for comfort with Emma. If she hadn't chosen you instead...' He allowed himself a wry smile. He had been the brother who compromised the heiress, but Hugo had been the brother who married her—for Hugo was the brother she loved. Hugo and Emma had been married for five years now, their happiness shadowed only by the deaths of Emma's father and of John, the eldest Stratton brother. Now Hugo was the head of the Stratton family, a baronet, and enormously wealthy. He had no need of the family estate at Stratton Magna.

Unlike Kit.

'Believe me, I do appreciate your generosity,' Kit continued, smiling still. He was determined to retain the upper hand in this encounter. 'I can guess what you were thinking, you and John, when you decided to leave Stratton Magna to me. But, as the oldest surviving brother, *you* should have inherited the family estate, not I. If I had known what you were planning to do, I might have warned you of the risks you were running.'

'Might you?' said Hugo with biting sarcasm. 'If I'd known what *you* were planning to do, I might have held my tongue. As it is—'

'As it is, Stratton Magna is mine now and I can have my revenge on Lady Luce without breaking my word to you. I swore to you, then, that I would never gamble for more than I could afford to lose. Until I inherited the estate, I was in no position to come back to England and face her. Now, I can,' Kit finished simply.

'You could have come back for good when John died,' Hugo said pointedly.

Kit sank back into his chair. It was now well over a year since John and his wife had died in that terrible carriage accident. The family had expected Kit to remain in England after the funeral, but he had not been prepared to oblige them. 'I had…other things on my mind,' Kit said, staring down into his wine. 'Distractions, you might say, one of whom is now in London.' He looked up at his brother. He could see that Hugo's anger was waning now. 'You may be sure that I learned my lesson well over Emma. Resolved then to devote all my attentions to ladies of…er…experience who would pose no threat to my single state.'

'Provided their husbands did not catch you in their beds,' put in Hugo sharply. 'You might not have come off with a whole skin if they had challenged you.'

'As it happens,' Kit said with studied nonchalance, 'I *was* caught out a couple of times. And I did come off with a whole skin.'

'Good God!' Hugo was laughing in spite of himself.

He had always found it difficult to remain furious for long. 'And how many of the poor cuckolds did you kill?'

'None,' said Kit with a bland smile. 'That would have been ungentlemanly. I *was* guilty, after all. And the ladies in question were—'

Hugo shook his head decisively. 'Enough of your diversions, Kit. We are not here to discuss your successes in the petticoat line. Heaven knows, half of Europe seems to be aware of those. We are here to discuss this preposterous proposal of yours. You cannot be serious. You could lose everything to that woman. And after the last time, surely you—'

'After the last time, I have absolutely no intention of losing to her,' Kit said emphatically, rising to his feet. He put a hand on his brother's arm. 'Nothing you can say will change my mind, Hugo. You cannot imagine how demeaning it was for me to be forced to come to you, cap in hand, to beg for the money to pay those debts. I knew that you would have to take it from the dowry of the lady I had compromised. Can you imagine how that felt? I may have been only twenty-two at the time, but, believe me, Hugo, it rankled. And it rankles still. I was a hair's breadth away from utter disgrace.'

Hugo paused, gazing up at the huge portrait of Emma above the fireplace. He clearly had his temper well in hand now. 'I do understand, Kit,' he said at length. 'But it was all a very long time ago. Everyone has forgotten what happened. You will simply stir it all up again if you challenge the woman. Let it lie.'

'No. I cannot. I have spent five years waiting for this moment and I intend to relish it.' He raised a hand as his brother made to speak. 'Don't be so ready to assume that I will lose this time. Believe me, I have no intention of doing so.'

The corner of Hugo's mouth twitched slightly. The long scar on the side of his face was barely noticeable now, except where it twisted his smile. 'And precisely how do you plan to ensure that, brother? Are you become a Captain Sharp in your time on the continent?'

Kit smiled ruefully. 'No, though I have learned to recognise them pretty well. I have no need to cheat. All these years of play have improved my game immeasurably. You know well enough that I was always lucky with the cards and the bones. Nothing has changed there. I am just more practised than before. I have no doubt that I shall win...especially as I hear that Lady Luce seems to have lost her own knack for the cards. Did I not hear that she is called "Lady Lose" nowadays?'

Hugo nodded, somewhat unwillingly.

'Good. That improves the odds even more. Lady Luce tried to ruin me then. Would have done it, too, if you had not paid my debts. I owe you. And I owe her. With Stratton Magna at my back, I shall see her in the gutter. And I shall rejoice at her downfall.'

Hugo was shaking his head despairingly, as if he did not understand how Kit could harbour such hatred for another human being. And for so many years. But if Hugo had spent years exiled on the continent, he too might have just such a ruthless attitude to Society. Kit had long ago concluded that people were there to be used for his own advantage. It did not pay to become close to anyone. That way lay disaster.

The third Earl Luce was pacing his mother's opulent drawing room. 'Mama,' he said at last, 'you cannot continue like this.'

The Dowager Countess took a generous mouthful of

best madeira, savouring it as she swallowed. 'For God's sake, William, stop behaving like a caged elephant.'

The Earl stopped abruptly. He glanced at his reflection in the ornate, gilt-framed mirror—he was nothing like as large as an elephant. How dare she suggest anything so offensive?

She raised her lorgnette and peered at him. That piercing stare had unnerved him since he was five years old. Now, more than forty years later, it still did.

'Continue like *what,* precisely?' asked Lady Luce acidly.

Her son cleared his throat, ready to do battle on the one subject where he knew he had the whip hand. He was intending to enjoy this. 'You cannot continue to gamble with money you do not have, Mama,' he began. 'You—'

Lady Luce used the arms of her chair to push herself into a standing position. Even then, she was considerably shorter than her son, and looked more than twice as wide in her old-fashioned hooped skirts. 'And who, pray, is going to stop me?' she said in an awful voice.

'I am,' he said, as stoutly as he could, but avoiding her gimlet eye. 'I cannot afford to continue to pay your debts, Mama. You seem to forget that I have a family of my own to keep.'

His mother snorted. 'How could I forget? Never seen so many confounded brats. You're as bad as Clarence.'

'Mama! How can you say such a thing? It is highly improper for a lady to mention illegitimate children, even if their father is a royal duke. And you know very well that I have never been unfaithful to Charlotte.'

'No, because no other woman would look twice at you,' snapped his mother, 'even if you did have the money to dangle after them. It's quite your own fault that you have sired ten children. And I do not see why my style of living should be curtailed to pay for them, just because you cannot keep your—'

'*Mama!* Please!'

His mother looked hard at him and smiled nastily. She was clearly enjoying his embarrassment. One day, he would…

He turned his back on her and went to the window. If he did not have to look at her, it would be easier to tell her what she was to do. 'My children are not in question here,' he said, trying to keep his temper under control. 'My father provided you with a very generous jointure. You do not even have to pay for the upkeep of this house. You have the means to live in considerable comfort, but you choose to gamble instead, relying on the assumption that I will always stand behind your debts.'

'Balderdash,' said his mother roundly. 'You left me hanging in the wind when—'

Lord Luce spun round furiously. 'That was five years ago, Mama, and it only happened once. You knew that I could not raise such a huge sum just then.' He raised his hand to stop her from speaking. 'Besides,' he went on rapidly, 'you came about soon enough, when you won all that money from Kit Stratton, did you not? You had no need of my backing.'

'Did I not? I'll have you know, you miserable apology for a whelp, that—'

'No, Mama, you will not. You will listen to me. You will learn to live within your means. If you come to me just once more to pay your gambling debts, it will be the last time, I promise you. I shall let it be known that I will not pay in future. And who would accept your vowels then?'

'You would not dare,' she spat. 'Your name would—'

'Balderdash,' he said, enjoying the feel of the word on his lips. Let her have a taste of her own medicine. 'Society will agree that I have been too indulgent for too long. You may be an "original," Mama, but Society tires of such entertainments in the end. I am the head of the family and I mean what I say.'

His mother stamped over to him and poked him in the chest. 'Do you, William? Do you, indeed? Then understand this. I shall behave exactly as I please. If I choose to gamble, I shall do so, and nothing you can say shall prevent me. I shall stake my jointure and leave all my other bills unpaid. And I shall make a point of telling all of London that the Luce estate stands behind me, since otherwise I should end up in the Fleet. How would that please your sense of propriety, eh? The Dowager Countess Luce in debtors' prison because her son would not pay her debts. What would all your fine friends think to that? And your sons, too. I am sure it would make for splendid sport at Eton.'

The Earl's shoulders slumped. She had won again. She was not a woman, she was a witch.

'Well?' she said.

'Mama, you must understand that I cannot afford it,' he said, adopting a pleading voice. 'The income from the estate has been poor ever since the end of the war. If there are any more major calls on me, I shall have to start selling the unentailed properties. Surely you cannot wish me to do that? It is all I have to leave to the younger boys.'

Lady Luce grunted. 'I might think about it,' she said grudgingly.

His tactics had worked. That was as near to a concession as he had ever won from her. 'Perhaps if you had another interest, something to divert your mind—' he began.

'There's nothing wrong with my mind,' she snapped.

'No, of course not,' he said, trying to grapple with the brilliant idea that had just struck him, 'but…a young companion might be just the thing.'

She fixed him with a steely gaze.

He quailed a little but continued. He could not refuse an opportunity to bridle the Dowager, however temporarily. 'Let me look about for someone suitable,' he said. Then he added, as a clincher, 'I will undertake to pay all the costs of her keep. Your jointure shall remain at your sole disposal, as in the past.'

His mother gave him a very strange look. Then, to his surprise, she nodded briefly. 'Yes, you are right. I could do with a young thing about the place.'

Victory! The Earl bowed over his mother's hand. His wife's bosom friend, Lady Blaine, would be bound to know of a suitable candidate. He would enlist her aid this very day. Now, he must make a speedy exit before his mother changed her mind.

He had just reached the door when she said, airily, 'Just make sure she plays a good hand of piquet, William. At my age, I do not have time to start teaching gels how to play cards.'

'Miss Beaumont?'

Marina spun round. She was being addressed by a liveried footman who was taking no pains to conceal his disdain at the sight of her shabby travelling costume and worn bonnet. Marina raised her chin a fraction. She might be poor and ill clad, but she was most certainly a lady. She would not allow herself to be daunted by a mere servant.

She narrowed her eyes as she looked at the young man. She was almost as tall as he was, she noted absently. 'I am Miss Beaumont,' she said in a frosty voice.

The footman could not hold her stern gaze. After a moment, he looked away. 'Will you come this way, miss?' he said, indicating the carriage that stood waiting to convey her across London to her employer's house.

It was only a small victory—but it mattered to Marina. If she was to live in Lady Luce's house, she must ensure that the Dowager's servants treated her with respect. 'Please see that my baggage is stowed safely,' she said, pointing to the two old valises that contained everything she owned. The footman did as he was bid, picking them up as though they weighed nothing at all. 'Thank you,' Marina said with a smile.

The footman seemed taken aback for a few seconds, as if he were suddenly seeing a completely different person. Then he remembered his place and helped Marina into the carriage where she sank back against the cushions with a sigh of relief. She had arrived in London, at last. And in a very short time, she would be making her curtsy to the Dowager Countess Luce, the old lady who wanted a gay young companion to brighten her declining years. Marina had decided during the journey from Yorkshire that she could fill the role pretty well. She had often acted as companion to her grandmother in her final years, reading to her, playing or singing for her, even playing cards with her. In those last years, Grandmama had become most exacting, almost as if she were still entitled to be treated as the sister of a viscount. Lady Luce could not be any worse. Reclusive elderly ladies were all much the same, weren't they?

Marina closed her eyes, trying vainly to shut out the noise and the overpowering smells. She had never imag-

ined that London could be so full of raucous sounds—
the cries of hawkers, each trying to outdo his neighbour,
the shouts of draymen anxious to make their way
through the bustle of traffic, the ring of horses' hooves
and carriage wheels, the underlying hum of a huge, pul-
sating city. At home, she had been used to the sounds
and smells of farmyard animals, the cries of wild birds,
and the howl of the wind across the moors. Nothing like
this. She resisted the temptation to hold her nose or put
her hands to her ears. If she was to live in London as
companion to Lady Luce, she would have to become
accustomed. She might as well start now.

Armed with this new resolution, Marina sat up and
looked out of the window. She had no idea where she
was, but the streets seemed to have become a little qui-
eter. They were certainly more genteel than before:
fewer hawkers, more gentlemen's carriages. The houses
had large windows and imposing entrances, some
flanked by columns like a Greek temple. This was much,
much grander than anything she had known in Yorkshire.

While Marina was studying the architecture on one
side of the street, the carriage drew up at a house on the
other. She had arrived! The footman, more deferential
now, had jumped down to open the door on the far side
and stood ready to help her out. As she stepped down,
the front door was opened by a stately old man in black
who was almost completely bald. What little hair he still
possessed was white as snow and sat round his pate like
a frill of cream round a pink pudding. He looked like
something out of a fairy tale, Marina decided, though he
should have been wearing a wizard's robe rather than a
butler's uniform.

'Welcome to London, Miss Beaumont,' the butler said

in an expressionless voice. 'Her ladyship is waiting for
you upstairs in her drawing room. Will you come this
way, please?' He turned and began to lead the way towards the imposing staircase.

Not now! Not yet! Marina looked down at her travel-
stained clothing and her darned gloves. She needed time
to make herself presentable before she was introduced
to Lady Luce. The Dowager would take one look at her
in this state and send her back to Mama by the first
available coach.

Marina took a deep breath and paused just inside the
door. 'I am sure her ladyship does not wish to meet me
until I have rid myself of the dust of the journey,' she
said in a voice that surprised her with its steadiness.
'Have the goodness to bring me to a room where I may
wash and change my dress first. The footman may bring
my valises.' Marina looked back to where the footman
was extracting her luggage from the carriage.

The butler stopped short, then turned back and stared
at her in apparent amazement for a few seconds. Finally,
he coughed and resumed his earlier vacant expression.
'As you wish, miss. Will you come this way? Charles,
bring Miss Beaumont's bags up to her room straight
away.'

'Yes, Mr Tibbs,' replied the footman quickly, hoisting
both bags with one arm so that he could close the front
door noiselessly behind him.

Marina smiled to herself, a very little. She had just
learned her second lesson. And so had Lady Luce's servants.

Chapter Two

Marina looked round her small, sparsely furnished bed-chamber. She supposed she should be glad that she had not been banished to the attics, with the servants. As a lady's companion, she would be neither servant nor gentry, but something indeterminate in between. She must maintain her distance from the servants. Lady Luce and her guests would, in turn, maintain their distance from the companion. Marina would be alone.

The butler had informed her, in a somewhat fatherly manner, that she had been given a bedchamber on the same corridor as her ladyship's so that she would be within easy reach, should Lady Luce have need of her services at any time. Marina had deduced that she was to be at her ladyship's beck and call, twenty-four hours a day.

She shrugged her shoulders. What else had she expected? Her own grandmother had been equally exacting—and more than a little querulous towards the end of her life. Marina would just have to summon all her reserves of patience and understanding, and set about ministering to another old lady's whims.

I shall pretend she is my own grandmother, Marina

promised herself as she changed her gown. I learned forbearance then. I can surely do the same for another demanding old lady, especially as, on this occasion, I am being paid for my trouble.

She smiled at the thought of the money she would send to her mother the moment she received her first wages. Mama had said Marina would need to provide for her wardrobe, but surely she could manage with what she had brought from Yorkshire? A companion did not need many gowns to accompany her mistress when she took the air, or to wind her lady's knitting wool. Marina had long ago decided to confine herself to what she already had. Her first duty was to her own family.

She considered her image in the glass that had been thoughtfully provided. It would do. Her grey gown, though creased from its time in her valise, was clean and neat, and set off with a fresh white collar. She looked like a lady, not a servant, she decided, with a small smile of satisfaction. Her dark brown hair had been neatly re-braided and pinned to the back of her head. Her newly washed complexion glowed with health. Her head was bare—she might be almost at her last prayers but, at twenty-three, she was not yet condemned to the spinster's cap—and she wore no jewellery except the mourning ring that had been on her finger almost since the day she had learned of her father's death. She nodded at her reflection in the mirror. Lady Luce would see, in her, the model of a demure, biddable lady's companion, well worth the wage she was to be paid. The Dowager would have no reason to send Marina back to her family. That must be avoided at all costs, for Mama desperately needed every penny Marina could spare.

And now she must go down to meet the lady who

would have the ordering of her life for months, perhaps years to come.

Marina took a deep breath, straightened her shoulders and made her way out into the corridor. Tibbs, the butler, was hovering not far away, waiting for her.

'This leads to her ladyship's chambers,' he said, indicating a door near the head of the staircase. 'No one else sleeps on this floor, except when her ladyship has guests. Though now there is yourself, miss,' he added, apparently as an afterthought.

'Does not the Earl stay here when he is in London?' Marina asked.

'No, miss. Her ladyship and her son...' He coughed. 'His lordship has his own house in town. He always stays there.'

'I see,' said Marina. It was understandable that a grown-up son would not wish to live under the eye of his mother, even for a day or two. The butler seemed to have been about to say something about the pair, something that had sounded for all the world like the beginning of backstairs gossip. Marina, not being a servant, should deliberately shut her ears to it. And yet she found herself wondering about the Earl and his relationship with his mother. Was she too demanding for his comfort? Elderly ladies often were. And a gentleman's patience could be quickly exhausted.

The butler led Marina down to the floor below and to a room at the front of the house. With a grand gesture, he threw open the door and announced, in stentorian tones, 'Miss Beaumont, your ladyship.'

Marina passed through the door that Tibbs was holding and heard it close quietly at her back. This sumptuous straw-coloured drawing room seemed to be empty.

She could see no one at all. But surely…? The butler had seemed in no doubt…

Marina hesitated by the door.

'Don't just stand there, girl. Come into the light where I may see you.' The sharp voice came from the depths of a chair by a large window overlooking the street.

Marina moved forward to find the source of that peremptory command. Only when she had reached the far side of the room could she see that the voice had issued from a tiny figure who was dwarfed by the chair she sat in. Lady Luce was richly dressed in plum-coloured silk, but in the style of more than forty years earlier, with wide skirts and an abundance of fine lace at her throat and wrists, and a powdered wig on her head. Although her skin was dry and wrinkled, the delicate lines of her bones showed that she had once been very beautiful. Now she resembled nothing so much as a miniature exotic fruit, so shrivelled and fragile that it might shatter if it was touched.

'Good gad, they've sent me a beanpole,' Lady Luce exclaimed.

Marina could feel herself blushing. It had been a matter of regret throughout her adult life that she had inherited her father's height and build. Her slight figure made her seem even taller than she actually was. Compared with Lady Luce, she must seem a veritable giantess. Marina curtsied. 'How do you do, ma'am?' she said calmly, trying to manage a smile for the tiny—and extremely rude—Dowager Countess who was to be her employer.

The Dowager did not immediately reply to Marina's polite greeting. She was looking her up and down, her sharp old eyes missing nothing of her new companion's dowdy appearance. 'Thought one of the Blaines would be better turned out,' she said. 'Wouldn't give a gown like that to a scullery maid.'

This was not a good start to their relationship. The Dowager must be instantly disabused of the idea that Marina was 'one of the Blaines,' or that she could afford to be better dressed. Marina knew she must set matters straight between them, even if Lady Luce sent her packing as a result. She had no choice.

'I think you must be labouring under a misapprehension, ma'am,' Marina began. 'My name is Beaumont, not Blaine. I am only distantly related to the Viscount's family, through my grandmother, but she was not acknowledged by them, not after her marriage.'

'Hmph,' snorted the Dowager. 'Nothing "distant" about it. Your mother and the new Viscount are first cousins, are they not?'

'Yes, but not—'

'You're a Blaine,' said the Dowager flatly. 'The old Viscount's father was a tyrant and a blackguard, but that don't change the bloodline, not in my book. Your grandmother was daughter to one Viscount, and sister to the next. You're a Blaine, all right.'

It was clearly going to be difficult to argue with Lady Luce, perhaps even to get a word in, Marina decided. But, on this delicate subject, she must try.

'Forgive me, ma'am,' she began again, 'but you must understand that the Beaumonts have never been acknowledged by the Viscount's family, not even when my grandmother's brother succeeded to the title.'

'That's because he was just like his father,' interrupted the Dowager, with a grimace, 'which was only to be expected, since all the Blaine men—' She broke off to scrutinise Marina's face for a moment and then said, 'I see you know nothing about your noble relations, young lady. Well, I may choose to enlighten you—perhaps—one day. But there are other, more pressing matters. For a start, we must do something about that frightful monstrosity you are wearing.'

Worse and worse, thought Marina, but before she had a chance to say a word in defence of her wardrobe, the Dowager was laying down the law on dress, just as she had on the subject of blood.

'It is fit only for the fire,' pronounced Lady Luce. 'Or the poorhouse. Though, even there, I dare say the women would turn their noses up at it. Have you nothing fit to be seen, girl?'

'I do have one evening gown, ma'am. Apart from that, I have very few gowns, all similar to this one. What spare money we have must be spent on my brother's education. Harry is at Oxford,' she added, with sisterly pride, 'and he is destined for the Church.'

'Don't approve of spending every last farthing on boys,' said Lady Luce quickly. 'You educate them, and where does it get you? Eh? Take your every penny and fritter it away. If it's not land drainage, or enclosures, or something equally unnecessary, it's fast living and loose women.'

'Harry does not—'

Marina's protest was cut short by another disapproving snort. 'Not *your* brother. Don't know the first thing about *him*. He may be a pattern-card of rectitude, for all I know. But the sons of noble families...' Lady Luce shook her head. Her message was clear. The sons of noble families were not to be trusted with money. Presumably that also applied to her own son?

'A lady has to be independent enough to lead her own life, in just the way she wants,' said Lady Luce, warming to her subject. 'Especially once she is widowed,' she added meaningfully.

At last, Marina understood. Lady Luce's unusual views on female independence were clearly to be applied to her own case, and probably to that case only. It was unlikely she would care about the plight of Mama, or any other gently bred widow who had fallen on hard times.

'You give 'em an heir and your duty is done,' said Lady Luce. 'Least a husband can do in return is to provide for a comfortable widowhood. But husbands seem to think that the heir should have charge of everything, even his mother!' She stopped, looking up at Marina once again. 'And just what do you think you are laughing at, young madam?'

Marina had not realised she had begun to smile at the old lady's spirited defence of her own interests. 'I beg your pardon, ma'am,' she lied quickly, 'I was thinking only that you reminded me of my own dear grandmother. I miss her greatly.'

'Balderdash,' said Lady Luce roundly. 'You were thinking that I was talking dangerous nonsense, but that I could be forgiven my revolutionary views because of my great age. Well? Were you not?'

Taking a deep breath, Marina said, with sudden resolution, 'Yes, ma'am, I was. I admit it. But I see now that your arguments should not be dismissed on such spurious grounds. You are obviously a redoubtable opponent, for woman or for man, and your great age has nothing to do with the case.'

Lady Luce gasped. For a second, Marina held her breath, thinking how foolhardy she had been to speak so. The Dowager would ring a peal over her head and then despatch her post-haste back to Yorkshire. But nothing of the sort happened. Her ladyship stared sharply into Marina's face, now mercifully straight, and then said, with a crack of laughter, 'Yes, you'll do. Once we have done something about your wardrobe, of course. I shall see to that tomorrow. You are not fit to be seen as you are. Turn round.'

Obediently, Marina turned her back.

'Again,' said the Dowager.

Marina turned to face her once more.

'Sit down, girl,' said Lady Luce, nodding towards a low stool at the side of her chair. 'It's giving me a stiff neck trying to look up all that way.'

Marina allowed herself a small smile as she obeyed. The Dowager's bark was extremely frightening, but Marina now fancied that her ladyship's bite was a little lacking in teeth, like a pampered old lapdog, yelping and snapping uselessly at every visitor.

'Now, Miss Beaumont. Tell me about yourself,' began her ladyship. She was obviously pleased to see that Marina, once seated on the stool, was shorter than she was. 'What do they call you?'

'Marina, ma'am,' replied Marina, puzzled. How could Lady Luce have agreed to employ a companion when she did not even know her given name?

'Marina. Hmm. Unusual name, is it not?'

'I am not sure, ma'am. I was named for my father's mother, I believe.'

'Foreign, was she?' Lady Luce's voice betrayed her distaste.

'I understand so. I never knew her. My father's family had served in the army for generations. All the women followed the drum.'

'Your mother, too?' Lady Luce's voice had a clear undertone of disapproval now. She probably felt that such behaviour was not appropriate for a niece of the Viscount Blaine.

'Yes, ma'am. But after the Peace of Amiens, my father decided that his wife would be better in England, since my brother and I were so small. We settled in Yorkshire.'

'And your father? What was he?'

'He was a captain in the 95th Rifles, ma'am. He died nine years ago, at the battle of Ciudad Rodrigo, along with my uncle.'

Lady Luce nodded in understanding. Marina wondered whether she, too, had lost loved ones in the wars. Many titled families had.

'But your mother was provided for?' Lady Luce clearly had no qualms about enquiring into the most intimate detail of her companion's circumstances. And she would doubtless persist until she received her answer.

'No, ma'am. At least, not well.' That was true, though it was not the whole truth. 'My mother supplemented our income by taking pupils.' Seeing her ladyship's look of surprise, Marina added, 'My mother is very well educated, ma'am. Her father was a great scholar. He educated his daughter exactly as he educated his son.' She smiled fondly. 'Unlike my mother, my uncle had no inclination for scholarship. He was army mad, almost from his cradle. A great disappointment to my grandfather.'

'Hmph,' said Lady Luce. It was not clear whether she approved or not. 'And who was he, this scholar grandfather of yours?'

Marina was beginning to dislike her ladyship's sustained questioning very much, but she did not think she could refuse to answer. 'He met my grandmother when he was the Viscount Blaine's private secretary, I believe, ma'am.'

Her ladyship smiled suddenly. 'And he was remarkably handsome, too, was he not? Tall, with fine features
and dark hair, and a beautifully modulated speaking
voice?'

'Why, yes. Grandmama did describe him in much that
way,' Marina replied. 'Did you know him, ma'am?'

Her ladyship continued to smile, a rather secretive
smile, and a faraway look came into her eye. 'Aye, I
knew James Langley. All the girls were mad for him, I
remember. Handsomest man we had ever seen…but
quite unsuitable…quite.' She looked sharply at Marina
as if looking for some resemblance. 'Your grandmother
kicked over the traces for his handsome face, did she,
eh?'

Marina blushed and nodded dumbly. Her ladyship's
salty turn of phrase was not what she was used to in
Yorkshire with her very proper mama.

'And her father cast her off as a result?'

Marina nodded again.

'Just what I'd expect from that family. Don't hold
with such cavalier treatment. Don't hold with it at all.'
Lady Luce shook her head so vigorously that a little
cloud of powder rose from her wig. 'If I had had a
daughter—'

The door opened to admit the butler. Bowing stiffly,
he announced, 'His lordship is below, your ladyship, and
begs the favour of a few minutes' conversation with
Miss Beaumont.'

'Does he, indeed?' said Lady Luce, frowning.

Marina was astonished. What on earth could Lady
Luce's son want with the companion?

'I suppose I must humour him, in the circumstances,'
her ladyship said, grudgingly. 'Conduct Miss Beaumont
below, Tibbs.'

Wonderingly, Marina followed the butler out of the room and down the staircase to the bookroom on the ground floor. Perhaps the Earl wished to look over his mother's companion, to decide whether he thought her suitable? But what if he did not? Marina doubted that her son's objections would make any difference to Lady Luce, not once she had made up her mind.

The Earl was standing by the window, looking out into the street. He was several inches shorter than Marina, and noticeably corpulent. Unlike his mother, he wore the newest fashions, even though tight pantaloons did not flatter his figure at all.

He waited until the door had closed before turning. He made no move towards Marina. And he did not attempt to shake hands.

Marina understood. To the Earl, she was only a servant. She curtsied, waiting for him to speak.

Like his mother, he surveyed her keenly. Marina caught his lofty expression and responded automatically by lifting her chin. Had not Lady Luce just insisted she was a Blaine?

'Miss Beaumont,' he said, in an affected drawl, 'you have arrived at last. We had looked to see you somewhat sooner than this.'

Marina did not attempt to make excuses for the timing of her arrival. His lordship might travel post, but she could not afford such luxury. She looked calmly across at him, waiting.

'However, it is of no moment now. We have more important matters to discuss.'

Marina's surprise must have been evident in her face, for he said, 'I take it Lady Blaine did not tell you about my requirements?'

'No, sir. Lady Blaine said nothing at all about the nature of the post. She wrote only—'

The Earl clearly had no interest in what Marina wished to say, and no compunction about interrupting a lady who was no better than a servant. 'What her ladyship wrote is of no interest to me, Miss Beaumont. What matters here are the instructions that I shall give you. Your role in this household is to prevent my mother from indulging in extravagant foolishness. No doubt you have heard that she has a predilection for gambling?'

Marina shook her head. 'I know nothing at all about her ladyship's manner of living, sir.'

The Earl snorted. He sounded worse than his mother. 'I see,' he said. 'Very well. The facts are these. My mother is overfond of gambling. On occasion, she has been known to risk considerably more than she can afford. Your role, Miss Beaumont, is to ensure that she does not.'

Marina gulped. How was she supposed to ensure such a thing? Surely Lady Luce would never have agreed to have her son's agent foisted on her? 'I do not understand, sir,' Marina said.

'It is quite simple,' snapped the Earl. 'Even a woman should be able to grasp it. I am employing you to stop my mother's gambling. The means I leave to you.'

Ignoring his rudeness, Marina tried to grapple with his astonishing statement. 'I had understood that I was employed by the Dowager Countess,' she began, but she was permitted to go no further.

'Ostensibly, but all the costs of your position fall to me. *I* am employing you. And your role will be as I have described.'

Marina swallowed hard. The task was impossible, surely? And the Earl was obnoxious. 'Is the Dowager

Countess content with this arrangement?' she asked quietly. It would sound presumptuous for a mere companion to speak so, but the question had to be asked.

The Earl was beginning to look angry. 'I require you to say nothing to her on the subject. If you do, you will be discharged instantly.'

Marina paled.

Lord Luce smiled nastily as he continued, 'Remember, Miss Beaumont, that it is I, not my mother, who pay you. And that it is to me you will answer, if you fail in your appointed task. That is all I wish to say to you. You may go.'

There was nothing more to be said. Marina automatically dipped a brief curtsy and left the room. Her heart was pounding madly. She understood at last why Lady Blaine had written that short, cold letter to Mama. At the time, Marina had wondered why her haughty relation should suddenly offer to recommend her to a comfortable position, after decades of estrangement. But since pride was a luxury that the Beaumonts could not afford, Marina had had to accept the crumbs from the rich man's table. Now, too late, she could see that the crumbs were laced with poison.

She was trapped. And she was alone in London. She could turn to no one for advice. If she was loyal to Lady Luce, the Earl would dismiss her. If she acted as the Earl's instrument, Lady Luce would soon suspect and send her packing. After all the money that had been spent on her passage to London, it seemed she would soon become a burden to Mama all over again. She would have squandered her only chance to help her family.

She shook her head defiantly. No. She must do her duty. Somehow, she must find a way to satisfy both the

Earl and his mother, and to earn the money to send home
to Yorkshire to keep Mama from penury.

She must.

She would.

Chapter Three

'Good gad! I thought you said you had an evening gown. Is that the best you can do?'

Face flaming, Marina stood rigid as the Dowager's sharp little eyes travelled over every detail of her drab appearance. She was wearing the best of her meagre Yorkshire wardrobe, a dove-grey gown made high to the neck, but relieved with a tiny ruff of precious lace. It was plain, and not in the least fashionable, but it was clean and neat. And, unlike most of Marina's other gowns, it bore no visible evidence of mending.

Lady Luce's distaste was manifest in the narrowing of her eyes and the slight thinning of her lips. She rose from her chair, shaking out her wide silken skirts. The fall of fine lace at her bosom quivered indignantly. 'I suppose that *is* your evening gown?' she said in withering tones.

'You are correct, ma'am,' replied Marina, refusing to drop her gaze. She would not be made to feel ashamed of her appearance. Her dress was perfectly adequate for a near-servant. 'This is quite my *best* gown,' she added daringly, remembering the lesson she had learnt when she first arrived. The Dowager relished a sharp opponent.

Lady Luce gave a snort which might have been suppressed laughter. With a tiny shake of her powdered head, she said, 'We shall see to your wardrobe tomorrow, as I promised. Don't suppose it will matter much tonight. Shouldn't be taking you to Méchante's in the first place, of course, not a gel like you.' She turned for the door, talking all the while. 'Too prim and proper by half. Just what I'd expect from William.'

'Excuse me, ma'am,' began Marina, daring at last to interrupt her ladyship's meanderings, 'but who is Méchante and why—?'

'Why should you not go there?' Lady Luce spun round to face Marina. She seemed remarkably nimble for her years. Her eyes were full of wicked laughter. 'My dear, Méchante—Lady Marchant—is not a proper person for a lady to know. She is the daughter of a Cit, and her history is…ah…more than a little colourful, besides. Most of the company at her card party tonight will be male. As to the *ladies* you may meet there…' She chuckled. 'Suffice it to say that you would do best to pretend never to have set eyes on them. You would be wise to make yourself as unobtrusive as possible. Try to blend into the background.' She looked Marina up and down once more. 'In that gown, it should not be difficult.'

Marina stared, but Lady Luce was already making for the door which opened, as if by magic, just as she reached it. The butler stood in the hall, waiting. No doubt he had been listening to every single word. Before morning, Marina's plight would be the talk of the servants' hall. She could feel herself flushing yet again as she followed Lady Luce to the door, head held high and eyes fixed on the Dowager's ramrod-straight back. The servants might mock in private, but they would never

detect the slightest sign of weakness in Marina's outward
behaviour.

Throughout the short journey through the still-bustling
streets, Marina worried at the information about the dubious Lady Marchant and her card party. Méchante—
Marina knew it meant naughty, or wicked, in French. If
the lady's past was as colourful as the Dowager had
hinted, she probably deserved her nickname.

Marina quailed inwardly at the thought of this first
test. Why did it have to come quite so soon? She began
to rack her brains for ideas to stop the Dowager's gambling but came up with nothing practicable. If she
claimed she was ill, the Dowager would simply send her
home. If she tried to intervene in the game itself, the
Dowager might well dismiss her on the spot. And if she
betrayed the Earl's instructions, the Dowager would
probably stake every penny she had, and more, just to
spite him, for she had made no secret of the fact that
she despised him. Marina chewed at her bottom lip. It
did not help.

'Pull yourself together, child,' said the Dowager
sharply. 'Méchante won't eat you, you know. You might
even enjoy yourself…get rid of that Friday face. You *do*
play cards, I take it?'

'Yes, ma'am,' replied Marina quickly. As a companion, she might be lacking in many ways, but she could
certainly hold her own at the card table. Her father had
delighted in teaching her how to play cards, and she had
been an apt pupil, but she had never yet had an opportunity to discover whether she had inherited his appalling luck. Nor did she wish to. Captain Beaumont's gambling losses had been the major cause of his family's
poverty. 'However, I never gamble. I believe that—'

'What you believe is of no importance. You will soon

discover that everyone gambles, whether they can afford it or not.' She stared hard at Marina for a second. 'I collect that you have no money?'

'I believe that gambling is wrong, whether one has money or not,' said Marina stoutly. 'It ruins too many lives.'

The Dowager continued to stare, narrowing her eyes assessingly, but she said nothing until they had reached their destination and were preparing to alight. 'Do not share your puritanical opinions with the guests tonight, Marina,' she said. 'It would do no good. And it could do you a great deal of harm.'

Marina nodded dumbly and followed Lady Luce into the brightly lit entrance hall of Lady Marchant's extravagant London house.

'Why, Lady Luce, is it not? Good evening, ma'am.'

The Dowager stopped so suddenly that Marina almost collided with her. As it was, she stepped on the hem of her ladyship's train and had to extricate herself carefully from the fine material. By the time Marina looked up once more, Lady Luce was staring coldly in the direction of the handsomest man Marina had ever seen. He had stationed himself between Lady Luce and the staircase and his presence seemed to fill the marble hallway. He was extremely tall and dark, with beautiful features that would not have looked out of place on a statue in a Greek temple. His exquisitely cut clothes seemed to have been moulded to his form, yet he wore them with an air of nonchalance.

'Such a pleasure to meet you again, ma'am.' The gentleman's drawl had an unpleasant edge to it, Marina noticed, and his finely shaped mouth curled in disdain as he looked down at the tiny lady whose path he was blocking. 'It must be…what?…all of five years? I look forward to making your acquaintance again. You *do* still play, I take it?'

'Oh, I play, Mr Stratton, you may be sure of that.' Lady Luce's voice was acid. 'I had not thought Méchante was quite so short of guests, however, as to need to invite just *anyone* to make up her numbers. I see that I shall have to take more care in deciding which invitations a lady should accept.' With that, she marched forward, forcing her tormentor to make way for her. He did so with easy grace, Marina noticed, and he continued to watch with narrowed eyes as the Dowager mounted the elegant branching staircase to the reception rooms above. He spared not one glance for the grey companion.

By the time the Dowager reached her hostess's drawing room, she was white with anger. Her thin lips were pressed tightly together as if to prevent her from speaking words that she might regret.

'Ma'am—'

'Have nothing to do with Kit Stratton, child,' said Lady Luce sharply before Marina had time to begin her question. 'He is dangerous. More dangerous than you could ever imagine.'

'But—'

'Good evening, Méchante.' Lady Luce was holding out her claw-like hand to a voluptuous blonde dressed in a gown of diaphanous pink silk. It was doubtful whether Lady Marchant wore much by way of petticoats beneath her gown. It seemed to cling to her almost like a second skin.

Marina had never seen anything so brazen. She caught herself staring and forced herself to look away. Their hostess's nickname was well deserved. She seemed to relish it, too. At Lady Luce's impudent greeting, Lady Marchant smiled contentedly, accentuating her slanting green eyes. There was something remarkably feline about that look, Marina decided. She was probably devious, as well as wicked.

Marina longed to ask questions, but could not. Who was the haughty man in the hallway? His name seemed vaguely familiar, but she could not place it. What was between him and Lady Luce? Enmity, for sure, but why? Marina had no opportunity to say a word, far less ask a question, for Lady Luce and her hostess were already mingling with the throng of guests. There was no sign of the incredibly handsome Mr Kit Stratton.

Marina forced her thoughts back to practical matters. She must not stand alone in the doorway as if she were an outcast. She must heed the Dowager's warning and blend into the background. The huge draped velvet curtains would provide just what she needed. They were far enough away from the candelabra to cast quite a deep shadow. In her grey gown, Marina would appear to be almost a shadow herself.

Safe in her dark corner, Marina surveyed the company. Almost all the guests were men. There were soldiers in scarlet coats, some of them quite senior, some of them so young that they still had the downy cheeks of a girl. Marina was forcibly reminded of her younger brother, Harry, and how very proud he had been on the first application of his cut-throat razors.

Of the non-military gentlemen, a few were dressed in expensive and well-cut coats, but most reminded her of Lord Luce. They looked well fed and well-upholstered and, in more than one case, well on the way to an early grave.

The ladies—no, that was too flattering a term—the women were few. Apart from Lady Marchant and Lady Luce, there were only three, none of them in the first blush of youth. They wore fine but slightly grubby gowns, all very low cut indeed. Two of the women had painted their faces. Lady Luce was right. Méchante's house was one that no virtuous young lady should ever enter. Why then had she been so insistent that Marina should accompany her tonight?

The noise in the room was almost deafening. It seemed that all of the gentlemen were well into their cups and each was almost shouting to make himself heard above his fellows. Marina found herself shrinking somewhat into the velvet shadow and wishing that she had been able to avoid coming to this place.

Where was Lady Luce? She and her hostess seemed to have disappeared. Marina supposed they must have gone into an adjoining room. Should she follow her employer? Or should she stay here where, for the moment at least, she seemed to be relatively safe? She hesitated, but only for a moment. It was her duty to protect the Dowager, somehow, from her gambling folly. What if she were gambling in the very next room?

Marina straightened her shoulders. She must follow her employer and do her duty.

'Well,' said a male voice at her elbow.

Marina smelt the nauseating mix of stale alcohol and sweat even before she turned. Where had this man come from? She was being accosted—there was no other word for it—by a middle-aged man in a rusty-black evening coat. He was quite as raddled as the worst of those in the room. His skin was almost as grey as her gown; he had the eyes of a man who had not slept for days on end.

She gave him the look that had cowed many an upstart in Yorkshire and made to pass on. It was not to be. The man's hand grabbed her arm and forcibly brought her to a halt.

'Not so fast, missy,' he said, in a drawl that sounded half drunk, half affected. 'And who might you be?'

Marina tried to shake him off, but failed. 'My name is of no moment, sir,' she said in icy tones. 'I will thank you to let go of my arm.'

'Indeed?' His red-lidded eyes narrowed nastily. He looked her up and down. 'This one has her nose in the air,' he said at last. 'Don't see why.' His contempt was obvious from the set of his lips. 'With looks like yours, you should be glad that any man deigns to take notice of you. Don't reckon you're worth a guinea of any man's blunt.'

Marina gasped. She knew just what he thought her to be.

With a final, rather undignified wrench, she pulled her arm free and ran through the doorway, praying that her employer would be in the room beyond. She was disappointed. The adjoining room held only card tables where little groups of gentlemen were deeply engrossed in piquet and whist. At the table nearest the door, one of the gentlemen, clearly disturbed by her hurried entrance, indicated irritably that she should be silent.

Marina felt herself flushing. She halted her headlong dash. The man who had accosted her might not think her a lady, but she would try to behave as she had been taught. Even in a house such as this.

Head held high, she walked slowly and calmly through the room to the doorway on the other side.

It was another room for gambling, but considerably less decorous than the previous one. A noisy dice table stood near the door; on the far side, there was a roulette wheel, with a number of players clustered eagerly round it, including two more painted ladies.

Marina suppressed a shudder. There must be a way out of this nightmare. Where on earth could Lady Luce have disappeared to?

Kit watched with narrowed eyes as Lady Luce mounted the stairs to the galleried landing. Five years seemed to have changed her very little. She was as rude as ever, but he had expected nothing less. Did she suspect his intentions? Possibly. She was bound to know of the change in his circumstances. Society tabbies such as the Dowager made it a point of honour to know everyone's business.

He took out his gold snuff box and tapped it with a manicured fingernail. Mechanically, he opened it and took a minuscule pinch. His eyes were still on the landing above.

Where was she? Would she dare to play when she knew he was here, watching, waiting his chance?

Of course she would. Lady Luce was a soulless harridan but she was no coward. She might avoid Kit if she decently could but, faced with a direct challenge, she would never retreat. All he had to do was wait for the right opportunity. One day, it would come. Perhaps even tonight?

With a little nod of satisfaction, Kit mounted the staircase. Unlike Lady Luce, he did not take the branch leading to the reception rooms. He had long ago made it his business to spy out the layout of Méchante's labyrinth of a house. He knew precisely where the high-stakes games would be played. And, like a skilled hunter, he knew that the best tactic was to conceal himself and lie in wait for his prey.

* * *

Marina was bewildered. She had made her way through room after room encountering only drunken gamblers with too ready hands. It seemed to have taken hours to come this far. Now she was back on the landing, but still there was no sign of Lady Luce.

At the far side of the landing, a door opened. A slurring voice said, 'So this is where you are. Don't think you fool me by pretending to run away. I learnt the tricks of your trade before you were born. And I know exactly what you have in mind. Exactly.'

Marina whirled round, took one look at the man weaving his way round the gallery towards her and instinctively backed away. Feeling a doorknob against her side, she quickly entered the room, leaning back against the door with a sigh of relief.

Here was yet another gambling room. This one was much smaller than the others and was generously hung with deep blue damask. A pointed archway in the wall led through to the adjoining room, also blue. In each, there was a large oval table where a group of gamblers was playing in complete silence. Marina looked in horror at the piles of coin, notes and vowels heaped on the green baize. The guests here were playing for very high stakes.

From her position by the door, Marina could not see any sign of Lady Luce. Perhaps she was not gambling, after all?

At the table in front of Marina, Lady Marchant was acting as banker. Marina took half a step forward, but stopped when Lady Marchant gave her a slight shake of the head. Obviously, Marina's presence was unwelcome here.

What was she to do?

Behind her, someone tried vainly to open the door. A

second later, it was pushed sharply into Marina's back. Surprised, she stumbled forward.

Lady Marchant frowned and shook her head angrily at the interruption, motioning to Marina to leave the room immediately. Unjust though it was, Marina knew better than to protest. She turned to do as she was bid. What choice did she have?

She stopped abruptly. There in the doorway, propping himself up against the jamb, was her drunken pursuer, the man she had been trying so hard to avoid. He was leering at her, waiting.

He thinks he has me now, Marina thought. But I will not allow myself to be used like a common street-walker.

She pulled herself up to her full height—which was a little taller than the drunk—and stared haughtily down at him. Her flashing eyes dared him to approach her. But in his befuddled state, would he heed her warning?

Through the archway, there came a cry of triumph. It was Lady Luce's voice. She was in the very next room!

Marina spun on her heel and cried out as she collided with a man directly behind her. He must have risen from Lady Marchant's table just as Marina turned.

For a split second, Marina felt herself falling, but then strong arms gripped her and held her upright. She found she was staring at a gold cravat pin in the shape of a swooping bird of prey, its cruel head set off by a blood-red ruby eye. She could not move. She was standing transfixed in a man's arms while the warmth of him invaded her limbs. Her mind was refusing to function. She could think of nothing but the obvious fact that he was even taller than her father.

Then she glanced up into his face.

It was Kit Stratton. And he had the hardest eyes she had ever seen.

Chapter Four

Kit set the grey lady back on her feet. It crossed his mind that she had no business to be in a house like Méchante's where all the females were either members of the muslin company or hardened gamesters like Lady Luce.

The grey lady seemed remarkably tongue-tied. Perhaps she was simple? That would certainly help to account for her presence here.

Kit looked over the grey lady's head to the swaying figure in the open doorway. Even in his cups, the man had a predatory look. Kit glanced down at the grey lady, wondering what the man could have seen in her. She was hardly worth pursuing, unless to puncture that strange air of 'touch-me-not' surrounding her. Yes, that must be it. It might be amusing to watch how she dealt with her would-be lover.

The drunk took a step towards them. 'I'll thank you to unhand my woman,' he said, enunciating each word with exaggerated care. 'I saw her first,' he added, as if to clinch the matter.

Kit stiffened at the man's brazen challenge. Not even drink could excuse it. He stepped smartly round the grey lady and confronted her pursuer, bending down so that their heads were almost touching. He forced himself to ignore the stink. 'You are out of your depth here, my friend,' he said in a low, menacing voice, 'and I find your presence offensive. Go and put your head under the pump.'

The man goggled up at him.

It seemed that hard words were not enough for this man. Kit seized him, spun him round and quickly twisted one arm up his back. Then he propelled his squealing victim out on to the gallery and threw him to the floor. Kit smiled grimly at the sound of bone crunching against wooden balusters. Stone would have been preferable, he thought, closing the door on the sprawling figure.

The grey lady had turned to watch. She was looking at Kit through narrowed eyes. Clearly, he had been wrong about her. There was nothing in the least simple about this female.

'Good manners require me to thank you, sir, for saving me from a fall,' she said in a voice of cold, educated politeness. She did not meet his eyes. 'As to the other—' she glanced briefly towards the closed door '—I shall try to pretend that I was not witness to such a vulgar display.' With a moue of disgust, she turned and moved serenely through the archway.

She holds herself like a duchess, Kit noted absently. How very strange.

He felt a sudden desire to laugh. For once, he had rescued a damsel in distress instead of ravishing her. And his reward? She had simply looked down her nose at him. He should have known better. Women were all the same. Next time—why should there be a next time with such a woman?—if there was a next time, he would make her sorry she had ever tangled with Kit Stratton.

*   *   *

Marina was glad to be able to seek out her protector on the far side of the arch. Kit Stratton was Lady Luce's enemy. Everything about him shrieked danger. Beneath that fine, polished veneer, the man was a flint-hearted savage. It had taken every ounce of her self-control to conquer her body's weakness and give him the set-down he so richly deserved. She was proud of her actions. She had shown she was a lady still.

At the table, they were playing Faro. Lady Luce had clearly been there all the time, hidden by the dividing wall.

Marina's heart sank when she realised her employer was acting as Faro banker. This was no mere flutter. This was serious gambling. Heavens, why did this have to happen? And why Faro? Faro was the game that she hated above all others, the game that had ruined her father. It could be a game of infernally high stakes and incredible losses. Men played and played, always hoping to recoup their losses on the next card, until eventually they had nothing left to stake. Faro had led many a man to blow his brains out. Her father might eventually have done the same, if he had lived through the war.

No one had taken the least notice of her entrance. She leaned back against the wall alongside the arch, trying to steady her rapid, anxious breathing. She forced herself to think logically and sensibly. She must not panic. Surely Lady Luce would not play for higher stakes than she could afford? And besides, as banker, she would certainly have the odds in her favour. There must be a good chance that she would leave the table a winner. At that thought, Marina began to feel less uneasy and craned her neck a little in order to watch the play without disturbing those at the table.

There were five players besides Lady Luce. All were

men. All had their backs to Marina. Lady Luce was gathering up a pile of coin and notes. Her crow of triumph had been justified, to judge by the amount she was pulling towards her. So far, she looked to be on top. With expert fingers, she broke a new pack and began to shuffle the cards. The discarded pack had been swept to the floor.

The only noise to be heard was the slap of the cards. The players seemed to be frozen in their seats. Then a deep voice broke the silence from beyond the archway. 'You seem to have remarkable luck, ma'am,' it said. 'Do you dare to raise the stakes for this next deal? Shall we say a minimum of twenty guineas? Or would you prefer to pass the bank?'

Marina did not need to look round in order to recognise the speaker. It was Mr Kit Stratton. His tone was light, but mocking. It was as near an insult as it was possible to be.

Marina saw the spark of indignation in Lady Luce's eyes and the sudden frown as she looked across at her rival. 'By no means, Mr Stratton,' she said in remarkably even tones. 'I have no intention of surrendering the bank just yet. But I certainly agree that the stakes have been too low. Did you suggest twenty? Why, I would not dream of proposing such a paltry sum. What say you to fifty?'

The gentleman sitting opposite the Dowager rose immediately. 'Too steep for me,' he said and left the room.

Mr Stratton strode forward and very deliberately put his hand on the back of the vacant chair. He and Lady Luce stared each other out. Marina knew, even from behind, that he was daring her employer to continue. She also knew that Lady Luce would never back down against this man.

What was Marina to do? She racked her brains, but for some reason she seemed unable to think straight. In her very first day in her new post, she was failing to prevent her charge from gambling for enormous stakes. What on earth was happening to her?

At length, Mr Stratton's voice replied, 'Fifty? Certainly. Unless you wish to go higher?'

Marina prayed silently that Lady Luce would not accept this further challenge. Surely it was bad enough with the stakes they had already agreed?

Lady Luce smiled slowly, first at Mr Stratton, and then at the other players. 'Gentlemen,' she said, 'as banker, I will accept any stakes that Mr Stratton cares to name.' She looked across at him once more. The gleam in her eyes suggested she was sure of her victory now.

For what seemed a long time, Mr Stratton said nothing at all. Then, in a very quiet, calm voice, he said, 'Madam, you do me too great an honour, but it would be ungentlemanly to disappoint you. A lady's whims must always be humoured. Shall we say…two hundred pounds?'

This time the gasp echoed round the room. Two more of the gentlemen made to rise, muttering excuses. Such stakes were almost unheard of.

Mr Stratton did not move an inch as the players left the table to congregate by the archway. He laughed, though Marina could detect no mirth at all in the sound. 'It shall be a snug little party, then, my lady,' he said, pulling out his chair.

Marina was beginning to feel quite light-headed. She put a hand against the wall for support. This could not be happening. Two hundred pounds was a fortune—and it was to be staked on the turn of a single card. She moved a couple of steps nearer, in hopes of drawing the Dowager's attention to herself. Perhaps she could signal to Lady Luce, distract her, somehow make her stop?

The movement caught Lady Luce's eye. 'So there you are,' she said caustically. She pointed to an empty chair at the far end of the table. 'Sit down, and do nothing. This is too important to allow of any distraction.'

Marina moved across the room and sank into the chair. The Dowager's sharp glance indicated very clearly that she must neither speak nor move.

She closed her eyes and rested her chin on her hand. If only she could *do* something. Her only hope was that Lady Luce would win. Her overpowering fear was that Mr Stratton—bold, ruthless Kit Stratton—would ruin her mistress.

And herself into the bargain.

Kit watched the tiny hands deftly shuffling the cards. Keeping his eyes fixed on the cards helped his concentration. It also helped him to spot any sign of cheating though, in this case, he expected none. Lady Luce was much too proud to stoop so low, even if she knew how, which he doubted. No. This would be a straightforward test of skill and nerve. Kit's well-trained memory for cards would probably cancel out some of the banker's inbuilt advantage.

After that, it was all down to luck.

Lady Luce gathered her cards together and pushed the pack towards Kit. 'Do you care to shuffle them yourself, sir? Perhaps one of the other gentlemen would cut?'

Kit stretched out a hand. 'I am sure the cards are well enough mixed already,' he drawled carelessly, not bothering even to glance at his opponent. 'I will gladly cut, however. Then, perhaps, we may get to the business of the evening?' He cut the cards to her with a decided snap.

Marina saw how the Dowager's lips thinned under the lash of his scorn. Mr Stratton seemed to be seeking to force a quarrel on her, in addition to everything else. How could two people have come to detest each other so? It was quite beyond Marina's understanding.

'Stakes, gentlemen, please,' said the Dowager in a hard voice.

Without hesitation, Mr Stratton extracted a fat pocket-book and, peeling off two banknotes, laid them on the nine in the livret of cards on the players' side of the table. Lady Luce watched impassively, waiting for the other two gentlemen to decide on their wagers. The bald man nearest Marina scribbled a vowel but then sat undecided, his hand hovering between the five and the six in the livret. The very young man at the far end was much more decisive, quickly pushing a heap of notes and coin on to the queen.

As the bald man's hand continued to hover, Lady Luce cleared her throat ominously, staring across at him. He coloured slightly and dropped the scrap of paper on to the six.

Marina held her breath, waiting for the first card to be faced. Her father had always said that it was an omen for the whole game. Normal Faro deals consisted of two cards—the banker won on the first, and the players on the second—but the first and last deals were banker's cards only. Papa had been convinced that if the banker won on that first card, the players would lose heavily throughout the game. Marina had never really believed it—it had not prevented her father from losing his shirt—and yet she found herself offering up a little prayer that the Dowager's card would win. It needed to

be a six, or a nine, or a queen. Best of all if it matched
Mr Stratton's nine. She wanted to see him lose.

Lady Luce took her time. Indeed, she smiled round at
the three men before she even touched the deck. She
seemed remarkably confident.

She faced her first card and laid it to the left of the
deck. Nine!

Lady Luce gave a little nod of satisfaction and col-
lected the stake from Mr Stratton's losing card.

He did not even blink. Marina decided he now looked
even more like a marble statue—beautiful, cold and
stony-hearted. Greek gods had been said to amuse themselves by treating human beings as pawns in their Olym-
pian chess games. Kit Stratton looked as if he felt exactly the same about his opponents.

He threw two more bills on to the nine in the livret,
never once raising his eyes to look at the banker or at
any of the other players. He seemed to be focused totally
on the cards.

Marina recognised that stare. She had seen it on her
father. Mr Stratton was almost certainly a practised
player with the ability to remember every card played.
She had been taught to do the same herself. The knowledge helped improve the odds, especially towards the
end of the game when few cards remained to be dealt.
Kit Stratton was very definitely playing to win.

The Dowager faced the cards for the next deal. A king
for the banker, followed by a two. No winners. With so
few players, there could be several such barren deals. If
the banker moved quickly through them, it would be
more difficult than normal to memorise the cards. Marina set herself to doing so, too. The task would help her
to remain calm, especially if Mr Stratton were to win.

Three more barren deals followed in quick succession.

Marina knew exactly which cards had been played. Did Kit Stratton? It was impossible to tell from his face.

Lady Luce faced a six on to the banker's pile to the left of the deck. The bald man groaned and muttered an oath as his stake joined the heap in front of the banker. He started to scribble his next vowel even before the players' card had been dealt. The man at the far end drew an audible breath. Another nine! Lady Luce placed it carefully on the heap of players' cards. Then she picked up the two bills that Mr Stratton had lost earlier and, holding them between finger and thumb as if they were contaminated, dropped them on to the nine in the livret.

Mr Stratton smiled down at the money for just a second before returning to blank-faced impassivity. He laid his hand flat on the bills, fingers spread in possession. He had well-kept hands, Marina noticed, momentarily distracted from the cards. Strong, too. Marina doubted they were gentle hands. He would like nothing better than to put those long fingers round the Dowager's throat and squeeze the life out of her.

What on earth had made her think that? Marina was suddenly horrified by the picture his lean fingers had conjured up. He was only a gambler. Ruthless, yes, but a gentleman, surely?

Without raising his hand, Mr Stratton slid all four bills from the nine to the ten. The moment he lifted his hand from the table, Lady Luce dealt another banker's card. Another nine!

The bald man gave a crack of laughter. He made to comment on such amazing luck, but the Dowager frowned him down. It was not surprising that she wanted no distractions in this duel. She dealt the *carte anglaise* with careful deliberation. This time, the players' card was a queen. The young man won. With a quick sideways glance, he pocketed his winnings and moved his original stake to join Mr Stratton's on the ten.

He, too, senses that this is a battle to the death, Marina thought. And he has chosen to side with the men, and with youth, against one solitary old woman.

Marina forced her thoughts back to the cards. Thirteen had been played. She could remember every one. Kit Stratton had staked four hundred pounds on the ten. There were still thirty-nine cards to be faced. And among them were four tens.

Marina was having difficulty remembering the cards. It had never happened to her before. She had prided herself on that ability, yet now, when it really mattered, it seemed to be deserting her. It was something to do with those strong, lean hands. She could not take her eyes from them. What was it about them? Mostly, they lay relaxed and utterly still on the baize table while Kit Stratton watched the deal of every card. He was like a hawk—a detached, ruthless hunter, ready to launch itself on any quarry that became even slightly vulnerable.

There were only nineteen cards left. And still not a single ten had appeared.

Beyond the archway, a knot of onlookers was gazing across at Lady Luce and her cards. Clearly, Lady Marchant's table had broken up in order to watch the excitement of the duel between Mr Stratton and the Dowager. Lady Luce frowned across at her unwelcome audience, and then returned her attention to the players. The bald man was leaning back in his chair, trying to appear nonchalant. The youngster was all excitement. He did not speak, but his eyes kept flicking back and forth from the money lying on the ten to the banker's set face.

There were beads of sweat on his furrowed brow. His fate was bound up with Kit Stratton's…and the elusive ten.

Lady Luce faced another pair of cards. The bald man's card won. Impassive, the Dowager pushed his winnings across the table and waited while he decided on his next wager. The pile of paper and coin in front of her was now pitifully small. She desperately needed a winning card.

Marina could see the increasing tension in the Dowager's fixed smile. Her lips were becoming thinner and thinner. Her hands were absolutely steady, however, as she turned up the next card. A nine to the banker. Useless.

And then the players' card. A ten.

There was a tiny gasp, quickly muffled, from one of the watchers by the archway. The young man at the table was grinning from ear to ear, but Mr Stratton had not moved a muscle. He was still gazing at the cards.

The Dowager pushed her last two bills across to the young man. With what seemed to be an apologetic glance at Mr Stratton, he pocketed his winnings and moved his stake from the ten to the queen. Lady Luce had no more bills. Rather than count out two hundred pounds in coin, she reached for pen and ink to scribble a vowel for Mr Stratton's winnings.

His raised hand stayed her.

Marina held her breath, knowing instinctively what was to come.

With a long finger, Kit Stratton indicated that his winnings remained on the table.

This time, Marina herself could not stifle a groan. Kit Stratton was riding his luck. If he won again, the Dowager would have to pay him seven times his stake. That was nearly three thousand pounds!

Lady Luce reached towards the cards. Marina closed her eyes, not daring to look. There were still three tens in the pack under the Dowager's hand.

A groan from the bald man made her open her eyes once more. The bald man had lost. And Kit Stratton had won with another ten.

This time, Marina knew exactly what he would do. That long finger moved again. All his winnings—against a prize of fifteen times his stake!

Three more deals, and no more tens appeared. The young man lost on his queen. The bald man won on a king.

Kit Stratton sat as if turned to stone.

There were only seven cards left.

Marina forced her whirling mind to concentrate on the cards. What were they? She ought to know.

She frowned into the silence, pushing every other thought out of her mind. Her brain cleared quite suddenly, as if a curtain had been drawn back from a chalkboard on which the cards had been written. Two aces, a two, a three, a knave…and two tens.

The bald man had two hundred pounds on the ace. The young man had put his stake on the six. Clearly he had no ability to remember cards.

Mr Stratton's hand lay carelessly on the green baize, his index finger extended towards one corner of the ten.

It seemed that no one dared to breathe while they waited for Lady Luce to face the next pair of cards. An ace for the banker. And a three for the players.

Lady Luce reached out to remove her winnings from the ace. Marina offered up a silent prayer of thanks. Now, let the same happen with the ten. Please.

The bald man was not prepared to retreat. He looked a little shiftily at the other players and then placed a stake on the ten. It seemed he had decided that Kit Stratton's luck was in.

With calm deliberation, the Dowager faced her next card. It was a useless two. She paused a moment, then quickly turned over the *carte anglaise*.

Ten!

The bald man gave a little crow of triumph. It was followed by a pregnant silence as everyone in the room watched to see what Kit Stratton would do. He could take his money now—six thousand pounds—or he could let it ride, in hopes of redoubling his winnings to thirty times his original stake.

For several seconds he sat as still as a statue. What was he thinking? There were only three cards left. Such an experienced gambler must know that the banker now had two chances of winning while the players had only one. The bald man had quickly pocketed his money. He was wise to do so, Marina judged. Surely Kit Stratton could not win again? Only the most hardened gamester would play on.

It seemed that Kit Stratton was a gambler to the core. With total nonchalance he tapped his pile of winnings into place. He never once raised his eyes from the cards.

But, for the briefest moment, an ironic smile pulled at one corner of his mouth.

Marina's heart was racing. That twitch of the lips had told her everything. Kit Stratton was well aware that the odds were against him, but he was prepared to run with his luck in order to defeat a woman he detested. And if he did not succeed now, he would make sure there were other occasions. He was the Dowager's enemy.

Marina looked towards Lady Luce. Under her old-fashioned face-paint, her skin was grey. Yet her eyes sparkled angrily. She had accepted Mr Stratton's latest challenge. Better to risk an unlikely loss of twelve thousand than to pay out on a certain loss of six.

Surreptitiously, Marina crossed the fingers of her right hand. She was not superstitious—she prided herself on being too well educated for such things—but she could not resist the impulse. She must not cross the fingers on her left hand, for that, she remembered a little guiltily, would bring bad luck. She forced herself to watch. Like the Dowager, she would show she was no coward.

Three cards remained—an ace, a knave, and a ten.

Lady Luce's tiny wrinkled hand hovered over the pack. Then, like a cat pouncing on a mouse, she faced the first of them with a snap. The ace.

Marina dug her crossed fingers into the palm of her left hand. Two cards only. The chances were equal now.

Lady Luce smiled calmly across at the players, but Mr Stratton continued to stare at the table. He could not see the banker's defiance as she turned the card that could be her ruin.

Ten.

Kit Stratton had won twelve thousand pounds.

With a gesture of disgust, Lady Luce faced the final, useless card. It was over. She had taken on the challenge and she had lost. She visibly straightened her back and waited for her adversary to speak.

He did not. He sat, as still as ever, staring at his winning card. Then, very slowly, his eyes narrowed and his mouth stretched into a taut, venomous smile. It made the hair on the back of Marina's neck stand on end. There was something almost devilish in Kit Stratton's expression.

He raised his head a fraction and stared at the Dowager, with that nasty smile tugging at the corner of his mouth. Marina was reminded of a cobra, its head rising before its victim as it prepared to strike. How could she ever have thought him handsome? Hatred and the lust for vengeance had put hideous lines into that remarkable face. She wanted to look away, but she could not. Opposite Mr Stratton, the Dowager was ashen. She seemed to have shrunk. She looked suddenly very old, and very frail.

Mr Stratton seemed to be waiting for Lady Luce to speak, to concede defeat. Yes, he would enjoy that. He wanted to humiliate her to the uttermost.

Lady Luce did not manage a smile, but she nodded casually towards her opponent as if nothing out of the way had occurred. Then she began to gather up the cards with deft, steady hands.

Marina's own hands were nothing like as steady. She kept them hidden in her lap. She must *do* something.

Slowly, languidly, Kit Stratton rose from his seat. He was enjoying this. From his great height, he looked down on Lady Luce, still smiling nastily. After a moment more, he spoke in a soft, sibilant voice. The cobra again. 'Success is mine on this occasion, I see,' he said.

Lady Luce scribbled a vowel and pushed it across the table. She said nothing. Her self-control was unbelievable.

'But I am in no hurry to collect what is due to me.' Mr Stratton narrowed his eyes balefully and lowered his voice even more. 'I shall look for settlement of this in, shall we say, seven days?' He bowed from the neck, never taking his eyes off the Dowager. 'I shall now bid you good evening, ma'am.'

Lady Luce said nothing. There was no need. The expression of loathing on her face was eloquent. Marina thought she could also detect a hint of fear.

Kit Stratton put the sheet of paper in his pocket and turned to leave. He had triumphed. Marina had fallen at the very first hurdle. The Earl would dismiss her forthwith. Her only chance of employment would be ruined, at a stroke, by this handsome, hateful man. Someone must stop him.

Almost without knowing it, Marina rose from her place and moved to put herself between Mr Stratton and the archway into the adjoining room. 'Sir…' she began, putting a hand on his arm to stay him. He turned sharply to look down at her. She had never seen eyes so cold, so hard. He was ruthless, implacable, and full of hate. Nothing would move such a man. 'Sir,' she began again, hardly knowing what she was going to ask of him, 'will you not—?'

She was not permitted to finish her sentence. With a sneering curl of that beautiful mouth, Kit Stratton lifted her fingers and removed them from his coat, dropping them instantly as if they were diseased. 'No, *madame*,' he said hoarsely. 'Whatever it is you would ask of me—' he looked her slowly up and down '—the answer is no.' He had a fine cambric handkerchief in his left hand—it seemed to have been conjured out of the very air—and, quite deliberately, he flicked it across his immaculate sleeve where Marina's touch had sullied it.

Marina was outraged. How dare he?

One eyebrow quirked upwards by the tiniest fraction. He was pleased at her reaction. What a villain he was! Marina could not think of words harsh enough to describe such a man. He was—

He was gone.

And with him went all Marina's hopes.

Chapter Five

Kit passed out through the silent onlookers who fell back to make way for him. There was awe on some of their faces. Probably none of them would have dared to take such risks.

Out on the landing, the drunk was long gone. The entrance hall below seemed to be deserted.

Kit walked slowly down the elegant staircase, his mind a blank. He could barely remember what he had done, except that he had had his revenge at last. He ought to feel elated, exhilarated, triumphant—but he did not. He felt nothing. Absolutely nothing.

He turned to watch Méchante's luscious figure descend the stairs, swaying seductively. The silk of her gown was almost transparent, leaving little to the imagination. In recent years, Kit had come to prefer his women a little more restrained. Unlike Méchante, Kit's current mistress did not peddle her wares to every man in sight. The Baroness Katharina von Thalberg offered herself only to him—and to her husband, of course. Kit could hardly object to that.

He waited for Méchante to join him, mentally comparing her with his delectable Katharina and finding his hostess a little wanting. Yes, he would go to Katharina. Losing himself in her body would give him back a measure of sanity after this night's madness.

'Must you go, Kit?' Lady Marchant purred. 'May we not drink a glass of champagne to your victory? And to old times? I have a fine vintage on ice in my private apartments.' She gazed at him with wide green eyes and stretched up to whisper in his ear, pressing her body sensuously against his. 'My guests can do without me for an hour or so.'

Kit's body did not react at all to her blatant invitation. Bedding a beautiful woman was a pleasure as normal—and as fleeting—as winning a hand of cards. But Méchante left him cold. She had been his mistress once, five years ago, and she had betrayed him.

He lifted her hand to his lips so that she could not read the expression in his eyes. 'No, my dear,' he said silkily, 'I never go back. And I never share.'

'Be careful, my friend.' Lady Marchant was not purring any longer. There was an edge of malice in her voice and her feline eyes had narrowed to slits. 'Your Katharina takes too many risks. Her husband may not be quite so forgiving, now that you are no longer in Vienna. There, he was just another minor aristocrat. Here, he is a diplomatic representative of the Hapsburg Empire. A scandal would ruin him.' She dropped a tiny, impudent curtsy. 'And it could happen so very easily, do you not think?'

Clever. And still dangerous. She was well named. Kit looked her full in the face. Yes, they understood each other. 'I thank you for your invitation, Méchante. And for your wise words.' He bowed again and turned to take his hat and cane from the servant. 'Now, I must bid you goodnight. A most interesting evening. I am indebted to you.'

Her brittle laugh followed him down the steps and into the crisp night air.

It was very late. Katharina would have tired of waiting for him. She would have gone back to her husband. She would have been mad to stay till now.

Kit closed the door quietly behind him and made his way up the stairs of the snug Chelsea house he had rented for their assignations. He would sleep here for a few hours. Tomorrow—later today, rather—he would find Katharina and apologise. She would forgive him… probably. And if she chose to exact a penance, well… that would be enjoyable, too.

He smelt her perfume even before he opened the door to their bedchamber. He breathed it in deeply, trying to conjure up memories of her body under his. Such a pity that she had gone.

'Kätchen!'

The Baroness Katharina von Thalberg lay sprawled across the huge bed, idly leafing through a magazine. She turned in surprise at the sound of her pet name and, for a second, a tiny frown creased her brow. *'Du kommst spät,'* she began, rolling over on to her back to look up at him with huge dark eyes full of hurt and accusation.

'Auf Englisch, Kätchen,' he said wearily. She had every right to complain of his lateness, but he was in no mood for one of her scenes. She need not have waited, after all. He returned to the charge. 'You are in London now. Here, you must speak English.'

The Baroness made a face. 'So you say,' she replied. 'I do not see why so. We are alone, are we not? We may speak in any language we choose. *Français, peut-être?'*

Kit pressed his lips together to suppress a sharp retort. She could be remarkably provocative, his little Austrian. And this was the wrong time. 'No, *madame*. English,' he said firmly, beginning to strip off his coat. He stretched his long body on the bed beside her, propping himself up on one elbow. 'But words are dangerous. They can betray us…in any language.'

He ran a lazy finger down the inside of her deep décolletage until it came to rest in the shadow between her perfect breasts. He began to stroke her skin as gently as if he were wafting a feather fan across a rose petal. Katharina closed her eyes in ecstasy.

'And what need have we of words?' Kit whispered. His lips were so close to her cheek that each word was a caress on her skin. She sighed out a long, shuddering breath.

Kit gazed down at the ravishing picture she made. His body was beginning to heat. At last.

'You have it exactly, my dear,' he said softly.

Lady Luce's hand was shaking as she raised the brandy balloon to her lips and tossed off the contents. 'I should have left that house the moment I saw him,' she said bitterly, collapsing into her favourite chair by the window. 'He is the very devil. With the devil's own luck.'

Marina nodded her understanding. There was no need to ask who was meant. It was strange to see the Dowager so…deflated.

Lady Luce groaned. 'And as for William…' She shook her head angrily at the thought of her son. 'He will positively relish raking me down. Not that he will be given the chance,' she added, straightening her shoulders a little. 'Thought he could fool me. Foisting a gel like you on his mother to keep her in order. Who is the fool now, I say?'

So the Dowager had known all along. Marina was not at all surprised. The old lady was very sharp. And her son was…not his mother's equal. Not that it made any difference, as far as the companion was concerned. The Earl might be somewhat lacking in brains, but he had the ability to send Marina packing.

The Dowager held out her balloon to be refilled. Obediently, Marina fetched the decanter and splashed some of the amber liquid into it. Lady Luce snorted. 'That's not even a mouthful.' She shook the glass impatiently until Marina added considerably more. 'Better,' she said. 'And you should have some, too.'

'Oh, no, ma'am. I never drink spirits. I—'

'Fetch another glass. You will need it. You have a difficult day ahead of you. William will see to that. Just the sort of thing he enjoys.'

The Dowager was right. In the next twenty-four hours, Marina was like to be dismissed. Her stomach turned over at the thought of the coming interview with Lady Luce's dreadful son. She sipped tentatively at her brandy and gasped as it burned its way down. 'Good grief,' she choked out at last. 'Do people really drink this for pleasure?'

Lady Luce laughed. She reached out her scrawny hand and placed it over Marina's smoother one. 'You have courage, Marina. I'll give you that. And I'll not let that arrogant son of mine bully you, or send you packing.'

Marina looked up in surprise.

'Why did you think I took you to Méchante's tonight? Did you think it was chance?' She shook her head at

Marina's obvious incomprehension. 'I have no intention of permitting William to order my life. Not in any way. I took you to that gambling den to show him—and you—that I shall play whenever, and wherever, I wish. He cannot stop me. And setting up a chit of a governess to watch over me will not stop me either.'

Marina felt herself blushing. 'I...I did not...'

'No, you did not. I'd have discharged you myself if I had thought for a moment that you were William's tool. As it is, he promised me a companion, all expenses paid. I shall hold him to our bargain.'

Marina gulped. Life was like to become extremely unpleasant if the old lady and her son used her as a pawn in their endless trials of strength. And with a loss of twelve thousand pounds to sharpen the contest...

Lady Luce held out her glass for another refill. Then she sat for a long time, cradling her brandy and staring vacantly towards the wall.

She must be thinking about the money, Marina decided. She cannot possibly find such a huge sum. Especially not in one week.

'He was determined on his revenge,' said the Dowager, musingly. 'I suppose I cannot blame him. He was word-perfect, too. I should have known he would be.'

'I beg your pardon, ma'am? I'm afraid I do not quite follow...'

'No reason why you should. And I wasn't talking to you, in any event.' At Marina's sharp intake of breath, she softened the merest fraction. 'Oh, you will come to learn it all in the end, I suppose. Best that I tell you myself. Can't have you hearing gossip from the servants. Wouldn't get the facts right, I dare say.' Lady Luce chuckled a little at her own wit. 'There is not much to tell. Several years ago, when Kit Stratton was barely out of leading strings, he lost five thousand pounds to me. I was in pretty deep myself at the time and could not afford to give him time to pay…or even an opportunity to recoup his losses. I demanded payment in seven days. I used those very words. He has been waiting his chance for revenge ever since.'

The story did not sound in the least plausible to Marina. Gentlemen lost thousands of pounds at play all the time. Why should Kit Stratton be bent on vengeance? Against a woman, too?

Her doubts must have been obvious, for Lady Luce looked somewhat shamefaced. 'He paid,' she said hoarsely, 'on the nail. I found out later that his brother Hugo had given him the money—out of his wife's dowry. They had been married less than a week. Kit was sent abroad soon after.'

'Oh,' breathed Marina. No wonder Kit Stratton had felt humiliated. And what of the brother? What had Hugo Stratton thought of it all? Had Hugo Stratton really sent his brother into exile? He— Hugo Stratton? *Now* she knew why the name had seemed familiar!

The Dowager was beginning to ramble. It must be the effects of too much brandy. 'Can't say I blame the boy. My own fault. Let him think I was doing it out of malice when it was really William's fault. Insisted he couldn't afford to tow me out of River Tick. I couldn't admit *that* to young Stratton, could I? But to use the very same words…' She raised her glass yet again.

'Do you know Hugo Stratton, ma'am? The brother?'

'What? Yes. No. Well…we are barely acquainted, but everyone knows about him. He's as rich as Croesus since his brother died, never mind the money from his wife. Doesn't come up to London much. Got out of the habit after the war, they say, because he hated being stared at.'

'Stared at?'

'He was badly wounded. Waterloo, I think.' The Dowager frowned. 'Why all this sudden interest in Sir Hugo Stratton? What is he to you, miss?'

Marina swallowed. 'I think he may have served with my father, ma'am,' she said quietly, gazing down at her skirts. 'In Spain. I think he fought in the battle where my father and my uncle died.'

Lady Luce said nothing. She simply reached for the brandy decanter and tipped a generous measure into Marina's glass.

Marina tried in vain to find a comfortable position in her bed. It must be nearly dawn. Her head was pounding, but she could not possibly sleep. What on earth had possessed the Dowager to give her brandy? Her brain was refusing to function.

She tried again.

Kit Stratton was Sir Hugo Stratton's younger brother. And a Captain Hugo Stratton had been her uncle's closest friend. They had served together for years. According to Uncle George, Hugo Stratton was the best friend, and the staunchest comrade, that a man could wish for. It was partly due to Captain Stratton's influence that Marina's father had joined the 95th. It was not Captain Stratton's fault that the brothers had died so soon after.

Kit Stratton could not be as bad as he was painted. It was not possible. Not if he was Hugo Stratton's brother. And he must be. It was an unusual name. Perhaps Kit had had other reasons for his hatred of the Dowager. Perhaps his insult to Marina herself was simply an unconscious continuation of his harshness at the card table. Perhaps…

There was no way of knowing, unless she found out for herself.

Yes, that was the answer. She would seek out Kit Stratton and ask him to forgive the Dowager's debt. If necessary, she would ask him to do it in memory of her uncle and her father—and for his brother Hugo's sake. No gentleman could possibly deny such a request.

The thought of such an interview made her stomach churn. She would have to abandon the last shreds of her pride to make her appeal, and if he treated her with the same degree of contempt as before… She shivered. She was not sure she could bear that.

Was he a gentleman at all?

It was true that the Dowager had rambled on for what seemed like hours about Kit Stratton's way of life, his mistresses, his fine clothes, his carriages, his horses… He had all the outward attributes of a very wealthy gentleman. But did he have a sense of honour to go with his high-couraged horses?

Marina smiled weakly. The horses had provided her solution. She rather wished they had not. Kit Stratton exercised his horses in the park every morning, come rain, come shine, no matter how great his indulgence the night before. According to the Dowager, it was one of his few saving graces.

He would be in the park tomorrow morning. No—in just a few hours. She had only to go there and confront him. As a gentleman, he could not fail to listen to a lady's pleas.

That was not true.

He could spurn her without a moment's hesitation. He had done so once already, knowing perfectly well that she was a lady. He could do so again, unless she could find some way of breaking through his armoured exterior.

Her own pride did not matter. It was her duty to protect her family—and to do so, she must retain her position with Lady Luce. To save the Dowager, she must challenge Kit Stratton.

Why did he have to ride such a huge animal? Kit Stratton's bay stallion must be seventeen hands or more. Marina felt completely dwarfed by horse and rider. Would he even condescend to rein in to greet her? He could not mistake the fact that she wished to speak to him.

Kit touched his crop carelessly to his hat, using his other hand to bring his horse to a stand with practised ease. There was a sardonic gleam in his eye as he looked down at her. 'You are about betimes, ma'am,' he said. His gaze wandered lazily around the park before coming back to rest on Marina's shabby figure. 'And you appear to have…mislaid your maid.'

'A companion does not have a maid,' snapped Marina, 'as you know very well, Mr Stratton.'

His eyebrows shot up. Then he nodded slowly, once. 'No. She has the tongue of a shrew instead, it would seem.'

Marina was suddenly sure she was blushing. Confound the man! This was not at all what she had intended for this interview. She swallowed hard. She must start again. 'Mr Stratton,' she said, as evenly as she could, 'I should be most grateful if we might have a private word. About…about last night. I—'

He frowned. 'You are come as Lady Luce's envoy? Believe me, ma'am—'

'No! No! She knows nothing of this, I promise you. I have my own reasons for wishing to…to consult you. You see…'

His expression was changing even as she spoke. He was almost smiling, but there was nothing in the least pleasant in it. Marina felt a sudden urge to flee. She swallowed again. He was doing everything he could to make her position impossible. He had not even dismounted, as any true gentleman would have done. That thought gave rise to a spark of anger. Heedless of risk, she fanned it. He was trying—deliberately—to overset her. He despised her, a poor plain companion, for daring to approach rich, handsome Kit Stratton.

'You mistake me, sir,' she said crisply. 'I am not come at Lady Luce's bidding but at my own, to ask a…a favour of you.' There. It was out. And Kit Stratton's face was dark with anger. 'Not for her ladyship's sake—I know that is impossible—but for—'

'A favour?' Kit snarled. 'A favour for whom? For you, ma'am? Believe me, I do not do favours for ladies. Not unless they have earned them.' He glanced quickly over her thin person, his eyes narrowing.

Marina stood stock still. She could neither move nor speak. This could not be happening. Was he really saying that—?

'I see that you take my meaning, ma'am. Good.'

He leant down towards her. The fresh, clean scent of his cologne assailed her. It seemed completely at variance with the black-hearted man who wore it. She forced herself to stand her ground.

'If you wish to…discuss the matter of last evening's events, ma'am, I will be pleased to give you a hearing. I shall be free at…eleven o'clock this morning. You may present your petition then. In private.' He gave her an address in Chelsea. To Marina, a stranger in London, it meant nothing.

He sat back into his saddle and took up the slack in the reins. 'I shall expect you at eleven. Do not be late.'

Chapter Six

Kit looked up from his newspaper as the long-case clock in the hall began to strike the hour. He had done her the courtesy of being here, because she was a lady. But he had known she would not come.

He turned back to his newspaper. He would just finish the report he had been reading, and then he would leave for his club. No doubt the story of his winnings would have done the rounds by now. He was like to hear about nothing else for a se'enight.

He leaned back into his leather wing chair, relishing the peace of the cramped Chelsea sitting room.

Five minutes later, a quiet knock on the door was followed by the entrance of the tiny woman who looked after the house. 'There is a…a person to see you, sir,' she said, bobbing a polite curtsy. 'She will not give a name. She—'

'The lady is come by appointment, to discuss a matter of business,' Kit said firmly, to quell the speculation in the housekeeper's eye. He rose to his feet. 'Show her in, Mrs Budge.'

The grey lady was liberally spattered with mud. Kit looked quickly towards the window. He had been so absorbed, he had not noticed the rain. Had she walked all the way? Had she no sense at all? She was already unattractive enough, even without the addition of brown mud to her grey appearance.

And still she thought to sway him?

He shook his head wonderingly. She seemed ill prepared for the mammoth task she had undertaken.

He raised his brows enquiringly. 'Good morning, ma'am,' he said politely. She had stiffened noticeably. Surely she did not feel insulted by his treatment of her? A woman—a lady—who had come to a private meeting in a gentleman's house?

He waited for her to speak. He would not help her.

'Good morning, sir,' she said at last. The poke of her drab bonnet dipped a fraction.

Was that a token bow? It seemed he would receive nothing more. Kit returned it in kind, from his much greater height. She dropped her eyes. She was nervous, clearly. He waited once more.

'It was good of you to see me,' she said, as if their meeting was the most normal thing in the world, rather than an outrage against the rules of Society. 'You said I might… The truth is, I wanted…I wished to ask you to forgive Lady Luce's debt. Oh, I know it is a fortune, but you are a very rich man, whereas she is old and—'

'And poor?' finished Kit sardonically. 'If your mistress is poor, ma'am, it is because she has gambled away her substance. She has no one to blame but herself. Do you not agree?'

She looked guilty but said nothing. Her silence was beginning to annoy Kit. He realised, in that moment, that he did not know her name.

'Do you not agree, ma'am?' he said again. 'Pardon me, but I have not had the honour of an introduction.'

He bowed politely. 'You are Miss Smith, I suppose?' he found himself adding sarcastically. There was something about this lady that vexed him intensely.

She lifted her chin and looked shrewdly up at him. 'No, Mr Stratton, I am Miss Beaumont,' she said calmly, holding up her muddy skirts so that she might drop him a disdainful curtsy.

She had the pride of a duchess—in the garb of a scullery maid. If he was not careful, she could best him in this encounter. And that he would never permit. Not from any woman.

'Well, Miss Beaumont,' Kit began quickly, motioning her to the second wing chair, 'just what have you to offer me that is worth twelve thousand pounds?'

She stopped short in the act of sitting down. The colour had drained from her face in an instant. She had become almost as grey as her gown.

'I *beg* your pardon?' she said in a voice raw with hostility.

Kit allowed himself to smile down at her. She recoiled gratifyingly, but she did not look away. She had a degree of courage, this grey lady.

'Many a man has allowed himself to be leg-shackled for a mere fraction of twelve thousand pounds, Miss Beaumont. It is, as you said, a fortune. And yet you would have me forgo it.' He took a step towards her. They were so close now that the muddy hem of her dress was trailing on his boots. 'You place a very high value on what you have to offer, Miss Beaumont,' he said, making his voice almost a caress.

Her head came up sharply and colour flooded back into her cheeks. She made to slap his face.

'No, Miss Beaumont,' Kit said, catching her wrist with his left hand and twisting it behind her back. 'I am afraid I do not permit ladies to strike me.' He looked down into her face. She had hazel eyes, flecked with gold. They were wide with fear. Was she so naïve that she did not know what she risked, visiting him like this?

He pulled her hard against him, unintentionally twisting her wrist a little in the process. Her lips parted on a tiny cry of pain.

He immediately relaxed his grip, but his gaze was caught by those invitingly parted lips. She needed to learn her lesson, once and for all. He brought his right hand up to cradle her head and lowered his mouth to hers.

She was not willing.

Her free hand clawed at him, her nails mercifully sheathed in her cheap gloves. Without raising his mouth from hers, he quickly imprisoned both her wrists in one lean hand.

Now she was truly caught.

Gently, unthreateningly, he began to pull at the strings of her bonnet. Her lips parted a little more as if to bid him welcome. She was yielding to him at last. He had expected no less. Women always yielded…sooner or later. He started his assault in earnest…

Without warning, a heavy boot kicked him hard on the ankle.

Kit drew in a sharp, painful breath. Automatically, he pulled away, but he knew better than to let go of his attacker.

What a picture she made! Her bonnet was askew and her dress was filthy, but her slim bosom was heaving and her eyes were ablaze with fury. She had a perfect complexion, he noted absently, especially when she was aroused. What a pity that anger, rather than desire, was the cause.

'I will thank you to let me go,' she said hoarsely. She sounded hard put to it to retain even a vestige of politeness.

Kit slid his hands up her arms until she was firmly gripped once more and held her at arm's length. She was unlikely to attempt another kick from that position. 'My dear Miss Beaumont, do you take me for a complete fool? I will let you go when I have your word to behave like a lady, and not before.'

Anger changed to embarrassment. She was actually blushing!

'You have it, sir,' she said stiffly. 'Do I have yours that you will behave like a gentleman?'

Kit was surprised into a shout of laughter at her temerity. What an astonishing woman!

He shook his head somewhat ruefully, but did not slacken his hold. 'Whoever told you I was a gentleman, Miss Beaumont? I fear you have been misinformed.'

She stared up at him. Her eyes were still blazing, but it did not seem to be anger now—or not wholly. 'I do not believe you, sir,' she said staunchly. Then she simply turned her head to stare down at the hand that was grasping her left arm. 'If you please, Mr Stratton…' She stood absolutely still, waiting.

Kit shrugged his shoulders and let his hands fall. What did it matter? He did not care to kiss a woman who was more than half wildcat. And who would fight him every step of the way. This interview needed to be brought to a speedy, and final, conclusion.

He crossed to the bell-rope and pulled vigorously. The door opened almost immediately. 'Send the boy out for a hackney, Mrs Budge,' he ordered. 'My visitor is leaving.'

The moment the door closed again, Miss Beaumont

began to protest. 'Mr Stratton, I have no desire for a cab. I shall leave on foot, as I came. Besides, we have not finished our business—'

'Miss Beaumont, there is nothing more for you to say,' said Kit firmly, advancing on her until she backed away. A low chair prevented her further retreat. 'I suggest you sit down. Good. Now, in the matter of the hackney, there is nothing to discuss. It is not my habit to permit ladies to walk the streets of London alone. In that, at least, I am a gentleman. The boy will pay the jarvey to take you wherever you want to go.'

She made to protest again but he stopped her with a raised hand.

'As to our *business*… You want me to forgive Lady Luce's debt. Twelve thousand pounds, payable in seven days. Very well, Miss Beaumont, I will do so.'

Her eyes widened in surprise, but she said nothing. Perhaps words were beyond her. That would certainly be the case in a moment or two, he'd stake his honour on that.

'There is a price, of course,' he continued, 'but you knew that when you accepted my invitation to visit me here, did you not?' He paused, waiting for a reaction. There was none. 'The price, Miss Beaumont, is you. In my bed. Willingly.'

That had done it. She was truly terrified now. She had learned her lesson at last. She would not trouble him again.

Not after this.

'You—' Her voice cracked. She cleared her throat and tried again. 'You are very direct,' she said hoarsely. 'May I ask how this…arrangement is to be achieved?'

Her response was much braver than he had expected. It was hardly surprising that she would not look straight

at him now. Still, he must play this little charade to the
end.

'Nothing easier, Miss Beaumont,' he said on the ghost
of a laugh. 'You will write to me here, naming the day
for our…meeting. It will, of course, take place *before*
the debt falls due,' he added, watching her face for signs
of duplicity. 'On the agreed day, you will be walking
early in the park, just as you were today. A plain, closed
carriage will draw up beside you. It will have a white
silk scarf tied to the handle of the door. You will step
into it.'

'And how, pray, is my absence to be explained to
Lady Luce?' Miss Beaumont asked witheringly. 'She
will wish to know where I have spent the day…and the
night. And then she will dismiss me on the spot.'

Kit delivered his *coup de grâce*. 'Oh, do not fear that
I shall detain you long, Miss Beaumont. Our…business
can be quickly dealt with. Darkness is not required, you
know. You will be home long before you have been
missed.'

Her head came up then. She was terrified still, but her
fear was overlaid with loathing. There was a hint of
something more, too—

The door opened. The interruption could not have
been worse timed. 'The cab is at the door, sir. The driver
has been paid.'

'Thank you, Mrs Budge. Tell him to wait. The lady
will be out in a moment.'

As the door closed, the grey lady rose from her chair
and stared proudly across at Kit. 'I will go now, Mr
Stratton,' she said quietly, 'but I shall take the liberty of
telling you that you are not worthy to be called Hugo
Stratton's brother. For he is a man of honour. While
you…'

She turned on her heel. In the space of a heartbeat, she had whipped open the door and disappeared down the hallway.

By the time Kit reached the front door, the hackney had almost turned the corner, its wheels throwing up great splashes of muddy water as it raced away.

Marina leaned back against the creaking leather. She would *not* faint. Not now. She had kept her self-control throughout that appalling interview. There was no point in giving way, not now that it was over.

Kit Stratton was a fiend. He was the very devil.

Had not Lady Luce used those exact words? But she, Marina Beaumont, thinking she knew better, had not heeded the warning. She had broken all the rules to visit him in his lodgings— No, that was wrong. No man of means would live *there*. Even a stranger to London could tell that. Her erstwhile host probably used that modest little house to entertain his mistresses. If Marina accepted his bargain, he would probably bring her there to…to… Oh, she had been well served for her arrogance. Kit Stratton had offered to forgive the Dowager's debt in return for Marina's honour.

He must have known she would not—could not—agree. He must have known.

Why then had he made her such an offer? It made no sense. He neither liked nor admired her.

What a stupid fool she had been, driven by her desperation to find some way of retaining her post. She had seen his arrogance, but she had thought she could find a way to move him, by appealing to his better nature.

Madness! Kit Stratton had no better nature. He had no feelings at all.

She closed her eyes, willing the memories to leave her. They returned, stronger than ever.

She had been in his arms. She had fought him...but not enough.

In all her life, she had never been kissed with any degree of passion. She had not known how it would feel. She had not imagined that she would respond, against everything she had been taught. Kit Stratton had been forcing himself upon her. She should have repulsed him but, for one incredible second, she had felt herself softening under his assault and welcoming the touch of his lips.

He had been right to treat her like a street-walker. She had behaved no better!

His final offer had proved it. He would take her innocence without thought for the consequences, as if her virtue was worth no more than the turn of a card on the Faro table. She would spend an hour—perhaps less—in his bed. And then he would send her back to Lady Luce, a little used, to be sure, but the bearer of a gift of twelve thousand pounds.

Would Lady Luce be grateful? Marina doubted it. If she ever found out, the lady would probably laugh.

No. Nothing would ever make Marina accept Kit Stratton's humiliating offer. Not even—

The hackney drew up outside Lady Luce's house. The front door opened just as Marina was stepping down on to the flagway.

The Earl's corpulent figure seemed to fill the doorway. 'So there you are at last, Miss Beaumont,' he said ominously. 'I shall not ask where you have been. We have much more important matters to discuss.' He looked her up and down, taking note of her dishevelled state. 'There is no need for you to change for this interview,' he said with a sneer. 'Our business will take but a very few minutes. How you dress thereafter will be your own affair.'

Kit poured himself a second glass of madeira and downed it in a single swallow, as he had the first. He looked across at the window and shook his head at the drab grey skies. He had gone too far. She had been foolish and naïve in her quest, but still…he had gone too far. She was, after all, a lady, but he had treated her like the veriest doxy. That final remark about how long… Had he really said something so unforgivably crude?

He must be losing his mind. He was definitely losing his self-control and he *never* did that with women. Never.

Not for more than five years.

Since that mad moment when he had compromised Emma Fitzwilliam, he had never allowed himself to utter a word or move so much as a finger without carefully calculating how the lady in question would react to his advances. He had thought he knew how to read them all.

But Miss Beaumont was not predictable. She had not succumbed to his practised lovemaking. She had thrown his words back in his face. And she had even compared him unfavourably to—

Hugo! How did Lady Luce's grey companion come to know of Hugo Stratton? They could never have met, could they? She would have been little more than a child when Hugo returned from the wars. And then he had married Emma Fitzwilliam.

If the grey lady had had dealings with Hugo, they must have taken place since his marriage to Emma. Well, well. That did not sound in the least like his upright brother. But no...it made no sense. What could Hugo want with such a woman when he had Emma?

Emma was blonde, beautiful, vivacious, loving—a perfect wife. Miss Beaumont was grey and rather gaunt. She did not seem to know how to laugh. And she prickled with pride. What could Hugo ever see in her?

The unexpected.

She was not like any of the women Kit had bedded. She fought him. And she spoke of honour, and of the worth of a gentleman.

She could not be Hugo's mistress. There must be something else between them. It was a puzzle. And it would plague him until he had resolved it.

Kit rose and made his way to the door. No point in staying here. Katharina was long gone and could not be with him again for several days. Sometimes, unfortunately, a husband had to take precedence. Kit might as well go to his club and face the inevitable gossip.

The cold brass handle served to remind him that the weather outside was foul and that he had no carriage in Chelsea. He opened the door to order another hackney, this time for himself.

Had she gone straight back to Lady Luce? Would she ever dare to venture out alone again? She would not be found walking early in the park again, that was certain. She had fled from him like a frightened doe.

He thought back through their tense encounter and found he was no longer quite so sure. He had never discovered precisely why she was so intent on begging him to forgive the Dowager's debt. To be honest, he had given her no chance to explain anything. He had simply pounced on her.

It would be madness for her to meet him again, knowing, as she did, what would happen between them. But how could he be sure—certain sure—that she would not accept his challenge?

His answer was clear enough. He must leave orders that any letter was to be brought round to his lodgings immediately.

And he must be prepared to hire himself a plain, closed carriage.

Chapter Seven

Marina only just succeeded in reaching her bedchamber. She did not even have the strength to reach the bed before her legs crumpled under her. She sank to the floor and dropped her head into her hands.

She was dismissed!

So much for the Dowager's promise of protection. That had gained her nothing. Lord Luce was insisting she leave his mother's house before the day was out. Mr Kit Stratton would wait in vain for her letter—Marina would be long gone.

How would she ever explain to Mama? Was there even enough money in her purse to pay her fare back home?

Damn Kit Stratton! It was all his fault!

'Twelve thousand! Are you saying that stupid chit stood by and watched while you lost twelve thousand pounds?'

'She did not stand and watch,' Lady Luce snapped. 'She was seated throughout.'

He ground his teeth.

'You need not play the martyr, William. The debt is mine, not yours.'

'Indeed? And you have twelve thousand immediately to hand, do you, Mama?'

For once she said nothing, pressing her lips together in a tight, angry line.

'No. Nor do I. I shall have to go to the moneylenders until I can sell the unentailed land. And there will have to be strict economies. For both of us.' He looked down at her, frowning darkly. 'Your useless companion leaves today, of course, and this house—'

'What? You have absolutely no right to dismiss her. How dare—?'

'I pay her, Mama. She is become an expense I can no longer afford.'

And his mother had long been another such, he thought grimly. It would be so very satisfying to tell her so. If only he could—

'Petty revenge, William. You seek to humiliate your own mother. I had not thought even you could stoop so low.' She looked at him with scorn.

Lord Luce was shocked into silence for a moment. He would almost have said she hated him. 'Mama, I...' he began. He cleared his throat and tried again. 'Mama, I truly cannot afford to pay Miss Beaumont. But, by all means, let her remain for a few days more. I admit it would be unkind to pack her off in this appalling weather.'

His mother looked at him in sudden surprise. Then she nodded.

'Perhaps you will tell her, Mama? If I am to arrange the money in time, I must set about matters immediately.'

He made to leave, then stopped, hesitating. 'Mama,'

he began in a softer voice, 'please stop doing this. I grant that you have a right to choose how you order your own life. If I have seemed to interfere, I…I apologise. But if you continue to gamble, you will ruin us all. Truly. I beg of you to stop. For the sake of your grandchildren. Please.'

He looked pleadingly across at his mother's tiny figure. There was no sign of softening in her features. This time, his tactic had failed.

'I see. No doubt we shall meet again in church tomorrow,' he said with freezing formality. 'I bid you good day.' He bowed and left her.

Lady Luce walked over to her favourite chair and slowly took her seat. For several minutes, she stared vacantly at the window and the street beyond. The driving rain was pouring down the panes so that it was difficult to see out.

The Dowager's bony hand reached for the bell on the table beside her. Almost before the sound had died away, the butler appeared.

'Have you seen Miss Beaumont this morning, Tibbs?'

'Why, yes, m'lady. She was with his lordship earlier, and then—'

'Never mind that,' snapped the Dowager. 'What was she doing before that? I sent my woman to her room and she was not there.'

'She…er…she went out early, m'lady. Walking, I supposed.'

Lady Luce snorted. 'When did she return?'

'Er…just after his lordship arrived, m'lady. He interviewed her in the bookroom.'

'I see. What are you waiting for, man? Go and fetch her! What is the point of having a companion who provides no company? Go and fetch her at once!'

* * *

Marina paused at the foot of the stairs to straighten her skirts. At least she was no longer mud-spattered, as she had been during that degrading interview with Lord Luce. She would have looked even worse, if Kit Stratton had not sent her home in a cab. Should she be grateful? It had kept her dry. And she had not got lost, as she had done on the way to Chelsea. Then again, if she had been forced to walk, Lord Luce might have been long gone by the time she arrived back. A curse on Kit Stratton! Everything was his fault.

Tibbs had already announced her. She had no option but to face her second accuser.

'So there you are at last, miss!' snapped Lady Luce, the moment the door closed behind Marina. 'Perhaps you would be good enough to explain where you were this morning?'

Oh, dear. Marina had been *almost* sure that her lady-ship would not wake before noon, that her absence would not be noticed. Yes, she had been a fool, on that count also.

'I assumed that you would sleep late, ma'am,' she said, 'and so I went out for a walk. I—'

'A walk? In the pouring rain?' Lady Luce's tone was scathing.

Marina lifted her chin. 'I am well used to the rain, ma'am,' she said with quiet dignity. 'In Yorkshire, it rains a great deal. If one ventured out only when the weather was fine, one would take no exercise at all.' Marina looked directly at the old woman, marvelling at her own ability to fence with half-truths. Kit Stratton's devilry was rubbing off on her, it seemed.

Lady Luce snorted in disbelief. 'Very well,' she said sharply, 'but in future I expect you to be here when I send for you.'

'In f...future?' Marina hid her hands in the folds of her drab gown to conceal their sudden trembling.

'Sit down, girl. You are as white as a sheet...and if there is one thing I cannot abide, it is missish young females who swoon at the slightest reverse.'

'I shall not faint, ma'am,' said Marina, trying to sound as if she was fully in control of herself. 'It...it is just that his lordship said I must leave at once. I—'

'His lordship was incensed by your behaviour. Not unnaturally,' she added, in a voice that tried, but failed, to convey a degree of sympathy with her son's feelings. 'But he does not dispute that it is for me to decide whether you shall go or stay.' Lady Luce gave a tight little smile that made Marina's heart sink. 'For the moment, I wish you to stay. Is that understood?'

'Yes, ma'am,' said Marina meekly. What on earth was going on? The Dowager had won the battle with her son—that was clear—but why had she bothered to fight?

'Now,' said the Dowager briskly, 'there are a number of matters that I must attend to this afternoon.' She looked disdainfully at Marina's shabby gown, wrinkling her nose in distaste. 'The first of them shall be to find you a suitable gown.'

'Ma'am—'

'You are to be ready to accompany me in ten minutes. Do not be late. That is all.'

There was nothing further to be said. Marina rose quickly, dropped a curtsy to the Dowager's back, and hurried away to find her bonnet and pelisse.

'Well? Do you, or do you not?'

Marina came suddenly back to earth. What had the Dowager just said to her? 'I beg pardon, ma'am. I fear I was wool-gathering. You asked...?'

'I asked, miss, whether you were satisfied with this gown, or whether we must seek another,' said Lady Luce testily. 'Well?'

Marina looked at herself in the glass. It was a very simple muslin gown, totally plain, but in a most becoming shade of pale green. She could not remember when she had ever worn anything but browns and greys, serviceable colours for a young woman who walked, and worked, in all weathers. This was sadly impractical...but she loved it. 'It is delightful, ma'am, but—' Marina tore her eyes from her reflection '—I fear I cannot afford to buy any gowns at all until I have my first quarter's wages. And since Lord Luce said I was to leave, I do not think I should—'

'Balderdash!' her ladyship declared. 'You will leave when—and if—I say. And I refuse to have a scullery maid for a companion. What would your cousin, Lady Blaine, say if she saw you?'

'But Lady Blaine has never laid eyes on me, ma'am, and—'

'For heaven's sake, child, will you never learn when to stop protesting? I say you shall have it. And the evening gown also. They are a gift. You will not be required to pay for them.'

'Oh.' Marina let out a long sigh. How wonderful. And now she would not have to meet Kit Stratton in her dowdy grey dress. He would not—

What was she thinking of? She was not going to meet that handsome devil at all. Never again. She had made up her mind to that, the moment she left his squalid little love-nest. She would not forfeit her honour, even to save her position with Lady Luce...even to save Mama from penury. It was impossible. Mama would be repelled by the very thought of such a sacrifice.

But Mama need never know.

Marina tried to close her mind against the siren voices trying to lure her to her doom. Mama might never know, but Marina herself would be only too aware of her transgressions. She did not think she would be able to live with herself, no matter how worthy the cause. She—

'Marina! I am waiting!' The Dowager was becoming angrier by the minute. This time she was clearly waiting for Marina to change back into her old gown, so that they could leave the modest dressmaker's that the Dowager had thought appropriate for a penniless cousin of the Viscountess Blaine.

'I beg your pardon, ma'am. Excuse me. I shall be ready in a very few moments.'

And this time, she was, having ruthlessly suppressed every urge to lapse yet again into wondering about the maybes and might-have-beens of her life.

It was much more difficult during the rest of the afternoon, however, for her ladyship rambled on and on about the places they visited, the people they saw, and the problems of life in London. Marina tried to play her companion's role. She smiled, she nodded, she murmured agreement at, she hoped, the right moments, but she was not seeing what Lady Luce saw, nor sharing her ladyship's thoughts. A terrifyingly handsome male face kept intruding into her mind. The skin of her arms and shoulders tingled as though his hands still held her. And her lips felt soft and yielding, waiting for the next brush of—

She groaned.

'Are you ill, child? You cannot feel faint, surely? Not on account of a short carriage ride and two new gowns.'

Marina forced a smile.

'I warn you,' said Lady Luce sternly. 'If you take to collapsing on me, I shall send you back to Yorkshire, no matter what your noble relations may think.'

This time Marina did not rise to the Dowager's bait. She remained calm and matter of fact. 'I have never fainted in my life, ma'am, and I do not intend to start now.'

Marina sank, fully clothed, on to her pillows. Peace at last! The blessed silence wrapped around her like the softest goose-down coverlet. Now she could try to resolve her future, without the Dowager's never-ceasing commentary on Society life and living.

That was not really fair...and Marina knew it. In more settled circumstances, Lady Luce's sharp-tongued comments would have been most entertaining but, today, too many of them had been directed at Marina herself. And she had deserved them all. She had never been one for allowing her thoughts to wander into might-have-beens. Indeed, her mother had often said that Marina was too commonsensical for her own good. Here, in London, she was supposed to be a paid companion, anxious for her lady's comfort, not a day-dreaming fool who had constantly to be recalled to her duty.

It was all Kit Stratton's fault!

He had disrupted her peace by his scandalous proposals and his even more scandalous behaviour. She had tried all day to banish his image, his voice, his touch...

She had failed. If she closed her eyes now, she could see him still, his beautiful features made sinister by the hard, calculating gaze he was bestowing on her.

She forced her eyes open. The image retreated. She dare not allow herself to sleep lest it come again. She was afraid of what she might do if she permitted Kit

Stratton to invade her dreams. Here, waking, she had some shreds of morality to cling to. There, if he took her in his arms again, she might be tempted to forget them all. For just one more taste of those lips…

She jerked upright. Heavens, she was starting to doze. She must not. Not until she had reached her decision.

She sprang up from her bed and began to pace about the room. That was better. Sleep was banished now. She must think, and weigh, and decide.

She could not yield her person to Kit Stratton. It was wicked, and immoral, and against everything she had been taught. A woman should remain pure until she married. She should give herself to her husband alone, in order to bear his children. Marina had seen quite enough of the treatment meted out to fallen women, even in rural Yorkshire. It was a terrible fate.

And it could be hers if she gave herself to Kit Stratton.

He would use her and discard her. He would not suffer—it was the way of the world that men walked free while women bore the burden of both their sins—and he would probably condemn her for yielding to his threats.

And yet the yielding might be so sweet…

She touched her fingers to her lips, remembering the feel of his mouth on hers, the way the heat of him had seemed to light an answering fire in her limbs—

No! She must not! Kit Stratton was a practised seducer, an out-and-out rake. He had known exactly what he was doing to Marina. No doubt he had intended to make her melt in his arms, to welcome his advances. She must not imagine that he had *felt* anything for her. She was just one more poor gentlewoman to be conquered…and forgotten.

Marina's pacing was becoming more and more frenzied. She forced herself to stop, holding on to a simple

wooden chair for support. She must not permit him to
rule her like this. She must find a way of giving him his
own again. She must outwit him.

There must be a way. And it must be done soon, before the Dowager's debt fell due.

She would find a way to best him if she had to spend
all night devising it. He had thought to trick her into his
bed, had he? Well, she had a trick or two up her sleeve
also, and she could play as dishonourable a hand as any
man alive.

She had found her solution.

Her father had taught her to cheat at cards. While she
had never used her skills for real, she had become most
adept. Her father and her uncle had laughed aloud when
she trounced them, time and time again, so perfectly that
neither of them could ever catch her out. Oh, how care-
free they had all been then. She could still see her father's smiling face and long, lean body, so well suited
to the dark green of the rifle brigade. On their last leave,
the two men had made much of her, a gawky fourteen-
year-old with no pretence to beauty. For those few
weeks, she had felt so very special. And then, in the
depths of a Yorkshire winter, the terrible news had
come. The laughter had disappeared for good from her
mother's eyes. In a single day, Mama had lost her only
brother and the husband she loved, but Marina never saw
her weep, even when they discovered that Papa's gambling had left them almost penniless. Mama simply became silent and serious, devoting all her energies to finding a way of supporting her two young children. By
calling on all her scholarly abilities, she had succeeded,
though it had been hard for them all.

Marina twisted the mourning ring on her finger. It was
all she had of her beloved father...apart from his lean

Rake's Reward

looks, and an ability to fuzz the cards. She would use her skills against Kit Stratton, in a way that would have made even her father marvel!

She carried her candle to the little table by the window and sat down, pulling a sheet of paper towards her. She dipped her pen in the standish and wrote the salutation with a firm hand. *To Mr Christopher Stratton. Sir...*

She stopped, pen poised. What was she to say? He was expecting a letter naming the day for an assignation, not an invitation to a game of cards. And where was it to take place? It would be madness to go alone to his Chelsea house—if she wished to leave there with her virtue intact. Perhaps she could challenge him at Méchante's? She would need to persuade the Dowager to take her there again—and soon—and not to betray that fact that Marina would be writing vowels with no money to back them. Perhaps—

Marina laid down her pen in disgust. Her common sense seemed to have deserted her completely. Was she going out of her mind? There was no way, no way at all, in which she could cheat Kit Stratton out of twelve thousand pounds in the next five days. Not unless she went alone to his house. There, she could—

No. There must be another solution.

She picked up the pen once more and rolled it round in her fingers. They were long, and clever, and—with a little practice to regain their old skills—they could produce a card as from nowhere, but in this case they would not provide the answer. She had been prepared to consider a thoroughly dishonourable course of conduct, in order to avoid even worse dishonour, but—

But there *was* another way. Less sure, perhaps, but still...

She dipped her pen once more and began to write,

pausing now and then over her choice of words. The letter must appear totally innocuous, to anyone other than Kit Stratton. That was vital.

She wrote until, at last, she was sure she had achieved her aim. She sat back in her chair to read her completed letter.

Sir, it began, *With reference to our recent discussions, you will appreciate that the property I have to offer is too valuable to be traded, except against payment in advance. I would therefore ask you to forward to me the paper in your possession at your earliest convenience. I will undertake to make all necessary arrangements for the conclusion of our business as soon as I am in receipt of the document in question.*

She nodded in satisfaction and added her signature to the sheet. He would not mistake her meaning. Of that, she was sure. He would send the Dowager's vowel for twelve thousand pounds, expecting Marina—as a woman of her word—to surrender her virtue to him. But she would not.

She could not!

Somehow, once she had the vowel in her possession, she would find a way of depriving Kit Stratton of his prize. The reward for his infamy should not be Marina's virtue.

Even if she had to behave in a thoroughly dishonourable fashion to achieve it, she would make sure his wicked plans were thwarted. She would begin practising at once to regain her skills with the cards…just in case they were needed.

And she would laugh in his face when she triumphed.

Chapter Eight

Kit looked up, annoyed, as the study door opened. He had given specific orders that he was not to be disturbed.

'Hugo!' he cried, his frown clearing immediately. 'What are you doing back in town? How long do you stay?' He strode across the room to shake his brother's hand.

'A short time only, perhaps a week or two.' Sir Hugo Stratton smiled enigmatically. 'Business, Kit,' he said.

Kit raised an eyebrow. He knew his older brother well enough to recognise that smile. 'You mean that you have heard about my…er…exploits and wish to satisfy yourself that nothing untoward is afoot. You really ought to stop concerning yourself about me, you know, Hugo. I am well able to look after myself now.'

Hugo laughed. 'That is what worries me. You do look after yourself. But someone has to look to the family's reputation, and by all accounts, *you* are not…' He stopped suddenly and put a friendly hand on Kit's shoulder. 'Why don't you tell me what has been happening since last I saw you?'

Kit nodded. In this mood, his brother would not be thwarted. It was easier just to give in gracefully. 'I will.

Just give me a moment to finish this letter.' He sat down at his desk again and set about folding and sealing the papers he had been working on when Hugo arrived. 'Pull the bell, will you, Hugo? I must send this off.'

The door opened just as Kit rose with the thick letter in his hand. 'See that this is delivered this afternoon,' he said, handing it to the butler. 'And make sure that the messenger remains anonymous.' The butler bowed impassively and withdrew.

'Can't afford to let the good Baron know the source of his wife's correspondence, can you?' commented Hugo wryly. 'I should do the same in your shoes, I suppose.'

Kit grinned. 'I might have known you would have heard about Katharina. How do you do it? You are supposed to be buried in the country.'

Hugo laid a finger along his nose and tapped twice. 'Family secret,' he said, failing to keep the amusement out of his voice. 'As head of the family, I have to have some advantages, you know.'

Kit shook his head resignedly and moved to pick up the heavy crystal decanter. 'I collect that Emma's formidable aunt has been gossiping again. Might I ask what tales she has told you this time?'

'You are too sharp for your own good sometimes, Kit,' replied Hugo, taking a glass of madeira and settling himself in the armchair opposite Kit's mahogany desk. 'You are right, of course. Emma's Aunt Warenne has been keeping us up to date. She says that your Baroness is a diamond of the first water. And that she has a remarkably possessive husband.' Hugo looked questioningly at his brother.

'There is no need to worry, Hugo. He is possessive, I grant you, but he is a very poor shot.'

Hugo choked over his madeira.

'Do take care, brother,' said Kit impudently. 'I really have no desire to take over your role as head of the family, even temporarily.'

'By all accounts, you are unlikely to live long enough to do so,' replied Hugo. 'Even your possessive Baron could have a lucky shot, you know. I can understand that you wished to make her your mistress in Vienna, but it is bound to be much more dangerous to continue the liaison here in London. As a diplomat, the Baron has a very great deal to lose.'

'True,' said Kit. Hugo was clearly waiting for him to say something more, but Kit kept all his attention on his glass.

With a sigh, Hugo continued, 'The *on dit* is that, since it took you almost a twelvemonth to seduce her from the path of virtue, you were unwilling to give up the spoils when her husband was called to London.'

Kit said nothing. He continued to savour his madeira.

'I take it that the Baroness was the reason you would not return to England after John's death?'

Kit swirled the wine in his glass. 'She seemed to be…unaccountably attached to her virtue for a considerable time after I returned from the funeral,' he said at last. 'I am glad to say that she has tired of it now.'

'Does it never occur to you, Kit, that seducing virtuous matrons is…is wicked?'

Kit tried to stifle a chortle.

'Yes, very well, perhaps that was a rather melodramatic way to put it, but… Let me tell you, Kit, that if any man tried to seduce Emma, I should put a bullet in him without a moment's thought.'

Kit looked up. One corner of his mouth tugged into a slightly mocking smile. 'But I'd wager your Emma would never be seduced. That's the difference, you see, Hugo. Katharina's seduction was long and drawn out because she *enjoyed* the chase. Make no mistake, she had decided almost at the outset that she would succumb…eventually. Fortunately, I was the only one to see that. Most of the Embassy fellows were sure she was virtue incarnate. Wagered I'd never succeed with her. She won me a tidy sum, I'm delighted to say.'

'How very calculating that sounds,' said Hugo, with obvious distaste. 'But if she means nothing to you, why did you follow her to London?'

'Because it suited my other plans. If Society was convinced I was deep in love with the beautiful Baroness, the tabbies were unlikely to dwell on what else I might have in mind. I prefer my…er…victims to be taken unawares.'

Hugo laughed shortly. 'And she was, I collect. To the tune of twelve thousand pounds. Was that not a bit steep, Kit? She won only five from you, after all.'

'True,' said Kit evenly, 'but five years of exile adds a great deal to the debt, in my opinion. I think twelve thousand would be a fair settlement.'

'*Would be?*' queried Hugo. 'You don't say Lady Luce will not pay?'

'Cannot? Will not? What does it matter? I am sure that she *cannot* pay without calling on her son for help. And he is far from willing to support her gambling. All London knows that. On the other hand, how would it look if he—?'

'If he left her hanging in the wind?' finished Hugo. 'We all know the answer to *that*. No one would receive either of them. Luce can't allow that to happen, not with his top-lofty shrew of a wife. She would make his life a misery, without a doubt. Never met a woman so dev-ilish high in the instep. Or one with so little cause.'

'One of the dangers of parson's mousetrap, Hugo,' said Kit.

Hugo shook his head despairingly at his brother. 'Not if you marry a woman who loves you, Kit. Don't you think you—?'

Kit rose quickly from his seat and headed for the door before the conversation could take an even more un-welcome turn. He should never have mentioned mar-riage in the first place. 'I've arranged to meet some friends at the club,' he said lightly. 'I take it you will accompany me? If we don't leave now, we shall be late.'

Hugo cast his eyes up to the ceiling, but he did not try to pursue the topic any further. Kit was relieved. He had the greatest of respect for his brother, and he cer-tainly did not wish to be at outs with him. On the other hand, if Hugo continued to drop these heavy hints about marriage…and love…

Women! They created nothing but problems!

Struck by a sudden thought, Kit wrenched open the door and called impatiently for his butler. 'That letter I gave you,' he said sharply, before the man had time to catch his breath. 'Have you despatched it yet?'

The butler flushed guiltily. 'I was just about to sum-mon a messenger, sir, and—'

'Don't bother me with your lame excuses, man. Hand it over.'

The butler produced the letter and retreated with rather more haste than normal.

Kit strode across the room and threw the letter down on his desk. 'It is your fault, you know, Hugo,' he said with a wry grin. 'You reminded me—unwittingly, I ad-mit—that it does not do to respond just when, or how, a lady expects. I think that, on this occasion, the lady shall be made to wait a little longer. You never know, it may do her good.'

He turned to where Hugo stood, intrigued, and clapped his brother on the shoulder. 'And now,' Kit said smoothly, 'if you are ready, shall we go?'

'Beware, Kit,' said Hugo. 'One day it may be you on the receiving end of such cavalier treatment.'

Kit looked hard at his brother and shook his head. 'Not I,' he said firmly. 'Not from any woman alive.'

Approaching the receiving line, Marina followed dutifully two steps behind Lady Luce. It was a very grand affair indeed. Marina's simple amber silk gown, which she had thought so splendid when she first tried it on, was very dull by comparison with the finery of the other guests. She would be able to merge into the background, yet again.

Introductions completed, the Dowager led the way into the ballroom and stood for a moment surveying the scene. She called Marina close with a beckoning finger. 'Do you see those two ladies over by the window?' she whispered, indicating with her fan a pair of richly dressed matrons. 'The one wearing that appalling puce gown is William's wife, Charlotte. Never did have an ounce of taste! Never a beauty, either.'

The Dowager's daughter-in-law was both plump and plain, but she had a decided air of consequence, even from a distance.

'She was passable when she was younger, I'll admit. Lost her figure—and her looks—through too much child-bearing. Much too much. Ten children, indeed! An heir and a spare should be enough for any man.'

Marina was hard put to stop herself from laughing

aloud. But the Dowager's next words banished any hint of mirth.

'So—what do you think of your exalted cousin?' Seeing Marina's obvious surprise, the Dowager said, 'The lady standing beside Charlotte is the present Viscountess Blaine.'

Marina saw a thin woman with an overlong nose and a modish but very unflattering hairstyle. She was wearing too many jewels. 'She looks…' Marina could not find any words. Even to the Dowager, she could hardly say that Lady Blaine looked like a horse.

'Quite,' said Lady Luce with a tight smile. 'Come. Let me make the introductions.' She strode across the room much faster than seemed possible for such a tiny person, forcing the other guests to make way for her. Marina followed in her wake, more than a little reluctant to face one of the relations who had treated her family with such contempt.

'Good evening, Charlotte. Good evening, Lady Blaine.'

The two younger women returned Lady Luce's greeting without any sign of pleasure. Both ignored Marina completely.

'I should like to present my new companion, Miss Beaumont,' said Lady Luce neutrally.

Both ladies turned to glance at the companion for a second. They were clearly far from satisfied with what they saw. Neither offered a hand.

The Dowager eyed Lady Blaine with disfavour. 'Surprising that you have not met before, is it not?' she said. 'Considering Miss Beaumont's mother is full cousin to your husband. But then, he has been out of the country for some months, has he not?'

The younger Lady Luce had started in surprise and

now lifted her lorgnette to inspect Marina more closely. Marina felt as if she were being examined for flaws like an insect impaled on a pin. She lifted her chin, turning all her attention to the Dowager and Lady Blaine.

'So this is the gel I recommended to you,' said Lady Blaine at last.

She had the kind of voice that reminded Marina of fingernails scraping across a chalkboard. How could anyone bear to be in the same room with her?

'I hope she is giving satisfaction,' continued Lady Blaine, for all the world as if Marina were not present. 'You must understand, ma'am, that I recommended her only because of the urgency of your son's request. I could think of no one else who could be procured at such short notice. If I had had a little more time, I am sure I could have found someone to suit you admirably.'

The Dowager's eyes narrowed dangerously. 'You have made yourself quite useful enough, my dear,' she said. 'I suggest you take your satisfaction from that. Leave the good deeds to those more accustomed to them. Come, Marina.' The Dowager moved Marina away before Lady Blaine's affronted gasp could be turned into words.

'Ignore her,' continued the Dowager. 'She has no breeding. Blaine married her for her money, of course. The men of that family always marry money and spend it on their mistresses.'

What an outrageous old woman she was! To be able to say such things! As a poor relation, Marina must always mind her tongue, but living with the Dowager would certainly never be dull.

The Dowager immediately began to point out other notable guests and to regale Marina with salty stories of their exploits. It was most entertaining. 'That beanpole

of a gel over there,' she continued, pointing most im-
politely with her fan, 'is Lady Blaine's eldest. Milly, or
Tilly, or some such. Her face has too much of the dead
horse for perfect beauty.'

Marina's eyes widened. How could she?

'Gel like that will never take. Especially since her
mother persists in dressing her in white. Makes her look
positively ill with that sallow complexion. The woman
has even less taste than Charlotte.'

Marina tried not to nod. Her brother would be
ashamed to learn that his sister could do anything quite
so uncharitable, however satisfying it might have been
to learn that her cousin was even less attractive than
herself. In Miss Blaine's case, a handsome dowry might
provide some slight compensation.

'Oh,' breathed Marina, catching sight of a couple
dancing the waltz, 'who is that beautiful fair-haired
lady?'

'What? Oh, that one,' said the Dowager, suddenly less
animated than before. 'That, child, is Lady Stratton, who
was Emma Fitzwilliam before her marriage. She is
waltzing with her husband, Sir Hugo Stratton. Don't
hold with it myself. Living in each other's pockets like
that.' She shook her head.

The dancing couple turned at that moment so that Marina could see Sir Hugo's face. Even though this man
was much older, and his face was visibly scarred, the
likeness to Kit Stratton was very strong.

'Oh,' breathed Marina, 'is he—?'

'Yes, he is Kit Stratton's brother,' said the Dowager
grimly, 'and as plump in the pocket as any man in London. Emma Fitzwilliam was the catch of the Season
when he married her. No doubt her money helped to
compensate for the scandal.'

'Scandal? I...I don't understand, ma'am.'

'No. Why should you? You're too young to know. It is just one more reason to beware of Kit Stratton, that is all. He ruined Emma Fitzwilliam, but he refused to marry her. Left that task to his elder brother. That's why he has spent the last five years abroad.'

Marina looked back at the couple on the floor. Sir Hugo Stratton and his wife were smiling at each other in a way that made Marina's heart turn over. Whatever might have been the reasons for the marriage, there was no doubt in Marina's mind that it was a love match now.

'Good gad!' exclaimed the Dowager a moment later. 'There's no avoiding the man, even here. Keeps turning up like a bad penny.'

Kit Stratton had just entered the room and was threading his way through the crowd of guests. Marina's stomach lurched at the sight of him. Her palms had become damp inside her borrowed evening gloves. Why did he have to be here? Why now? Would he recognise her?

He stopped some distance from them and sketched an elegant bow to a haughty dame in a feathered turban. Their exchange was very brief. Then, with a barely suppressed grimace, he left her for the dance floor, where he tapped his brother on the shoulder and impudently stole his partner. Sir Hugo simply smiled on the departing couple and strolled off, stopping here and there for an animated conversation with some of the other guests. He did not glance back even once towards his brother. Instead, he looked lazily round the ballroom, as if to assess how many of the guests he knew. His glance flickered over Marina and the Dowager, hesitated barely a moment, and then moved casually on.

'There seems to be no bad blood there,' Marina said, unwisely voicing her thoughts.

'Hmph,' snorted Lady Luce in disgust. 'It's all for show, I don't doubt. Come, Marina,' she added, turning for the door. 'I have no intention of remaining here a moment longer. I had not expected the air at this ball to be quite so polluted.'

With a final lingering glance towards the colourful throng of swirling dancers, and Kit Stratton's tall, elegant figure, Marina followed her mistress to the exit, totally unaware that she was not the only lady taking an interest in that arrestingly handsome gentleman. Miss Tilly Blaine, half-hidden by a pillar, was gazing on Kit Stratton with wide, glowing eyes, as if she had never beheld anything so beautiful.

Marina spent a disturbed night and then an uncomfortable day, trying vainly to give all her attention to Lady Luce's At Home. At least neither the younger Lady Luce nor her bosom bow, Lady Blaine, had put in an appearance.

As soon as the drawing-room door closed behind the last of her callers, the Dowager sank back into her favourite chair and straightened her powdered wig. 'Thank heavens for that,' she said. 'I was beginning to think that pair of harpies would never leave.'

Marina smiled but said nothing. The Dowager had obviously enjoyed the afternoon's verbal sparring with her visitors. The problem with the last two was their failure to fight back when lashed by the Dowager's acid tongue.

'And what, pray, are you smiling at, miss?' asked the Dowager.

Marina considered for a second or two, and then said, 'I was musing on the definition of a harpy, ma'am. I was always taught that they were fearsome mythical beasts, with murderous claws. But it seemed to me that there was nothing in the least mythical about Mrs Varity and her daughter—'

Lady Luce choked on a laugh. Mrs Varity was a remarkably large woman and totally unsuited to figuring in any myth, except in the guise of a well-padded cushion.

'And their claws seemed to have been drawn long before they even entered the house,' finished Marina, undaunted. 'I cannot think why that should be so. After all, it is not as though your guests are received with anything other than the utmost kindness.'

Lady Luce struck Marina on the wrist with her fan. It was quite a gentle blow, however, and the lady's eyes were sparkling with appreciative amusement. 'That is quite enough from you, young lady,' she said. 'I fear I am nurturing a viper in my bosom, keeping you here.'

'I fear so, ma'am,' agreed Marina, nodding gravely.

'Hmph! And I will not have you defending that Varity woman, either. She only came in hopes of finding out exactly what happened at Méchante's t'other evening. Wanted to crow over my losses, that was all. Like a cock on a dunghill!' She opened her fan and waved it aimlessly to and fro for a moment. 'I fancy I showed her the dangers of that!'

'Indeed, ma'am,' said Marina, non-committally. In fact, Mrs Varity had quit the field in full retreat, and Lady Luce was clearly relishing her victory. Now might be the time to tackle her on the touchy subject of Kit Stratton. 'Are you expecting Mr Stratton in the next few days, ma'am?' she asked quietly.

'What business is that of yours?' snapped Lady Luce, her geniality gone in an instant. 'Fallen for his pretty face, have you, eh?'

'No, no!' Marina felt sure she was blushing. 'It was just… I was wondering whether, as a gentleman and so very much your junior, he might not decide that it was…unseemly to collect on the debt.'

'Not he!' cried her ladyship, with an explosion of harsh laughter. 'Kit Stratton does not have a gentlemanly bone in his body. He would sooner cut his own throat than—' She looked up as the door opened. 'What is it *now*, Tibbs?'

The butler bowed stiffly, indicating the salver he carried. 'A letter has been delivered, m'lady. By hand. The messenger did not wait for a reply.'

Lady Luce stretched out her hand towards the salver.

'It is for Miss Beaumont, m'lady,' said the butler, offering the tray to Marina.

It had come! At last!

Lady Luce sat back in her chair with a grunt of disapproval. Marina could feel those sharp little eyes boring into her as she took the letter and calmly nodded her thanks to the butler. In a moment, the Dowager was going to question her about it. What could she say? Penniless companions, newly arrived in London, did not receive letters by special messenger—especially if they had no acquaintance in the city. She should have been prepared for this.

Marina weighed the letter in her hand. It was heavy enough to contain an enclosure. And it must be from Kit Stratton. The handwriting was bold and firm. Definitely not a lady's hand. Feeling the Dowager's increasing curiosity on her, Marina stuffed the letter hurriedly into the pocket of her gown.

'You may open your letter if you wish, child,' said her ladyship airily. 'You must be wishing to know who has written to you.'

Marina shook her head quickly. Too quickly. 'Oh, I know that already, ma'am,' she said. 'There is only one possibility, since I have no friends in London. There is a…a London clergyman who may become a patron to my brother, Harry,' she said, trying to make the hasty lie sound convincing. 'You may recall that he is to enter the Church when he leaves Oxford. The reverend gentleman promised that his wife would seek me out when I came to London. It is most kind of them both, I think, since they know nothing of Harry's sister. The letter can only be from her.' Marina tried to smile confidently at the Dowager. Would she be believed? It seemed a remarkably unlikely story. What if the Dowager asked Marina to produce this clergyman?

Lady Luce looked assessingly at Marina for a moment. Then she said sharply, 'You are here as companion to me, my girl, not to be running off to some do-gooding parson. Bad enough to have to listen to them on Sundays, without other days of the week as well.'

Marina tightened her lips to hide her smile. Lady Luce made no secret of her trenchant views on the clergy. If she disliked a sermon, she made sure that the whole congregation knew it. She had done so on the previous Sunday, smiling in satisfaction while her son squirmed with embarrassment. Marina had felt it, too, but in truth the Dowager's outrageous behaviour had been the least of her worries. She had spent Sunday, and most of Monday, wondering whether Kit Stratton would reply. At least she had her answer now.

'You may visit this parson in your own time,' Lady Luce continued. 'Not in mine. Is that understood?'

'Yes, ma'am,' said Marina meekly.

'Oh, get along with you now. Go and read your letter,

since it is burning a hole in your pocket. I shall not need you until dinner.'

Marina could scarce believe her luck. It seemed the Dowager believed her story. And as for the degree of indulgence she was showing…

'Thank you, ma'am. You are very kind,' she said, rising from her chair to drop a curtsy. 'I—'

The Dowager waved an impatient hand. 'I suggest you go before I change my mind,' she said tartly.

Marina retreated, as quickly as dignity permitted. The butler was hovering in the hallway, so she mounted the stairs at a measured pace until he was out of sight. Then she scampered up the remaining flight and along the hallway to the safety of her room, trying not to slam the door in her haste.

The letter was sealed with a wafer that did not wish to be removed! She cursed softly, trying to tear it apart. At last, the thick paper was undone. Yes, there was an enclosure. Kit Stratton must have taken the bait!

In her haste, Marina dropped the outer letter on the floor. No matter. She would read it in a moment. First, she must be sure that she had the Dowager's vowel in her hand.

She spread the folded sheet on the little table and smoothed her hand quickly across it. Disappointment hit her like a blow. It was the same black handwriting as the address. Why had Mr Stratton written her two letters?

The answer came in a moment. The inner letter was addressed not to Marina, but to the Dowager herself. And Marina was clearly intended to read it. That was the only reason why he would have left it unsealed.

Marina glanced quickly down the sheet, hardly daring to breathe. Then she let out a tiny cry of triumph. It was as good as forgiveness of the debt. He wrote that he would return the Dowager's vowel when he called upon her at the end of the week—and that he would not demand the money.

Marina closed her eyes and clasped the letter to her bosom. It seemed almost too good to be true. She had set a trap—and her quarry had walked straight into it. Her future must now be secure.

For almost a minute she sat immobile, while pictures rose in her mind of Mama, comfortably circumstanced at last, and beaming gratefully at her daughter. In just a few short weeks, Marina would be able to send home her very first contribution to that small, spartan household. How wonderful that would be.

Provided Kit Stratton could be tricked out of the second part of the bargain!

Marina opened her eyes with a start. She still had to deal with Kit Stratton's designs on her virtue. But at least she had secured the Dowager's debt. That was the first, vital step.

She bent down to retrieve Mr Stratton's outer letter. What would he have to say to her?

The letter was very short indeed. It contained barely two lines. There was neither salutation, nor signature.

White scarf. Tomorrow. The letter is post-dated and can be publicly revoked.

It made no sense. What on earth…? Marina scrabbled around on the table for the inner letter and forced herself to read it carefully, one sentence at a time.

Then she understood.

The letter was dated two days hence and addressed to the Dowager Countess Luce. Its tone was curt and formal. *Madam*, it said, *Your intermediary has prevailed upon me not to collect on your recent debt. I shall call*

*upon you tomorrow, as agreed. Your vowel shall be re-
turned to you then. Christopher Stratton.*

In her haste, she had overlooked that one significant
word—tomorrow. And the date. The letter was worth
nothing, nothing at all, until that day. She had been
duped.

How arrogant, how stupid she had been to think for
one moment that she could outwit a practised deceiver
like Kit Stratton. He had taken her stratagem and turned
it back on her. She had demanded payment in advance
and he had provided it, but so cleverly that she could
not make use of it until after she had delivered on her
side of the bargain. Nor could she now retreat, as all her
senses were urging her to do. If she did not meet him
on the morrow, he would no doubt make their bargain
public immediately, using Marina's letter as proof of his
allegations against her. It would cost him nothing. He
had no reputation to lose. But Marina would be cried a
liar, a cheat and a wanton, to boot. Lady Luce would
discharge her on the spot—she would have no choice.
Marina would be forced to return to Yorkshire with not
a penny to her name—a name that would be dragged
through the mud in London and, eventually, in Yorkshire, too.

Marina would be an outcast. Mama would be shamed,
dreadfully shamed. There would be no more pupils—no
father would permit his child to enter such a household.
They would have to rely on Harry for their very bread.

Harry! What of Harry? He would probably suffer, too.
He might even be asked to leave Oxford, for who would
give a living to a man with such a sister?

A tear squeezed its way out and down Marina's cheek.
Angrily, she brushed it away. What was the point of
tears? She had brought all this on herself, by her own

stupidity in sending that incriminating letter. And signing it, too! If her family suffered, she alone was to blame. Oh, why had she ever set eyes on Kit Stratton?

He had won. It mattered not how many curses she called down on his head. He had won.

He expected her to be in his carriage on the morrow. And, heaven help her, she now had no choice but to comply.

Chapter Nine

Marina had not slept.

As soon as she heard the first stirrings of the household below, she rose and began to make ready for her fateful meeting with Kit Stratton. She felt like the condemned preparing for the scaffold.

She stripped off her nightdress and washed every inch of her skin with the freezing water left from the night before. The cold should have brought her body to life, but it did not. She barely shivered.

Then she hunted through her meagre supply of underthings to find those with the least evidence of mending. She shivered then, to be sure. He would see them…all of them, but her pride would not permit him to discover the full extent of her poverty. He must be made to remember that she was a lady and—in that at least—his equal.

She shuddered again at the sight of the pretty green gown hanging from the rail. Had she really considered wearing such a thing for this meeting? She had truly been mad.

Hastily she donned the most severe of her drab Yorkshire gowns, plain, long-sleeved and high to the neck.

Only then did she pause to look at herself in the glass. Her face was almost as grey as her gown. The mass of chestnut hair curling around her shoulders contrasted starkly with her pale skin, like a wig on a corpse. With shaky fingers, she braided her hair and pinned it back into her usual neat knot. That was better. No…it would not do. She unpinned it and did it over again, much tighter. Her hair would be barely visible now, especially under her bonnet.

But he was bound to insist that she remove it. And then every other stitch of clothing she was wearing…

Swallowing her fears, Marina forced herself to look around the gloomy interior. The carriage was far from elegant. And it had a vague, musty smell to it, as if it had lain long unused in some damp coach house. Involuntarily, she wrinkled her nose.

'I apologise for the carriage, Miss Beaumont.' Mr Stratton was leaning carelessly back in his seat to let his frank gaze wander over her body. 'It is not mine, you understand. Mindful of your reputation—' He quirked a sardonic eyebrow at Marina's start of surprise. 'Oh, yes, ma'am. Mindful of your *reputation*,' he said again, with emphasis, 'I have hired this anonymous vehicle, rather than use my own. It is not quite what I should like…but then you will not be in it for long, will you?' He leant forward and slid one lean hand out behind the closed window blind. After a moment, he sat back once more, carefully folding the white silk scarf that had been attached to the door handle. 'I would not, for the world, draw attention to your presence here,' he said in a soft, almost menacing voice.

Marina stared dumbly at the floor. It was none too clean.

'Remove your hat and gloves, if you please.'

Marina looked up with a start and then complied, struggling a little with the strings of her bonnet. She had made the bargain. He would make sure she kept it.

'Now, give me your hand.' His long fingers enfolded hers in a strong grip. With a single movement, he pulled her from her seat and on to his lap, lowering his mouth to hers.

Without thinking, Marina tried to push him away.

He raised his head and looked down into her eyes. His expression was unreadable. 'Willingly, Miss Beaumont,' he said softly. 'That was what was agreed. Have you so soon forgotten?'

'Willingly in your *bed*, Mr Stratton,' snapped Marina, 'not in a dirty, smelly carriage.'

Kit gave a great shout of laughter. '*Touché,* Miss Beaumont,' he said, grinning. 'Perhaps you would like to resume your seat?'

Without giving Marina a chance to respond, he grasped her round the waist and placed her back on her seat as though she weighed nothing at all. Then, still grinning broadly, he lounged back in his own place once more.

It was the first time Marina had ever seen genuine humour in his face. For once, his eyes had softened. His whole expression was alive with amusement. He seemed years younger…and devastatingly handsome. If this was the face he showed to his conquests, it was no wonder they all succumbed. Marina, too, could feel the pull of his attraction. She wished—

She turned away before her resolution failed her and busied herself with replacing her bonnet on her tightly braided hair. Even without her gloves, it seemed that her fingers wanted to tie themselves in knots.

Kit leaned towards her, smiling mischievously. 'Shall I help you, ma'am?' he said, stretching out a hand. 'I am accounted…adequate in dealing with ladies' clothing.'

Appalled, Marina batted his hand away and turned even further from him. He was doing it quite deliberately. He was determined to ensure she was thoroughly unsettled. As if his mere presence was not enough to do that.

At last her bonnet was tied and her gloves restored to her hands. She clasped them together in her lap and sat round in her seat. She would not let him see how much he affected her. 'May I ask where we are going, sir?' she said quietly.

He nodded approvingly. Confound the man! It was as if he could read her mind and was awarding her marks for self-control.

'I am taking you to my house in Chelsea, ma'am. It is far enough away from the fashionable streets and perfectly suited for the…business we have to conduct. I take it you do not object?'

'I was not aware that I had any choice in the matter,' Marina replied acidly.

'No, but it does no harm to observe the niceties of polite conversation, do you not think? It serves to make a tedious journey pass the more quickly.'

He was laughing at her! For just a second, she saw it in his eyes, before his expression became a bland mask, as usual. With difficulty, she suppressed an urge to slap that handsome face into awareness of her anger. But there was no point. She had tried that tactic before, and failed. Last time, he had—

Last time, he had kissed her.

The carriage slowed. Kit lifted the blind a fraction to

see where they were. Then he reached into a pocket and produced a lady's veil. 'I suggest you drape this over your bonnet, ma'am, just in case. One never knows who might be walking by. I would not wish your reputation to be sullied because you had omitted to wear a hat with a veil.'

Oh, how dare he? He was blaming her for what was about to happen. More than ever, she wanted to hit him, but she forced herself to drape the veil over her bonnet instead. It covered her face completely. It was unlikely she would be recognised, even by someone who knew her well.

He was already standing on the flagway, holding up a hand to help her down.

Marina hesitated. There was something about those lean hands... She was afraid to touch his fingers, afraid of what she would feel if she did.

'Come along, ma'am,' he said impatiently. 'Let us be done with this business of ours.' He looked narrowly at her, as if he could read her thoughts through the veil. 'Unless you wish to renege on our bargain?'

Marina rose, gathered her skirts and climbed down unaided, marching towards the door without once looking at Kit Stratton. She lifted the knocker and let it fall back on to the door with a hollow clang.

In the echo, a voice whispered in her ear, 'I was persuaded you were no coward.'

Marina shivered. She could feel his breath against her neck and the warmth of his body at her back. She could not escape. Oh, why did the door not open?

After what seemed an age, it did. The tiny housekeeper stood there, hostility writ clearly in the lines of her body. Even the black bombazine of her dress seemed to bristle. For several seconds she stood blocking the entrance, staring up at Marina with narrow, searching eyes.

'Thank you, Mrs Budge.' Kit's voice was cool but authoritative. His housekeeper stood aside to let the visitors enter.

Kit placed a hand—ever so lightly—in the small of Marina's back and guided her into the little sitting room where they had met before. Marina told herself to remain calm, to ignore the tingling of her skin and the sparks shooting down into her belly. She would find out all about them, soon enough. Soon, she would be in his bedchamber…in his bed.

He shut the door firmly on the housekeeper, giving instructions that they were not to be disturbed. Perhaps he wanted to— Oh, surely not here?

'No, Miss Beaumont,' Kit said laconically, 'I am not about to ravish you on this hideous Chelsea carpet. I hope you will grant me a little more finesse than that.'

He was reading her mind again!

'Pray be seated. May I offer you some refreshment?'

Marina shook her head dumbly. It would choke her.

Kit sat down opposite her, stretching out his long legs towards the fireplace. He seemed much too large for the tiny room.

'I must admit, ma'am, that I am surprised you have come.'

She sat up even straighter in her chair, but said nothing.

'You mean to keep your side of the bargain, then?'

Slowly, she raised the veil from her face and looked haughtily across at him. 'Of course. I would not break my word,' she said levelly. 'Even to you.'

He sat quite still, watching her. She was white and drawn. In the half-light of the small windows, she was not in the least attractive, apart from those huge, luminous eyes. A victim on the tumbrel could not have looked worse. How had it come to this? He had been so sure that she would break her word. Women always did. But this one had proved him wrong. He ought to let her go. So what on earth was he doing?

Collecting on a bargain, made and sealed. He had agreed to forgo twelve thousand pounds, and his revenge on Lady Luce, besides. Some recompense must be due for that. And there was something about this woman...

He sat silent, staring at her and wondering at his own perfidy. Was he truly about to allow an innocent gentlewoman to sell her virtue to him for twelve thousand pounds? In all his twenty-seven years, he had never paid a woman to share his bed. Never.

He had pursued them, certainly. Over many months, on occasion. Indeed, it had taken nearly a year to pluck his lovely Baroness from the arms of her husband. His friends in Vienna had called her unassailable. They had taunted him. In the end, he had been forced to prove that even she could be made to fall in love with him. Like a ripe plum, she had been ready to drop into a waiting, caressing hand. His hand. But, in truth, she had fully intended to fall...if not with him, then with another. That virtuous demeanour had been a façade, covering a lusty, passionate nature. She suited him; and he her. When she had come to London with her husband, it had suited him to follow. It had been time for him to return. And it suited him to have her here, whenever he wanted her.

That was not quite true. At present, he did not have his beautiful Baroness.

He had Miss Beaumont instead.

She was prepared to surrender herself to him. No doubt she thought she had made a bargain with the devil,

but she would keep it, because she had given her word.
A most amazing woman. If only she had the looks to
match that remarkable character...

He ought to let her go. Now. But then that old harridan would have won. As she had done five years ago.

A second defeat was unthinkable. Miss Beaumont
must be held to her bargain.

He should never have offered the bargain in the first
place, for Lady Luce would be the gainer, while all the
costs would fall on her hapless companion. Only a man
sunk in the depths of infamy would take her. Was he
that man?

Miss Beaumont was turning a ring around her finger
under her glove. Or rather, she was trying to do so, with
precious little success. Was she at all aware of what she
was doing?

Kit rose and began to pace. There was too much furniture in the room. In the end, he gave up and went to
stand at the window, looking out into the street. It had
begun to rain again.

'Miss Beaumont,' he said into the heavy silence.

She started in her seat. The hand with the ring went
to her mouth in an unconscious gesture of anxiety.

Kit came to stand over her. 'Miss Beaumont, you have
kept your side of the bargain. I must admit that I did not
expect you to do so. I honour you for your courage.' He
paused for a few seconds. 'I must tell you, ma'am,' he
began again, 'that I now have no desire to complete our
mutual...business. I make it a rule never to mount more
than one mistress at a time. Yesterday, as it happens, I
was fortunate enough to...' He let the words tail off,
watching her intently. 'I see that you take my meaning.
If you permit, I will now escort you back to the park so
that you may return home.'

'I...I do not understand. The debt... We agreed—'

'The debt is paid. You may deliver my letter to Lady Luce tomorrow. On Friday, I shall call and return her vowel, as I promised. The debt shall be cancelled.'

'I—'

Kit put his hands under her elbows and lifted her gently out of her chair. He could feel that her body was shivering. 'Do not be afraid, ma'am. I, too, keep my promises. You may be sure of that.' She looked quite bewildered. Her huge eyes were dark as she stared up at him. There was the beginning of a spot of hot colour on each of her cheeks, marring that beautiful complexion.

Slowly, he lifted the veil from the top of her bonnet and arranged it over her face once more.

'Come, Miss Beaumont,' he said softly. 'Your carriage awaits.'

She said nothing more while they mounted into the carriage and took their places as before. She said nothing throughout the drive back to the park.

Kit looked at her tense, shrouded figure. What was it about her? He was giving up a debt of twelve thousand pounds. And for what?

For a woman who was a worthy opponent, a woman who had as much courage as any man.

He smiled to himself as he watched her. He would make sure her honour was protected. She deserved no less. For Lady Luce, on the other hand, he had determined that there would be no protection. He would forgive her the debt, to be sure, but the whole world would learn that he had done it. He, Kit Stratton, would be seen to be thoroughly magnanimous. And she, the Dowager Countess Luce, would be publicly beholden to him for twelve thousand pounds of charity. The world would expect her to be exceedingly grateful to Kit Stratton.

She would be humiliated beyond bearing.

It was not the revenge he had planned for, but, on reflection, it might prove to be just as sweet.

Marina was very, very cold. The cracked leather at her back felt like sheet ice, reaching its freezing fingers through to her bare skin. That would account for the shivering that she could not prevent.

He was taking her back to the park. She had been in his house—at his mercy—and he was returning her, intact. She was not even worth an hour's distraction from his latest mistress!

She glanced across at him from under lowered lashes. She had not so far dared to look at him, even through the veil. She was afraid of what he would see in her eyes.

He seemed to be miles away. His face wore an expression of intense but distant concentration, as if he was solving a particularly knotty, abstract problem. How to checkmate a king, perhaps? Or overcome an attacking queen?

The rain had stopped. She had not noticed before. In Chelsea, it had been pattering half-heartedly on the roof, suggesting yet another muddy walk back to Lady Luce's house. Perhaps, now, it would not be quite so bad. She should be able to pick her way through the mud and the puddles.

A knowing smile started to play around Kit's mouth. Marina knew at once that he had solved his puzzle, and was now enjoying his anticipated victory. She never, for a single moment, doubted that he would win. He would always win, especially where women were concerned. He was the devil.

That lean hand moved the blind a fraction, just as before. 'We shall arrive in a moment or two, Miss Beaumont,' he said. 'You will be able to make your own way from here, I hope? You will understand that I dare not take you to your door, lest…'

Why was he suddenly so polite? It made Marina want to scream. An hour ago he had been set to ravish her in this very carriage. 'Thank you, Mr Stratton,' she snapped, unable to hide her burgeoning temper. 'I am quite able to manage without your…your services.'

Muffled laughter greeted her rather feeble sally. Marina felt she had achieved a small victory.

But it was short-lived. This time, he did not pull her on to his lap. He threw himself on to the seat beside her, tossed up her veil, and caught her gasp of alarm in a brutal, demanding kiss.

It was a kiss of possession. He was showing her that she was his, that he could have taken much more than her lips, that she would have been unable to resist. And to her eternal shame, it was so. She knew she ought to fight him, but her limbs were filled with a wondrous, glowing languor. His invasion of her mouth was no punishment, but a joy, tempting her towards delights that she could never have imagined. The warm scent of him seemed to surround her like a sun-filled arbour. She could have struggled free of his encircling arms, if her treacherous body had been willing to try. But it would not.

She slid her arms around his neck and yielded to an overwhelming desire to return his kiss.

It was Kit who broke it at last.

The carriage had stopped. Marina had no idea how

long it had been stationary. Her whole being had been drowning in the magic of her first truly passionate embrace. Now she was gasping for breath and her heart was pounding. What had she done? How had she allowed it to happen?

She gazed up into Kit's face, but his eyes were hooded and his expression blank. He was breathing quite easily. The kiss that had made such an indelible impression on her whole being seemed to have left him quite cold. Humiliation rose in her throat as if to choke her. Her face felt hot. She realised she must be quite scarlet.

She must get away from him!

Hastily pulling down her veil with one hand, she grabbed the handle of the carriage door.

Kit put a restraining hand on her arm. 'The path is on the other side, Miss Beaumont,' he said calmly. 'I would not have you descend into the mud.'

Marina's hands clenched into fists. Again, that incredible urge to scream like a demented fiend. She rose and pushed past him, not trusting herself to speak another word.

Unable to rise in the cramped interior, Kit bowed to her. 'You will understand that I may not alight to help you down, Miss Beaumont,' he said politely. 'I trust you will forgive me for that.'

Marina flung open the door and stepped down into the blessed freedom of Hyde Park. She half turned back to him. He was almost invisible in the gloom. 'For that, most certainly, Mr Stratton,' she said in a low venomous voice. 'But for nothing else.' Reaching up, she slammed the door on him with all the force she could muster.

She would almost have sworn that she heard an appreciative laugh from inside the carriage as she started to hurry away.

It was impossible to deal with such a man. Impossible for her. She must have nothing more to do with him.

Head lowered, she hastened towards the gate. Thank heavens there was almost nobody about. Only a single gentleman on horseback, taking his morning exercise.

She reached the gate just as the gentleman trotted up behind her on a fine bay mare. He pulled his horse aside politely so that Marina would not be splashed. Automatically, she looked up at him to nod her thanks.

Oh, no! Surely not! Please let her be mistaken!

He stopped in the act of raising his crop to his hat, a very strange look flitting across his features. Then with a tiny shake of his head, he completed the salute and walked his mare through the gate.

Marina looked after his retreating figure. It had almost seemed as if he recognised her. But that was impossible. They had never even been introduced, and besides… She reached up to straighten her concealing veil.

Part of it had caught on the top of her bonnet. Much of her face must have been visible from the moment she alighted from Kit Stratton's carriage. The rider of the bay mare had seen her step down, she remembered that clearly. He must have crossed her path deliberately just now, in order to get a closer look at a woman who was so obviously defying convention. By his expression, he had recognised her face, even if, please God, he did not yet know her name.

What would he do with the information he had acquired? Would he broadcast to the world that a very tall, grey-clad lady had emerged alone from a closed carriage in the early hours of the morning? He had only to describe her thus for her name to be forthcoming from many of Lady Luce's acquaintances.

Marina shuddered. The sheet of ice had returned to her back.

She would have to abandon her resolution to avoid Kit Stratton. He alone might be able to save her from public disgrace, provided she could appeal to him very soon.

For the gentleman on the bay mare was Sir Hugo Stratton.

Chapter Ten

Nothing of it made any sense, Marina thought, throwing aside her bonnet and gloves and sitting down at her little writing table. The whole episode had been like a series of riddles, each more indecipherable than the last. First he had attacked her in his carriage. Next, he had spurned her, on the far from convincing grounds that he did not deal with more than one woman at a time. Finally, he had attacked her in his carriage all over again. So much for his claim of being faithful to his newest mistress.

For some reason, he had been toying with her. Men could be just as fickle as women, surely? And Kit Stratton was definitely that. In his Chelsea house, he could barely bring himself to touch her. In his dark and musty carriage, he had—

That must be it. It had been so dark in the carriage that he would not have been able to make out her features. He had probably told himself that he was kissing someone else, his latest mistress, perhaps.

She felt used. Could it have been worse if he had actually bedded her? As it was, she had screwed her courage to the sticking-place, and then he had rejected her, in the most obnoxious manner. Most humiliating of all, he had kissed her so beguilingly that she had responded—eagerly—in spite of the insults he had been heaping upon her. She burned with shame at the thought of what she had done, how she had felt... Her conscience reminded her that she had sinned, yet she knew that, given another chance, she would willingly sin again...

There must be no more chances.

Marina turned her ring round her finger, trying to devise a new, more terrible curse to throw at him. She was not very good at curses. Her mama had made sure that she learned none of the bad language used by the common soldiers. And what good would it do, anyway? She still had to ask—nay, beg—Kit Stratton to persuade his brother not to betray her to the world.

She dare not see him. She must write to him. Again. As before, her future would hang on his reaction to her request.

She pulled a sheet of paper towards her and steeled herself to write the most difficult letter of her life.

With a mischievous glance at her husband, Emma Stratton put a hand on Kit's shoulder to pull him down to her level so that she could plant a smacking kiss on his cheek. 'How lovely to see you, Kit,' she said, gazing flirtatiously at him through her long lashes.

Kit smiled indulgently at his beautiful sister-in-law. 'If the tabbies could see you now, Emma...' he warned, doing his best to inject a hint of menace into his words.

'And what do you mean by that remark, pray?' she replied, in mock outrage. The wicked sparkle in her eyes betrayed her.

From his stance by the window overlooking the busy street, Hugo wagged a finger at her. 'You know very well, you minx. They will never stop seeking scandal between you and Kit.'

Emma threw her husband a speaking glance and sank into her spindle-legged chair in a single, elegant movement. 'What, I? A respectable matron, the mother of three stout children? Fie on you, sir!'

Kit took her hand in his and raised it to his lips, grinning wickedly all the while. 'But who is to say they are all yours, Hugo? After all, we are so very much alike...' He left the thought unfinished. He did not need to remind Emma, or her husband, that she been compromised all those years ago as a result of mistaking Kit for Hugo in a midnight garden.

'You wretch, Kit,' she cried, rapping him hard across the knuckles with her fan.

'Seriously though, Kit,' said Hugo, strolling across the Aubusson carpet to where his wife sat and resting his hand gently on her shoulder, 'it would be wiser not to mention the likeness between us. You might just set them thinking. You know how easily rumours start.'

'I'd like to see how they would account for it, Hugo, when I have been in Vienna almost since the day of your wedding. I may have something of a reputation with the ladies—' Hugo raised an eyebrow, and Emma giggled '—but there are some things even I...'

Emma clapped her hands over her ears, but then she spoiled the moment by collapsing in gales of laughter. The two men were soon laughing, too.

Emma said, weakly, 'This is vastly improper. You are quite as bad as each other, you know.'

'Very true, my love, very true,' said Hugo, nodding. 'We shall now talk of subjects fit for my lady wife's drawing room. Will you not be seated, Kit? Tell me, did you see the lady who was with the Dowager Lady Luce at the ball t'other evening?'

'Why do you ask?' said Kit carefully.

Hugo grinned. 'Sparring for wind, brother? I ask, because I expect you to know every lady in London. You must have seen her. She is so much taller than all the other ladies that every eye must be drawn to her.'

'As it happens, Hugo, I did *not* see her at the ball, but I do know who she is.'

'Ah,' said Hugo, nodding expectantly.

'She is Lady Luce's companion. Her name is Beaumont.'

'Of course!' Hugo slapped his thigh. 'I should have guessed. The likeness was there all the time.'

Emma frowned across at him. 'Hugo, you are talking in riddles. What likeness? Who is Miss Beaumont?'

'I am not totally certain, Emma, but I think my friend, George Langley, was her uncle. You know he was killed at Ciudad Rodrigo, but I may not have said that his sister's husband, Tom Beaumont, died there too.'

'Oh, how dreadful!' cried Emma. 'A husband *and* a brother!'

Kit rose abruptly and strode across to the window.

Hugo nodded in sympathy. For a few moments he sat in silence, remembering.

Emma put a gentle hand on his arm. 'What makes you think she is related to them, love?' she asked softly.

'There can be no doubt. Not for anyone who knew Tom Beaumont. She has a great look of him. Same height, same build, same features. But what on earth is she doing as companion to that old harpy? Surely—?'

'I suspect her family is become very poor, Hugo,' said Kit in a harsh voice, turning back into the room. 'I take it the army did nothing for the widow?'

'I am afraid I do not know,' Hugo replied, flushing a little. 'You will recall that, after the battle, I was…in some difficulty.'

Kit nodded quickly. The last thing he wanted was for his brother to be forced to recall the accusations of cowardice that had been heaped upon him by his malicious commanding officer. They had long since been proved false, but the memories would still be painful.

'I had no chance to do anything for Mrs Beaumont at the time. I was not even permitted to write to her,' Hugo added bitterly. 'And when I eventually came home, it was years too late. I did not even know where to begin to look. Somewhere in the north, I fancy.'

Kit turned back to the window, his mind racing. He had so nearly done something thoroughly dishonourable to a lady who should have been under his family's protection. No wonder Miss Beaumont had shown such courage under his assault. She came from heroic stock. He clenched his fists in frustration and swallowed a groan. Miss Beaumont needed help, not harassment. But it was unlikely that she would accept anything from him. After all, she had said— Yes, of course, she had said he was not worthy to be Hugo's brother… The connection had been clear, almost from the start, if only he had thought to pursue it. And now…

Emma had been talking eagerly to her husband. 'And I shall certainly take her up,' she finished triumphantly. 'Lady Luce shall have nothing to say in the matter.'

Hugo gave a crack of unwilling laughter. 'That would be the first time, my love. Do you not agree, Kit?'

'What? Your pardon, Hugo, I was not listening. You asked…?'

'It is of no moment. Emma and I were just discussing

Miss Beaumont. Emma is determined to help her, yet I...I must admit I have doubts.'

'Oh?' Emma bridled visibly. 'Why?'

'Believe me, my love, I shall ensure that she and her family are not left in penury, but there is no need for you to become involved. She is only a companion, after all.'

'Hugo! What a wicked—!' Emma broke off, looking shrewdly into her husband's face. 'No. You would never say anything so unkind. Or so top-lofty. You are trying to hide something from me.' She clasped her hands in her lap, fixed her angelic blue gaze on his face and waited. A knowing little smile began playing round her mouth.

Kit waited, too. What on earth could Hugo know to Miss Beaumont's detriment? Unless—

'Emma, I am asking you not to take Miss Beaumont under your wing. At least, not immediately.' Hugo raised his brows, waiting for her response. His expression was grave. Eventually, Emma nodded, somewhat unwillingly, Kit thought. 'Believe me, I have good reason for my caution,' Hugo continued, unbending a little in the light of his wife's acquiescence. 'Suffice it to say that I saw her earlier today, somewhere no lady should be.'

Kit just managed to conceal a start of surprise.

'But she may have—' began Emma, eager to defend a possible protégée.

'Patience, my love, patience. Give me time to discover a little more about Miss Beaumont. I promise that if I find that she had good reason for her...actions, I shall positively insist that you help her.'

'Very well,' Emma said. 'I shall have patience, since you ask it of me. But do be quick about your enquiries, love,' she added with an impudent little grin, 'for I am already longing to meet your mysterious Miss Beaumont.'

In spite of his concern, Kit almost laughed. Emma was truly outrageous. She could play the part of the obedient wife to perfection, but underneath...!

Hugo was laughing, too, and shaking his head at his beautiful, wilful wife. 'So much for marriage vows, eh, Kit? Obedience, indeed!'

Rising quickly, Emma dropped a kiss on her husband's forehead, before he could move from his seat. 'Never fear, husband,' she said gaily. 'I shall not break my vows—or not today, at least—since I am promised to Lady Dunsmore and—' she glanced at the gilt mantel clock and gave a little shriek '—heavens, I shall be most dreadfully late.' She hurried to the door but Kit was before her, ready to open it for her. 'Goodbye, Kit. I leave you to my lord and master. No doubt you are well used to his imperious ways.' She left the room in a swirl of lemon muslin and jonquil ribbons. It seemed suddenly duller without her.

Hugo was still smiling when Kit came back to join him by the huge fireplace. 'An extraordinary coincidence, is it not, Hugo, that this young woman should be the daughter of your old friend?'

'Not quite that, Kit. Her uncle, Langley, was my friend. We served together for years. Her father was some years older and only recently transferred into the 95th, so I did not know him all that well. On reflection, though, I am not so surprised if the family is poor. Beaumont was always gambling and he very rarely won.'

'Ah,' said Kit. That could explain much about Miss Beaumont's attempts to protect her mistress from the evil consequences of gambling. Yet another reason to condemn his own behaviour, too.

'It sounds as if you know more about Miss Beaumont than you are prepared to say, Kit. I collect that I am right in thinking she is not a fit person for Emma to know?'

'No, Hugo,' said Kit immediately, 'you are not right. Miss Beaumont is most definitely a lady. What makes you think otherwise?'

Hugo glanced suspiciously at his brother, but Kit was still determined to give nothing away. He had schooled his features into a bland expression and simply waited, as Emma had done, until the silence forced Hugo into speech.

'Oh, very well, since you are so intent upon knowing. I saw her in the park, very early this morning. She was quite alone. She alighted from a carriage with its blinds drawn, apparently after having some kind of altercation with the person inside. I assumed her companion to be a man. And I can think of no acceptable reason for her being there. Certainly, when she saw me, she looked remarkably guilty.'

'You spoke to her?'

'No. We have not been introduced. I recognised her from the ball.'

'Through her veil?'

Hugo leaned back in his seat and eyed his brother sceptically. After a moment, he said, 'I shall not ask how you come to know that. But I am now more than ever sure that I should discover more about Miss Beaumont before I permit Emma to know her.'

Cursing himself for his stupidity, Kit flung himself out of his chair and strode across to the window, before his loose tongue could betray him even more. Was there anything he could say to retrieve the situation? If Hugo began to make enquiries about Miss Beaumont, rumours were bound to start to fly. And it would be Kit's fault. He must say something to buy a little time, if nothing more.

He turned back from the window and said, 'Hugo, I fully understand your desire to protect Emma's reputation, but you have no need to be concerned about Miss Beaumont. She is a lady, and a virtuous one.'

Hugo still looked unconvinced.

Goaded, Kit continued, 'I give you my word that I have not seduced her.'

'But you *have* met her,' Hugo said flatly. 'Alone, I take it?'

Confound it! Hugo had always been able to read Kit as no other could. He would not be satisfied with less than the truth…or some part of it. 'She sought me out to ask me to forgive Lady Luce's debt,' he said baldly.

'Ah, I see.' Hugo gazed into the fire for several moments, considering. Then he looked up again, and said, 'That is not, perhaps, surprising…given her background. And I can fully understand why she slammed the carriage door in your face. She would have been far from pleased by your refusal.'

'She was as mad as fire,' Kit agreed, smiling sardonically as he remembered how passionately she had responded to him, and how furious she had been at her own weakness. There was nothing to be gained by denying his involvement, but it would not do for Hugo to learn the whole. 'However,' he continued, 'given your revelations about who she is, I fancy I ought to grant her request.'

'Twelve thousand pounds? That would be remarkably generous, Kit. Especially given your feelings about the Dowager.'

'Nothing has changed there. It will please her not one

whit to have to admit that Kit Stratton has generously forgiven such an enormous gaming debt.' He nodded reflectively, watching his brother's reactions from the corner of his eye. Hugo's worried look had faded. 'Now that I come to think on it, it should be worth all of twelve thousand pounds to see the proud Lady Luce thus humbled.'

Hugo closed his eyes and shook his head despairingly. 'Having failed to dissuade you once before on that topic, I shall not interfere again. As to Miss Beaumont, I suppose I should—'

'You *are* satisfied, I hope, Hugo?' said Kit quickly.

'I accept your word, naturally. And since it appears that no one saw her with you except myself… Very well, Kit. I would not damage a lady's reputation without cause. I shall say nothing.'

'Even to Emma?'

'I shall suggest that she calls on Lady Luce.'

Kit choked. 'She would not dare!'

Hugo grinned, shaking his head. 'Of course she would. Emma will see it as a challenge. She will set about reconciling the two families, and taking up Miss Beaumont, just as she always intended. No doubt Emma will discover more about the virtuous companion in half an hour than I could do in a week of asking. I would say, Kit, that you should resign yourself to enjoying much more of Miss Beaumont's company than you had expected. Unless you wish to forgo your visits to Fitzwilliam House?'

'Certainly not,' Kit said promptly. 'If Miss Beaumont should happen to be here when I call, I dare say I shall learn to adjust.'

Checking yet again that the wafer was firmly affixed to Mr Stratton's letter, Marina let herself in to the Dow-

ager's drawing room. She knew exactly what she was
planning to say, having spent another sleepless night
worrying about whether her ruse would work. Now, she
was about to find out.

Marina walked quietly across to the window, and the
Dowager's chair. Lady Luce's eyes were closed, but Marina did not think she was asleep. It was too early for
that.

'Don't just stand there, girl,' snapped the Dowager,
without opening her eyes. 'There is nothing wrong with
my hearing, even when my eyes are shut.'

Marina fought back a nervous laugh. She must appear
normal. Holding out the letter towards the Dowager's
motionless figure, she said, 'A letter has been delivered
for you, ma'am.'

Lady Luce half opened one eye. Then she sat up
straight and took the letter, studying the handwriting.
'Don't recognise that fist,' she said, casting a suspicious
look at Marina. 'Brought round this morning, was it?'

'I am not sure quite when it was delivered,' said Marina, who had decided to stick as closely as possible to
the truth. 'Clearly, no reply is expected, since the messenger did not wait.'

'Hmph.' Lady Luce broke the seal and spread the
sheet, then raised her glass to read.

Marina held her breath.

'The blackguard!' cried her ladyship almost immediately, throwing the paper to the floor and gripping the
arms of her chair with her claw-like hands. 'How dare
he? He *condescends* to make me a gift of twelve thousand pounds, because *my* intermediary has asked it of
him! It is a foul lie! I would not send an intermediary
to give him the time of day! And then he is pleased to

inform me that he will call tomorrow to return my vowel. To laugh in my face, more like!' She paused to draw breath, temporarily exhausted by her tirade.

'May I read the letter, ma'am?' Marina asked as calmly as she could.

'If you must,' said the Dowager, with a dismissive wave in the direction of the paper on the floor.

Marina retrieved the letter and glanced at it, as if she were reading it for the first time. 'Perhaps one of your friends spoke to Mr Stratton without asking your leave, ma'am,' she suggested gently, watching for any signs of a further burst of fury. 'If so, he or she has saved you a vast deal of trouble.'

'Confounded impudence,' muttered Lady Luce. 'If I find out who has dared to interfere in my affairs, I shall—' She stopped and looked searchingly at Marina. 'Why are *you* defending this so-called intermediary? Mmm?'

'I know very few of your friends, ma'am, so I am hardly in a position to defend them. I was thinking only that, since the debt has caused so much difficulty with... between yourself and the Earl, it was a blessing that it no longer had to be paid.'

'Blessing? Believe me, my girl, it is no blessing to be beholden to Kit Stratton.'

With that sentiment, Marina was in total agreement.

'And if the price is to permit that young ne'er-do-well to lord it over me, I shall never accept—'

The door opened. 'Earl Luce, m'lady,' announced the butler.

Lady Luce uttered a very unladylike curse.

Heavens! Now I am truly in the suds, Marina thought.

The Earl strode into his mother's drawing room with a look of grim satisfaction on his face. The Dowager eyed him with disdain as he bowed over her hand. 'Good morning, Mama,' he said politely. 'I trust I see you well.'

Without waiting for a reply, he turned to Marina and looked her up and down assessingly. 'I did not expect to find you here still, Miss…er—'

'Beaumont,' snapped the Dowager. 'I will have you know, William, that Miss Beaumont is going nowhere at *your* behest. She is worth a dozen of those milk-and-water misses by whom you set such store. And I intend that she shall stay.'

Marina's eyes widened in surprise. Did Lady Luce really mean—?

'We will discuss that later, Mama. In private,' said the Earl, so angrily that his jowls shook. He paused, took a deep breath and tried to regain control of his plain features. 'We have weightier matters to discuss at present— your little…difficulty, Mama. I know you doubted my ability to raise so much money in so short a time. But you were wrong. I have brought you a draft for twelve thousand pounds.' He patted his pocket. 'At no small inconvenience to myself, I may add. I had to go into the City to conduct the final negotiations for this loan myself—' his distaste for the whole process was very evident '—but of course I had no choice. No matter how great the burden on my estate, I could not let it be said that my mother would renege on a debt of honour.'

Marina could see that the Dowager was grinding her teeth more and more with every word he said. She waited for the inevitable explosion of wrath.

Lady Luce looked up at her son's face. He clearly thought he had gained the upper hand at last. 'You have put yourself to a vast deal of trouble, William,' she said crisply, 'and without there being the least need. I do not

need you to lecture me about honour. I suggest you take
your twelve thousand pounds and put it to good use. Buy
Charlotte a new gown. Anything would be preferable to
that puce monstrosity she was wearing t'other night.'

'But you owe—'

'I owe nothing, William,' said Lady Luce, raising her
voice a little so that the sarcastic tone was very marked.
'I no longer have a debt to Kit Stratton. I can handle my
own finances perfectly well, without interference from
you. And now, if you will excuse me—' she rose from
her chair and began to make her way to the door, her
full skirts swaying as she moved past him '—Miss Beaumont and I have an engagement this morning.'

'But I went—'

'Good day to you, William,' said the Dowager firmly,
without turning round. 'No doubt you will find your own
way out. Come, Marina.'

Marina did not dare to meet the Earl's eye. He looked
as if he was about to suffer a seizure. And no wonder.
The Dowager, it seemed, would do anything to spite her
son. Anything. Even if it meant accepting a favour from
a man she detested as much as Kit Stratton.

Chapter Eleven

There had been no engagement, of course, though Lady Luce had called for her carriage and driven around the park in order to make good on her remark to her son. And she had spent almost every moment of their outing in berating, first, her son and then Kit Stratton. It was difficult to judge which of them she hated more. Marina had guessed that it was very much a matter of timing. The Dowager had used Mr Stratton's offer to outmanoeuvre her son, without thinking about the consequences. Those would come on the morrow, when Mr Stratton called on her to return her vowel.

Marina doubted that her ladyship would be able to control her temper in the face of such provocation, even though she now had no way of repaying the debt. It would have been quite amusing, had it not been so serious for Marina herself. The problem of Sir Hugo Stratton remained. Marina had had no reply to her latest letter to Mr Kit Stratton. Perhaps he would simply ignore her pleas? After all, why should he have any desire to oblige her? She had left him with the impression that she despised him—at least, that had been her intention.

She remembered, then, that low laugh as the door was

slammed in his face. That could not be the reaction of a vindictive man.

She would have to be patient and await his response. Somehow, she was now sure that there would be one. He was not a man who would simply ignore a cry for help, especially from a lady.

How on earth did she know that? She knew nothing about him, except that he was an out-and-out rake, and that none of the matchmaking mamas would trust their daughters anywhere near him, even though he was lately become very rich indeed. The Dowager was of the firm opinion that he would be a rake until the day he died, that, since the title was settled on Sir Hugo and his sons, there was no need for Kit to set up his nursery at all. Indeed, according to the Dowager, 'twould be better so, since a ne'er-do-well such as Kit Stratton did not deserve to inherit anything at all.

Remembering how her uncle had spoken of Hugo Stratton, Marina was not surprised that provision had been made for the scapegrace youngest son. Uncle George had always said that Hugo Stratton was the most honourable and upright of men, and that he cared for those who were less fortunately circumstanced. Strange, then, that Kit should be so very different in temperament. He—

Her musings were interrupted by a sharp tap on her door with a summons from Lady Luce. She required Marina's presence in her drawing room immediately. Company had arrived.

It could not be Kit Stratton. That was certain. He was not expected until the morrow and, given the animosity between him and the Dowager, it was highly unlikely that he would set foot in her house one moment before it was necessary.

* * *

'Ah, there you are, child,' said Lady Luce as the door closed behind Marina. Her ladyship sounded remarkably amenable for once, Marina decided.

Lady Luce turned to a visitor who was concealed by the back of the sofa. 'Come in, do,' said Lady Luce again, beckoning Marina forward. 'I wish to present you to Lady Stratton.'

Lady Stratton! Sir Hugo Stratton's wife—beautiful, elegantly clad in rich blue velvet with a feathered hat perched on her golden curls—sat perfectly composed on Lady Luce's damask sofa.

Lady Luce said formally, 'You will allow me to present Miss Beaumont, who is recently become my companion. She is related to the Blaines, but her family hails from Yorkshire. I dare say London is more than a little overwhelming after all those empty moors.'

Lady Stratton smiled up at Marina and extended her hand. 'Oh, I doubt that Miss Beaumont will allow a little dirt and noise to overset her,' she said. 'Miss Beaumont, I am delighted to make your acquaintance.' She pressed Marina's hand in a way that seemed significant.

Marina frowned a little, and stared into the loveliest pair of blue eyes she had ever seen. There was nothing to be read there other than innocence—and a hint of amusement. If Lady Stratton was come as envoy for her brother-in-law—and what other reason was there?—she was not about to reveal it. Marina could not help responding to that seductive smile and the friendliness in those beautiful eyes. Maybe—

'Oh, do sit down, child,' said the Dowager testily. 'I cannot be doing with you towering over us in that way.'

Lady Stratton laughed. 'I have often wished to be taller myself, ma'am,' she said, 'for my husband mocks my lack of inches. His brother is even worse, I have to say. But then, what else is one to expect from such a rogue as Kit?'

The Dowager snorted.

Marina had by now become well used to interpreting her mistress's eloquent snorts and grunts. This time, it betokened a cynical agreement with her visitor's comments.

Lady Stratton looked, with considerable amusement, towards her hostess. Then she said, perfectly politely, 'Our families have not been much in the habit of social intercourse, ma'am. That is partly because we spend so much of our time in the country. My husband is not much taken with London Society, as you may know. However, we are fixed here for a little time and I was hoping to persuade you, ma'am, to honour us with your presence at a small musical soirée we are holding on Saturday.' At the sight of the Dowager's visible hesitation, Lady Stratton leaned forward and said, 'Oh, do say you will come. And Miss Beaumont too, of course.'

Lady Luce hesitated still, but it was clear, to Marina, that she was not immune to her elegant visitor's enormous charm. Looking shrewdly at that lovely face, the Dowager said sharply, 'Will your brother-in-law be present?'

Lady Stratton's musical laugh filled the room. 'Oh, I doubt it, ma'am. I very much doubt it. Kit does not make a habit of frequenting the salons of respectable ladies, even those to whom he is related. Besides, his presence would be like to frighten off most of my guests!'

Even Lady Luce could not contain her amusement at that. Marina frankly laughed, inspired by their visitor's open gaiety.

'Yes,' said Lady Stratton, turning towards Marina, 'an outrageous thing to say, was it not? Even if it had the merit of being true. Have you met my brother-in-law, Miss Beaumont?'

'I fear she has,' said the Dowager acidly.

'Indeed? How very interesting.'

Marina closed her eyes for a moment, praying that Lady Stratton would not pursue the point. If she discovered that Marina had visited Méchante's gambling house, she would immediately withdraw her invitation.

'Tell me,' continued Lady Stratton, smiling in a way that seemed to envelop Marina with her charm, 'what did you think of my brother?'

'I…I…' For a moment, Marina was completely at a loss. 'He is…most striking,' she stammered. 'So very tall.' Good grief! What was the matter with her? She was rambling like an idiot. 'That is…he…'

Lady Stratton reached across and laid her hand on Marina's. 'You are very tactful, Miss Beaumont, and I thank you for it, but there is no need, I assure you. I am only too well aware of Kit's shortcomings, which are many. He is certainly both tall and striking. I have known impressionable young ladies who swooned at the mere sight of him. That was before he went abroad, of course. These days, innocent young damsels are usually forbidden to look on Kit at all, lest one glimpse of those handsome features should corrupt their morals completely.'

Marina could hardly believe her ears.

The Dowager chuckled wickedly. 'Quite right, too,' she said. 'Kit is a great deal too handsome. And, by all accounts, he has a most persuasive way with the ladies. Can't say I've seen it m'self. Seems an arrogant young puppy to me. Plays a fine hand of cards, though.'

That brought Marina back to earth with a jolt.

Lady Stratton rose, drawing on her fine kid gloves. 'I

must go. It has been a pleasure to talk to you, ma'am. Kit warned me that you were both forthright and honest. I only wish there were more in London of like mind. Society affairs can be so very dull, do you not agree?' She extended her hand to Lady Luce, who was nodding in agreement. 'I may expect you on Saturday, I hope? Both of you?'

Without so much as glancing at Marina, Lady Luce said, 'Yes, ma'am. You may. And if I should chance to see that brother of yours there, I promise you that I shall not permit our morals to be corrupted in any way. Who knows, if we really tried, we might reform him.'

Smiling, Lady Stratton shook her head. 'That, I fear, is most unlikely. All London knows that Kit Stratton is quite beyond redemption.'

Kit's Chelsea housekeeper had never before set foot in one of the grand houses in the west end of London. She was not altogether sure that she should be here now, but the Baroness had been very specific in her instructions and very specific about the rewards that Mrs Budge would receive if she carried them out.

The French maid who had brought Mrs Budge up the back staircase seemed to have a very high opinion of herself, almost as if the back stairs were not good enough for her. Mrs Budge knew better. A servant was a servant. A member of the nobility—such as the Baroness von Thalberg—would always have the power to order the lives of servants and to dismiss them on a whim. No wonder, then, that poor servants had to make a shilling or two in any way they could. How else would they live when times were hard?

Mrs Budge curtsied carefully towards the Baroness's back. She was attending to her toilet at the dressing table and appeared to be applying very skilful and almost invisible make-up to her beautiful features. Her sharp eyes were watching her visitor's every move in the mirror.

At last, she put down her brush and turned on her stool. 'So, Budge,' she said, in her pretty European accent, 'what brings you here, at this hour of the morning? I very much hope it is worth the inconvenience you are causing me. I am already late for a most important engagement.'

The housekeeper did not like the menacing undertone in that low, sensuous drawl. She curtsied again. 'M'lady,' she said, a little hesitantly, 'you wanted to know about any female who came to the house. There was a woman—a lady, I should say—who came to visit the master on Saturday last—'

'And today is Friday,' interrupted the Baroness silkily. 'You have taken a remarkably long time to bring me news of it.'

'Beg pardon, m'lady, but I did not think anything of it at the time. The young lady is no beauty. The master said she had called on business and I believed him. Couldn't see no other reason for him to entertain such a plain beanpole.'

'He took her upstairs?'

'No, m'lady, no. They were in the downstairs room. Only there.'

'And what did they discuss?'

'I...I don't know, m'lady. The door is very thick, and I—'

'Spare me your lame excuses. What else *do* you know?'

'She left alone. In a hackney. There was a letter came, shortly after. I think it must have been from her. Leastwise, the master gave instructions about dealing with letters, just after she left. We don't get his letters. Not as a rule.'

The Baroness frowned in annoyance.

'Then the master brought her back again. On Wednesday morning, very early, it were.'

'And they went upstairs?' asked the Baroness again.

'No, m'lady. They were in the downstairs room for only a few minutes. Then they left again.'

'Together?'

'Yes, m'lady.'

'I see. And what is this…person's name?'

'I…I don't know, m'lady. But she has written again. That is why I came. You said you…you said you would be grateful. I have brought you the letter.'

'Ah,' said the Baroness, extending her elegant white hand.

Mrs Budge took the sealed letter from her pocket and, after a moment's hesitation, gave it to the Baroness. 'I thought…once you have read it, it can be resealed and delivered to the master,' she said quickly. 'He will think it was delayed in the post.'

The Baroness was not listening. She broke the seal without any attempt to protect the paper beneath. Spreading the sheet, she quickly scanned the few lines it contained, before turning back to Mrs Budge. 'Unfortunately, there is no signature, only initials—M.B. I wonder…'

Frustrated by that news, Mrs Budge took a step towards the dressing table, stretching out her hand to retrieve the letter. 'I am sorry there is no name, m'lady, but I have brought you all the information I have. If you would please to return the letter, I—'

The Baroness picked up the single sheet and tore it to

shreds with careful precision. Then she screwed the fragments into a ball and threw them into the fire.

Mrs Budge gasped in horror as she saw her employer's letter twist and blacken in the flames. 'M'lady—'

'The letter was not delayed in the post. It was lost. Our mysterious M.B. will wait in vain for the succour she so desperately desires. And how well served she will be.'

Mrs Budge was more than a little puzzled by those enigmatic words. What on earth could have been in that letter? It was too late to find out now. She should have opened it herself before bringing it to the Baroness. 'What shall I say to the master?' she asked weakly.

'You will say nothing. No such letter ever arrived. Does anyone else in the household know anything of it?'

'No, m'lady.'

'Very well. I am indebted to you, Budge. Wait there.' She opened a drawer in her dressing table and fumbled among the contents.

Mrs Budge waited hopefully.

'Here,' said the Baroness, dropping a single guinea into Mrs Budge's waiting palm.

Mrs Budge looked at the coin in surprise. She had expected rather more for such valuable information, especially as she was risking her place by bringing it at all.

'Your face betrays you, Budge,' said the Baroness. 'I should have been much more generous, believe me, if you had provided a name or something of their conversation. I suggest you bear that in mind for the next occasion.' She picked up a silver bell from her dressing table and rang it vigorously. 'Now you may go. Make sure that no one sees you leave. And, if you find a name for this M.B., bring it to me at once. Then, you *will* be rewarded.'

Mrs Budge swallowed hard and curtsied, tucking that single guinea into the bottom of her pocket. It was too late to wonder whether she had been wise to accept the Baroness's bribe to spy on her employer. She turned to leave. The French maid had reappeared, ready to show her out.

'Wait.' The single word was very sharp.

Mrs Budge turned back obediently, but the Baroness was paying no attention to her. She had moved to her gilded writing desk and was already dipping her pen in the standish. The housekeeper assumed she was writing a note to the master, to be delivered when he next visited Chelsea. She waited patiently. Another service meant— or should mean—a further payment.

The Baroness wrote quickly, barely pausing to consider her words. Then she folded and sealed the letter with a plain wafer. 'You will deliver this immediately, Budge, if you please.'

Mrs Budge looked at it. It was not the Baroness's usual expensive writing paper. This was much coarser to the touch. Moreover— 'But I have never heard of this place, m'lady,' she protested, without stopping to think. 'How am I to find this Mr Johnson?'

The Baroness frowned her into silence. 'That is hardly my concern,' she said silkily. 'You will take the letter to that address and deliver it personally into the hands of Mr Johnson. No one else.'

Mrs Budge nodded, waiting expectantly. This sounded much more lucrative than waiting for the master to drop information about M.B.

'You will not wait for a reply. And you will tell Mr Johnson nothing—not one word—about the identity of the sender of the letter. And nothing about yourself, either. Do you understand?'

The housekeeper nodded again. She might do precisely as the Baroness ordered, but she would also do her best to find out the identity of the mysterious Mr Johnson. She might be able to sell the information later, perhaps to the master himself.

The Baroness handed over another guinea. Mrs Budge weighed the coin in her hand, letting it be seen that she thought the amount inadequate.

'There will be a further payment once the letter has been safely delivered.'

'But if I am not to wait for a reply, m'lady, how will you know that—'

The Baroness smiled very slowly. It was a little frightening. 'There is no need to concern yourself about that, Budge. I shall know for certain soon. Oh, yes. Very soon. And so, I fancy, will M.B.'

'Mr Stratton has called, m'lady.'

The Dowager, dressed very carefully in her widest and most imposing hoops, sat rigid in her chair. 'Show him in, Tibbs.'

Rising automatically, Marina discovered that her legs were shaking beneath her. She gripped the back of a chair with both hands until she had enough control to stand unaided. Kit Stratton must not see how much his presence affected her. She tried to fix a polite smile on her face.

'Mr Stratton, m'lady,' announced the butler, as he threw open the door.

Kit Stratton strode into the room, his tall, commanding figure seeming to dwarf everything around him. His bow to the Dowager was masterly. His bow to Marina—a little less deep, a little less slow—had a hint of irony in it.

The Dowager nodded slightly in acknowledgement of his salutation but she said nothing. She did not offer refreshments. Nor did she attempt to break the awkward silence that reigned in her drawing room.

He looked down on her tiny figure with the hint of a smile twisting one corner of his mouth. 'I am come in the matter of your debt, ma'am, as we agreed a se'enight ago. It was twelve thousand pounds, I believe?'

A slight blush began on the Dowager's scrawny neck. She looked away for a moment and then resumed her rigid stare. Still, she said nothing.

Kit Stratton withdrew a paper from an inside pocket of his beautifully tailored corbeau coat. He unfolded it, scanned it for a second, and then laid it on the table at the Dowager's hand. 'Your vowel, ma'am,' he said simply.

Lady Luce looked at him with distaste.

He was waiting for her answer. He might have decided to forgive the debt but he was clearly seeking a modicum of contrition from his opponent. Marina could see that his little smile was becoming more pronounced, as was Lady Luce's flush of embarrassment.

The Dowager reached out and picked up the vowel, crushing it into a ball with her wizened fingers. 'I am beholden to you, sir,' she said, with a tiny nod of acknowledgement.

Marina was willing the Dowager to say what was necessary to persuade Kit Stratton to leave. It would take only a few well-chosen words.

Say them, Marina prayed. Please say them.

Lady Luce said nothing.

Mr Stratton almost laughed. It was not a pleasant

sound. 'You are indeed beholden to me, ma'am,' he said. It was not exactly a threat, but...

'Twelve thousand pounds,' said Lady Luce at last, in strangled tones.

'Indeed,' he said, waiting.

'You are well aware that I do not have the money to pay you, sir.' The words sounded as though they had been forced from the Dowager's lips. The flush had vanished. She was now extremely pale under her heavy make-up.

Now he smiled. It was a very superior smile. 'I am perfectly well aware of that, ma'am, though I am pleased that you find yourself able to acknowledge it. I do not propose to demand payment from you. You have your vowel. The debt is at an end.'

Marina sensed that the Dowager was itching to strike his arrogant face. She seemed to be keeping her seat with difficulty.

He calmly turned away from Lady Luce and looked at Marina. 'I hope I see you well, ma'am, and that you are settling in since we last met—' Marina held her breath '—at Méchante's.'

'She will do very well,' said an acid voice from behind him. The Dowager had risen from her chair, clearly annoyed that he should even notice her companion. 'What I wish to know now, young man,' continued the Dowager, having regained his attention, 'is the identity of this *intermediary* you have the effrontery to mention. I gave no one leave to intervene on my behalf and I shall remonstrate with him at the first opportunity.'

'Shall you?' he said silkily.

Behind him, Marina quaked. Surely Mr Stratton would not betray her? Please.

'You will find that rather difficult, I fear,' he continued, 'because I have absolutely no intention of revealing his identity to you. I must have some recompense—must I not?—for the loss of twelve thousand pounds.'

The Dowager was so shocked that her mouth fell open in a most unladylike manner.

Marina felt a little bubble of laughter rising in her throat, but she crushed it before it could burst forth. So much for the Dowager's attempt to enter the lists against Mr Stratton. She had been unhorsed at the first pass and now lay winded at his feet.

'And now I must leave you, ma'am. No doubt we shall meet again at Méchante's.'

The Dowager seemed still incapable of speech.

He turned to Marina once more. 'Perhaps you would be so good as to show me to the door, ma'am?'

Marina's eyes widened, but the Dowager, recovering a little now, nodded angrily. 'Show him out, gel. Show him out, do. This ridiculous interview has gone on quite long enough.' Deliberately, she turned her back and marched across to her chair by the window.

He smiled knowingly and moved to open the door for Marina.

'Thank you, sir,' she said, a little breathlessly, waiting for the door to close behind them. She had only a few seconds to thank him for intervening with his brother to save her from disgrace—and no time at all to choose her words. 'Mr Stratton,' she said in a soft, urgent voice, 'I must thank you for responding so promptly to my letter. I am very much in your debt.'

Kit frowned. She was in his debt over the Dowager's vowel, but not over his response to her letter. That had been far from generous. What was she about, to say such a thing? Of course, now that he had formally forgiven the Dowager's debt, he no longer had any hold over the companion, but it was the outside of enough for her to take him to task about it with such sly, double-edged words.

Kit looked down at her, hard. She had an air of innocence about her, which made him suddenly very angry. He had forgiven this debt out of regard for her courage…and perhaps her innocence. The words she had just spoken were very far from innocent.

But he could not rail at her in Lady Luce's hallway, however much she might deserve it.

Forcing himself to assume a bland, neutral tone, he said, 'I am not in the habit of allowing ladies to remain in debt to me, ma'am.'

Her immediate response was a fiery blush. And she would no longer meet his eyes. Kit cursed silently. How could he have made such a thoughtless remark? Not even her devious words could justify what he had said. He seemed to be losing his touch where Miss Beaumont was concerned. She was bound to imagine he was referring to the crude price he had earlier demanded of her. It would matter not a jot that he had told her, in terms, that he had no intention of bedding her. And it was even more unthinkable now that she was under his family's protection. Surely she had the wit to understand that?

'You need have no concerns on that score, ma'am,' he said, rather more curtly that he had intended. 'There are no debts between us. You should know that very well.'

The blush had faded to a spot of heat on each cheek. It reminded Kit that her skin was as flawless as a perfect peach. His hand rose, almost of its own volition—

She stepped back smartly. His questing fingers met only thin air.

'You are very direct, sir,' she said, her gaze fixed on a spot somewhere beyond his shoulder. 'And on certain points I fear we do not agree. As a gentleman, you must allow a lady to reach her own conclusions on indebtedness. Must you not?'

Kit bristled. 'I—'

The butler appeared at the foot of the staircase. Private conversation of any kind became impossible. Kit took her hand and began to raise it as if for a kiss, but then stopped with deliberate rudeness. 'You are too kind, ma'am. And now, I will bid you good day. The butler will show me out.' With a tiny bow, he walked nonchalantly down the staircase where he retrieved his hat and gloves, and left without a single backward glance.

Chapter Twelve

'Tell my woman to fetch down my plain evening cloak, Tibbs.' The butler bowed. 'And have the carriage brought round immediately.'

'At once, m'lady.'

Marina had risen from her seat on the stool by the Dowager's favourite chair.

'Where are you going, miss?'

'I thought to fetch my bonnet and pelisse, ma'am, since you have ordered the carriage.'

Lady Luce looked narrowly up at Marina. 'Sit down,' she said curtly. 'That will not be necessary. I shall not need you this evening.'

'Oh,' said Marina, wonderingly. It would be impolite to say anything more, however much curiosity she might feel.

The Dowager was not fooled. 'I congratulate you on your restraint, Marina. Unfortunately for you, your face is too expressive. Yes, I am going to Méchante's. And, no, I am not permitting you to go there again. It is not a fit place for a young lady such as you.'

'But a week ago—'

'A week ago, certain people required to be taught a

lesson,' she said forthrightly. 'I do not believe in be-labouring a point, once it has been taken. Even to William,' she added, perhaps a little untruthfully. Marina had noticed that the Dowager did not seem to mind how often she scored the same points against her son.

'There you are at last, Gibson,' said the Dowager sharply as her aged abigail entered the room, carrying the cloak which she immediately began to arrange around her mistress's shoulders. 'Now, while I am out this evening, I wish you and Miss Beaumont to work on the gown you were making earlier today. If it is to be wearable by tomorrow, you will both have much to do.'

'Yes, m'lady. I shall fetch it at once.' The abigail curtsied herself out, but not before the Dowager had added, to her retreating back, 'And do not forget what else I told you to do, Gibson. I am expecting to see a distinct improvement there, remember.'

Marina was following none of this. What on earth was going on?

It was too late to ask. Tibbs had arrived to conduct the Dowager to her carriage.

The abigail returned carrying her own workbox, and Marina's, too. 'I took the liberty of bringing this down for you, miss,' she smiled, the wrinkles on her cheeks very pronounced. 'Save you the trouble.'

'That was kind of you, Gibson,' said Marina, her eyes caught by the gown that was draped over the abigail's arm. It could not be one of the Dowager's. It was much too flimsy and stylish. And the colour was ravishing—a subtle shade of peach, shot with pale gold.

Gibson settled herself comfortably on the settee, clearly relishing the privilege of using the Dowager's drawing room. 'We can work here for the moment, miss, since the light is better. We can go up to your room later, so that you can try it on.'

Try it on? Marina had to swallow hard before she could speak. 'This gown is for me?'

'Why, yes, miss. Did her ladyship not tell you?' At Marina's shake of the head, she said, with a wry smile, 'Her ladyship does enjoy her little jokes.' She looked Marina up and down with her shrewd old eyes. 'I doubt it will take too long. Not with two of us to do the stitching. It wants but the setting of the sleeves and the flounce around the hem.' She opened her workbox and began to search for matching thread. 'Now, if it had been a gown in the old style, we should have been here for days. I know that these newfangled fashions can be very revealing, but they are much, much easier to sew.'

Marina could only nod.

'And with your figure, miss, this simple cut will be ideal. You wait and see. I promise you will be amazed at what I shall do for you.'

'Good evening, Kit.'

Kit was not surprised to be met by Méchante, almost on the doorstep. She had an uncanny knack of knowing exactly who was in her gaming house and where she was likely to be least welcome. After his last rejection of her advances, he should have known to expect a further assault, the moment he set foot in her house again. She was not a good loser.

He forced himself to smile down at her. 'My dear Méchante,' he said in a light, playful tone, 'how delightful to be welcomed by one's hostess. On the doorstep, no less. To what do I owe this singular honour?'

She smiled up at him with glowingly sensuous green

eyes. She was trying very hard to provoke a reaction. She seemed to need to prove that she could.

He continued to smile with the same studied friendliness. She did not light even the tiniest spark of desire. She must know it, too. He caught the moment when her expression changed from seduction to calculation.

'Are you for Faro tonight, Kit?' she said abruptly. 'Your favourite opponent is here.'

Kit raised an eyebrow. 'Is she, indeed?' He did not need a name to know precisely who was meant by Méchante's remark. 'I must own I am a little surprised, considering…'

Méchante laughed. It was a rather brittle sound. 'Considering that she has only just rid herself of last week's debts. Was that what you were about to say?'

Kit gave a tiny shake of his head. 'No. I was not about to say anything of the kind. If you wish for information about my dealings with the Dowager, you must address your questions to her, and not to me.'

Méchante tried again. 'Come, Kit. You can tell me, can't you? After all, it was in my house that the debt was incurred.'

He shook his head again, more forcefully this time. 'No. If she wishes you to know, she will—no doubt—tell you.'

'Oh, very well,' Méchante said testily. 'But if you wish to enter the lists against her in future, I shall insist on knowing everything. From now on, that is a condition of entry to my house—devised especially for you, Kit.'

He bowed slightly. 'I shall—of course—take note of your wishes, though I do not promise to frequent your house if you insist on such terms. As it happens, I have no intention of playing Faro tonight. It is a night for skill, I fancy. A simple hand of piquet will suffice. Will you join me?'

'Thank you, but no. Piquet is not my game. I wish you good fortune.' With an elegant curtsy, she led the way up the staircase to the landing and disappeared into the hubbub of noisy guests in the main reception room.

Kit strolled thoughtfully up the stairs, looking around him. There was no one about. The upstairs hallway was empty. The piquet room was beyond the main reception room. He looked towards the door to the Faro rooms. It was closed. He paused with his hand on the newel post. He might just stroll in to see how the game was progressing. If Lady Luce was there, he would resist the temptation to take a hand against her. She would be desperate to challenge him, and even more desperate to win, but it would not do to indulge her.

The first Faro chamber was empty. Surprising, Kit thought. Normally, both tables would be full. He strolled through to the inner chamber. There, every chair was taken. Lady Luce was seated immediately opposite the banker, a man Kit did not know. Judging by the pile of coin in front of her, she had been winning. She was not 'Lady Lose' on this occasion.

Kit propped himself casually against the side of the archway, watching the play. The game would soon be over.

As soon as the last card had been dealt, a player at the far end of the table hailed Kit with a drunken wave. 'Kit, old fellow. Won't you join us? Just the sort of man I like to play against. Generosity itself, what?'

Lady Luce's shoulders tensed visibly but she did not turn round. She seemed to be studying her fingernails.

Kit moved across to the table and leant a hip against it, spreading the fingers of one lean hand on the green baize, only inches from the Dowager's elbow. 'Not to-night, I thank you,' he drawled. He paused, watching Lady Luce's rigid figure. She seemed determined to ignore him. He would not permit that.

'Good evening, ma'am,' he said in a voice of the utmost politeness, but without altering his careless stance. 'I note that you appear to be rather more successful this evening than…on previous occasions.'

The Dowager raised her head a little and looked sideways at him through her lashes. 'Good evening, Mr Stratton,' she said sourly. 'You are not prepared to hazard your reputation at the Faro table, I collect?'

'I see no need, ma'am. I have nothing to prove there. *My* reputation is safe enough.'

'Indeed?' said Lady Luce with a tight smile. 'I had heard—' She broke off, looking round at each of the players in turn, gathering their attention. In the sudden hush, she said, 'I had heard that, in the matter of fidelity at least, reputations were becoming…just a little tarnished.'

What on earth did she mean by that? What could she have heard? The slight murmurings around the table suggested that the rumours—whatever they were—had already gone beyond the Dowager.

Slowly, Kit straightened, making her a tiny, mocking bow. She really was a very small woman. 'I have no doubt, ma'am, that the application of a sufficient quantity of gold will restore any lustre that may be missing. You need have no concern on that account. I will bid you good evening.' Before she could reply, he turned his back and sauntered out of the room.

On the far side of the archway, Méchante was standing, holding a glass of champagne and smiling with satisfaction.

Kit nodded towards her and continued on his way. He refused to let either of those confounded women see even a hint of weakness.

But underneath Kit's studied nonchalance, his fury was mounting. Lady Luce had suggested he was being unfaithful to Katharina. How dare she? It seemed that the old harridan would stop at nothing to inflict injury on Kit, even downright untruths. He had *not* been unfaithful to his Baroness, except— Miss Beaumont. That must be it. The Dowager must have learned about his clandestine meetings with Miss Beaumont and put her own interpretation on them. It was extraordinary, but what other explanation could there be? He would need to find a way of quashing the rumours before Katharina heard them, as she doubtless would. Lady Luce must be persuaded to—

No. Lady Luce was not the person most at fault in this case. Hugo had been sworn to secrecy on the subject of those meetings. Apart from him, no one knew that Miss Beaumont had visited Kit. There was only one possible source of the rumour that the Dowager had been spreading—Miss Beaumont herself.

If the woman had been naïve enough to confide in the Dowager, she would soon learn to regret her lack of discretion. And Kit would take the greatest pleasure in telling her exactly how foolish she had been.

'She is to play later. And to sing. She is not in the least retiring in that respect. I fancy she may be quite accomplished. She looks remarkably well this evening, too. Do you not agree, Hugo?'

Following his wife's gaze, Hugo murmured something that could have been assent. 'Something different about

her. Cannot quite put my finger on it. She looks...
younger.' His voice had a questioning note.

'Men,' said Emma with a laugh. 'Of course she looks
different. She has a new hairstyle. Much more flattering
than that tight knot she used to wear.'

'You are probably right, m'dear,' agreed Hugo. 'She
is not exactly handsome, but she looks like a woman of
breeding. Something to do with the way she holds herself, I fancy. She will turn heads, in spite of her lack of
conventional beauty. Pity she is so tall.'

Emma nodded slightly. 'I am too short, and she is too
tall. There is no pleasing you gentlemen. However, you
are right. There are very few gentlemen here who would
be tall enough to look her in the eye.'

Hugo chuckled wickedly. 'What you need, my dear,
is a visit from brother Kit.'

'Heavens, no! If Kit were to show his face here, half
the ladies would faint from shock and my reputation
would be in shreds.'

'Are you sure?' said Hugo softly.

Emma closed her eyes and nodded, as if the picture
was too painful to contemplate.

'In that case, my love, I suggest you prepare to be
shredded, for your brother-in-law has just walked
through the door.'

Emma's softly voiced cry of 'Oh, no!' was the only
sound to be heard in the sudden and complete hush pervading the huge white and gold reception room of Fitzwilliam House.

Kit Stratton stood in the open doorway surveying the
assembled company as if his arrival were the most natural thing in the world. He was wearing immaculate
black evening dress, with no jewellery save for a gold
pin in his intricate neckcloth. He looked bored. He did

not smile even when his eye lit upon his brother and his beautiful sister-in-law. He strolled easily across the crowded room, the guests standing aside to make way for him. Some of the older ladies stepped back very smartly indeed, as if afraid that his nearness might taint them. Kit appeared not to notice.

He bowed gracefully to Emma and then raised her hand to his lips. 'My dear Emma,' he said, 'my apologies for arriving so late. I trust I have not disrupted your entertainment?'

Emma frowned warningly at him, but Kit was not in a mood to accept her hints. 'I am surprised that you have chosen to attend such a dull affair, Kit,' she said smoothly as he let go of her hand.

Over her shoulder, Hugo added, in a voice intended for Emma and Kit alone, 'Especially as Emma definitely did not invite you, brother.'

Kit suppressed a smile. 'Perhaps you would care to introduce me to some of your guests, Emma?' He knew that her immediate reaction would be confusion. She would be well aware that many of her guests would be affronted to have Kit Stratton presented to them.

But Emma was more than ready to pick up the gauntlet that Kit had thrown down. 'I am sure, dear brother,' she said, 'that I shall be able to present you to some of my guests, at least.' She tucked her hand through his arm. 'Come.'

Kit glanced sideways to see that Hugo had a very knowing look on his face. He clearly believed that his wife would have the better of Kit in this encounter.

Emma led Kit directly to Lady Luce, whose tiny figure had been hidden by those around her. He had barely a few seconds to compose his features. After last night's little encounter, it was unlikely that the Dowager would be in the mood for exchanging polite nothings.

The grey companion seemed to be missing on this occasion, which was a pity. Kit had hoped that Emma's soirée would provide him with an opportunity to confront Miss Beaumont with what she had done. He had determined that she would not learn just how furious her indiscretions had made him. After all, she had probably done more harm to her own reputation than to his. None the less, he did not care for any woman to make free with his name or to interfere in his private life.

'Ma'am, I think you are already acquainted with my brother-in-law, Mr Stratton?'

Lady Luce frowned up at Kit's bland countenance. 'So, young man, you have decided to create another scandal, have you?'

Kit bowed without a word.

'You should be ashamed of yourself,' continued the Dowager. 'Half your sister's guests will be finding that they suddenly have pressing engagements elsewhere. You will ruin her party. You mark my words. Is that not so, Lady Blaine?' she added, half turning to her companion.

Lady Blaine tried to look down her long nose at Kit.

'You will allow me to present Mr Kit Stratton,' said the Dowager mischievously, visibly relishing Lady Blaine's discomfiture. In normal circumstances, Lady Blaine would never have permitted such an introduction.

Kit reached forward and impudently took Lady Blaine's hand, raising it as if for a gallant kiss. He restricted himself to another elegant bow. 'Delighted, ma'am,' he said coolly.

'Mr Stratton,' said Lady Blaine, in the coldest, most arrogant voice he had heard in years. 'Ma'am,' she went on, turning back to Lady Luce, 'as it happens, I do have another engagement—'

'Balderdash,' said Lady Luce rudely. 'This is a musical soirée and the entertainment has barely begun. You cannot leave just because this young…ne'er-do-well has appeared uninvited.'

Kit was having difficulty in keeping his face straight. He did not dare to meet Emma's eye. Lady Blaine looked as if someone had placed a bad smell right under her nose.

'Besides,' continued Lady Luce, 'did you not say that your Tilly was about to perform? I do hope she is in good voice. Can't abide those screeching females who never know when to stop.' She looked round for the young lady in question. Everyone else followed suit.

Miss Blaine was standing by the instrument, dressed in a white muslin gown that was not in the least flattering to either her complexion or her thin figure. Her eyes were wide. She was absolutely immobile, as if she were transfixed by a beautiful vision. And her gaze was resting adoringly on Kit. It was a look he had seen too many times, on too many impressionable young females.

'Not sure that she looks capable of performing,' said the Dowager loudly. 'Looks to me as if she were about to swoon…or perhaps she is wandering in her wits.'

Lady Blaine choked and started across the room towards her daughter, but it was too late. Too many of the guests had heard Lady Luce's caustic words and had turned to look. A low murmuring had begun. In a few hours, the tale of Miss Blaine's infatuation would be all over London. Only the young lady herself seemed oblivious to what was going on in the room. She continued to gaze wide-eyed at Kit. Her lips had fallen open on a tiny sigh of delight.

Her mother took her by the shoulders, giving her a little shake. Her low angry words were inaudible but their effect on Miss Blaine was clear. She flushed bright red, hanging her head as her mother ushered her out.

Lady Luce snorted eloquently. 'Can't abide missish females with highty-tighty mothers,' she said, 'especially ones who never seem to lose at the card table.'

Emma quickly looked away, trying—Kit fancied—to hide her amusement. 'Excuse me, ma'am,' she said. 'I must find someone to take Miss Blaine's place. She was just about to sing.'

'Oh, Marina will do that,' said the Dowager airily, stopping Emma with a hand on her arm. 'She won't disgrace me, I promise you that. Where on earth has she got to?'

Marina? A most unusual name. Could she be referring to the grey companion? Kit had never learned Miss Beaumont's given name. But her initial was certainly M.

Emma was looking round the room. After a moment, she pointed with her fan. 'Over there, ma'am. If you will excuse me, I will go and ask her if she will favour us with some music now, rather than later.'

Kit watched Emma make her way through the press of guests, with a word here and a touch there to clear her path. She had the happy knack of charming everyone, almost without effort. Hugo was a lucky man.

Emma stopped beside a tall lady who was almost completely hidden by a pillar. She was dressed in a kind of filmy creation of pinkish-gold, with dark hair dressed high on her head, making her appear even taller. After a moment, she stepped out and, moving with exquisite grace, made her way calmly across to the instrument. Kit could not take his eyes from her. She seemed to be floating across the room.

It was only when she sat down at the instrument that
the light fell full on her face. The Dowager's grey companion was not beautiful. But there was something about
her that drew the eye. She looked…

Kit could not find the right words. He was seeing
something in Miss Beaumont that, for all his experience,
he had overlooked before. It was very strange.

And then she began to play.

Chapter Thirteen

Miss Beaumont played beautifully. Under her fingers, the instrument seemed to sing. Kit found her performance strangely moving, though he was careful to ensure that anyone watching him would conclude that he was thoroughly bored. It would do no good for Miss Beaumont's reputation if the polite world suspected that Kit Stratton had even the slightest interest in her.

It was rather more difficult to maintain that bland façade when she began to sing, for her voice was even more remarkable than her playing. He tried to remember whether her speaking voice had had that mellifluous, caressing quality. He did not think so. It had been low, cultured, pleasing—but it had not touched a chord in him in the way her singing voice now did. Was it because of what she sang? He was not sure. Both the words and the simple melody were new to him. She sang of the beauty of nature, of wild open spaces—like her home in Yorkshire, he supposed—and of the joy of being alive. He felt he could smell the heather on the moors as she sang. And she looked almost beautiful, too, seemingly transfigured by the simple act of making music. He would hardly have believed it possible. All thought of berating her vanished from his mind.

Emma took his arm as the first song ended. 'How can you, Kit? You are listening to the most ravishing performance you are ever like to hear, and you make no attempt to hide your boredom. Do you have a tin ear? Or are you merely a barbarian?'

Kit looked down into Emma's teasing face. He must not admit the truth, even to her. There were too many people around who might overhear. On the other hand, he was not prepared to lie about the beauty of Miss Beaumont's singing. That would be unworthy. 'Apologies, m'dear,' he said absently. 'I fear my thoughts were quite elsewhere. I was not listening. But if you tell me that Miss er…that the lady's performance was ravishing, I shall of course agree with you. It would be ungentlemanly to do otherwise.'

Emma rapped her fan across his knuckles. 'Ungentlemanly, indeed!' she said, trying not to laugh. 'The lady's name is Beaumont, Kit, since you appear to have forgotten. And you really should not attend musical evenings if you are not prepared to *try* to listen to the performances.'

Kit bowed, trying to appear suitably contrite.

Emma was not taken in. 'For your penance, brother dear, you shall stand by my side for Miss Beaumont's next song. And, at the end of it, I shall expect you to give me a considered opinion on both the music and its performer.'

Kit groaned theatrically but did not attempt to escape. He leaned back slightly against the pillar, feigning a lack of interest that he did not feel.

Miss Beaumont's second song was quite different from the first. It was an Italian ballad that had been much

in vogue in Vienna, though Miss Beaumont—Marina?—
adopted a considerably faster tempo than had been usual
in Austria. The added pace seemed to turn it into a different piece altogether—gay, infectious and bursting
with life. Kit wondered whether Miss Beaumont knew
how much of her inner self she was exposing by singing
as she did. Underneath the prim, proper and rather serious exterior of the companion, there was a completely
different person, a woman full of joy and laughter.

As he listened, rapt, Kit decided that this other Miss
Beaumont needed to be brought out into the light of day.
The stern Miss Beaumont appeared never to laugh. It
was time that she learned.

Marina bowed her head in acknowledgement of the
applause. She knew she had performed well, in spite of
her relative lack of practice since arriving in London.
She had been taking a chance on that first song, but it
was unlikely that anyone in polite Society would ask her
about it. They would not wish to admit that they did not
recognise it. Marina smiled to herself, just a little. It had
been Grandmama's favourite song, written especially for
her, and Marina had every right to sing it whenever, and
wherever, she might choose.

Lady Stratton came to join her as she rose to leave
the instrument. 'Miss Beaumont, that was delightful,'
she said, pressing Marina's hand. 'I cannot tell you how
moving it was. Even Kit was touched by the power of
your song.'

Marina followed her hostess's glance. Kit Stratton was
still leaning carelessly against a pillar, as he had been
throughout Marina's performance. He had looked anything but moved. Every time Marina had looked in his
direction—and she had tried very hard to resist the temp-

tation—he had seemed to be resigned to enduring a far from pleasurable experience.

Marina's doubts must have been obvious, for Lady Stratton said impulsively, 'You do not believe me? Come. You shall hear it for yourself.' She put her hand through Marina's arm and steered her across the room to where Kit was standing.

Marina swallowed hard and steeled herself to greet him with easy politeness. He straightened as the pair approached.

'Kit,' began Lady Stratton, 'I was just telling Miss Beaumont how much you had enjoyed her singing. I fear she was not convinced.'

Mr Stratton looked narrowly at his sister-in-law. Marina felt instinctively that he did not welcome her arrival at all.

'Miss Beaumont,' he said with a tiny bow, 'I congratulate you on your performance. I have never heard that Italian piece performed in quite that way before. Most…diverting.'

Marina had not truly expected effusive praise from Mr Stratton but, in this case, she would have preferred it if he had said nothing at all. His manner was more than a little condescending. She might owe him thanks for swearing his brother to silence about their meeting in the park, but she would not permit him to treat her with disdain. He acted in that way with all his other women—if Lady Luce was to be believed—but Marina was not prepared to become one of their number. Mr Stratton must be made to realise that.

Lady Stratton forestalled Marina's reply. 'Oh, dear. My Aunt Warenne is signalling to me. I fear that can only mean that she has detected something amiss with my arrangements.' She smiled warmly at Marina. 'Pray excuse me, Miss Beaumont. I am sure I can trust Kit to entertain you in my absence.'

An awkward silence ensued while Marina tried to think of an excuse to leave. It would appear unpardonably rude if she simply deserted him. Yet—

'May I ask you about that first song you sang, Miss Beaumont? My education must be much at fault, for I cannot say that I remember hearing it before.'

Oh, dear. What could she possibly say? If she told him that she was the composer, good manners would force him to compliment her on her talent, even though it would be a downright lie. She could imagine exactly how he would behave—in that insufferably superior way of his, assessing whether she merited the attention that the great Kit Stratton was bestowing on her, deciding whether she was worth bedding.

Heavens! What had made her think of that?

It was the way he was looking at her. His gaze was intent. His eyes were much bluer than she had remembered. In the gloom of the carriage, she had seen little. Here in the light of dozens of candles, it was different— quite, quite different. He could not attack her here, in the sight of all his sister's guests.

Marina found that she had raised her hand to her lips, as if reminding herself of how it had felt to be kissed by Kit Stratton. How could she have done such a thing? With all his vast experience of women, he was bound to be able to read her every move. Marina began to feel very hot, in spite of her low-cut gown. She hurriedly clasped her hands together, where they could do no more mischief. She felt the heat rising up her neck. She must...must think of some way of replying to him.

Mr Stratton was all chilly politeness. 'Are you quite well, ma'am?' he said evenly, ignoring her lack of response. 'It is very hot in this room. Perhaps you would like a little air?'

Was he proposing to escort her outside? Surely not. Publicly agreeing to a tête-à-tête with Kit Stratton would ruin her for ever. 'I…I am quite well, sir, I thank you.' She had regained control of her voice at last, thank goodness. 'And I do not think it will be necessary for me to take the air.'

'No?' He frowned briefly. 'I find myself wondering if it is the air or the company to which you object, ma'am.'

Marina's eyes widened. Surely a rake could not be insulted by a lady's refusal to be alone with him? But it seemed that he was. He had stiffened quite perceptibly.

Without thinking what she was doing, Marina reached out and laid a consoling hand on the smooth cloth of his evening coat.

It was as if her fingers had touched a living flame.

She jerked her hand away with a gasp. Under that silken exterior, there were tense muscles and warm, breathing flesh. She felt she had reached through to his naked skin.

This time, she blushed to the roots of her hair. Her whole body seemed to be on fire. She could hardly breathe.

He, of course, was fully in control. Confound him!

After a moment, he bowed with impeccable politeness and said, 'Will you allow me to fetch you something to drink?'

'I…I am a little thirsty after singing,' she said at last.

He nodded. 'Champagne?'

Wordlessly, she shook her head. Her fingers were twisting at her ring, as usual.

'No, perhaps not. Lemonade, then. Excuse me for a moment.'

Marina was left alone, trying to marshal her wayward
thoughts. Being close to Kit Stratton was very dangerous. He was temptation. She could not stop thinking
about the feel of his body, and the touch of his lips on
hers. In spite of herself, she had wanted it to happen all
over again. Here! It was madness. This was a man who
had mistresses by the dozen, the most beautiful women
in Europe. His only reason for kissing Marina had been
to prove that he could, and that she could not help but
respond to him.

It was not Kit, but his brother who came to join her.
She tried to be glad of it. Kit Stratton was handsome,
charming, but cold as ice. Ladies made fools of themselves over his perfect face, as Miss Blaine had done
earlier. At least Marina had not done that.

'Miss Beaumont,' said Sir Hugo genially, handing her
a goblet of cool lemonade, 'you will forgive me, I hope,
for taking my brother's place. I wished very much to
have a moment alone with you this evening, to tell you
how much I valued your uncle's friendship. And your
father's, too, though I did not know him so well. I had
hoped to write to your mother after the battle but it…it
did not prove possible. I hope you will believe that I am
most heartily sorry for it. Tell me if you will, how does
your mother go on? And you have a younger brother,
too, I understand?'

'A most interesting evening—even without the Baroness. I must say, child, that you performed very well
indeed. Everyone said so.'

Marina was not paying attention. The Dowager's remark provoked her into betraying her thoughts. 'Everyone except Mr Stratton,' she said sharply. In an attempt
to retrieve her slip, she added hastily, 'I cannot think

why he attended a musical soirée in the first place. He
was obviously bored throughout. He did not even have
the good manners to pretend to be entertained.'

The Dowager looked hard at Marina but said nothing
for a moment. Then she changed the subject. 'I noticed
you were deep in conversation with Sir Hugo. He was
most taken with your performance. Heard him say so
m'self.'

'He was most kind, ma'am. He spoke to me of my
father, and of my uncle, who was his great friend. He
said that he had always been sorry to have lost touch
with Uncle George's family. He plans to write to Mama
and—oh, ma'am, he says he should be able to offer
Harry a living, once he is ordained. You cannot imagine
how much that could mean to us. It is quite wonderful.'

The Dowager raised her eyebrows. 'Thought your
brother already had the offer of a living,' she said flatly,
'from his London clergyman friend. His wife wrote to
you, did she not?'

Heavens! Why had she ever told that stupid lie? 'The
family have left London for the present. Did I not mention it, ma'am?' Marina began, cudgelling her brain for
a plausible story. 'And it…it was not exactly an offer.
There was no definite promise of a living, though there
was a…a vague hope of something. Whereas Sir Hugo's
offer,' she continued more confidently, 'is real. I have
Sir Hugo's permission to write to tell Mama—and
Harry—at once. I shall do so the moment we reach
home.'

Emma sank into her favourite chair with a sigh of
relief and closed her eyes for a brief moment.

Hugo smiled lovingly down at her. 'Your evening was
a great success, my love,' he said. 'I am sure you could

become one of Society's foremost hostesses if you chose.'

Emma looked sceptically up at him. 'That is not what Aunt Augusta thinks, I may tell you, Hugo. She blamed me for Tilly Blaine's outrageous behaviour. Insisted that I do something about it. Though what that was supposed to be, when the girl's mother was standing by, I cannot imagine.'

'Your Aunt Warenne was, no doubt, somewhat put out by Kit's arrival. You were lucky she did not insist on showing you the door, Kit.'

Kit turned back from the window where he had been idly watching the carriages below in the light of the flambeaux. He grinned at them. 'Emma's Aunt Warenne terrifies most men, I admit, but I have found that she mellows on closer acquaintance.'

Emma groaned. 'Even Aunt Augusta is not proof against your brother, Hugo. He should be locked up. He is a danger to womankind.'

Kit bowed ironically. 'I take that as a compliment, sister dear.'

Emma tried to look stern, but failed. 'Oh, stuff!' she cried inelegantly. 'Seriously, though, Kit, what am I supposed to do if chits like Tilly Blaine swoon at the very sight of you?'

'Ignore them,' he replied harshly. 'As I do. After a few moments on a cold hard floor, they tend to come to their senses.'

Emma shook her head despairingly. 'You have no heart, Kit Stratton. One day, perhaps, you too will discover how it feels to admire someone who does not return your regard. And you will be well served.'

'If I have no heart, as you suggest, my dear Emma, I will be unable to experience any such thing.'

Emma's response sounded remarkably like a growl. 'I never could abide logic-chopping gentlemen.'

Hugo grinned at his brother. 'I suggest you pour Emma a glass of wine, Kit. Perhaps if you present it to her on bended knee, she may be persuaded to forgive your impertinence.'

Kit laughed. 'The wine, by all means,' he said, pouring three glasses and carrying one to Emma.

She looked up at him, waiting, but he did not kneel. He gave her a dandy's exaggerated bow instead. She shook her head and took the glass from him. 'Hugo should have learned by now that you never take his advice, however good it may be.'

'Nonsense,' said Kit roundly. 'He advised me to attend your soirée, and I did so.'

'What? Hugo, you—!'

'And I am heartily glad that I did. It was a most entertaining evening. I found some of the music beautiful…in spite of my tin ear.'

Emma was looking daggers at her husband, who was trying to appear a picture of innocence.

Kit grinned wickedly. 'Come, dear sister, do not be angry. Hugo was only trying to reconcile Society to my outrageous behaviour. He appears to believe—I cannot imagine why—that they may be prepared to accept me if I do the pretty at gatherings like these.'

'Society will accept any single man with a good pedigree and a substantial income,' said Hugo cynically. 'Now that you are become so much more eligible, your notorious affairs will simply be viewed as youthful indiscretions.'

Kit said nothing, though he knew it was true. His recently acquired wealth had made a world of difference.

Emma sipped her wine thoughtfully. 'And do you plan to fulfil Society's expectations, Kit?'

'In the matter of a wife, do you mean?'

Emma coloured a little at his blunt reply. 'Yes, I suppose I do. You used to say—'

'I used to say that I had no intention of marrying. Displays like Miss Blaine's have done nothing to change my mind. How could any man wish to shackle himself to such a silly chit?'

'Perhaps you would not think so harshly of her if she were a beauty. It really is not her fault that she is thin and plain, you know.'

'That may be true, but she need not accentuate her lack of looks in the way she does. A woman may be thin and plain, and yet look remarkably well.'

Emma looked up at him with her head on one side. 'You are referring to the musical Miss Beaumont, I collect? And you are right. With that lovely gown and her more flattering hairstyle, she looked…not handsome, but…' She was searching for the right word.

'Striking?' put in Kit softly.

Emma paused before replying. 'Yes,' she said slowly. 'She was certainly striking. Particularly when she sang.'

Kit said nothing.

'I think,' said Hugo seriously, 'that there are hidden depths to Miss Beaumont. She did not say so in terms, but it appears that her family have suffered considerable hardship since her father was killed. Mrs Beaumont has been forced to take in pupils. And there is a son at Oxford, which must put a strain on her resources. It is no wonder, really, that Miss Beaumont has had to find a place as a companion. They probably need every penny she earns.'

'But you will help them, Hugo?'

'I have already promised to do so, my love. I told Miss Beaumont that I would be able to offer her brother a living, as soon as he was ordained. If you had seen the look on her face, Emma...'

'Which living did you promise her, Hugo?' Kit enquired politely.

'Why, Stratton Magna, of course,' said Hugo. 'It is the richest living in our gift, and the only one vacant, so—'

'I think you mistake, brother,' said Kit quietly. 'Stratton Magna is not in your gift. You may be head of the family, but Stratton Magna belongs to me.'

For a brief moment, Hugo looked nonplussed. 'You are right,' he said, with a thread of embarrassed laughter in his voice. 'But you know how we are placed with regard to the Beaumont family. We...I permitted them— my friend Langley's only kin—to live in penury for nearly ten years. Giving Harry the living of Stratton Magna would lift the family out of poverty—and without the appearance of charity. Would you have me withdraw the offer, Kit?'

Kit looked at his brother, and then at Emma, whose beautiful eyes were filled with concern. He permitted himself a little smile. 'No, Hugo. I would not. But have you considered how Miss Beaumont will react when she learns that she is beholden to me?'

Chapter Fourteen

En route to Fitzwilliam House once more, Marina leaned back into the velvet squabs of Lady Stratton's carriage. Such luxury for a mere companion.

She closed her eyes, relishing the moment. Lady Stratton, and Sir Hugo, too, were being so very kind to the penniless girl from Yorkshire. Not only had Lady Stratton persuaded the Dowager to permit Marina to visit Fitzwilliam House in the mornings, but she had also invited Marina to two of her evening parties. The Dowager had muttered a little at first, but had soon been forced to concede that she had no real need of her companion, since the evenings in question would be spent visiting the sort of gambling houses that were closed to gently bred young ladies.

Marina was not at all sure how Lady Stratton had done it. But the effect was that Marina's life in London was becoming more akin to that of a proper lady than a paid companion. And she had a wardrobe to match, for Lady Luce had gleefully made good on her threat to spend her son's money at the dressmaker's. She might exercise her scathing wit on the indecent modern fashions, but everything she had chosen for Marina was extremely flattering.

Looking down at the dark blue pelisse she wore, Marina smiled. It was so very satisfying to be dressed in glowing colours and beautiful fabrics, even though the dressmaker who had made them was far from top of the trees. That did not matter a jot. To Marina, it still seemed like a fairy tale. The Dowager had gone so far as to ban any garment in grey or brown, so Marina had quickly packed away her Yorkshire gowns before they could be despatched to the workhouse. That would be very wrong, for Mama had worked hard to produce the money to pay for those gowns. Besides, Marina might yet be forced to return home by a change in the Dowager's fickle temper.

Or by disclosure of her disgraceful meetings with Kit Stratton.

She gulped as his handsome face rose yet again in her mind. She could see him laughing with Lady Stratton like any normal gentleman, rather than like the wicked rake he was. She ought to despise him.

But she could not.

She wanted to condemn him out of hand for living a life of deep depravity and for attempting to lure her into it.

But she could not.

Everything that had happened between them had been her own doing, at least in part. She had gone to meet him—alone. She had visited his house. She had melted in his arms...

She was just as guilty as he.

And when she saw the laughing face he turned on his family, she had felt only envy. If only he would—

Marina dropped her head into her gloved hands. What on earth was happening to her?

She had been kissed by Kit Stratton. And she was lost.

'Why, Miss Beaumont!' Mr Stratton paused in the act of entering his sister's drawing room. 'What a... delightful surprise.'

Marina rose somewhat shakily from her chair. Oh, why did he have to appear now, as if she had conjured him out of her daydreams? And why had Lady Stratton not yet arrived? She was usually so very punctual.

He was waiting for her to say something. Waiting. He had cocked an eyebrow at her. Her obvious confusion seemed to be a source of amusement to him.

Marina straightened her back. 'I have leave to visit Lady Stratton in the mornings when Lady Luce does not require my services. Lady Stratton has been very kind.'

'So I should hope. She considers that the Strattons neglected your family after the death of your father.'

'Oh, no—'

'Miss Beaumont,' he said, in that deep, arresting voice that seemed to make her fingers and toes tingle, 'allow me to warn you that there is absolutely no point in disagreeing with Emma when she has made up her mind to something. If she has decided that our family owes a debt to yours, you would be well advised to accept it.'

How dare he? Marina knew he was arrogant, but this was the outside of enough. 'Indeed?' she said. She could not trust herself to say more.

'Indeed.' He looked her up and down then. It seemed that he had only just noticed her modish appearance, for his eyes widened a fraction. Did that signify approval?

Marina lifted her chin. She would not permit his presence to overset her. 'I am waiting for Lady Stratton, sir.

She suggested that we might practise our music together this morning. She had not mentioned that she expected any visitors.'

'No, she would not. Brothers, Miss Beaumont, do not count.'

Marina refused to react. He was clearly enjoying his attempts to bait her.

'As it happens, she did not expect me. I have come to take Hugo to Jackson's boxing parlour.' He looked shrewdly at her. 'You do not wrinkle your nose at the Fancy, Miss Beaumont. Emma would, I assure you.'

Marina returned his gaze frankly. 'I have a brother of my own, sir. I long ago learned not to notice such things.'

'Ah. Yes, of course.'

She felt as if he had just patted her on the head. Suddenly, she wanted to hit him, or kick him, as she had in his Chelsea house when he— Oh, God, why did that encounter keep pushing itself into her mind? Why were her thoughts for ever raging out of control? She—

'Oh, I am so sorry to have kept you waiting, my dear,' cried Lady Stratton, entering the room like a small whirlwind. 'I was— Kit! What on earth are you doing here at this hour?'

'Nothing of great import. I was planning on a visit to Jackson's boxing parlour. Promised to introduce a friend there this morning, but I wondered if Hugo might like to join our company. Some time since we have sparred together.'

Lady Stratton grimaced theatrically. 'It is one of the sad facts of life, Miss Beaumont, that ladies must put up with the singularly unattractive pursuits of their menfolk. I cannot, for the life of me, understand what pleasure they derive from using each other as punchbags.' She glanced at her brother-in-law. 'And you have no need to grin, sir! Oh, go away, do! You may continue your discussion with Hugo.'

He bowed to her with exaggerated care. 'Your wish is my command, dear sister.' He turned a fraction towards Marina. 'Miss Beaumont, you will allow me to say that I am delighted that the Dowager is permitting you a little time for yourself. Whether such freedom is best employed in the company of my quiz of a sister—' Lady Stratton only half succeeded in suppressing a shriek of outrage '—is a matter on which I am not qualified to pass an opinion. Day to you, ma'am.'

The door closed on him just as the book thrown by Lady Stratton reached the spot where his head had been. 'Wretched, wretched man!' she exclaimed, but she was almost laughing as she spoke.

It was not possible for a lady in Marina's position to make any comment. She tried to force a smile. Lady Stratton might laugh at her brother's wit, but Marina knew it hid his cold, ruthless heart. She had seen him at his most dangerous, drawing the Dowager towards financial ruin and Marina herself towards...

Towards what?

Hugo shook his head. 'I'm afraid not, Kit. I have an engagement this morning that I cannot break, though I should be happy to accompany you on another occasion. Jackson will tell me I am sadly out of condition. And he would be right, too. Haven't been in the ring for weeks.'

'In that case,' Kit said, 'I am glad you cannot come. What is the use of a brother who cannot provide a decent level of opposition?'

Hugo grinned. 'Let us make an appointment to meet

in a week's time, brother. Then I'll show you opposition.'

Kit stretched out his hand. 'Agreed,' he said. 'Five guineas to the winner?' They shook hands on the deal.

'Kit, there's something I have been meaning to ask you.' There was a noticeable hesitation in Hugo's voice suddenly. 'I… Have you heard any rumours lately?'

Kit's brows rose. 'Have to be more specific, I'm afraid, Hugo. I hear rumours all the time. What sort of rumours?'

'About…your Austrian lady friend.'

Not Marina, then. Katharina. What on earth could Hugo have heard? Kit permitted himself an exaggerated sigh. 'Ah, I see. No, I have not. But I trust you will tell me what they are.'

'I would not do so ordinarily, but she… You deserve better, Kit, than to be made to look a fool by that… female.'

Kit knew instinctively what was coming. He felt an instant surge of anger, first—and unfairly—against Hugo for being the bearer of such tidings, and then against Katharina for being the cause of them. But he refused to allow his bruised pride to show. Even to his brother.

'You may tell me the whole, Hugo,' he said evenly. 'Do not attempt to spare my feelings. In this case, I have none, believe me.'

Hugo stared at him for a second before continuing, 'It is rumoured that the Baroness has taken another lover. No, I do not have a name, I'm afraid, but I have heard it now from a number of sources. They could be wrong, of course, but…'

'But you do not think so.'

'No. Especially as it… You ought to be aware, Kit, that one of those infernal scandal sheets is making much of your affairs, and of the fact that the Baroness is known to have strayed.'

'You have seen it?'

'No. No, I have not, though others have. Do you want me to try to—?'

'Thank you, Hugo. No. I am grateful for the information. There is nothing more for you to do now. I shall deal with matters in my own way. I trust that Emma knows nothing of this?'

'I am not aware that she does,' said Hugo carefully, 'but her Aunt Warenne is always one of the first with the latest *on dits*. I should think it is only a matter of time…'

'In that case, I had better be on my way. It seems I shall be…sparring with more than one opponent today. Wish me luck, Hugo?'

'With your experience, shall you really need it?'

The Baroness was white with anger but she did not raise her voice. 'So you have the impudence to come to me for payment, do you, Budge?' Her foreign accent was becoming more pronounced with every word. She waved a paper at the housekeeper. 'After this?' she hissed.

Mrs Budge quailed, but stood her ground. 'I carried out your orders exactly, m'lady, I promise you. It has been almost a week now and you said—'

'I gave you clear instructions to say nothing about the writer of that letter. Do you deny that you disobeyed me?'

'No, m'lady. I mean, yes, I…' She shook her head slightly, trying to regain control. 'M'lady, I said nothing about you to Mr Johnson or anyone else. I simply delivered the letter you gave me.'

The Baroness spread the paper she held and glanced down at it. 'Are you telling me that you had no conversation with Mr Johnson?'

'Er...no, m'lady, not exactly. We...we exchanged the time of day, so to speak.'

'Quite,' said the Baroness sourly. 'I should have known better than to trust an English servant. Especially one who dares to ask for payment after betraying me.'

'M'lady, I swear—'

The Baroness thrust the paper towards Mrs Budge. 'Read it, then, Budge. Read it. And then tell me that you are not responsible. If you dare.'

Mrs Budge scanned the paper, her hand shaking a little at the violence of the Baroness's onslaught. Then she lifted her chin and looked resolutely at her accuser. 'M'lady, this is nothing to do with me. I did not tell Mr Johnson that you and the master are... And I certainly said nothing else about you.' At the Baroness's snort of anger, she added, daringly, 'How could I have done so, when I knew nothing about your other affairs?'

'How dare you?' spluttered the Baroness. 'Get out of my house before I have you thrown out. Get out, I say!'

Mrs Budge almost ran out of the room before the Baroness could make good on her threat. Clearly she would receive not a penny more from the Austrian woman.

What would happen now? The Baroness might well betray her treachery to the master, who would be bound to dismiss her if he found out. And Mrs Budge could not afford to lose her place, or the income it provided.

Yet there might be another way of earning money, at least for now. The Baroness had accused her of betrayal and was treating her as if she were guilty. So...she might as well reap the rewards.

She would pay another visit to the well-informed Mr

Johnson and, this time, she would not be nearly so circumspect about what she told him. The next edition of Mr Johnson's little scandal sheet would give the haughty Baroness a seizure—she hoped—besides making the woman the butt of London gossip for the rest of the Season.

She pursed her lips and nodded at her own cleverness. Good. Very good.

And, just in case that did not do the trick, she would ensure that a copy of Mr Johnson's interesting history would find its way to the Austrian Embassy, for the personal attention of the noble Baron von Thalberg.

Instinctively, Kit ducked back into the shadows. He had no desire to be seen in the vicinity of Katharina's house. There were quite enough rumours flying already.

Then he recognised the black-clad woman who had emerged. It was his own housekeeper.

Now, that was very interesting. What possible reason could Mrs Budge have for visiting Katharina at her home? He had given the woman no message to deliver. In truth, he had had no communication at all from Katharina for over a week, which was not surprising if his little Austrian was indeed playing him false, as Hugo had suggested. Clearly, it was time they parted. He had made it plain enough, throughout their liaison, that he was always faithful to his mistresses—while they lasted—and that he expected the same courtesy from the ladies in question. Since Katharina appeared to have ignored his warning, their rupture could not now be delayed.

For a moment he toyed with the notion of entering the Baron's house and giving Katharina her *congé* face to face. What a scandal that would create! The diplomat's wife receiving one of the greatest rakes in London—alone in her drawing room, too. Did he dare?

Yes, he did. He would do it—were it not for the scandal that would then descend on Emma and Hugo, as well as himself. That would be mightily unfair on them. Kit would have to find another means of dealing with the duplicitous Baroness. A lesser man might do the deed by letter, but Kit had no intention of adopting such a cowardly tactic. He would confront her with her deceit and leave her in no doubt of why she was to be banished from his bed.

His eye was caught by Mrs Budge's raised hand. She had walked only a few yards from Katharina's door and was trying to hail a hackney. Even more interesting! Where could she be going that justified such expensive transport? No doubt Katharina had paid her, but what was her errand? It made no sense for Katharina to employ Mrs Budge to take messages to her new lover. There were plenty of other servants in the household who could be bribed to do that. What was the service that only Kit's housekeeper could perform for the faithless Baroness?

He looked around rapidly for another cab, but there was none in sight. He cursed roundly. A passing gentleman looked at him in surprise and disgust, hesitated, and then walked on.

Kit grinned ruefully at his own loss of control. The housekeeper's hackney was out of sight. It would be impossible to follow her now. He might as well continue with his original errand and call at his friend's house, next but one to Katharina's. He would be waiting to be taken to Jackson's boxing parlour for his introduction to the great man. A turn in the ring was even more necessary now, Kit decided. He really needed to vent his wrath on someone this morning, or he would explode.

Mrs Budge would not escape scot-free, however. At some point convenient to Kit, the housekeeper would be faced with an interview that she would find more than a little uncomfortable.

Chapter Fifteen

'I did not come here to be insulted,' hissed the Baroness, rising indignantly from her seat in the cramped parlour.

'No, Katharina, you came here to see if you could cozen me into believing that these rumours were a pack of lies.' He fixed her with a stern gaze. 'Well? Did you not?'

She did not reply. She tried to meet his eyes, but failed. To cover her confusion, she began to pace around the room.

'Spare me these theatricals, my dear. You should know they will achieve nothing. I asked you here to tell you face to face that our...understanding is at an end. You know why.'

She threw a sharp glance at him and deliberately turned her back.

'Does your husband know that you are playing him false yet again?'

She spun on her heel. 'How dare you say such a thing! You, of all men! As if you were blameless!'

'My dear Katharina, it was but a simple question. I ask because I have a warning for you. Once, you were discreet. Now, it appears, you are not. If these rumours should reach the Baron's ears and he should be minded to defend his honour—it is not impossible, you know, since he is neither as old nor as blind as you would like to believe—I shall refer him to your latest *cher ami*. I have no intention of facing a bullet at dawn for Cullen's—' He stopped abruptly, waiting until she looked him in the eye once more. 'I am sure your English is quite adequate to supply the appropriate word.'

He smiled coldly at her, before striding across to the fireplace to pull the bell. 'Mrs Budge will show you out.' He folded his arms and leaned casually against the mantel until the door opened.

'Show my visitor out, Mrs Budge,' he said sharply.

The housekeeper curtsied and took her stance by the open door.

'Goodbye, my dear. Be grateful that I did you the courtesy of a meeting. It is more than you deserve. A woman who uses servants to spy on their own master deserves no consideration of any kind.'

The Baroness threw him a look seething with hatred, before marching through the open door.

'I hope you paid her well,' he called after her, relishing the housekeeper's suddenly ashen face, 'for she is most certainly going to lose her place.'

The Dowager smiled grimly. 'Splendid. Absolutely splendid,' she said with satisfaction. 'It will be delightful to see that woman get her just deserts.'

Marina had no idea what her mistress was talking about, but it must have something to do with the scandal sheet that lay in her lap. What woman could she be referring to?

'Kit Stratton has excelled himself this time. I should

not have believed that he had it in him. And his Austrian…er…mistress will be mad as fire. I wonder…' Her
smile broadened. 'I wonder if someone will see fit to
show this to her husband. We might have a real diplomatic incident then. Oh, it is famous.' She chortled nastily, enjoying the thought. Then, seeing Marina's puzzlement, she threw the paper across to her. 'Read it, if
you wish. But don't come over all missish when you do.
It's the way of the world.' She nodded to herself. 'And
when the world pauses to think about it, they will soon
work out the identity of the mysterious M.B.'

M.B.! Marina felt as if all the blood had suddenly
drained from her body. She barely had enough strength
in her fingers to spread the cheap paper. She was betrayed! Now that her initials had been printed in a scandal sheet, it would take no time at all for her identity to
be discovered. She had been a fool to depend on Kit
Stratton's aid. And much too quick in thanking him for
ensuring his brother's discretion. Sir Hugo must have
spoken of what he had seen…or perhaps the culprit was
Kit Stratton himself. She had been mad to think him a
gentleman.

She felt as if a black cloud had settled around her. It
was only a matter of time now until she was completely
disgraced.

She glanced furtively at the Dowager who was still
smiling in grim satisfaction. Why? She had hinted that
she knew the identity of M.B., but that was impossible.
If she had known the truth, she would not be talking to
Marina in this odd way. She would be telling her to pack
her bags.

There was something very strange about all this.

Marina bent to the paper.

The piece was short but devastating. A certain Mr S.

had been seen to have an assignation with a mysterious tall lady. The scandal sheet, drawing on its private sources, was not in the least surprised to learn of that, since the gentleman's 'close friend,' a foreign lady of exalted position, was known to have been seeking solace in other quarters of late. The mysterious lady was known to the editor (he said) but he would not injure her reputation by naming her at this stage. Her initials, however, were M.B.

Marina swallowed hard. She looked across at her employer. For a second, everything became hazy, as if she were about to faint, but then her vision cleared again. She did not dare to say a word. She was sure her voice would crack.

Lady Luce seemed to have noticed nothing. She was totally caught up in her enjoyment of the scandal to come. 'I shall not drop any hints for a day or two,' she said, 'for I wish to see how many are astute enough to work it out for themselves. And to see how Kit Stratton will react. If he has an ounce of common sense, he will take himself off to Vienna again, before the axe falls. But then, he always was a stubborn, arrogant man. Thinks he can talk his way out of anything.'

She rose from her chair, chuckling, and made for the door. 'I dare say it will be better than a play.'

Marina expelled a long breath as the door closed behind the Dowager. She must think! What was she to do? Should she warn Mr Stratton of what the Dowager was about? But how could she? She did not understand it herself. Besides, he would accept no advice from a mere female, especially one like Marina, whom he clearly despised.

The Dowager seemed to think that the axe was about

to fall on Kit Stratton. If Marina had an ounce of sense, she, too, would simply stand by and watch.

The horse stumbled. Automatically, Kit gathered him up, mentally upbraiding himself for his failure to pay attention to his mount, or the terrain. The last thing he wanted was an injury to his favourite bay.

'Sorry, Caesar, old fellow,' he said soothingly. 'Your master is not worthy of you today.' He reined the huge stallion back to a gentle walk. At this pace, Caesar would now look out for himself, and, since they had the park to themselves at this early hour, Kit could indulge himself in a little reflection.

It was now two days since he had parted from Katharina. He had no regrets. Indeed, it was surprising how little impact her absence was having on his life. He had enjoyed her beautiful body—what man would not?—but he did not *need* her. He never had. It was unusual for him to be without a mistress, to be sure, but he was in no hurry to replace her.

In truth, none of the women in London Society attracted him in the least. They lacked beauty, they lacked wit, they lacked—

He shook his head. What on earth was the matter with him? The ladies in London were easily the equal of those in Vienna. Why was he suddenly so difficult to please? London offered mistresses a-plenty to choose from, married ladies who presented no threat to his independence, who would be more than willing to share his bed in return for an expensive bauble or two…and the chance to boast of having captured the handsomest rake in London. Kit grimaced a little at the thought. He knew only too well how Society spoke of him. Sometimes, his looks were a curse.

He began to review the potential candidates. Méchante, for example, would not hesitate, even now, in spite of the way he had insulted her. She had been an accomplished lover, once. And he could not deny that she was coldly beautiful. But, like all the rest, she cared only for herself. She had no redeeming qualities. There was absolutely nothing there to admire.

The same was true of all of them.

He frowned. All except—

Miss Beaumont was the only woman who had anything in the least admirable about her. She did not have looks, but she did have courage. It was a pity that she appeared to have duplicity, too. He should have taxed her with it, when he had the chance. At Emma's party, for example. Why had he not?

Because he had been so bewitched by the way she sang that he had not been able to bring himself to shatter the spell. She was no beauty, it was true, but in that simple shimmering gown, with her chestnut hair falling in loose curls about her face, she had stirred something in him that had given him pause. What kind of woman could make music like a female Orpheus? He had wanted to begin to understand that—and other things about her, too. He had been quite incapable of taking her to task, no matter how justified his criticism might be.

But was it?

He tried to remember precisely what she had said on the landing of Lady Luce's house. He could not. Something about his letter, but what exactly? He had been sure at the time that she was intending to insult him, but what if he was wrong? Women were sometimes so very difficult to read.

Except in bed, of course, he thought with a smile,

remembering the many neglected, resentful wives who had come to purr under his hands. There, he had never had any difficulty at all.

'Mama, I must speak to you.'

Lady Luce raised a questioning eyebrow. 'Indeed, William? And what, pray, is so urgent?'

'I have news about Kit Stratton, ma'am.'

'Very well. I am listening.'

'I think I should speak to you alone, Mama.'

Marina rose immediately.

'Tush!' said the Dowager. 'Miss Beaumont is my companion and knows a great deal more than you give her credit for. Sit down at once, Marina. Anything that my son wishes to say to me, he may say in front of you.'

The Earl looked both uncomfortable and angry. His neck had turned an unbecoming shade of purple. 'Very well,' he said in a strained voice. 'If that is what you wish, ma'am. But I warn you that what I have to say is not for the ears of a gently reared young lady.'

The Dowager threw him an eloquent look. It suggested that, in her opinion, her son's views on what young ladies should and should not know left much to be desired. However, she said nothing. She merely nodded at him, impatiently.

He cleared his throat and began rather pompously, 'You will know, I suppose, ma'am, that Mr Stratton has had a number of…er…liaisons.' He glanced furtively towards Marina and then looked hurriedly away. 'It is rumoured that his return to England was simply to follow his Austrian mis—er…his Austrian, when her husband was sent here. For all I know, it may be true. However, you will be interested to know that she has tired of him and that he—a man who has always prided himself on being the one to end these little…affairs—appears to be on the point of receiving his *congé* from the lady. It will be the first time, I dare swear.' He smiled down at his mother. 'I was sure you would relish the news.'

'And I did relish it, William…the *first* time I heard it. That was several days ago. Where on earth have your wits been all this time? Or is it that you have been relying on Charlotte for your information? She is always the last to know.'

The Earl's colour mounted once more. 'If you are not interested in what I have to say, Mama, I shall take my leave.'

'Stuff!' said his mother sharply. 'Stay where you are. Now, *I* shall tell *you* about Kit Stratton.'

Marina held her breath. What more did the Dowager know? She had been smiling to herself almost non-stop since the moment she had first read the scandal sheet's wicked tale. It looked as if she believed every word of it. And she seemed to be firmly convinced that she alone knew the identity of Kit Stratton's latest mistress, the elusive M.B. She was wrong, of course, but how was she to be set right? Did she really know another M.B.? So far, she had not chosen to share her secret with Marina. Would she reveal it now?

'While it may suit the lady in question to put it about that she is giving Mr Stratton his *congé*, it is certainly not true.'

'What? Mama, you—'

'Allow me to finish, William. As I said, it is not true. Mr Stratton ended the relationship himself, as soon as he discovered her perfidy. That was several days ago, William. Can't say I blame him. Was there anything else you wished to tell me?'

Lord Luce seemed incapable of speech.

'Then, since you do not appear to have seen it, I will give you a little light reading matter.' She took the scandal sheet, now rather ragged, from her pocket and handed it to him. 'I suggest you share it with your dear wife. Then you may puzzle together over the identity of M.B.'

Her son was rapidly scanning the sheet. His jaw had dropped open.

'Interesting, ain't it?' said the Dowager with something approaching a gleeful cackle. 'Let me give you a word of advice, William. Don't look too far afield for the mysterious M.B.'

'I beg your pardon, ma'am? I cannot think what on earth you can possibly mean.'

'That is because you refuse to use what little sense you were born with.' She was looking very hard at him. He seemed to be genuinely puzzled, as well as indignant. 'Oh, very well. I am becoming tired of waiting, in any case. At this rate, I shall be carried out in my box before anyone else discovers who she is.'

Holding her breath, Marina began to study the toes of her slippers.

'M.B.,' said the Dowager. 'It should not be so very difficult, especially for you, William. Think— No. Consider, if you will, the number of ladies of your acquaintance with surnames beginning with B. And then think, very carefully, about a family that is…allied with your own. That is where you will find M.B. Indeed, you yourself have been almost as close to the lady in question as Kit Stratton is rumoured to be.'

'What? Mama, I—'

The Dowager rose angrily. 'Do you never listen to a word I say, William? I told you to *think*, not to talk drivel. Oh, go away. Go away before I lose all patience with you.'

Patience was the last virtue that Marina would have attributed to the Dowager, but she was too full of anxiety to be able to appreciate the joke. The Dowager's description could fit Marina—pretty well, at least—but she was almost sure now that she was not the intended target. Lord Luce had never been close to her, not in any way. So who?

The Earl had risen automatically with his mother, good manners overcoming his wrath. He was refusing to acknowledge Marina's existence in any way, which was not surprising considering that she had just witnessed yet another humiliating scene between them. 'I will take my leave, then, Mama,' he said, bowing. 'I'm afraid I can make nothing of your riddles. I cannot think of any family of my acquaintance that would permit such disgraceful behaviour. A young woman alone with Kit Stratton? It would be scandalous.'

The Dowager nodded, smiling maliciously.

'I am sure no such person would be tolerated by my family. And as for your hints… Why, there is only one family that would fit your description, and the Blaines are quite above reproach—'

The Dowager snorted eloquently. 'Are they, indeed? You, obviously, do not stop to wonder why her ladyship always wins when she holds the Faro bank. Tongues are starting to wag about your precious Blaines, William.'

The Blaines? Oh, good God, was that what the Dowager had meant? Why did all Marina's problems seem to stem from the Blaines? Marina began to feel a little sick.

Her reaction was nothing to William's, however. He was gasping like a stranded fish. And his colour was mounting, yet again. Marina had never seen an apoplexy, but she was beginning to wonder whether she might be about to.

The Dowager made for the door, ignoring her son's plight. 'Come, Marina,' she said, beckoning. 'We have matters to attend to. Remember what I have said, William,' she added with affected geniality. 'M.B. A lady that you, too, have held in your arms. Intriguing, ain't it?'

In her haste to make up for her lateness, Marina did not really look where she was going. 'Oh, I beg your pardon,' she said quickly, automatically reaching out a hand to steady the young lady against whom she had stumbled. 'How clumsy of me.'

The young lady smiled a little vacantly, but it animated her plain features. It was the eldest Miss Blaine. 'No harm done,' she said. 'Why, you must be Miss Beaumont.' She suddenly blushed bright red. 'Forgive me,' she continued, in a tumbling rush of words, 'but since you are the only other young lady who is as tall as I am, I could not help but guess at your identity, even though we have not been introduced. We were both at…at Lady Stratton's party, but Mama and I had to leave because…because I—'

'Because you felt unwell,' Marina improvised, automatically trying to put Miss Blaine at her ease. 'It was not in the least surprising. I found it very hot myself.' She glanced up the stairs towards Lady Stratton's drawing room. 'Have you been calling on Lady Stratton?'

'Oh, yes. She is usually at home to visitors on Mondays. We called on Monday last, because Mama said I must apologise for…for making a scene. But Lady Stratton would not hear of it. She insisted we should call again. She is so kind and charming, do you not think? And so very elegant.' There was no mistaking the envy in Miss Blaine's voice.

'Yes, indeed,' Marina agreed, trying unsuccessfully to warm to the awkward young woman. 'She has been immeasurably kind to a mere companion, too.'

'But I thought…I understood that you were…related to Papa?' There was something about her tone. It suggested that, if Marina had been a mere companion, Miss Blaine would not be prepared to converse with her at all.

'Ye…es,' replied Marina, a little hesitantly.

'Well, in that case, I shall call you Marina. And you must call me Tilly.' She gave an embarrassed giggle. 'Dreadful name, is it not? But since ''Mathilda'' is even worse, I fear I have no choice in the matter. I often wish Mama had called me something more poetic—'

'Tilly!' Lady Blaine's voice thundered from the landing above them. 'Why on earth are you dawdling there? I expressly asked you to order the carriage. Do it immediately, if you please.'

'I was just about to do so, Mama, but I encountered Marina, and—'

'Miss Beaumont,' said Lady Blaine, with emphasis, looking down at Marina with profound dislike. 'No doubt she is here on an errand for her employer. Pray, do not let us keep you from your duties, Miss Beaumont. You will find Lady Stratton in her drawing room.'

Marina glanced at Tilly, but the girl was already hurrying off down to the hall to carry out her mother's orders. And it was unlikely she would ever again dare to address Marina in Lady Blaine's presence. The woman seemed to enjoy inflicting humiliation on others, even on her own daughter.

Picking up her skirts once more, Marina slowly mounted the rest of the stairs until she stood on the landing alongside Lady Blaine. From her greater height, she looked down into the older woman's face, registering the depth of dislike and contempt in her hard eyes.

An imp of mischief prodded Marina into a pert little curtsy and an insolent speech. 'How kind of you, Cousin. As it happens, I know my way.' Then she hurried along the corridor before the astonished Viscountess had time to utter a single word in reply.

'Miss Beaumont!' Lady Stratton was alone. She rose from her chair as the door opened. 'What a pity! Lady Blaine and her daughter have only just left.'

Taking a couple of deep breaths, Marina forced herself to behave as normally as she could. This was the wrong time, and the wrong place to turn her mind to—

'Do sit down, my dear. You look a little flushed. Are you perfectly well?'

'Perfectly, ma'am, I thank you. It was just that I was a little late and so I was hurrying.'

'There was no need, I assure you. Do remove your bonnet. I will ring for some fresh tea. You look as though you need a cup.'

Marina watched her hostess move elegantly across to the bell. Everything seemed so very normal. She was a guest in a lady's drawing room. They were about to take tea.

And Marina had at last discovered the identity of Lady Luce's M.B.! After three days of racking her brains, the answer had been dropped into her lap.

She closed her eyes in horror for a moment. There could be no doubt. The Dowager's hints had been clearly directed at the Blaines, even though she had never actually pronounced the name. The Dowager's M.B. was part of a family allied with her son's. She must have been referring to the close friendship between Lady Blaine and William's wife. It was just possible that, at some time, William had held the child Mathilda in his arms. The Dowager had probably been making mischief, as she so often did, by telling her son he had held the *lady* in his arms. She would enjoy taxing his rather weak intellect.

But could it really be true?

Yes. In the Dowager's eyes, at least. She seemed to detest the Blaines almost as much as she detested her own son. And it had been the Dowager who had drawn everyone's attention to Tilly Blaine's obvious infatuation with Kit Stratton.

A hint or two more from Lady Luce—or from that wicked scandal sheet—and the whole of Society would quickly identify Tilly Blaine as the mysterious M.B., the woman who was reputed to be Kit Stratton's new lover. Miss Blaine would be ruined.

It must not be allowed to happen.

It would be a monstrous injustice to an innocent girl whose only fault had been to betray her feelings for London's foremost rake. And it would be Marina's fault.

Something must be done to save Tilly Blaine, even if—

The door opened. She had not heard a knock.

Marina turned, expecting to see Lady Stratton's butler with the tea tray.

'Afternoon, Emma,' drawled that well-known voice. 'Have I arrived too late to greet your visitors? How very remiss of me.'

Chapter Sixteen

Marina was a mass of warring emotions. The sight of Kit Stratton's handsome, elegant person made her heart race and her mouth go dry. But she knew that she had every reason to be furious with him. Was he not, ultimately, responsible for having betrayed her—or at least her initials—to the world at large? Was he not responsible, at least in part, for the potential disgrace that was hanging over poor Tilly Blaine?

Given the slightest opportunity, she would have no hesitation in taking him to task. She rather doubted that anyone had ever done so before, particularly a woman, but in this case, she had cause. And she would not permit his overpowering masculinity to prevent her from doing her duty. She refused to give in to the disturbingly seductive memories that plagued her dreams. Dreams where Kit's strong hands had gently—

She forced herself to look coldly on him.

He bowed slightly. 'Forgive me, Miss Beaumont. For a moment, I thought Emma was alone. It had not occurred to me that you might be here at this late hour of the day.'

Marina bridled but said nothing. Of course he had

overlooked her. She was only a poor, plain companion, was she not?

Lady Stratton had crossed the floor to take her brother-in-law by the arm and draw him into the room. 'You do not fool me, brother dear,' she said archly. 'I know precisely why you have arrived at this late hour. You are deliberately avoiding my other guests, while allowing yourself to claim that you have done the pretty by your brother's wife.'

He grinned down at her. 'I make no attempt to deny it—especially as I recognised the arms on the carriage that was driving away. I must admit that the society of Lady Blaine is not at all to my taste.'

'But I thought the Viscount was a member of your club?'

'Yes, but so are many gentlemen. It does not mean that I seek out his company. Besides, he has been abroad since just after I returned to England. Visiting his plantations, or some such, I understand.'

'Oh,' said Marina, before she could stop herself. Her disapproval must have been apparent from her tone, for Mr Stratton threw her a very strange look. She felt she must be blushing, at least a little. But, on the other hand, she knew that she had right on her side on this occasion. She looked challengingly back at him. 'Are you surprised, sir, to learn that some people do not approve of the exploitation of our fellow men? The Church teaches us that we are all brothers. It cannot be right to enslave our brothers.'

Mr Stratton looked at Marina with frank curiosity. 'A follower of Wilberforce, I collect?'

She nodded.

'Most laudable,' he continued. 'But the slave trade is ended. Your battle is won, is it not?'

'No, indeed,' she countered hotly. 'We may no longer transport the poor souls out of Africa, but, in the plantations, they are still in chains. And—'

The door opened to admit the butler. 'Tea, at last,' breathed Lady Stratton, sounding relieved. 'You will take a cup, Kit?'

'Beg pardon, m'lady,' said the butler, setting the tray down on the pie-crust table, 'but Sir Hugo asked if you could spare him a few minutes, on a matter of urgency. He is in his bookroom.'

'How very awkward,' she said, but moved to the door with a little shrug. 'Miss Beaumont, I must ask you to forgive me for a moment. Might I prevail upon you to do the honours in my absence?'

'Of course.'

'And Kit will be on his best behaviour, I promise you.' She glared a warning at him, but it seemed to produce no reaction. 'I shall return shortly. Pray excuse me.' She hurried from the room.

Marina's heart had begun to beat very fast. She told herself to ignore it. As the door closed on the butler, she lifted the silver teapot and looked up at Kit Stratton with as much coolness as she could muster. 'Cream and sugar, Mr Stratton?'

'Thank you.'

He took the seat opposite Marina. His biscuit-coloured pantaloons were so tightly moulded to his body that Marina could see the flexing of his every muscle when he stretched out his long legs. She tried to concentrate on the sugar basin and then on handing him his cup.

'Thank you,' he said again, reaching out with one strong, lean hand. He did not touch her, but at that moment Marina's hard-won control began to crack, and her hand wavered slightly. If he had not taken the cup just then, the tea would have been spilt.

I must be going out of my mind, she thought. Why am I concerning myself about serving tea, when this man is about to bring utter disgrace upon me? And upon Tilly Blaine?

She took a deep breath and folded her hands in her lap. Her tea sat untouched on the table. 'Mr Stratton, I must ask you if you are aware of the rumours that are circulating about you and...about our meetings.'

His eyes narrowed. 'I collect that you are about to tell me, Miss Beaumont,' he replied non-committally.

That was almost too much. 'I should not need to do so, since you must be the cause of them.'

He raised an eyebrow.

That was the last straw for Marina's increasingly fragile temper. 'How dare you?' she raged. 'You led me to believe that you had done as I asked. I was fool enough to think that you were a true gentleman, that you would ask your brother not to betray what he had seen. I should have known not to trust you. Tell me, pray, was it you who betrayed my indiscretion to the scandal sheets? Or did you merely disclose it to your friends? I am sure they must have been vastly amused.'

Very slowly, he replaced his cup on the table. Then he leaned back in his chair and surveyed Marina through half-closed eyes. She could feel his contempt, but she would not be cowed, not by a worthless rake. She straightened her shoulders and returned his blatant stare.

'Very good, Miss Beaumont,' he said softly. 'And now, perhaps you would be good enough to explain these accusations of yours. I may add that I am not in the habit of betraying confidences.'

'Then why did you betray mine?'

'I did not,' he said flatly.

She barely heard him. She was now so angry that the words were tumbling out. 'You and Sir Hugo were the only people who knew I had been in your carriage. No one else saw me in the park that morning. It was obvious that your brother had recognised me. Why else would I write to you as I did? You allowed me to believe that all would be well, while—'

'You wrote to me? When?' He was leaning forward now, his whole body alert.

'You know when,' she responded tartly. How dare he pretend not to remember?

'Miss Beaumont,' he said slowly, 'I received no letter from you.'

'But—'

'No letter,' he repeated firmly. 'It is true that my brother recognised you in the park. I assure you that he has spoken of it to no one, not even to his wife. He felt he owed it to your father and your uncle to preserve your good name.'

'Then—'

'And I have spoken of it to no one except my brother, Miss Beaumont. If your name is circulating in the scandal sheets, it is none of my doing, I promise you.'

'Oh.' Marina let out a long breath and dropped her head into her hands. A moment ago, she could easily have flown at him; now her strength had evaporated. It could not be true. Could it? 'I do not understand,' she whispered at last. 'If neither you nor Sir Hugo spoke of it, how is it that—?' She did not finish the sentence. What did it matter who was guilty? Her shame would be just the same. She could not bring herself to look at him. She could not move.

Kit reached out and gently removed her hands from

her face, holding them in a comforting clasp. 'Miss Beaumont,' he said, trying to convey his sympathy in the tone of his voice, 'Miss Beaumont, look at me.'

It seemed a very long time before she obeyed. Her huge eyes were full of horror, as if she could see a terrible fate awaiting her.

'You believe the Strattons have betrayed you. I promise you we have not done so. But, from what you say, it appears that you have been betrayed. Tell me of this letter. When was it sent? Who delivered it?'

Miss Beaumont lifted her chin an inch. 'I wrote to you as soon as I reached home. I took the letter to the receiving office myself.'

'You are sure the direction was correct?'

'Yes, of course. I could not mistake it. After all, I had only just come from your house.'

'You directed it to me in Chelsea?' At her impatient nod, he said slowly, 'I see. That was unfortunate, I think.' It was unfortunate, too, that she had entrusted her letter to the post, rather than to a messenger, but it would not do to tell Miss Beaumont what he was beginning to suspect. She was distraught enough already. He must treat her with great care from this point. But he had very little time. Emma might return at any moment.

He tried to smile reassuringly at her. She had not withdrawn her hands, but he doubted there was anything to be read into that. He was not sure that she was aware that he held them. 'I did not receive your letter, ma'am. Would you be kind enough to tell me what was in it?'

'I...I cannot remember exactly, sir. I said that I thought your brother had recognised me. I...believe I asked you to intercede with him, in hopes that he might say nothing.'

'That was all?'

'I may have mentioned alighting from your carriage…to explain how it was that Sir Hugo saw me. I
am not sure.'

Kit frowned. Worse and worse. There was one last
question. It had to be asked. 'Miss Beaumont, did you
sign your letter?'

'Oh, no,' she replied quickly.

He breathed a sigh of relief.

'I used only my initials.'

Kit looked quickly down at the floor, trying to hide
his obvious dismay. Her letter was lost—and it contained
all the information needed to ruin her. She—innocent
and unworldly as she was—had thought she would be
safe as long as she did not sign her name. Confound it,
how many women did she think there were with the
initials M.B.?

'Miss Beaumont—'

'Mr Stratton, I…I apologise for my hasty words a
moment ago,' she said stiffly, avoiding his eyes. With a
sudden movement, she pulled her hands from his and
hid them in her skirts. She was blushing now, terribly
conscious that he had been holding her hands.

He was reminded yet again that she had a flawless
complexion. He found himself wishing that she would
look at him again. She had beautiful eyes, even if the
flecks of gold were now hidden by the depth of her hurt.

She spoke to her skirts. Her voice was so low that it
was difficult to make out her words. 'Mr Stratton, I think
it is worse than you know. A scandal sheet is circulating.
It says that you have a new m…mistress, a tall lady with
the initials M.B. There is much speculation about
my…about the lady's identity.'

Kit nodded. This was very serious—for Miss Beaumont. 'Do you have any reason to believe that you have been identified as M.B., ma'am?' he asked softly.

'Oh, no,' she cried, dropping her head into her hands once more. 'No reason in the world.'

Kit thought she was beginning to sound a little hysterical. It made no sense. She must know she was safe as long as M.B. remained unidentified.

'Lady Luce is certain that the lady in question is Tilly Blaine.'

Kit stared in total disbelief. Miss Blaine? Tilly Blaine?

'Her real name is Mathilda, you see, but everyone knows her as "Tilly" so the connection is not obvious at once, and—'

Kit began to laugh. He could not help it. The thing was just too absurd. Tilly Blaine! A gushing beanpole of a woman who talked—once started, she was almost impossible to stop—of nothing but poets.

Miss Beaumont shot to her feet, rattling the teacups in her haste. 'How dare you laugh, sir? Have you no thought for what Miss Blaine may be made to suffer? You—'

Rising politely, Kit calmly lifted the tea table out of range of her wrath. 'My dear Miss Beaumont,' he said smoothly, 'I have not the least doubt that nothing will come of it. For who would believe that I would ever—?'

'You conceited coxcomb!' she spat. 'You think of nothing but yourself. You say no one would ever believe that you—the great Kit Stratton—would have secret meetings with a plain girl like Tilly Blaine. May I remind you, sir, that you had two such meetings with me?'

Kit took a deep breath. What on earth had possessed him to say something so arrogant? A cock crowing on a dunghill showed more humility than he. Miss Beaumont would never listen to a word he said after this. He reached out to take her hand once more, but she pulled away as if she had been burnt.

At that moment, the drawing room door opened.

Emma had returned.

'Are you for Faro tonight, ma'am?'

'Perhaps,' said Lady Luce. 'Worries you, don't it, Méchante, to see my run of luck?' She allowed the lackey to relieve her of her dark evening cloak. 'Be grateful I am not Lady Blaine. After all, I *do* lose—sometimes. I fancy I might see whether my luck still holds tonight.'

Lady Marchant bowed her acknowledgement. 'As you wish, ma'am,' she said. 'My rooms are always open to you.'

The Dowager snorted and turned towards the staircase.

'What do you think about this latest rumour?'

'What rumour?' said the Dowager sourly, pausing on the step.

'Why, about Kit Stratton's latest mistress, the mysterious M.B.'

The Dowager looked narrowly at her hostess. 'You do not know who she is,' she said flatly, and with obvious satisfaction. 'How very frustrating for you.'

'Am I to understand that you do?' Lady Marchant's voice dripped venom.

'Naturally,' said Lady Luce evenly. She looked Méchante over for a long moment. 'But I do not propose to share that information. Not yet.'

Lady Marchant made to speak, but the Dowager forestalled her. 'I know there is no love lost between you and Kit Stratton. So I will give you a hint, for we are surely allies in this little charade. This time, Kit Stratton has gone much too far. This time, he might even find himself riveted. And I doubt he will enjoy the experience.' She laughed nastily. 'But I most certainly shall. I would gladly have paid him his twelve thousand pounds for this. Pity he will never know it.'

Méchante's eyes gleamed with malice. 'M.B. is a *lady*? A *single* lady?'

Lady Luce nodded. 'We should perhaps look forward to dancing at his wedding.'

'Oh, it is famous! I doubt I shall dance at his wedding, however. On his grave, more like.'

The Dowager's eyebrows shot up.

'My dear ma'am,' said Lady Marchant, 'I may not have succeeded in identifying M.B.—I admit my sources have been useless there—but I have not been idle, I assure you.' She continued confidingly, 'You will have noticed the increasing rumours about Kit and the Austrian Baroness? I fancy her husband is finding it…somewhat difficult of late to overlook her adventures. What is more, I have made it my business to ensure that most of the foreign diplomats—and especially the French Ambassador—are laughing at the Baron's inability to keep his wife in his own bed. His stiff-necked pride will never tolerate that, especially from a Frenchman. There must now be a good chance that Kit Stratton will have a bullet in him before he gets near the altar.'

'Balderdash! Kit Stratton is a crack shot.'

Lady Marchant beamed at the old woman. 'I do not believe that I said anything about a duel, ma'am. You must know there are other ways…'

The Dowager paused assessingly. 'Indeed there are. I thank you for the information, Méchante, and I shall watch developments with…interest. As it happens, I am holding a large party on Wednesday evening. Everyone will be there—the diplomats, the Strattons, the cream of Society… It could be very entertaining. Such a pity that I cannot extend an invitation to you, my dear, but I am sure you understand…'

Marina had just reached the end of her second page of notes about the arrangements for the Dowager's party on the morrow, when the butler entered with a letter.

'Lady Marchant's man brought it, m'lady,' said Tibbs, offering the salver to the Dowager. 'He did not wait for a reply.'

Lady Luce nodded a dismissal. She sat for a moment, weighing the letter in her hand. 'I wonder…' she said softly. Then she broke the seal.

From her seat on the low stool, Marina watched anxiously. She was quite certain that Lady Marchant was out to make mischief in any way she could. The Dowager had hinted that Méchante was become Kit's enemy. And what better way to attack Kit than by attacking M.B.?

The letter contained an enclosure. The Dowager lifted it fastidiously with the very tips of her fingers and laid it aside.

Oh, God, it looked like— Please, no! Not another!

The Dowager cackled gleefully. 'My alliance with Méchante! I had not expected it to bear fruit so soon. But so it is.' She took up the second paper again, more eagerly this time, and unfolded it. After a moment, she looked up and said, 'The Baroness will be furious. And as for the Blaines… You will enjoy this, Marina, after all the insult that their family has inflicted on yours. Listen. ''We have, in the past, been reticent about the identity of M.B., out of proper regard for a lady's reputation. But we now learn that her conduct does not merit such restraint. We have learned, with horror, that M.B. is known to have visited Mr S. at his house in Chelsea on at least two occasions and to have been quite alone with him there. We can only deplore such laxity of morals in the young females of today. Their parents should reproach themselves—'' So they should,' said the Dowager, dropping the paper into her lap and putting aside her reading glass. 'Much too high in the instep, in my opinion, for an upstart Viscountess. Time she was brought down a peg or two.'

Marina's mind was in a whirl. Her only thought was that someone had betrayed her visits to Chelsea. It must have been Kit Stratton. No. It could not have been Kit Stratton, for he had denied it. Not Sir Hugo either, for he was sworn to secrecy. But someone had done it. Someone… If only she knew who it was, she could perhaps—

No. There was nothing that she, a poor companion, could do. In any case, it was too late. Her conduct was known to the world. It wanted only the revelation of her identity to complete her ruin. And that could not be long delayed, for—

'Earl Luce, m'lady.'

The Earl strode in, carrying another copy of that infernal scandal sheet!

Marina felt her heart shrivelling within her like an autumn leaf. There was no hope now. The Earl detested her. When he found out what she had done—as he soon must—he would make quite sure that the whole world learned of her disgrace.

'Mama! I have brought you the latest news. I fear you will be greatly shocked. It is scandalous—'

Lazily, the Dowager picked up her own copy of the scandal sheet and waved it in her son's direction. 'Save your breath, William,' she said acidly. 'I learned of it long ago.'

The Earl let out a long, exasperated sigh.

Marina wished that the floor would open and swallow her up. Her blood was pounding so loudly in her ears that she felt as if her head would burst.

'Oh, sit down, do. Tell me,' the Dowager continued, with poorly feigned concern, 'how is Charlotte taking the news?'

'I have not told her. She is... You must understand, Mama, that Charlotte is in an...interesting condition.'

'What? Again? For heaven's sake, William, you cannot afford to support ten children, far less eleven. What on earth were you thinking of?'

'Let me remind you, Mama, that marriage was ordained by God for the procreation of children.'

'Hmph! Even you are not required to populate the earth all by yourself. You are a fool, William. Sometimes I wonder if—'

'Mama,' interrupted the Earl, with a sharp glance towards Marina, the unwilling witness of his humiliation, 'I came to ask your advice about this...this...' He waved his scandal sheet in the direction of the copy on his mother's lap. 'You say that you know who M.B. is. So, you must also know that it falls to me to take action in the matter.'

Lady Luce raised an eyebrow.

'Someone must do so, Mama. Her father will not return for at least another month and her brother is only a schoolboy. I cannot ignore my responsibilities. Remember that I am her godfather.'

Tilly's godfather! Marina closed her eyes and dropped her head. Her hands were tightly clasped to stop them from shaking. Automatically, she felt for her ring.

'So you have decided that I was referring to Tilly Blaine, have you, William?'

'Are you telling me that you were not?'

'I am telling you nothing at all. It is for you to draw your own conclusions.' The Dowager pursed her lips for a moment. 'I must say, however, that I should not be surprised at anything that family might do.'

The Earl stared hard at his mother but she said nothing more. She looked, Marina thought, like a cat who had just caught a live mouse and was waiting for it to attempt to escape, so that it could be caught all over again. Why did one old woman get so much pleasure from tormenting her only son?

'Very well. You leave me no choice, Mama. I shall go immediately to consult Lady Blaine. She will be profoundly shocked, of course, but I must have her agreement before I take the…necessary steps.'

Necessary steps? What on earth could he mean? What was he going to do?

The Dowager relaxed back into her chair. A tiny smile flickered at one corner of her thin mouth. She said nothing at all.

The Earl waited a moment. Then he said, 'As you wish, ma'am. I bid you good morning.'

A quick bow and he was gone.

The moment the door closed on him, the Dowager began to laugh. It was a hard, brittle sound, and to Marina's ears, it was filled with malice.

'Pompous ass,' said the Dowager at last, straightening her back once more. She lifted her lorgnette and turned her gaze to Marina. 'What is the matter with you, child? You look as white as a sheet. Do you tell me you are not enjoying this little tragedy? I told you it would be better than a play, did I not? Pity that William has proposed himself for the leading role, for his acting ability leaves much to be desired. I doubt there will be many curtain calls.'

'Ma'am.' Marina's voice was barely audible. She cleared her throat and forced herself to try again. 'Ma'am, may I ask what the Earl meant…about taking the necessary steps? I did not—'

'Lud! You really are a country mouse,' said the Dowager, shaking her head. 'I had not thought that Yorkshire was so very far from civilisation. Why, he will insist that Kit Stratton marries that gel. What else did you think he would do?'

Marina felt a chill of fear settling round her body. She could neither move nor speak. Kit Stratton would be forced into a totally loveless marriage. It did not matter that Tilly Blaine worshipped him, for she would soon discover that her new husband despised her. No doubt, she would learn to hate him. Oh, it was a terrible fate for both of them.

And it was Marina's fault.

She closed her eyes. Her anger at Kit Stratton's outrageous behaviour had melted away as if it had never been. Now she could see his handsome face looking down at her with sympathy in his eyes. She could almost feel his hand on hers, gentle and comforting, when he should have been accusing her of betrayal. Nothing he had done could possibly merit such a lifelong punishment. A woman who truly loved him would sacrifice herself to save him. A woman who truly loved him— and Marina could no longer pretend to herself that she did not—was bound to tell the truth, no matter what the cost to herself.

Oh, dear God, how had it come to this? She was in

love with the blackest rake in London. If anyone discovered it, she would be ruined.

Marina willed a shell of ice to form around her heart. It was the only way. She sat immobile, allowing it to grow. She had fallen in love with Kit Stratton, in spite of herself. If he so much as guessed her weakness, he would use it against her. She did not think she could bear that. She must lock her feelings away where not even the strongest flame could melt a path to them.

Otherwise, she was totally lost.

The Dowager was paying not the least attention to Marina. She was totally absorbed in her own train of thought. 'He will never succeed,' she said emphatically.

Marina was shocked back to the present.

'Kit Stratton will never agree to an alliance under duress. He went into exile five years ago to avoid marrying Emma Fitzwilliam—and she was both beautiful, and an heiress. He will certainly refuse to marry a plain, empty-headed ninny like Tilly Blaine. Especially when it is William who demands it. He will laugh in William's face.'

'But Miss Blaine—'

'Balderdash! Think, Marina. Everyone knows that Kit Stratton's mistresses are always diamonds of the first water. If Tilly Blaine was alone in his company, it would have been at *her* instigation, not at his. Can't say I'm at all surprised, after the exhibition she made of herself at Lady Stratton's. She will be responsible for her own ruin. And for making William look the fool that he is. Dare say the whole Blaine family will have to go abroad.' She nodded happily at that new thought. 'You and I will have our revenge, miss, and London Society will be well rid of them all.'

Chapter Seventeen

'**A**nd so she berated me, Hugo. You've never seen such fire, I tell you. Her eyes were ablaze. She looked to be about to launch herself at me, claws unsheathed like a tawny lioness. It was a pity that I had to quench the flames...and so callously, too.'

Hugo gave him a rather strange look, but said nothing.

'She must have thought me totally devoid of feeling but, in truth, the idea that I would have anything to do with Tilly Blaine was so absurd... However, I should not have laughed. I freely admit my fault, but—'

'That is all very well, Kit, but did you admit your fault to Miss Beaumont?'

'I... No, I could not. Emma returned just then, and it was impossible for me to say anything more. As it was—'

'As it was, Emma was well aware that something...out of the ordinary had taken place in her absence. She told me that Miss Beaumont seemed quite distressed. That is why I am here. You know well enough that I feel in some degree responsible for Miss Beaumont's welfare. So I must ask you, Kit, did you take advantage of her?'

'No. Of course not. I would not do such a thing. Not to Miss Beaumont. I held her hands, nothing more. And my aim was only to comfort her. She was distressed, but more for Miss Blaine's sake than for her own.'

'She is a remarkable woman, I think,' said Hugo.

Kit nodded thoughtfully. He had long since reached the same conclusion. She was in some considerable danger of losing her reputation, but she seemed more concerned for others than for herself. He had never encountered a woman like her. In that instant, he resolved to do what he could to protect her. It would be little enough. He should have found out precisely where his housekeeper had been and what she had done, but he had been so incensed by the woman's treachery that he had dismissed her the moment the Baroness was out of the door. He would never find her again now.

Kit's butler knocked and entered, carrying a letter on a salver. 'Excuse me, sir, but this has just been delivered. The messenger says it is urgent. He is waiting for a reply.'

'Very well,' said Kit, ripping open the seal. 'Take him to the kitchen. I will ring when I am ready.'

'Very good, sir.' Soundlessly, the butler bowed himself out.

Hugo had quietly taken a seat beside the fireplace. He was smiling. 'You have your servants very well trained, Kit.'

Kit looked up and grimaced. 'Here, perhaps,' he said, his voice full of self-reproach, 'but not in all my establishments. Good God!'

'What is it?' asked Hugo, rising.

'This letter. It is from Katharina…the Baroness. She writes that her husband knows about her affairs and that he is threatening her.'

'What does she want from you? Did you not warn her to refer her husband to her latest lover? Cullen, ain't it?'

Kit nodded. 'Apparently, I am the only one who can help her. She asks me to meet her but—' he looked again at the letter, to make sure that he had missed nothing '—she specifies neither time nor place. She says only that she dare not go to Chelsea.'

'Sounds smoky to me.'

'And to me,' agreed Kit. 'I have never been moved by impassioned pleas. "Do not fail me," she writes. What am I supposed to make of that?'

'Something underhand, I should guess. Shall you ignore it?'

'No.' He went to his desk and sat down. 'For the moment,' he said, beginning to write, 'I shall humour her. When she has stated her terms...'

'When she has stated her terms, Kit, you will not go alone to meet her.'

Kit glanced up and grinned briefly. 'Protecting my back still, brother?'

Hugo grinned back. 'You used to say that was what brothers were for, as I recall.'

Kit did not respond. He merely shook his head ruefully and continued with his letter. Hugo, well used to his brother's ways, returned to sit in his chair, seemingly content.

The butler returned just as Kit was sanding his letter. Odd. He had not rung. 'You are become a mind-reader, it appears?' he said, looking sideways at the man.

'No, sir,' said the butler impassively. 'Lord Luce has called. He insists on seeing you immediately.'

'Ah, that explains it.' Methodically, Kit sealed his letter and handed it to the butler. 'See that the messenger has that. And now…I suppose you had better ask my latest visitor to come in.'

Lord Luce entered the room like a ship in full sail, seeking an enemy to blast with his cannons. But he stopped short when he saw that Kit was not alone.

'You are acquainted with my brother, Sir Hugo Stratton, are you not, sir?' said Kit with withering politeness.

'Indeed,' said the Earl through gritted teeth. 'However, my business, sir, is with you. Alone, if you please.'

Hugo, who had risen to bow to the Earl, resumed his seat with calm deliberation. Kit tried not to smile. Hugo could be mighty stubborn when he chose and, in this case, he had clearly decided that Lord Luce's visit required a witness.

'My brother has my full confidence, sir,' Kit said. 'You may discuss any business in front of him. Pray be seated.' He waved the Earl towards a stout chair. 'How may I serve you?'

The Earl did not sit. He looked as if he were about to explode. 'You may serve me, sir, by making an offer of marriage to my goddaughter, Miss Mathilda Blaine! I need not demean her, or myself, by giving you reasons. You know them well enough.'

So that was to be the way of it, Kit thought. In the absence of the father, the godfather came to demand satisfaction. Pity that Luce lacked the necessary dignity to play the role of the wronged parent.

'I fear you are mistaken, sir,' Kit said, very deliberately. 'I have given Miss Blaine no reason—no reason at all—to believe that she might expect an offer from me.'

'You…you lying devil, Stratton! Two private meetings in your Chelsea hide-away. Is that not reason enough? Eh?'

Kit pursed his lips. 'Has Miss Blaine told you, in terms, that she was there?' Seeing Luce's hesitation, Kit continued, 'I take it that she has not.'

'Didn't need to. Her mother taxed her with it. She didn't deny it. How could she? You were seen together, dammit!'

'Might I ask, by whom?'

The Earl began to bluster. 'Don't matter who saw you. Whole of London will know. The gel will be ruined if you don't do right by her. And I intend to see that you do!'

Kit clasped his hands casually behind his back and began to pace slowly up and down in front of the hearth. 'How very unfortunate,' he said at last, shaking his head, 'that we find ourselves unable to agree on that point.'

'What? You—!'

'I have absolutely no obligation to Miss Blaine. Pray convey that message, with my respects, to the Viscountess. My respects to your lady wife, too, of course. Good day to you, sir.'

Kit moved to open the door. Hugo rose politely.

The Earl finally exploded. 'By God, I'll see that you suffer for this! Every door in London with be closed to you. To every last one of you!' He stomped out, muttering.

Calmly, Kit closed the door on the Earl and shrugged his shoulders. 'Nasty,' he said. 'I am sorry you had to be witness to that, Hugo.'

Hugo chewed at his lip for a moment. 'He means mischief, Kit. You must see that. What do you mean to do? I don't believe for a moment that you will allow that clown to blacken your name all over London.'

'Our name, Hugo. His threats were directed at us all, you and Emma included.'

'I will consult Emma, of course, but I do not take kindly to threats.'

'Nor I,' agreed Kit. 'And in this case, a lady's honour is involved.'

'Miss Beaumont's?'

Kit nodded. 'I cannot disprove Luce's allegations without compromising Miss Beaumont. And that I will not do.'

'Do you have a choice?'

'Certainly. I shall do nothing. I have absolutely no desire to be legshackled, Hugo. Even if I had, Miss Blaine is the last woman I should choose. Let Luce do his worst—if he dares. No one in his right mind would believe that I willingly sought an assignation—no, two assignations—with Tilly Blaine. Luce will be laughed to scorn.'

'That's a pretty risky tactic, Kit. And Miss Blaine could be ruined. Have you no thought for her?'

'Miss Blaine has brought it upon herself, Hugo. You heard what Luce said: the girl had a chance to deny the allegations, but she did not. She must *want* to be ruined.'

Hugo shook his head a little sadly. 'Wants to seize the faintest chance of marriage to you, more like.'

'More fool she,' retorted Kit harshly. 'I should make her the devil of a bad husband, Hugo.'

'Now that, I fancy, is the first sensible remark you have made all morning,' said Hugo with a fleeting grin. He made for the door. 'You will send to me at once if you hear from Luce again? Or from your Baroness? Good. Do not forget that Emma is expecting you this afternoon. And she will not accept excuses!'

Kit maintained his nonchalant pose until the door had closed behind Hugo. Then he sank into the chair behind his desk and distractedly ran his fingers through his thick

hair. Hugo had been remarkably restrained, Kit concluded, particularly as the Stratton name was bound to
be sullied by Kit's decision to ride out the coming storm.
What a coil! First, Katharina—and then, this Blaine
woman. She must be mad! No woman could believe—
surely?—that she could blackmail a man into marriage
on the basis of a few mistaken rumours. What kind of
marriage did she think it could be?

She probably did not think about it at all. Most women
were incapable of thinking beyond the altar and their
bride-clothes. Tilly Blaine must have spun herself some
mad fantasy based solely on his handsome face. Truly,
his looks were a curse!

Kit shook his head despairingly. Hugo had said—and
he was right—that inaction was a dangerous course to
follow. Luce would not have the sense to keep his mouth
shut. And there would always be those who would quote
the old adage of 'no smoke without fire'. Even while
they admitted that Kit Stratton had never been known to
trifle with single women, particularly plain ones, they
would wonder. And they would gossip. In the end, Kit
would be forced to offer for Miss Blaine.

He would have to go abroad again.

Would that not be an admission of guilt in the eyes
of Society? And what about Hugo and Emma? His disgrace would also be theirs.

If Kit left England, the scandal would be soon forgotten.

His choices were stark. He could flee. Again. Or he
could betray Marina Beaumont. That he would not do.

Marina hesitated by the steps. She was not sure that
she dared to enter Fitzwilliam House again after yesterday's altercation with Mr Stratton. She had been so

dreadfully embarrassed when Lady Stratton walked in on them. She had covered up her anger as best she could, but Lady Stratton was no fool. She must have been aware that her guests were at outs. It had been a relief to escape from the house.

Marina wondered how Mr Stratton had accounted for their quarrel. Perhaps he had simply pretended that nothing had happened? Perhaps Lady Stratton was too polite to ask?

It was impossible to know. Just as it had been impossible not to respond to today's urgently worded request that Marina call on Lady Stratton as soon as possible. Her ladyship had even sent the Stratton carriage to sit at the Dowager's door, to await Marina's convenience.

She was in no doubt about why she had been invited. The request had come in the name of Lady Stratton, to be sure, but it must have originated with the lady's brother-in-law. Kit Stratton knew—as did his brother—that Lord Luce's allegations about Kit and Miss Blaine were totally without foundation. The Earl had no grounds for demanding that Kit should marry Miss Blaine. But Marina was the only person who could prove it.

Marina took a deep breath and mounted the steps. The door swung open just as she reached for the knocker. She was expected. Replying mechanically to the butler's greeting, she followed him up to Lady Stratton's drawing room without another word. Her brain was too full of questions. What could she say to Lady Stratton, who had been so very kind to her? What about Sir Hugo, who knew the real truth? Lady Luce might be absolutely sure that Kit would not be forced into marriage with Tilly Blaine, but what if she were wrong?

Marina lifted her chin resolutely when she reached the

upper landing. She had been taught to be honest and to have consideration for others. In this situation, however, such simple rules would not suffice, for she could not save one party without harming the other. She was sorry for Tilly Blaine, but the only way to save the girl's reputation would be to sacrifice Kit. And Marina was not prepared to do that. It was not a matter of love. Absolutely not, for love was buried. It was a matter of honour.

'Miss Beaumont, m'lady.'

Lady Stratton hurried forward to take Marina's hand. She looked less composed than usual, but at least she was alone. Marina had been expecting—and dreading— a meeting with one or other of the Stratton men.

'Thank you for coming so promptly, my dear. The Dowager made no difficulty?'

'No, ma'am. She…she is much absorbed in domestic matters at present. And she is promised to a card party this evening. She said that she had no need of me.'

'Good. I would not wish to inconvenience her in any way. Will you not be seated? Do take off your bonnet and be comfortable. I will ring for some tea.'

Marina did as she was bid, wondering what was coming next.

She did not have long to wait. The tea tray was delivered by an impassive butler—followed by Mr Kit Stratton.

'Miss Beaumont,' he said formally, bowing.

Marina's throat was so dry that she could not speak. She managed to incline her head.

'Miss Beaumont, I trust you will forgive me,' said Lady Stratton, colouring a little, 'but I find that I am again required to leave you to consult with my husband. So very tedious, is it not? But I know that I can depend on you to do the honours on my behalf.' She whisked

herself out of the room almost before Marina had time
to draw breath to reply.

She was alone with Kit Stratton. Again! And he was
looking down at her with eyes full of accusation.

'Cream and sugar, Mr Stratton?' asked Marina. Her
voice was a croak.

'Indeed, ma'am. I have not changed my habits since
yesterday.'

He was not about to make this interview an easy one,
but Marina did not feel she had grounds for complaint.
He probably wanted to strangle her for what she had
done. Being a gentleman, he would confine himself to
wounding her with words.

She handed him his cup. She did not smile. Nor did
she speak.

The silence was broken at last when he said, 'I take
it that you are aware, ma'am, that Lord Luce called upon
me today?' He waited for her nod before continuing.
'And you are aware of the details of his errand?'

She nodded again. There was nothing she could say.

'Good. That makes our discussion that much easier.'
He paused, replaced his cup carefully on the tray and
turned in his chair so that he could look directly into her
eyes. 'I need to be sure, Miss Beaumont. You do not
intend to intervene in any way in this matter?'

That sounded very much like an accusation to Marina's ears. Did he really believe that she would remain
silent while he was forced into a loveless marriage? Was
that what he thought of her? How could it be that she
loved a man who believed her to be so base?

She stared back into those blue eyes, refusing to drop
her gaze. She would prove that she was no coward. 'Mr
Stratton,' she said in a low, determined voice, 'I may be
poor, but I am not without honour. It was not possible

for me to reveal the truth to Lord Luce this morning—'
she fancied she saw a momentary gleam in his eye at
that '—but I have every intention of telling him at the
first opportunity. The Dowager—I have no doubt—will
ensure that this scandalous rumour is exposed for the
falsehood that it is.'

His eyes narrowed. That fleeting gleam—if it had ever
been there—was long gone. He now looked absolutely
furious. Marina fought against her natural desire to
shrink from him.

He reached out and clasped her wrist in a grip so tight
it was almost painful. 'Miss Beaumont, you will allow
me to tell you that you are a fool. You would announce
to the world that you had private meetings with the worst
rake in London—twice. Just what do you expect to
achieve? Mmm? Other than your own ruin, of course.'

Marina felt as if his words were blows, battering her
defenceless body.

His merciless attack was not over. His grip tightened
on her flesh. 'Do you think to save Miss Blaine from
disgrace by your admission? You are too late for that,
my girl. She has all but announced to the world that she
is M.B.'

'No! She could not have—'

'I have it from her godfather's own lips, Miss Beaumont. Would you have me call him a liar?'

'No, but—'

'I am glad you spare me that, at least. Now,' he said,
pulling her a little closer, 'you will listen to me. I have
given Lord Luce my answer. The matter is decided. You
will not say a word about your part in it, neither to the
Dowager nor to anyone else. Your story would change
nothing, but it would certainly brand you as yet another
of Kit Stratton's misguided mistresses.'

'But—' She tried to struggle free. He must not be allowed to go through with this.

He reached out his free hand and placed a finger gently across her lips. 'Be quiet, Marina, and listen to me. Do you never do as you are told?'

That single touch changed everything. She could not utter a word. Though his strong hand gripped her frail wrist bones as fiercely as ever, that finger was resting on her mouth with the delicacy of a butterfly. She felt a sudden overwhelming urge to taste his skin.

Something must have shown in her face, for his hold on her wrist relaxed a fraction. His free hand left her mouth to stroke a stray curl away from her cheek, but his finger did not return to her lips. She closed her eyes to hide the longing that filled her at the loss of his touch.

'You will return to Yorkshire quite soon. In a week or so. You will say that you no longer need to be employed as a companion, since your brother is to receive a rich living. That is true enough, though it cannot now be at Stratton Magna. I could not allow— It might give rise to…difficulties if you were living on my estate.'

'*Your* estate! It is *your* living?'

'I shall arrange for it to be exchanged for another,' Kit said coolly.

In that moment, all Marina's longings were overtaken by a desire to strike his haughty face. He was calmly arranging her life—and her family's—without permitting her to say a word. And it was quite obvious that he was determined to allow himself to be blackmailed into marriage with Tilly Blaine. Stupid, arrogant—

'I see,' she said angrily. 'I collect that I am now permitted to speak? How very kind of you, Mr Stratton.' She jumped to her feet, wrenching her wrist from his grasp with a tiny mew of pain. 'Then you will allow me to tell you that I have absolutely no intention of taking orders from you, sir. Tilly Blaine is a fool, and dishonest, to boot, if she thinks to secure a husband by such lies. I shall tell the truth, to anyone who will listen. And if it should ruin my reputation…I have only myself to blame. Everything that happened was my own doing. And I am more than prepared to face the consequences of my actions. What is more—'

She was given no chance to continue. Kit seized her by the shoulders and shook her, hard. Her eyes widened in shock. Then he took her into his arms, and looked deeply into her eyes. 'Marina, you are, without doubt, the most courageous, and the most exasperating woman I have ever met.'

And then he kissed her. It was a kiss of anger, and of ruthless power. She knew it was intended to prove how weak she was, to show her that she could not stand against him.

She knew it. And yet she wanted to yield to him. The touch of his lips renewed the encounters of her dreams, when he had come to her in love and gentleness. Her body yearned for him. In spite of everything.

She was a fool!

'No!' she cried, pushing him away with all her strength as he raised his hand to her hair. 'No! I will not be a pawn in your games, Mr Stratton! Even a plain companion has a conscience, sir, and I intend to obey mine. Good day to you.' She grabbed her bonnet and ran out of the room without giving him the opportunity to say another word.

For perhaps the first time in his life, Kit was completely at a loss. At first, he could think of nothing but the proud set of her head as she fled from him. He had abused her…again. Where Marina Beaumont was concerned, his vaunted powers over women seemed to vanish. He had brutally restrained her, he had shaken her almost until her teeth rattled, and then he had kissed her as if he wanted to punish her. For what? For daring to stand up to him? For offering to sacrifice herself to save him from marriage to the dreadful Miss Blaine?

He must do something…or Marina would be ruined. She was a paragon, a woman in a thousand, and she would be cast down into the mire for trying to defend him.

He must find a way of stopping her.

His flight would not save her. Only her own silence could do that. And she would not remain silent while she believed she could stop him from marrying Tilly Blaine.

He slumped down into his chair and tried to think rationally. It took a long time, but eventually an answer came. It was far from palatable.

Marriage.

Society required him to offer for Tilly Blaine. Once their forthcoming marriage had been made public, nothing—nothing—could prevent it. Marina could surely be brought to realise that her confession would be useless. She was bound to agree to keep silent.

Provided his marriage had already been announced.

He shook his head despairingly. A week ago, he would not have believed it possible. He, Kit Stratton—the rake who had sworn he would never be shackled to any woman—no longer cared whether he was forced into marriage or not.

Kit crossed to Emma's little writing desk in the corner of the room. He would swallow his stiff-necked pride and demand—no, request—an urgent interview with Lord Luce.

And at that interview, he would offer marriage to Miss Tilly Blaine.

Chapter Eighteen

Almost tripping in her haste, Marina hurried down the stairs in response to the Dowager's summons. Lord Luce had called on his mama yet again, probably to gloat about his meeting with Kit Stratton. Now was Marina's chance to convince the Earl that he was wrong about his goddaughter and Kit Stratton. There might still be time to prevent the announcement of the engagement.

The Earl glanced up in annoyance when Marina entered the room but, for once, he said nothing. Perhaps he had realised, at last, that his protests would merely inflame his mother's temper more than ever.

'And so I was right,' said the Dowager with satisfaction, paying no attention at all to Marina's arrival.

'Not precisely, Mama,' said the Earl. 'It is true that young Stratton acted just as you predicted when I called on him yesterday. Refused point blank to recognise his obligations to the gel. Challenged me to do my worst. Dam…dashed impudent, too.'

The Dowager began to look very pleased with herself.

Marina could not believe her ears. He couldn't have! He was going to marry Tilly Blaine. Had he not said so,

just yesterday? Lord Luce must have misunderstood...
somehow.

'After discussing the matter with Lady Blaine, we...I
decided to give the fellow a little time to reflect before
I took any action.'

'Hmph! You mean Lady Blaine told you not to say
anything. She has the sense to see that there is no point
in trumpeting the ruin of her daughter's reputation. She
knows that the rumours will start soon enough by themselves. While you—'

'While I have been proved right, ma'am,' he declared.
'Young Stratton has now written to me requesting the
favour of an interview at my earliest convenience. He is
to call on me this morning. I have no doubt that he will
make an offer for Tilly.' He allowed himself a very superior smile. 'Lady Blaine is delighted, as you may
imagine. When I left her, she was writing to her husband, telling him the good news and how fortunate the
family had been to be able to rely on such an invaluable
intermediary as myself. She told me that no godfather
could have done more. Of course, I always knew I had
diplomatic skills, but—'

'Your only skill is in deluding yourself,' retorted the
Dowager. 'You think that you will be applauded by the
Blaines and all their set for this great *coup* you have
brought off, do you? I tell you it will not happen.'

'Excuse me, ma'am,' began Marina, trying desperately to attract the Dowager's attention. This wicked
charade must be stopped.

'Not now, Marina. I am talking to William.'

'But, ma'am, it is vital that you listen to me. Mr Stratton has been wronged. Miss Blaine was *never* alone
with him.'

There was an astonished silence. Lord Luce stood goggle-eyed.

'I beg your pardon?' exclaimed the Dowager at last, turning to stare at Marina.

'Miss Blaine is not M.B. I am.'

'Impossible—'

'Be silent, William. Marina? Explain.'

'It is quite true, ma'am. It was I who visited Mr Stratton at his house in Chelsea. Twice.'

'I warned you not to keep this…this hussy in your house, Mama. You should have—'

'I asked you to be silent, William. I have no doubt that Marina had good reasons for her actions—'

It was only then that Marina realised she would have to explain what she had done, and why. Her horror must have shown on her face for the Dowager continued quickly, 'We will speak of that later, my child. For the moment, we must concentrate on William's little escapade. So much for your great victory, eh, William? You cannot hope to marry her off now.' Marina was at a loss to understand why Lady Luce sounded so pleased.

'Nonsense,' said the Earl. 'I do not believe what Miss…what this person says, not for one moment. Come, come, Mama. Tilly has admitted that she was with Stratton. Are you suggesting that she lied? A Viscount's daughter? To her own mother?'

'Tell me, William,' said Lady Luce softly, 'what *exactly* did your precious Tilly say?'

The Earl looked a little self-conscious. Then he said, 'I was not present, of course. Lady Blaine said she taxed Tilly with being M.B. and…and Tilly would not deny it. So it must be true.'

'Balderdash! Tilly Blaine has the brains of a flea as well as the face of a horse. I'd wager a king's ransom she said nothing at all. Probably just stood there, looking guilty, with her mouth hanging open at the very idea of having been alone with Kit Stratton. Well?'

The Earl began to pace. His mother sent a conspiratorial glance towards Marina.

His pacing stopped abruptly. 'It is of no moment whether Tilly was with him or not. What matters is that he is prepared to offer for her. His letter leaves me in no doubt about that.' He patted his pocket. 'We'll never get a better offer for Tilly. She's well enough dowered, but for the rest... Can't pass up a chance like this. Her father will be delighted that I've caught her such a rich husband.'

If Marina had not heard his words, she would not have believed that any gentleman could be so wicked.

The Dowager did not attempt to mask her outrage. 'You are a blackguard, William. Your only interest is in being able to boast about your famous victory over Kit Stratton. I tell you I will not permit it. Kit Stratton may be a rake, but he is worth ten of you.'

'But you hate Kit Stratton, Mama!'

The Earl had voiced Marina's exact thoughts. Why should the Dowager take Kit Stratton's part against her own son? No matter how much she despised him, he was still her own flesh and blood.

'Not nearly as much as I hate you. And the family of the man who sired you.'

'What? But my father provided for you...this house, the—'

'Your father disowned you and rejected me. Did you never notice how little you resembled the family portraits?' She shook her head. 'No. I suppose you did not. A strong intellect has never been much in evidence among the Blaines.'

The Earl's jaw had dropped open. Deflated, he sank into a chair.

'I will not allow that accursed family to triumph over me again—even if I have to side with Kit Stratton to do it. I warn you, William. If you persist in trying to force this match, I will announce to the world that your father was the late Viscount Blaine.'

'You…you will only bring scandal on yourself,' he protested weakly.

'What of it? I am an old woman now. Everyone who mattered—my husband, our son—is dead long ago. Why should I care a rap what they say of me now?'

'I am still your son, too, Mama,' he replied, with surprising dignity, 'and my children are your grandchildren. You will ruin their lives for your petty revenge.'

'Petty, is it? Your father—your real father—seduced me and then threw me into the gutter. My family was about to disown me. I could have died if it had not been for Lord Luce. He married me and saved my reputation. And when our own darling son was killed in India, and my husband soon after, Lord Blaine—your *father*—came to gloat over my distress. Said your brother was a weakling, of weakling stock. Said I should be glad that a real man had sired *you*.' She glared at him. 'You are no son of mine. Look at you, with your tyrant's ways and your broods of children. You're a Blaine, all right.'

'No, Mama. Under the law, I am the rightful Earl Luce.'

She almost groaned. 'The title should have gone to Roland. He was the only true Luce.'

'My brother is dead, Mama. No amount of revenge will bring him back to you.'

'No, but the Blaines shall suffer as I have suffered. I mean what I say, William. If you force Kit Stratton to marry that Blaine chit—*your niece*, I should say—I'll denounce you at the altar if I have to.'

He rose from his seat and shook his head at her. 'Think carefully before you do anything so rash, Mama. Remember that you are known to be…unconventional. They will take it as the ravings of a lunatic.'

'Balderdash!'

'And nothing you might say will influence Lady Blaine, in any case. What will she care if you had an affair with her father-in-law? He is long dead. Whereas her daughter—and the prospect of imminent disgrace—is very much alive. No, Mama, your pitiful little blackmail will not serve.' He bowed abruptly. 'Good day to you, ma'am,' he said, and marched out.

Marina could not believe what she had just heard. It explained much, but it was like…like the plot of a Gothic novel. Such things did not happen in real life, did they?

The Dowager looked at Marina with defeat in her eyes. 'Shocked, child?' she said quite gently. It sounded nothing like her normal, robust delivery. 'I dare say your grandmama could have told you much about her family and their wicked deeds. The Blaine men have always been wild with women. Not their own women, you understand. Blaine women, both wives and daughters, must be totally beyond reproach in that regard. Dare say that's why your grandmother was cast out. She challenged her father. And her brother. They would never tolerate that. Never.'

'Is that…forgive me, ma'am, but is that why you let me stay? Because of what the Blaines did to my family?'

Lady Luce gave a wan smile. 'The Blaines have done enough harm already, to your family and to mine. Couldn't let William revert to his father's ways. He's already a bully. And he longs to be a tyrant. He'd be a womaniser, too, if he had the money or the looks.'

'He is *your* son too, ma'am,' ventured Marina, expecting one of the Dowager's bruising snubs for her pains.

'Perhaps, but I can't say I've ever seen any of myself in him. Always backs away from a fight.'

'He did not do so this time, ma'am. He seemed… determined to give you your own again.'

She snorted. 'Only because he thinks he is on safe ground.' She paused. 'This time, I fear he may be. The Blaines could win. Again.' Her thin hands were curled into fists.

'Ma'am…I think I should leave London.'

'Why? I need you here.'

'But Lord Luce is bound to tell Lady Blaine about… about what I have done. She…she despises my family. She will find a way to brand me as Kit Stratton's mistress, I am sure of it…though I promise you that I am not. You would not want a companion with such a reputation, ma'am. I should go now, before the rumours start.' And before Kit's betrothal is announced, she added silently to herself. If she was taxed about her dealings with Kit, she would be unable to conceal her feelings for very long.

'Certainly not. You will stay here. Lady Blaine cannot slander you without giving up all hopes of forcing young Stratton into marriage with her daughter.'

Marina knew that the Dowager was wrong. Lady Blaine did not have to say that Marina was M.B. She had only to say that Marina had allowed herself to be seduced by Kit Stratton. The tabbies would be only too happy to spread the scandalous rumour, especially when it came from such an impeccable source.

'Besides,' continued the Dowager, 'I think my threat may give her pause. William is much too sure of himself. The Blaines would not wish it known that the late Viscount was given to seducing innocent young ladies…and then abandoning them. Mark my words, Marina, I shall not allow them another victory.' She drummed her fingers on the arm of her chair. 'They are all promised for my party this evening. I think that a short private interview will be in order.' She smiled, in very much her old way.

'And now,' she continued blandly, 'perhaps you ought to tell me about the real M.B. and her dealings with that handsome young rake?'

Marina gazed at herself in the glass. She was still thoroughly agitated. If it had not been for Gibson's help, she would have been unable even to fasten her gown. And as for her hair…

She looked dreadfully pale, almost ghastly, in spite of the glowing pink of her new evening gown. She viewed herself with something approaching horror. She was about to be exposed as a harlot. And she would have to watch, from the sidelines, while the man she loved was forcibly betrothed to the daughter of a wicked, scheming family. There was nothing she could do to prevent any of it.

She made her way along the hallway and down the stairs, reminding herself to keep her head high and her back straight. The Dowager had summoned her to join her makeshift conference in the bookroom on the ground floor. Marina hated that place. It was the room in which the Earl had interviewed her on the day she arrived— and again on the day he had sought to dismiss her. It all seemed so very long ago. For it was before she had learned to love Kit Stratton.

She tried not to think about him, but it was useless. She had only to hear his name for her heart to start pounding and her skin to tingle in anticipation of his touch. It was unlikely she would ever see him again— in spite of everything the Dowager had said, she was sure to be banished to Yorkshire very soon—but she found herself longing for one more glimpse, one more touch of those strong fingers…

Foolish, foolish girl, even to think of such a thing! She had tried to save him. And she had surely failed. This interview would prove it.

Tibbs was standing guard by the bookroom door. He nodded at Marina and opened it.

'Miss Beaumont is here,' declared the Dowager. 'Good. We may begin.'

'I do not see why I should have to tolerate the presence of a woman like that,' snapped Lady Blaine, looking to Lord Luce for support. 'If you will excuse me, ma'am—'

'I will not. I would remind you, ma'am, that you are a guest in my house. I decide who shall go and who shall stay.'

Marina tried to hide her clenched fists in her skirts. Terrible though it was, this interview would have to end soon. The Dowager's guests were arriving. If only there were something she could do…

'I take it, ma'am,' continued the Dowager firmly, 'that Luce has told you the gist of our discussion this afternoon?'

Lady Blaine looked down her nose at the old lady. Eventually, she gave a tiny nod.

'Let us have the truth with no bark on it. You and

your family are proposing to use falsehoods to catch a rich husband for your daughter. You do not need me to tell you how dishonourable that is. Your daughter is no better than a slut!'

Lady Blaine was shocked into a protest. 'How dare you say such a thing? My daughter is innocent of any wrongdoing. She—'

'Your daughter allowed the whole world to see her behaving like a mooncalf over Kit Stratton. I don't call that innocent!'

'Of course it was!' retorted the Viscountess, who was now becoming extremely angry. 'With those remarkable looks, he seemed like a hero to Tilly, the sort of man who belonged in the settings of her favourite poems. She was daydreaming, nothing more!'

'Perhaps you should take her off to see some of the exotic locations she is so fond of,' said the Dowager quickly, 'instead of forcing her into marriage.'

'Her husband can show them to her,' said Lady Blaine flatly. 'After they are married.'

The Dowager nodded to herself. 'You are determined, then, ma'am? Very well. So am I. If you go ahead with this, I shall announce to the world that your dear friend, William, is the illegitimate son of the late Viscount. He is, in fact, your husband's older brother.'

'Half-brother,' corrected Lady Blaine.

The Dowager waited for her to continue, but she did not. 'Have you nothing more to say?'

Lady Blaine glanced at the Earl and then drawled, 'The whole world knew that my father-in-law sired children on the wrong side of the blanket. If you wish to add yourself to the list of his mistresses, ma'am, please do so. It will not affect my family—or our decisions— in the least. And now, if you please, I should like to join

your other guests. I came here on the promise of Faro
and I have every intention of playing.' She bowed her
turbanned head a fraction and then swept across the
room and out of the door.

The Earl made to follow.

'A moment, William.' When he turned back, the
Dowager said, 'I take it that Kit Stratton has made an
offer for Miss Blaine?'

'Yes. This afternoon.'

'And it has been accepted?'

'Yes. Nothing can be announced until the Viscount
returns, naturally, but we expect him very soon now.
Lady Blaine received a letter from him this very afternoon.'

'How very fortunate for her,' said the Dowager acidly.

Her son did not attempt to reply. He bowed politely
to his mama, looked with loathing on Marina, and strode
out of the room.

'Ma'am,' began Marina, putting a hand gently on the
Dowager's arm.

Lady Luce turned a strained face to Marina. This time,
she appeared to be completely defeated.

'Ma'am, I have had an idea. The other day, you
said...you implied that Lady Blaine cheats at Faro. Are
you sure of it?'

The old eyes gleamed. 'Absolutely sure,' she said
firmly.

'We may yet outwit them...if...if you are sure that is
what you want to do?'

The Dowager nodded immediately. 'Absolutely sure,'
she said again.

'Then...then I must ask you to trust me, ma'am, and
to follow my lead, however strange my actions may
seem. I do not know precisely what I shall have to do—

I must gauge the lie of the land first—but I shall certainly need your help. I can explain that later. Upstairs.'

The Dowager had started to move towards the door. Her guests would be wondering why she had not yet appeared. 'My help?'

'Lady Blaine is going to play Faro. And—with your help, ma'am—so am I!'

'Good evening, ma'am.'

'Mr Stratton!' Marina stopped in her tracks. What on earth was he doing here in Lady Luce's house?

He reached for her hand but she whipped it behind her back. She dare not let him touch her now. She dare not even think about him. She must focus only on what she was about to do.

He looked quizzically at her. 'I don't bite, Miss Beaumont. You are quite safe, you know. And I *was* invited.'

She nodded, wide-eyed. 'I beg your pardon, sir,' she said in a strained voice, and then stopped. She could think of nothing more to say.

'My brother and his wife are here, too. It seems that the Dowager has decided to offer the Strattons a truce. I wonder why?'

Marina was in no doubt that he understood perfectly. It was simply that he enjoyed baiting people, especially Marina herself. She tried to frown him down. 'Excuse me, if you will, sir. I am needed in the Faro room.' She turned to go.

'How very interesting,' he drawled, taking her arm and slipping it through his own. 'I was just on my way there. We can go together.'

'No! I—'

He put his free hand firmly on top of her fingers. She

could not escape from his grasp. 'Marina,' he said softly, 'you are exasperating...and you are beautiful—'

She gasped. That was a downright lie.

'And, on this occasion, you will do as I say. Come.'

He started towards the card room, forcing her to follow. What else could she do? The warmth from his body seemed to be spreading out from the spot where his fingers clasped hers. She could feel it coursing through her veins like fiery spirit, burning a track towards her heart. The Dowager's brandy had been nothing like this. From this, she did not think that she could ever recover.

He had said she was beautiful.

Kit knew perfectly well that he should not have done it. He was telling himself so, even as he pressed her hand.

It might be his last opportunity to touch her soft skin.

Soon she would be gone from his life. Settled and comfortable—he would see to that—but gone. He would not be able to keep up the necessary pretence if he continued to see Marina Beaumont.

He loved her—more than he had ever thought possible.

Hugo had been right, as he always seemed to be. Kit, the rake, the man who cared for no member of the female sex, had fallen in love with the bravest, the most infuriating, the most wonderful woman in the world. But he could not marry her. If only it could have been otherwise. If only Marina were—

There was no point in brooding over such a mad fantasy. He could never have married Marina. Not while a belted earl was publicly accusing him of seducing his goddaughter. A marriage between Kit and Marina would have made her an outcast. She would have been labelled a harlot—or worse. A man might learn to cope with exile and public humiliation. A gently reared lady never would.

And so he was betrothed to Tilly Blaine—an empty-headed chit who lived in a world of poetry and make-believe. He had never given the girl a moment's thought. Not even once. But now—or as soon as her father came home—he would be required to dance attendance on her, to squire her to parties, to play the part of the happy bridegroom-to-be. It would take every ounce of his self-control to play the part, but he would do it.

He would do it, provided Marina Beaumont was gone from his life.

He looked down at her. She was avoiding his eyes, but he could see the slight flush on her neck and feel the tremble in her fingers. She knew! She must know!

'Why, good evening, Kit.'

At the sound of that sultry voice, Kit felt an almost irresistible urge to utter the foulest curses known to man. He gritted his teeth. His muscles tensed, ready for the conflict to come.

'And it is Miss…the Dowager's grey companion, is it not? Will you forgive us for a moment?' The Baroness put her hand possessively on Kit's arm. He wanted to shake it off, to berate her for her rudeness to Marina, but it was too late. Marina had pulled away from him and disappeared without a word. Out of the corner of his eye, he saw that she had found the Dowager and that they were whispering together.

'Is she the best you can do, Kit? Really, I should have thought—'

'What do you want, Katharina? I came here to play cards, not to pull caps with you.'

'Why—' She broke off, looking suddenly concerned.

'I cannot talk now,' she whispered, nodding towards the stairs where her husband had just appeared. 'Later. I will think of something.' She whirled away.

Kit turned to watch the Baron's ramrod-straight figure ascend the stairs. He was in his prime, in spite of his prematurely greying hair. The gold-braided dress uniform sat well on his spare frame. He strolled past Kit without so much as a glance. Kit, conscious of the humour of the situation, bowed briefly from the neck. He had always believed that cuckolded husbands deserved some slight acknowledgement, even if only on the duelling field.

Having made sure that neither the Baroness nor her husband was before him, Kit strolled into the Faro room. He might as well play. He had lost the only thing that would ever matter to him. Perhaps if he lost his wealth tonight, the Blaines would be less eager to have him as a son-in-law.

He settled down to play with reckless abandon.

Chapter Nineteen

Kit had been playing for over an hour, and losing heavily. He had not cared a jot—in fact, he had been rather pleased—until Lady Blaine had taken over the bank. Against her, he felt a need to win.

The Dowager, on Kit's immediate right, had been remarkably polite to him, almost as if there had never been a feud between them. She was an unpredictable old woman, but she played a fine hand of cards. He would have sworn she could track the cards as well as he could himself.

The place on Kit's left hand had been vacant for a while. He had found himself wishing that Marina would take it, but he knew she would never do that. It would seem much too forward. She was sitting at the far end of the table, occasionally placing a small wager with a shaky hand. He supposed that the Dowager must have provided her with the stakes. Soon they would be gone. She was losing too often.

The bank's first deal was over. Lady Blaine had won very heavily throughout. Too heavily? Had Kit missed something? He had heard rumours…

Lady Blaine smiled nastily at the Dowager, sitting immediately opposite her. 'The luck would appear to be with the bank tonight, ma'am,' she said, pulling the heap of winnings towards her. 'Shall you attempt to recover your losses?'

To Kit's enormous surprise, the Dowager pushed back her chair and rose. 'No point in chasing your luck when it don't intend to be caught,' she said sharply. 'Don't worry, ma'am. I shan't leave you without an opponent. Marina! Come and take my place. Your luck cannot possibly be worse than mine.'

Marina rose obediently from her seat and came round the table. She appeared hesitant and concerned. 'Ma'am, I—'

The Dowager put her hand on Marina's shoulder and forced her to sit. 'Play,' she said shortly. Then she fixed her gaze on Lady Blaine and issued a clear challenge. 'Miss Beaumont takes my place and plays with my stakes. You will accept that, I take it, ma'am?'

Lady Blaine went rather red, but she nodded. She could not do otherwise in the Dowager's house. Kit found he was rather enjoying the old woman's mischief-making. Perhaps she was not such a harridan after all.

Marina did not look at him or acknowledge his presence in any way. Kit was not really surprised, but the devil in him decided that she should not be permitted to ignore him. He would make her do or say something, even if it was only to tell him to mind his business. It would be good to see the fire in her eyes again.

Lady Blaine had broken a fresh pack and was shuffling it rather absently; all her attention seemed to be focused on the other players at the table. No doubt she was hoping that more would come to fill the empty places. The greater the number of players, the greater her winnings be.

Kit looked sideways at Marina. Her hands were lying loosely on the green baize. She was staring down at them, apparently lost in thought. 'Have you played Faro often, Miss Beaumont?' he asked quietly. Once the play began again, it would be much more difficult to converse with her. He must make the most of this one chance. She might not be beside him for more than one game.

She did not look at him. For a moment, it seemed that she had not heard him or, at least, that she was not going to reply. Had he really offended her so grievously?

Finally, she spoke. 'I have rarely been in the kind of company that could afford to, sir,' she said in a low voice.

From the far side of the table, Lady Blaine was straining to overhear their conversation. 'I take it that you are experienced enough to shuffle the cards, Miss Beaumont?' she sneered.

At that, Marina looked up at last. A little uncertainly, she stretched out a hand to take the pack. 'I can try, ma'am, if you permit.'

Rather than put the pack into Marina's waiting hand, Lady Blaine put it down on the table. Then she smiled knowingly at one of the gentlemen.

Ignoring the snub, Marina simply picked up the pack and began to shuffle the cards. It was obvious that she was no card player. At one point, she almost dropped the pack.

'Perhaps you would cut, Mr Stratton, once Miss Beaumont has finished?' asked Lady Blaine condescendingly.

Kit nodded. He could not trust himself to speak civilly to the woman.

'May we join you?' said Hugo's voice from the back of the room.

Kit turned and rose from his chair to greet Emma. She

was looking decidedly pleased with herself. Was that a result of yesterday's successful scheming? He was almost sure that Emma had deliberately left him alone with Marina on the previous afternoon, though he had been unable to fathom just what she was trying to achieve. Women!

'Would you like to sit here, Emma?' He indicated the vacant place on his left.

'No, thank you. I prefer to sit at the end, next to Hugo. He counts the cards better than I do. You would never tell me how to bet, Kit. You enjoy watching me lose.' From any other woman, it would have sounded like an insult, but not from Emma. There was always that enchanting glint of humour in her eyes.

'As you say, ma'am.' Smiling, Kit made Emma an extravagant leg, before resuming his seat. Miss Beaumont did not seem to have moved an inch. She was still struggling to finish shuffling the pack.

He waited patiently, watching her hands. He would never have believed that she would be quite so clumsy. It did not sit with the elegance of all her other movements, but—

'If you have finished, Miss Beaumont?' Lady Blaine sounded decidedly testy.

Marina coloured a little and abruptly stopped shuffling.

'May I, Miss Beaumont?' Kit held out his hand for the cards.

Without raising her eyes, she placed the pack on his palm. She did not touch him by even a fraction.

'Thank you, ma'am,' he said softly. He cut the cards swiftly and pushed the pack back across the table to Lady Blaine.

'At last,' she said. 'I was beginning to think we would

never be able to play.' She looked round at the players. There were now seven of them. 'Stakes, ladies and gentlemen, if you please.'

Mechanically, Kit placed his bet. Marina did not move at all. 'Do you not wish to play, ma'am?' he asked quietly, hoping the noise at the table would prevent the banker from hearing his words.

She shook her head slightly. 'In a moment, sir,' she said. Her hand was toying with the little pile of cash that the Dowager had left behind. Then she pushed a banknote on to the three.

The game was unusually noisy. When Emma won, she exclaimed about her good fortune. When she lost, she groaned aloud. The second lady player followed suit. Marina, however, did not. She watched the banker win her stake from the three and simply replaced it, without a word. She lost again, and replaced it again. Why was she playing that single number, over and over?

Kit was waiting to see what she would do if she lost a third time, when he felt a touch on his left side. Katharina! Automatically, he started to rise, but she stopped him with a hand on his arm.

'Please do not let me disturb your game, sir,' she said in that husky drawl that he had once found so attractive. She slid into the seat and began to fiddle with the reticule on her wrist.

He tried to ignore her. She was probably trying to find her money so that she could join the game. If she had a little more consideration for her fellow-players, she would have done that before sitting down.

Another three was turned up. But this time, it was the *carte anglaise*. Marina had won. Kit felt absurdly pleased for her. He bent towards her, with a whispered word of encouragement.

From the other side, he felt a hand slip something into his pocket.

No one else was paying any attention at all to Katharina. They were too engrossed in the game. Soon, it would be over.

Marina allowed her winnings to ride on the three. So she was not a total novice, then. She knew enough about Faro to understand that she could win seven times her stake. Pity she did not also know that the odds were so much in favour of the banker.

Lady Blaine looked round once more, waiting for stakes to be placed. Then she turned over her next card with a snap.

'Lurched again,' said Hugo, with a laugh. 'I should never have listened to your advice, my love.'

Lady Blaine faced the *carte anglaise*. Nobody won.

'You never do,' Emma retorted, 'except when you are looking for someone to blame. It was not I who suggested you should put your money on the five.'

'Well, there will be no more now,' he said. 'I think that they have all been played out.'

'Are you sure?' said Emma, her hand still hovering over the livret.

'Almost,' Hugo replied with a twisted grin.

'When you are ready, ladies and gentlemen,' said Lady Blaine testily. She sounded like a bad-tempered schoolmistress.

Emma hesitated for a second more, then dropped her stake on to the six.

On Kit's left, Katharina rose. All the gentlemen at the table stood up politely. Lady Blaine looked furious that her deal was being interrupted.

Katharina's smile encompassed all the men, but ignored the ladies. 'I do not think I am in the mood for Faro, after all,' she said with a pout. 'Excuse me.'

Kit patted his pocket surreptitiously as he resumed his seat. No, he had not been mistaken. She had definitely slipped a note to him. Clever. If her husband asked, all those present would say that Katharina had barely spoken to Kit. She was being very careful indeed. Could it be that the Baron really was threatening her? She had always said that he had a fiery temper.

Lady Blaine had just dealt the final *carte anglaise*. Again, none of the players won.

There remained only one card to be played. It must be a three. And it would win for the banker. Kit felt a little sorry for Marina. She had not staked much on her threes, but she would have lost three times and won only once.

Lady Blaine faced the last card. It was a five! Kit could not believe his eyes. He was certain he had not miscounted, even though he had been distracted a little by the Baroness. The last card should definitely have been a three.

'I knew I should not have relied on you to count the cards for me, Hugo,' protested Emma somewhat archly, giving her husband a playful rap with her fan. 'You said all the fives had been played, you wretch.'

'I was sure that they had,' Hugo replied slowly. 'I must have made a mistake. However, it is of no moment. If you had bet on the five again, you would have lost on the banker's last card.'

'True,' agreed Emma.

Lady Blaine began to gather up the used cards and her large pile of winnings. As banker, she had done very well indeed.

Marina raised her head and looked straight across at

the Viscountess. At the same moment, the Dowager appeared in the doorway. All the gentlemen rose politely.

'I thought…' Marina stopped and frowned. She looked puzzled. 'Beg pardon, ma'am, but should there not have been another three?'

Lady Blaine gaped.

All the players round the table stopped dead and stared.

Lady Luce strode forward and stood behind Marina's chair, with her hand on the companion's shoulder to prevent her from rising. 'What was that you said, child?'

Marina turned her head to look over her shoulder at the Dowager. 'I…I…must have been mistaken. It could not have been… It seemed to me that there were only three threes played, but—'

'Of course you were mistaken, Marina. Not surprising, I should say, considering how little you know about cards. However—' she paused and directed a narrow-eyed stare at the Viscountess '—there have been too many instances of cheating at Faro recently, especially at private parties. Some hostesses, I know, will no longer permit it to be played in their houses. I will not allow any suspicion of impropriety to hang over mine.' She stretched out her hand imperiously. 'The cards, if you please, ma'am.'

Lady Blaine still sat immobile.

'If you please, ma'am,' said the Dowager again, louder still. 'You would not wish to be classed as one of those bankers who cheats to win, would you?' she added pointedly.

Kit leaned on his chair and stared at the floor so that no one would see his face. He had thought that Marina was clever, but this…this was brilliant. Unfortunately, it was also very dangerous indeed. In fact, it was madness.

Lady Blaine had no choice. She handed over the pack. Her face was ashen and her fingers were not quite steady.

'Thank you,' said the Dowager curtly. She marched to the end of the table and began to lay out the cards. The players crowded round to watch. No one spoke.

The cards spoke for themselves. A three and a seven were missing. There were two extra cards—a five and a ten.

Lady Blaine began to bluster. 'The pack must have been wrongly made up. I did not—'

The Dowager picked up the fives and tens and compared them with the rest of the deck. 'I fear not,' she said grimly, picking out two cards. 'These cards did not come from a new pack. They are slightly worn. And I fancy—' she held one of them towards the candelabrum '—I fancy there are pinholes in this one.'

Everyone gasped. Everyone except Kit. And Marina.

She was hanging back, trying not to be noticed. And she was refusing to meet his eyes.

The Dowager appeared to be outraged. 'I cannot believe that you dared to do such a thing as a guest in my house,' she said angrily to the speechless Viscountess. 'I will thank you to leave immediately. You will understand if I do not recognise you, or any of your family again. I may say that I do not expect that any other respectable members of Society will do so either.'

Lady Blaine rose to her feet, though she needed to lean on the back of the chair to do so. Her guilt was written on her face. None the less, she protested, 'It must have been a mistake. No other explanation is possible. You may choose to believe the worst, ma'am, but my true friends will not.' She made for the door, straightening her back as she went. She had not once looked at the pile of money lying on the table.

The Dowager looked round at her remaining guests. 'I cannot tell you how sorry I am,' she said.

Her tone was an odd mixture of regret and ill-concealed triumph, Kit decided, wonderingly. Was it possible…? Had she known all along? But how could she have made sure—?

It had to have been Marina. A three had been removed. And Marina had played only threes.

Either Marina had deliberately set out to expose Lady Blaine's cheating or…or she herself had fuzzed the cards in order to entrap the woman. In either case, it was breathlessly daring.

And his Marina was nothing if not bold.

Lady Luce shook her head sadly. 'I had heard the rumours, of course. I knew she had been winning often—perhaps too often—when she held the bank, but I never dreamed…' She sighed. 'However, so it is.' She moved round the table to the banker's place. 'What am I to do with all this?' she said, indicating the pile of money. 'Perhaps you would like it to be returned to you?'

'Certainly not,' said Hugo firmly. 'We lost it. We might well have lost it anyway. Perhaps you have a favourite charity, ma'am? A foundling hospital, or some such?'

'I have a better idea,' Kit put in, deliberately concealing his mounting fury under a veneer of mild amusement. 'Why not give it to the anti-slavery campaigners? After all, Lady Blaine's husband is due back from his plantations any day now. I am sure he would appreciate the gesture.'

That made Marina raise her eyes to his, at last. She was looking daggers at him.

'Splendid!' said the Dowager with a crack of harsh laughter. 'We shall see what the scandal sheets make of that!'

Kit did not miss the momentary glance of triumph that Lady Luce directed at Marina. His worst suspicions were confirmed. And now his anger threatened to overwhelm him.

The Viscountess Blaine was most definitely a cheat. But Marina Beaumont had risked everything in order to ensure that the woman was publicly exposed.

'My dear, you excelled yourself,' whispered the Dowager as soon as they were out of earshot of the others.

Marina shook her head. She had replaced the three, to be sure, but not the seven. Nor had she inserted the marked card. Lady Blaine had added that after the pack had been shuffled. Marina was at a loss to understand why the woman had taken such a stupid risk—she could fuzz the cards with such extraordinary skill that the players had no chance of winning, except when she permitted it. Without those missing cards, she would never have been exposed. But one would have been enough. Marina need not have cheated at all...

'You must have a remarkable way with the cards, child. Nobody suspected anything. That woman will never be able to lift her head again.'

'Kit Stratton knows.'

The Dowager's smile vanished. 'How can he know? He said nothing when you were shuffling the cards, did he?'

'No, ma'am. But he knows. I saw it in his eyes.' She would never forget that look, a mixture of shock and disgust. He knew she was a cheat. How could she ever face him again?

'That's as may be,' said the Dowager gruffly, 'but he will do nothing, even if he does suspect you. Why should he? Lady Blaine's guilt was obvious to everyone. And her disgrace will remove his obligation to marry their wretched daughter. Kit may be a rake, but he's a gentleman. No gentleman could be expected to maintain an offer for the child of a proven cheat. He should be calling down a blessing on your head!'

'But what of Miss Blaine? She is the innocent party in this. She will be ruined by his public rejection of her.'

'No, my dear, she will not,' said the Dowager, patting Marina's arm soothingly, 'for the betrothal was never announced. What is more, you are forgetting that Tilly Blaine lied in order to ensnare Kit Stratton. She knows she was never alone with him. She told her mother that she was.'

'But she—'

'No, Marina. Do not try to defend her. Even if her first reaction was misinterpreted—and I take leave to doubt that, myself—she has had two full days to tell the truth. She has not done so. She is a true Blaine.'

Marina did not try to argue. The Dowager was right. Lady Blaine and Lord Luce had conspired together to entrap Kit Stratton, and Tilly had done nothing to stop them. Her motives did not matter. The deed was wicked, worse by far than anything Marina had now done. Tilly was fortunate that the betrothal had not been made public. Her disgrace would stem only from her mother's.

'I think I should like to retire now, ma'am, if you would permit it.'

'Certainly not! What are you thinking of? You must

stay and you must be seen to enjoy the party. Play a hand or two of cards.'

'I could not,' breathed Marina, horrified.

'Of course you could. Not Faro, I agree—I shall permit no more Faro tonight—but a rubber of piquet, perhaps.' She looked hard at Marina. 'Just make sure you do not appear too expert,' she added in an undertone.

That should not be difficult, Marina thought, for her brain was in such turmoil that she would probably forget everything she had ever known about card playing.

'Come, let me find you an opponent,' said her ladyship, leading Marina towards Sir Hugo and Lady Stratton. 'I am trying to persuade this gel of mine not to dwell too much on that unfortunate incident with Lady Blaine. Can't seem to get it out of her head. What she needs is something to occupy her mind, like a rubber of piquet. Do you play, Sir Hugo?' The Dowager was being extremely direct.

'I do,' began Sir Hugo a little uncertainly.

'He does, ma'am,' interrupted Lady Stratton, 'but he has promised to take me down to supper. However, I am sure that Kit will be happy to oblige you.' She turned and beckoned.

No! Please, no! Marina wanted to run, but her legs were made of lead.

Kit bowed with his usual elegance. When Lady Stratton explained the Dowager's request, his expression remained totally impassive. Then he turned to Marina. 'I should be delighted to give you a game, ma'am,' he said, offering her his arm.

The Dowager beamed.

Inwardly, Marina cringed. This could not be happening.

But it was.

In a matter of moments, they were seated at a small table and Kit was breaking a new piquet pack.

'You will understand, ma'am, I am sure,' he said silkily, 'if I choose to take charge of shuffling this pack myself.'

They had been playing, in total silence, for nearly half an hour. Marina had lost almost every hand. Her discards had been weak and her card play even weaker. It was pitiful to watch.

But Kit was still furious with her. He feared that if she spoke a word to him, he would lose his temper. It was barely under control, as it was. More than anything, he wanted to take her in his arms and shake the life out of her. Set a cheat to catch a cheat. What on earth had possessed her to do something so foolhardy?

He gritted his teeth and led another card. She failed to follow suit. It was the last straw. 'If you wish to play piquet,' he snarled, 'you should learn the rules. You are required to play a club, if you hold one. And I am perfectly well aware that you do.'

Her hand trembled. She looked up at him with those huge eyes. They were full of guilt.

His anger vanished instantly.

'Marina,' he said softly, 'I should like to beat you. How could you do such a thing? You—'

She threw down the remainder of her cards. 'What I do, sir, is my concern alone. And since I am such an unworthy opponent for you, I will not trouble you further. How much do I owe?'

Her guilt had been replaced by indignation. She obviously thought he deplored what she had done. He did, of course, but only because of the risks she had been taking. He wanted to protect her, but every time he tried to get near her, she bristled like a porcupine.

'You owe me nothing,' he replied. Then, almost as an afterthought, he said, 'We failed to agree any stakes at the outset. However, since you have conceded defeat, I ought, I suppose, to exact a forfeit of some kind. Will you allow me to take you driving tomorrow?'

'No.' The word was quietly spoken, but it was final.

'Why not?'

She almost squirmed in her chair. She was clearly surprised by his question. Did she think he would take a dismissal so easily?

She clasped her hands on the table and fixed her gaze on them. 'You forget my position, sir. I am a companion, a servant. I know my place—and it is not in a gentleman's carriage.' She rose from her chair and walked calmly out of the room. Even in defeat, she still held herself like a duchess.

No, Kit thought, your place is not in my carriage. It is in my bed. And that is where you are going to be, my sweet Marina, even if I have to abduct you into it.

Chapter Twenty

'I thought I heard a carriage half an hour ago. Who was it?'

'It was Lady Stratton's carriage, ma'am,' said Marina, avoiding the Dowager's eye.

'Would she not step inside?'

'She…she was not *in* the carriage, ma'am.'

The Dowager said nothing. She simply stared at Marina and waited.

'She… I… She sent a message, inviting me to call on her at Fitzwilliam House. I declined.'

'What? Why on earth—?'

'Ma'am, I cannot become intimate with Lady Stratton. She is a great lady—as you are—and I am a nobody.'

'I should have thought,' retorted the Dowager, 'that, after last night's escapade, Lady Stratton would be extremely grateful to you.'

'But she does not know—'

'And you are certainly not a nobody. You are a Blaine.' She stopped short and gave vent to something that was almost a giggle. 'Then again, perhaps not,' she added ruefully. 'It might be unwise to make too much of your links to *that* family. The rumour mills are al-

ready working. Lady Blaine may have spoken of her
"true friends" but they seem to be deserting her in
droves.' She chortled. 'And I understand that another
edition of that nasty little scandal sheet is in preparation.'

'But how can that be? There has not been time—'

'There is always time, Marina, if one makes it one's
business to use it.'

It was worse and worse. The whole episode would
soon be all over London. And it seemed that the Dowager was conspiring to make that happen. Marina really
must escape from it all. She could not bear it any longer.
Kit had been saved, but at the cost of Marina's peace of
mind. She yearned for him, but she knew she must never
set eyes on him again. He would now remain in London—its foremost rake—and so she must leave.

The butler entered. 'Lady Stratton is below in her carriage, m'lady. She presents her compliments, and asks
if Miss Beaumont may be permitted to accompany her
on her drive this afternoon.'

'No,' breathed Marina.

'Of course,' declared Lady Luce roundly. 'Fetch your
bonnet and pelisse, Marina. And be quick about it. Her
ladyship will not wish to keep her horses standing.'

'You look pale, my dear. Are you quite well?'

'A…a little tired, ma'am, that is all,' Marina lied. 'Her
ladyship's card party finished very late.'

'And you, of course, were required to stay until all
the guests had left. The role of a companion is not an
easy one. And I doubt that Lady Luce is an easy mistress.'

'No, ma'am, you are wrong!' protested Marina. 'The
Dowager has been immensely kind to me…and…and…'

Lady Stratton patted Marina's hand. 'Forgive me for

speaking out of turn. It was wrong of me. Especially as her ladyship has been so generous in sparing you to me. What made her change her mind this afternoon?'

Oh, dear. Now what could Marina say? 'It...it was not Lady Luce who declined your invitation earlier, ma'am. I...I thought she would need me and so I took it upon myself to—'

'Very commendable, my dear. But you are here now. And is it not a beautiful day for a drive in the park?'

Marina nodded gratefully.

'I must tell you,' continued Lady Stratton, lowering her voice, 'that last night's scandal has done us a very good turn. Kit had engaged himself to Lady Blaine's eldest daughter—not with the blessing of his family, I may add—but there can be no question of a marriage now. Not with *that* family. No one will receive them in future, and— But you must know all this. Is not Lord Luce godfather to Miss Blaine?'

Marina was forced to admit that it was so.

'Then you must be aware of the methods that Lord Luce employed to entrap Kit. I have a great deal of respect for the Dowager, Miss Beaumont, but I find it very difficult to think well of her son. He has not behaved like a gentleman.'

There was nothing Marina could say. Everything Lady Stratton said was true.

'Hugo tells me that the Blaines will be going abroad as soon as the Viscount returns. It will be something of a shock to him, I expect.'

A wave of guilt hit Marina. She had never once considered the Viscount in all this. She had cared only for Kit. She was wicked, thoroughly wicked.

'I cannot say that it worries me overmuch,' continued Lady Stratton. 'Lord Blaine is a reprobate—just like his father was. His fortune stems from his sugar plantations, and it seems he don't much care what he does to increase it. Some of the tales I have heard are…upsetting. Kit thinks— But you are not interested in listening to my ramblings. Tell me, did you enjoy the party last night? After the Faro ended, I mean.'

'I…I hardly remember, ma'am. It was all so unsettling. If I had not mentioned the missing card—'

'If you had not mentioned your missing card, Lady Blaine would not have been unmasked for the cheat she undoubtedly is, and I should still be contemplating the nightmare of having Tilly Blaine for a sister. You will never know how grateful I am to you.'

Marina felt herself blushing.

'It seems that Tilly Blaine is the only member of that family who views it all with equanimity. She, apparently, is so delighted at the prospect of travelling in Europe that she is quite unmoved by her mother's disgrace. Strange girl. Her head is so stuffed with poetry that there is no room for common sense.'

It was quite late by the time Marina returned to the Dowager's house. She would have to hurry to change for dinner. Lady Luce frowned on a lack of punctuality.

Marina threw off her day gown and began to splash water on her face. There was no time to do more. Her hair… Oh, dear, her hair was beginning to come out of its pins. She would have to—

'May I help, Miss Marina?' The Dowager's maid had come in without a sound.

'Gibson,' said Marina thankfully. The old abigail was always wonderfully deft with hairpins. 'How thoughtful of you. I am desperately late, I fear. Do you think you could help me with my hair?'

'Not to worry, miss. Her ladyship said as I was to help you, since you had been delayed with Lady Stratton. Sit down here. It won't take but a moment.'

Marina did as she was bid and watched, entranced, as Gibson turned her dishevelled locks into a smoothly elegant style. 'Gibson, you are a marvel,' she said, and meant it.

The abigail coloured a little. 'That's enough of your nonsense, miss. Come, let us find you an evening gown. What about the green silk?'

'Well… Have you any idea, Gibson, what her ladyship's plans are for this evening? Are we going out?'

'I believe so, miss. Her ladyship did not say precisely, but she is wearing one of her fine gowns.'

'In that case, it had better be the green silk,' agreed Marina. 'And the matching slippers, too.'

By the time the dinner gong sounded, Marina was walking sedately down the stairs as if she had all the time in the world.

The Dowager, however, was not deceived. She looked Marina up and down. Then she gave a nod of approval. 'I must say that that gown is particularly becoming,' she said. 'It is perhaps a little low-cut, but at least it is not as flimsy as some of the gowns the gels are wearing nowadays.' She led the way into the dining room and took her seat. 'Pity that you will not have a chance tonight to display how well you look.'

Oh. It seemed that she was not to go out after all. Marina felt a pang of disappointment for which she was soon reproaching herself. What right had she to expect evening engagements?

'I am going to a card party. Alone,' said the Dowager flatly. 'After last night's performance, you would attract far too much attention.'

Marina had to admit that Lady Luce was right.

The Dowager then proceeded to talk incessantly throughout dinner. Marina found she was grateful, for she was not in the mood for conversation. Her mind kept reverting to images of Kit Stratton, no matter how hard she tried to banish them. He was not to marry Tilly Blaine after all. He—

It was not her business. Kit Stratton was nothing to do with Marina. Not any more. Her thoughtless actions had given rise to a great deal of grief but, thanks to the card playing skills her father had taught her—and a lot of luck—she had succeeded in undoing the harm she had caused. To Kit, at least. As for the Blaines… She must learn to live with what she had done there. Lady Stratton's artless revelations in the carriage suggested that the family's downfall was well merited. It even sounded as if Tilly had recovered from her passion for Kit. Remarkably quickly, too. Perhaps she would fall in love with an Italian poet…

'If you are ready, Marina…' The Dowager had risen, ready to leave the dining table.

Marina sprang to her feet. 'I beg your pardon, ma'am. I'm afraid I was wool-gathering.'

'Hmph,' snorted the Dowager, leading the way up to her drawing room.

'Excuse me, m'lady. A note has just arrived for you.'

Lady Luce did not respond to the butler until she had reached the landing. 'Bring it up here, man,' she said sharply. 'Can't read it at that distance.'

Marina tried not to laugh. The Dowager was on top form again.

The note was from Lady Marchant. And it produced a crack of laughter from the Dowager.

'Oh, don't look so downcast, Marina. This is priceless.

I promise you will enjoy it.' She sat down in her usual chair and glanced towards the decanter.

Marina had long ago learned to recognise the signals. She filled a glass and placed it on the table by the Dowager's hand. Then she took her usual seat on the low stool alongside.

'Very good, my dear, very good.' She spread Lady Marchant's note and raised her lorgnette to read it again. 'Yes, excellent. It seems that young Kit Stratton will not be the handsomest rake in London for much longer.'

'He is going abroad, too?' Marina was more than a little surprised. Lady Stratton had mentioned nothing of the kind.

'Oh, no. Nothing so simple.' She raised her glass and sipped slowly, smiling with pleasure. 'I may have forgiven you, child, for interfering in my debt to young Stratton, but I have certainly not forgiven *him* for his impudence when he returned my vowel. Arrogant young puppy….' She frowned at Marina. 'After the way he treated you, I should imagine you will be pleased to see him brought down a peg or two.'

There was an iron band around Marina's heart. With every word the Dowager spoke, it was tightening, until she could hardly breathe. 'What…what do you mean, ma'am?' she whispered hoarsely.

'Why, the cuckold's revenge, of course. It appears that the Baroness's husband does not take kindly to being made to look a fool. He has arranged—with the willing help of Méchante, I have no doubt—to change Kit's pretty face a little.'

Horror, and outrage, gave Marina back all her strength. She jumped to her feet. 'You must stop him!' she cried.

'Why? No one is going to murder young Stratton. Not

in Green Park. I dare say it will be just a discreet little
mill...a few cuts and bruises, nothing more. Kit will
soon mend.'

'But, ma'am, you cannot—'

'Stop fussing over nothing, Marina. You are too soft-
hearted by half.' She rose and swept out.

Marina was left alone. She could call on no one but
herself. There was no time to change, or to send a message, for the attack might take place at any moment. In
any case, she had no idea where to find Kit.

Except in Green Park.

'You are not going alone, Kit.'

Kit raised a weary eyebrow. Hugo was in one of his
stubborn, elder-brother moods.

'You accept that?'

'Yes, since you insist.'

'Good,' said Hugo. 'Now, this could be a clandestine
meeting with your Baroness, as she suggested, though I
doubt it. Since she insisted that you go alone, I shall be
your...coachman.'

Kit gave a crack of laughter.

Hugo laid a heavy hand on his shoulder. 'I'll have
you know, brother, that I can tool a carriage as well as
you can...and better than my coachman, too. No one
will give me a second look, especially if I wear a plain
dark coat.'

Kit nodded. Hugo was right, of course. 'I shall wear
the same,' he said. 'No point in offering a target for the
Baron's pistol, if that is what he has in mind. You think
he will try to shoot me, do you not, Hugo?'

'It's possible. We need to be prepared.' He paused.
'Unless you are willing to forget this appointment altogether? We could always go to the club, you know.'

'You know that is impossible, Hugo. We need to find out what is afoot. If I do not go on this occasion, they are bound to create another chance to attack me. Next time, I might not be forewarned. And I might not have my stalwart coachman to defend me!'

Hugo shook his head, laughing. 'Your coachman— with his pistol—will call to collect you in an hour. Go and find yourself a coat, brother. And make sure it is fit to be seen. If I am to bear your body home, I must have it elegantly clad.'

In the dusk, the shadows played tricks. Green Park seemed to be alive with movement, but it might have been nothing more than the wind among the leaves.

By the time Hugo had climbed down from the box, Kit had already found an urchin who would mind the horses for the promise of a shilling. At least one of them would return to pay the lad, surely?

'Couldn't see any movement,' Hugo said quietly, 'even from up there. If they're here, they must be well concealed. You have your pistol?'

Kit patted his pocket. 'And my cane. Katharina's note said that I must walk along the shrubbery path. She would come to meet me when she was sure I was alone.'

'Did she say which entrance you should take?'

'No. Why?'

'Because it gives us an advantage. You will start walking from this end. I will start from the other. They will not know which of us is Kit.'

'No, Hugo. This is my fight. I will not put you in the line of the Baron's bullet. I will go in alone. You may come to my aid if I need you. No doubt, you'll know soon enough.'

Hugo looked unconvinced.

'I mean it, Hugo,' Kit said grimly. 'I need to be able to give you back to Emma in one piece.'

Hugo frowned. 'At least, give me time to get to the far end. If I make my way into the shrubbery, I ought to be able to get to you the sooner.'

Kit recognised the sense in his brother's proposal, but still he hesitated. If anything happened to Hugo, there would be a widow and three fatherless children. Whereas he, Kit, had no one waiting for him. For Marina had rejected him.

'Kit? What do you say? You cannot object to that, surely?'

'Oh, very well. If you must. I will give you two minutes, and then I shall start along this path.' He held out his hand. 'God save you, Hugo.'

Hugo clasped Kit's hand firmly with one of his own and laid the other on Kit's shoulder. 'We have the advantage of surprise, Kit. Wellington would be proud of us. God bless you.'

He disappeared in the direction of the coach and the distant entrance to the shrubbery. Kit watched, counting the seconds. At the end of the agreed two minutes, he put his hand into his pocket, gripped his pistol and started along the gloomy path, swinging his cane.

Hugo had absolutely no intention of hiding in the shrubbery, waiting for Kit to be attacked, perhaps killed. Hat in hand, he raced along to the far end of the park, where the path met the roadway. There he paused to catch his breath, and to put on his hat once more, at exactly the kind of rakish angle Kit always used.

In the gathering gloom, no one would be able to tell them apart.

He pulled his pistol from his pocket and cocked it.

With his arm hanging loosely at his side, his pistol was hidden by his coat. He started forward at a measured pace.

It was just like the start of a duel.

He had covered no more than fifty yards when he heard a tiny rustle in the bushes to his left. He looked quickly down the path, straining to see in front of him. There was no sign of Kit. He must appear soon.

Hugo continued to walk steadily down the path.

'That's Stratton!' cried a man's voice from the bushes.

Hugo ducked automatically, but there was no bullet. Three hefty bruisers pushed their way out of the bushes. They were barring his way. And they had cudgels in their hands.

'So that is the way of it,' he said grimly. Unlike Kit, he had no cane.

From the corner of his eye, he caught a flash of colour among the trees. Good God, there was a woman in there!

'Behind you!' cried a female voice.

It came from the wrong direction.

Hugo whirled just in time to duck. The fourth man's club missed his head by a hair's breadth.

A woman screamed. And then another—a second voice.

Hugo ignored them. The force of his assailant's blow had bent the man almost double, exposing his neck. Hugo hit him with the pistol, but it spun out of his hand. He whipped round to face the other three—unarmed.

Kit had appeared as from nowhere. He was using his cane like a sword against two of the bruisers. Only one now faced Hugo.

Kit flashed Hugo a grin. 'I think the odds are fairer now, gentlemen,' he said calmly. 'Three against two.'

One of the pair risked a quick look behind him. A

mistake. Kit struck him hard on the wrist. With a howl of pain, the man dropped his cudgel and clutched his arm. 'Ye've broke it!' he screamed.

'Probably,' said Kit, squaring up to his last man. 'Let's see what you're made of, eh?' he snarled.

The man hesitated.

Kit stepped back a pace and looked towards Hugo. He was holding his own. Kit lunged forward. 'Now then!'

The man dodged.

Kit whirled, ready to parry the next blow.

A woman screamed again.

Kit looked towards the sound.

The man Hugo had felled was on his feet again. And he had an arm across a woman's throat.

It was Marina.

A murderous rage overcame Kit. In a split second, he had plunged his cane like a sword deep into his opponent's belly. The man dropped without a sound.

'Careful, Kit,' Hugo gasped, still struggling.

Hugo's voice stayed Kit's all-consuming fury. Instantly, he was icy calm. Waiting.

Two men were disabled. Hugo was about to overcome the third. But the fourth man had Marina.

'Let us go,' yelled the fourth man. 'Or I'll slit 'er throat. Swelp me, I will.'

Kit dropped his cane and took two paces forward, sliding his hand into his pocket. 'Let her go. Or I'll kill you.'

The man did not move. But his knife did. It glinted suddenly in the dim light. Kit heard a muffled groan.

'Let her go,' he said again, pulling the pistol from his pocket. 'Even at this distance, I can put a bullet in your head before you draw breath. Let her go.'

Hugo had his opponent in an armlock at last. 'Don't be a fool,' he yelled. 'He's a crack shot. He'll kill you.'

The man stood undecided.

The silence was rent by another scream.

Chapter Twenty-One

Marina struggled to turn towards the sound. Out of the corner of her eye, she caught a fleeting glimpse of a woman in the bushes, trying to fight free of a man. He seemed to have her by the hair.

'That's enough o' that, missy,' growled Marina's captor, pushing the knife higher up her throat. 'One more move an' I'll stick ye.'

Marina froze.

She was not afraid, even though she knew she might die here. All her senses seemed to have been heightened by the danger. She could smell her captor's unwashed body and fetid breath, overlaid with the sweet smell of the new leaves on the trees. She could hear his frightened breathing, and feel it on the back of her neck. His knife touched her throat with a cold promise of death.

And only yards away, she could see Kit's powerful shape, unmistakable in the gloom, preparing to shoot. He took another step forward.

'That's enough,' yelled Marina's captor. 'Any closer an' I'll kill her.'

Kit stopped. Slowly, he raised his pistol.

Marina felt her captor shrinking into her shadow.

There was no target for Kit but her own defenceless body. She held her breath. He would shoot only if he were sure. She loved him. So she must trust him.

She refused to close her eyes. If this was to be her last moment on earth, she wanted her gaze to rest on the man she loved.

'I think you might be wise to put up your pistol,' said a voice from the shrubbery.

Marina could not turn to see. It was a man's voice, though, and it had a foreign accent.

Kit did not take his eyes off Marina. Nor did his pistol waver by even a fraction. 'I think not, Baron,' he said grimly. 'You know my reputation. Tell your man that I can do exactly as I said. Tell him I will kill him if he does not let her go.'

'As I will kill you,' replied the Baron, moving out on to the path. Marina could see him now. His left hand was clamped around his wife's upper arm. When he pulled her out behind him, she moaned.

His right hand held a small silver pistol. And it was pointed at Kit.

No! Marina swallowed the scream that rose in her throat. She must not distract Kit. She must *do* something. But what? She had no weapons. She could not even kick out, for she did not have boots on her feet. She had run out, wearing the green silk evening slippers. They were now in shreds. Her feet were almost bare.

She could feel the man's panicked breathing slowing a little. He was beginning to think he was safe, protected by the Baron's gun. The hand holding the knife at her throat relaxed a fraction.

It had to be now.

She took a deep breath and rammed her elbow back

into the man's ribs with every ounce of strength she possessed.

He doubled up, groaning. The knife was no longer against her throat. She ducked away and threw herself towards Hugo, well out of Kit's firing line.

Kit had not moved. His pistol was still trained on Marina's attacker, now grovelling on the ground.

'Did he hurt you, Marina?' Kit's voice sounded hoarse.

'No. No.' Why was he concerned about her? He should be defending himself against the Baron. 'Take care, Kit,' she cried.

Kit smiled into the gloom. Without turning towards the Baron, he said calmly, 'If you were minded to kill me, sir, you really should have done it by now.'

The Baron hauled his wife a little closer. She whimpered.

'Do not imagine, sir, that I will lift a finger to protect your wife,' Kit said flatly. 'Our affair is long over. I suggest you would do better to address your complaints to her new protector.'

Marina closed her eyes in a moment of sheer terror. The Baron would never accept such insults. He was bound to shoot Kit now.

After a long pause, the Baron said slowly, 'Let these men go, Stratton. Your quarrel is with me.'

Kit glanced towards Hugo, who nodded and loosed his hold on his captive. The man hobbled over to where Kit's second victim lay on the ground and half-hauled, half-carried him off into the darkness. Marina's captor, and the man with the broken arm, simply took to their heels.

'Honour among thieves,' said Kit, turning slowly to face the Baron.

'And now it is stalemate, Stratton, I think.'

Marina started forward. If she could come between them—

Hugo caught her before she had gone a yard. He pulled her into the shelter of his arm and held her there. 'No, Marina,' he whispered into her hair. 'Do not interfere. Leave this to Kit.' When she still struggled to free herself, he laughed softly. 'Trust him, my dear. I promise he will come back to you.'

Marina was stunned into immobility. It sounded as if—

'Shall we play it out here? Or would you rather meet me on the field of honour, like a gentleman?' The Baron's tone made clear that he did not see Kit as a gentleman at all.

'As you choose, sir,' Kit said quickly. 'It will make no difference to the outcome.'

The Baron spluttered something in German. His wife groaned.

'Indeed,' said Kit. 'I am not your wife's lover now, sir. But I was. You have every right to try to kill me.'

'Are you saying, Stratton, that you have *no* such right?'

Kit said nothing.

Marina understood then. If they met on the duelling field, Kit would not fire on the Baron. He would just stand there, proud and defiant, allowing the wronged husband to have his revenge. It was Kit's concept of justice.

The Baron understood too, for he put up his pistol. 'I do not relish the idea of cold-blooded murder,' he said.

Kit nodded in the direction of the vanished bruisers. 'Do you not?' he said wryly.

'They would not have killed you,' replied the Baron

matter of factly. 'You would have become somewhat
less attractive to the ladies. That is all.' He had not released his ferocious grip on his wife's arm. 'Katharina
was happy to lure you here. She said she wanted to
watch your beating. I fancied it might provide a salutary
lesson—for both of you.' He looked down at her. There
were streaks of tears on her ashen cheeks. 'So. So. It
will do, I think.' He put his arm round her shoulder. It
was not a loving embrace. 'We will go now,' he said.
'My compliments to you, Stratton, and to your brother.
I had not expected anyone to overcome that nasty quar-
tet.' He gave a stiff military bow, its precision marred
by his hold on his wife. 'I am sure you understand that
we shall not speak again.'

Kit returned the Baron's bow, but the man had already
turned to leave. In a very few moments, they were out
of sight.

Marina straightened and Hugo released her. She
thought she felt a tiny, comforting squeeze before he let
her go.

'That was a close-run thing, Kit,' Hugo said, shaking
his head a little.

'Perhaps,' replied Kit.

Marina was almost sure he avoided his brother's eye.

'As for you, woman,' Kit said, advancing menacingly
on her, 'what in heaven's name did you think you were
doing?' He took her by the shoulders, as he had done
once before. This time, he did not shake her. He just
stood there, staring down at her, letting his gaze rove
over her features. 'You are, without doubt, the most infuriating, idiotic, ungovernable—'

Hugo cleared his throat ostentatiously.

'Oh, go and see to the horses, can't you? You're a
pretty poor apology for a coachman, I must say.'

Hugo burst out laughing. 'At once, sir,' he said with
a mock bow. 'Just as you say, sir.'

'Marina.' Kit lingered over the word, all the while
stroking her hair back from her face. 'Marina,' he repeated, 'you are quite maddening. How shall I ever be
able to cope with you?'

She did not reply. She was sure she had not heard him
aright. He must mean—

He drew her into his arms and began to kiss her face,
beginning at her hairline, and moving to her forehead,
her eyes... She groaned with the pleasure of his touch.

He stopped. 'Marina? Good grief, what am I doing?
You are hurt. And cold. Here.' He shrugged out of his
dark coat and wrapped it round her, imprisoning her
arms. 'Your neck. Let me see.' With amazing gentleness,
those strong, lean fingers lifted her chin so that he could
see where the knife had been. 'Confound it! Can't see a
thing in this light!' He tightened his grip on her. 'Come.
There is a light on the coach.'

She stepped on something sharp and gave a little cry
of pain.

'My God,' he exclaimed. 'Your feet!' He swept her
into his arms, ignoring her attempted protest, and carried
her out of the park to the waiting carriage. Hugo was on
the box. A grinning urchin was at the horses' heads.

Hugo jumped down to open the carriage door. 'Spot
of abduction tonight, is it, sir?' he quipped.

Kit flashed a smile in response. 'Drive back to Fitzwilliam House, my good man,' he said. 'Very slowly.'

Kit ignored Marina's protests that she had received
nothing more than a scratch. He took her throat in his
hands and gently, gently traced the red line the knife had
made. There was one tiny drop of blood. He swore under

his breath. He should have killed the villain when he had the chance!

'What is it?' Marina asked.

'You are bleeding,' he replied harshly. 'He cut you—'

'It was my own doing,' she said, putting her hand over his. 'I felt the prick of the knife when I pushed myself free. It is nothing.'

'You could have been killed, you beautiful idiot.'

Marina said nothing, but she smiled shyly. She seemed to be relishing his insults.

'And your poor feet…'

'That, too, was my own doing. I could have stopped to put on outdoor shoes…but then I might have been too late.'

'Too late for what, pray?' he asked, lifting her into the corner of the seat and raising her poor, bruised feet into his lap.

'To warn you that—' She stopped and looked inquiringly up at him. 'I suppose you will tell me that my warning was unnecessary. And that my arrival only served to put myself in danger.'

'Something of the sort,' he murmured, stroking the shreds of the green silk slipper from one foot.

A shiver ran through Marina.

Kit pretended not to notice. Slowly, he caressed the second slipper free.

She shivered again, more noticeably. 'What are you doing, sir?' she whispered hoarsely.

Kit began to stroke the bare skin of her foot where her stocking was torn and bloody. 'Trying to remedy the damage you have done, ma'am.'

He continued to run his fingers over her skin with a touch so light that, if she closed her eyes, she could not quite be sure that it was happening. She pushed herself back against the deeply cushioned seat, trying to escape from the feelings he was creating, yet at the same time longing for them to continue. In the end, she could not stifle a tiny groan.

'Mmm,' agreed Kit huskily. 'I fear these must be removed.'

Marina was floating. She barely heard his words. Her skin was alive, but her mind had been numbed by the magic of his touch.

He began to slide his fingers up to her ankle, and then to her calf. It was exquisite. She wanted to purr like a contented cat. When he raised her skirts to remove her ruined stockings, she could do nothing to resist him. He untied her garters, allowing himself a tiny caress of her inner thigh that had her moaning in her throat. Then he rolled the stockings down and gently peeled them from her bleeding skin.

She was still purring when he lifted her on to his lap and began to kiss her. She did not know where she was, only that she was in the arms of the man she loved, and that he was caressing her, kissing her, as if he loved her. A tiny, strident voice from her old self tried to scream that he was a rake, that he knew exactly how to seduce plain, innocent women like Marina, but she ignored it. The purring was too strong.

At first his kiss was light, hesitant, even unsure of her response, but as she began to kiss him back, everything seemed to explode. He pulled her close against his hard body, his hands stroking her spine and her hair. When it finally tumbled down her back, she heard a rumble of satisfied laughter, deep in his chest. Then the kiss was transformed. It was harder, more demanding, almost punishing, but she leaned in to him like a woman starving, craving for more. Innocent though she was, she responded to him with a lover's passion.

He groaned out her name.

If she never had another moment of passion in her life, she would remember the sound of her name in his throat.

His fingers had found their way to her bodice, had undone the tiny buttons and untied the ribbons of her chemise. Her breast was resting heavily in his hand. He groaned again, never lifting his lips from hers. And he began to roll her nipple between finger and thumb, gently at first, then more roughly. An arrow of heat shot through her, like the pull of a puppet's strings under his fingers, and she felt a sudden release of liquid fire in her belly. Her whole body was about to melt.

So this was passion—this unutterable longing for union, for fulfilment.

Kit broke the kiss, breathing hard.

Marina whimpered. She could not open her eyes. It had been so blissful.

'Forgive me,' he said huskily, pulling her head into the crook of his shoulder and applying his fingers to the buttons of her dress. 'I should not have done that.'

Slowly, she opened her eyes. They were huge and dark, and dazed with passion. He was not sure whether she was actually seeing him. He tried to concentrate on restoring her gown to a more decorous state, but it was almost impossible to do up those tiny buttons without touching the skin of her breasts. It was beautiful skin, like creamy silk overlaid with blush. And it was so very tempting…

'Kit,' she breathed through lips swollen from his kisses. 'Please—'

'No, my sweet,' he said, trying to hide the desire in

his voice, 'not here. Not in a dirty, smelly carriage, remember? In my bed. Willingly in my bed.'

She did not respond. He had lost her.

He knelt on the floor and, taking his handkerchief,
began to wipe away the grime and the blood from her
feet with featherlight strokes. He needed, desperately, to
prove to her how much she meant to him. He could think
of no other way.

'You must be bathed, Marina, to remove this dirt.
Emma will be able to give you some ointment, and ban-
dages—'

'Emma?' She sounded bemused.

'Emma. My sister. Hugo's wife. I am taking you to
her.'

'But you cannot!' she exclaimed. 'I am not your—
Oh, heavens! Look at me!' She put her hands to her hair,
desperately trying to put it into some kind of order. 'I
must go back to Lady Luce's house…where I belong. I
must… Oh, what will she think of me? How shall I ever
explain?'

Kit pushed the ruined stockings under the seat where
Marina could not see them. 'You will tell her the truth,'
he said, with emphasis. 'Or I shall. You ran out to save
a life.'

'But I—'

'And you succeeded. You are a very brave woman,
Marina Beaumont.'

Kit looked his fill at her. She was flushed with passion—and now with embarrassment, too. She was so
beautiful, he caught his breath.

A sharp rap on the roof brought him back to earth. It
took him a moment to realise that they were no longer
moving. He let down the glass and stuck his head out.
'Why have we stopped?'

'We are at Fitzwilliam House, y'r honour,' said Hugo respectfully.

'Are we, indeed? Well, turn this blasted carriage round and take the lady home.'

'Home, y'r honour?' Hugo queried.

'Yes. Back to the Dowager's house. The abduction has been postponed.'

Kit insisted on carrying Marina into the Dowager's house. His long dark coat was wrapped around her to protect her modesty from the servants' prying eyes, but there was no disguising the fact that her hair had come down and her feet were bare. He could almost feel her shame as he carried her up to the drawing room.

The Dowager had not yet returned.

'I could carry you up to your bedchamber,' he said.

'No!' It was almost a scream. 'It is bad enough that you have carried me here. I— Put me down, sir. And then, please leave.'

So that was to be the way of it. Well, it was time she learned otherwise. 'Marina, I will leave when you promise to stop behaving like an idiot.' He lowered her gently into a wing chair. 'What is the matter with you?'

'Lady Stratton said that your engagement to Miss Blaine was at an end. Is…is that true?' She was staring at her hands again.

'How could you think otherwise? After all, you were the one who secured my release, with those clever hands of yours. I don't believe I have thanked you for that.' He bowed formally. 'A woman like Tilly Blaine would drive a man to murder, you know. I need a woman who knows the value of silence—'

'Oh,' she sighed.

'And courage. My wife must—'

The door was thrown open. 'Good God!' exclaimed the Dowager. 'What are *you* doing here? I thought you were—' She turned and waved the butler away. Then she tottered across the room and almost fell into her chair.

Marina attempted to rise. 'Are you all right, ma'am? You—'

Kit pressed Marina back into her chair with a firm hand on her shoulder. 'Stay where you are. I will see to her.' He poured a generous measure of brandy and put it into the old lady's shaking hand. 'Drink this, ma'am. You will feel better for it.'

The Dowager, it seemed, needed no prompting from Kit. She tossed it off and immediately held out her empty glass to be refilled. With the second measure, however, she sipped in a more ladylike fashion, using her free hand to straighten her wig. 'That's better,' she announced.

Kit grinned across at Marina. His cynical mask had vanished, replaced by open delight...and love. Marina felt her insides melting at the intimacy of it. That icy husk around her heart—how vainly she had worked to nurture it!—had disappeared in the glowing warmth of his response. And he had talked of his wife... No, it was impossible.

'I suppose your being here would account for it,' said the old lady suddenly, setting down her glass.

'I'm afraid I do not quite... Account for what, precisely, ma'am?' Kit asked tersely.

Marina could see that Kit was determined to control his temper. He was finding it difficult.

'For your being here,' Lady Luce repeated. 'If you're here, you can't be there, can you? And that would account for it.'

The old lady was definitely rattled this time. She was talking in riddles. 'Did something happen, ma'am?' Marina asked gently. 'At your card party?'

The Dowager nodded a little shakily. 'Went to Méchante's after all. Some ruffians arrived. They were demanding money from Méchante. Apparently, for services she had arranged.' She cast a very scornful look in Kit's direction. 'I collect that they failed in their task. Naturally, she refused to pay, so they started to break up the house. Made a pretty good fist of it, too. It will cost her a small fortune to put all to rights.'

'Were you hurt, ma'am?' Kit asked quietly.

Marina realised that he was genuinely concerned. He knew, at first hand, that any one of those bruisers could have broken the Dowager's bones at a touch.

The Dowager shook her head. Then she gave a choke of laughter. 'Méchante was, though. They misliked the way she tried to order them out. She will be more than a little bruised tomorrow. Black eye, too, I dare say.'

Marina caught her breath, and then sighed. Perhaps Lady Marchant had received no more than she deserved.

'And you think *I* am well served, too, eh? Don't you?' added the Dowager tartly.

Kit said nothing. He was looking at Marina.

The Dowager appeared not to have noticed. 'Well, perhaps you are right. I had rather hoped those devils would change your looks, but…having seen them in action, I admit I was wrong to…' She pushed herself up from her chair. 'I want to go to bed. You, sir, should not be here. You must leave. Pull the bell.'

Kit did so and then politely offered her his arm. 'I had understood, ma'am,' he said quietly, 'that, even under your stern rules, a betrothed couple were permitted to be alone together.'

Lady Luce's gasp was so loud that it drowned out Marina's. For probably the only time in her life, the Dowager was totally at a loss for words. And as for Marina…

He led the Dowager towards the door. 'You should know that Miss Beaumont has done me the honour of agreeing to be my wife, ma'am. But I know you have had a distressing evening. Tomorrow will suffice for your congratulations. Marina will be removing to Fitzwilliam House in the morning. You will be very welcome to call on her there.'

'Kit! You—!'

'Later, Marina, my love. Later. Do not embarrass Lady Luce with such shameless protestations of affection. She needs her rest.' He smiled over his shoulder at her, but his expression was quite serious again by the time he had turned back to Lady Luce and her hovering abigail. 'Goodnight, ma'am,' he said, bowing. 'Sleep well.'

He closed the door firmly on them and returned to Marina. She was bristling. Again. She probably had cause.

'If I had been able, Kit Stratton, I should have run across the room and slapped that stupid smile from your arrogant face. How could you say such things?'

He tried to look sheepish. She was not deceived. She laughed. It was the glorious, joyous sound he had longed to hear. 'You are a rogue, sir, as well as a rake. And I have *not* agreed to marry you. You—'

He reached for her and drew her into his arms. Then he kissed her, thoroughly, until she had stopped resisting. 'Now, Marina, I am going to send for hot water and towels to bathe your feet and you, my sweet, are not going to protest. Indeed, you may sing to me while I see to your hurts. After that, I shall carry you up to your room—'

'No!'

'Accompanied, for propriety's sake, by one of the maids. Tomorrow, you will remove to Fitzwilliam House while I make arrangements to convey you home to Yorkshire and—'

'Stop, stop! You are impossible, Kit Stratton. I will not permit you to order my life like a…a…' She could not think of a suitably insulting description of his high-handed behaviour. And she did not really wish to try very hard. Not now, when there were more important things to be said. 'Besides, I have not said that I love you. Or that I will marry you—'

'But you do, don't you?' he said, planting tiny kisses on the side of her neck until she melted into his arms once more. 'And you will.'

'Only if you love me,' she whispered.

'To distraction,' he said and found her lips.

* * * * *

The Unknown Wife
by
Mary Brendan

Mary Brendan was born in North London and lived there for nineteen years before marrying and migrating to Hertfordshire. She was grammar-school educated and has been at various times in her working life a personal secretary for an international property developer and a landlady. Currently working part-time in a local library, she dedicates hard-won leisure time to antiques browsing, curries and keeping up with her two lively sons.

Prologue

'I don't want you to go out this evening. Stay home and spend some time with me and our children before they are put to bed.'

The woman might have been deaf for all the attention she paid to those beseeching words or the tall handsome man who had uttered them. Patiently he watched her from his study doorway as she teased abundant dark curls to drape alluringly over her elegant white shoulders. Her head turned this way and that as she assessed her reflected image in an elaborate hallway mirror.

'For pity's sake! Will you look at me? Answer me!'

The beautiful brunette swished about in a rustle of vermilion satin. 'What is wrong with you tonight, Benjamin?' she enquired. 'Is Mrs Smith out of sorts?

If you think I will oblige you with playing at happy families because your mistress is indisposed, you are more *stupide* than I imagined.' Her head fell back, exposing a pearly throat, and her low-lidded eyes held a feline intensity as she looked at him. 'Your *chère amie* might be unavailable, but my friend is not,' she purred with insulting indifference. 'Lord Ballantine is due any minute to take me to the opera.'

On hearing who was her escort this evening, her husband approached her with light, rapid steps and gripped a soft arm.

'Your *cicisbeo* can wait…or move on to the next silly strumpet on his list. You are not to be Ballantine's only conquest tonight, I'm sure. As for my mistress, she is not indisposed and would, as ever, be pleased to see me. Which is more than can be said for my lady wife.' He closed his eyes, grimaced regret as an apologetic hand smoothed over pink pressure marks marring her fine skin. 'It is time you and I attempted to put things right between us. The children are old enough now to sense this interminable disharmony. They did not ask to be brought into this world or live in such a bleak atmosphere.'

'The children! Always it is the same. We should live our lives to please the children! Sometimes I wish I had returned to France. Chancing my fate on the tumbrils with my esteemed family might have been preferable to enduring your disgusting touch.'

Her husband smiled thinly, his fingers detached from her arm. 'You? Enduring my disgusting touch? When was that, my dear? Tell me, can you really recall the last time you allowed me into your bed? I'm damned if I can remember enjoying my conjugal rights in five years.'

Beneath an impeccable *maquillage* the woman's face whitened. 'And I am damned, *mon cher,* if I can remember *ever* enjoying my conjugal rights. You have your heir,' she breathed. 'A daughter, too. Leave me be. I have performed all the duty I can or I will for you.' She stepped past him, heading for the street door. By the foot of the stairs her pace faltered. 'Why are you hiding there? Are you spying on your mama? Quick! Up to bed with you, this instant. Tomorrow you are back to school, and not a moment too soon.'

The small boy said nothing, merely fixed the woman with a velvet-brown gaze. She flinched beneath that unwavering, penetrating stare at the same moment his eyes slid past to watch his father through stripes of banister.

'Upstairs with you now!' The woman's voice was strident with unease. 'Do you want the school masters to be told you need a good lesson in manners and discipline?'

The boy's eyes whipped back to his mother, but already he was overlooked, for a butler had portentously materialised in the hallway.

'Lord Ballantine's carriage awaits, ma'am,' the aged servant informed neutrally.

'*Méchant...*' the woman murmured beneath her breath with a slanting glance at her son. Whilst majestically draping a sable stole about her petite figure, she announced, 'I am the daughter of a count whose august bloodline is centuries old, yet I have a son who is insolent and a husband who is too cowardly to punish him.'

'And I am the son of an earl whose noble ancestry far outstrips yours, yet I have a wife who invites scandal because she acts like a common—' The man's lips compressed into a skewed line as from a corner of his eye he saw his son's fingers clench on oak.

'You are a younger son...a nobody...' she mocked over her shoulder.

The butler hobbled to close the great doors, then merged tactfully into shadow. Just a waft of expensive French perfume hinted at a woman's recent presence.

The man held out a hand. Within a moment crisp cotton was held away from bare feet as the boy padded over cold flags to his father and immediately curved against his hip. Long patrician fingers cradled a fair fragile head close to his waist. When he spoke his voice was hoarse with tears.

'When you are a man, Etienne, choose your wife

carefully. Reason and respect must reign. Marrying for loyalty or duty…or even love is unwise. Doing the right thing is often very wrong.'

Chapter One

Had he been anywhere but Ireland those limpid doe eyes attached to his quite solemnly, quite boldly, might have unsettled him. He had coupled with many women, in many countries, but Ireland? Curse it for a dank and dismal hell! He'd never before set foot on a squelching sod of it. And yet…and yet…squinting through lashes rimed with ice, through eyes filmed with cold, he could detect something familiar in the child's face.

The child was still, looking back with quiet instinct, uncaring of the drizzling sleet sleeking his fair hair against his head. The stallion snickered, blew steam at the side of his pink-cheeked face. A hoof batting against the boy's cap, catching ice on the ground, finally took the rider's attention. Moments before the lad had hurtled into the road chasing the

hat and laughing, for an icy blast had exposed his
tender head. The gangly, tumbling figure had made
horse and rider rear back and slew to the right, almost
overturning them both.

A dark visage creased fiercely beneath the bite of
the elements and its owner's thoughts. But the man
was glad now he hadn't bellowed abuse, although the
lad deserved scolding. He might have run him down
and broken his own neck in the bargain. Brusquely the
man flicked, then snapped, leathered fingers at the
hat. Obediently it was retrieved with a childish peek
at the softening snow. He wasn't afraid. He smiled
instead; a faltering curving of lips that arched blond
eyebrows into a sleet-spangled fringe.

A broad, brown hand shot out and the cap was
knocked clean of its freezing granules.

'You should be careful. I could have knocked you
flying. This stallion might have pulped a little chap
like you.'

The boy was unabashed, just darting eyes enliven-
ing a complexion drawn with cold. Dark features
suddenly swooped close to his as the rider plopped the
hat on the child's soaking skull.

'What's his name?' the boy asked, stroking the
stallion's flank.

'Storm.'

'What's your name?'

The man seemed as though he might ignore the

trembling wistful enquiry, and the small, bone-white fingers still on the flank of his sleek black mount. 'It's polite to say, what is your name, *sir,*' he corrected tersely, but he began to introduce himself anyway. 'Etienne—' The rest was lost to a woman's guttural Irish tone.

'Mother Mary, did I turn me back for one minute to speak with Mrs O'Flaherty and find you gone. Now, what will your ma be sayin' if she finds out all today's mischief…an'— Faith! Look, you're drenched through, so y'are…' A woman clutching at her bonnet and dragging her cloak hard about her stamped over the unyielding street towards them. Grabbing at the lad's hand, she tugged him gently backwards towards the shelter of shop doorways, roaring and making a fist for a cart that drove too snugly by him. There was no more than a sharp stare angled from beneath an awning of bonnet brim to acknowledge the stranger astride his powerful stallion.

Etienne watched as the boy trudged away stabbing the toes of his boots into frozen earth mounds formed by cartwheels. Clods were successfully loosened, tossed off the tip of his boots into the air. Far back in Etienne's mind a childish reminiscence stirred, twitching his thin lips. He reined back, cursing for the hundredth time that he'd not taken the coach for hire at the Fiddle and Flute. But for the blacksmith failing to shoe the lead quick enough for him he would have been travelling in relative comfort towards Waterford. Now he felt unsettled, irritable, and he knew it wasn't just to do with being wet, hungry and cold. An odd feeling that something portentous had occurred wouldn't be shrugged off along with the ice burdening his caped shoulders. Settling his beaver low on his brow, he cursed and kneed the horse forward. It was just a child; an Irish peasant's brat. The boy was nothing to do with him. He'd never before set foot in Ireland, he reminded himself as he sent his mount into a furious gallop.

'Have you invited me here simply to watch me die of influenza?'

Connor Flinte, Earl of Devane, turned from the slurry obscuring the view through his mullioned window and grinned at the man entering his vast and cosy library. He watched his guest's busy fingers despatching a shower of melting ice from his long dark hair.

Connor's rapid step showed genuine welcome and affection as he closed the space between them to shake hands. 'Is that any way to greet your host? Your long-lost comrade? Some carping gratitude for me fine hospitality, I'm thinking!' Connor chided with liberal Irish charm and intonation.

'Well, you have to admit, Con, this weather is appalling, even for February. Is Ireland always so...so damned *wet?*'

The Earl of Devane quirked an ebony eyebrow at him. 'Wet? Get away with you. This is nothing. You should see it when the rains get here. Seriously, it's good to see you, Etienne. Why did Gallagher not announce you?' Connor frowned at the door. His conscientious butler was nowhere to be seen.

'Oh, I told him not to bother. He seemed a bit flustered. Your porch roof is leaking; as I arrived he was organising the positioning of the buckets with a couple of footmen. It reminded me that the roof of Redgrave Park needs attention.'

'Are you away from here and straight to Redgrave Park? Or have you a mind to stop off in Mayfair?' Connor asked his former comrade-in-arms. 'If you are going to London, I have an errand to beg of you. Would you deliver an urgent letter to my man of business in Cheapside?'

Etienne's expression became decidedly wolfish. 'Oh, I think I might detour through Mayfair en route to Suffolk. And of course I'll be your post boy.'

'How is Lady Avery? Still besotted with you?' Connor asked with a mix of admiration and humour in his voice as he contemplated the beautiful widow who had been this man's mistress for at least half a decade. Plenty of men as wealthy and influential as this one had tried to win her affections and lure her away. Nevertheless she remained steadfastly loyal to her Colonel even, so rumour had it, during those long months that he spent abroad on army duties.

'I believe she's very well,' Etienne replied with a grin. 'Judging from her last *billet-doux,* she'll be delighted to see me. It would be churlish to disappoint her after six months' absence.' His smile sobered. 'I should make it my business to see Miss Caroline Greenwood, too, before I set out to check on Redgrave Park.'

At Connor's enquiring look he elaborated. 'It's time to think about a wife and heirs. Last time I was in town, I paid Miss Greenwood some attention. She seems amenable and is pretty enough. She doesn't blush, stammer or giggle too often. I'll want a decent hostess who is able to conduct herself properly. She's young…about nineteen, I would guess. That apart, she fits the bill.' He chuckled. 'And her parents are more than willing to foot the bill. They've been hinting at a hundred thousand deposited in my bank account as the chit's dowry. Her father has kept regularly in touch. Now I'm home for good I imagine they think I'll take up where I left off. I expect I will.'

'How very romantic,' Connor murmured.

Etienne shot him a look from beneath thick dark brows. 'What's romance got to do with any of it?' he countered in an equally sarcastic vein. 'We've established that Lady Avery is just as fine as ever she was. My marriage won't worry her.'

As though remembering his role as host, Connor indicated his guest should take a seat in a comfy fireside chair, positioned close to glowing coals. He drew his own armchair up to the lofty stone chimney-piece—so enormous was it, he could have put the chair down within the soot-stained cavern. With a weary sigh, Etienne dropped his tall frame into the cushions. One long muscular leg stretched out in negligent ease as his head lolled back to dent soft hide. A dark hand was thrust into a trouser pocket; the other accepted the crystal brandy balloon extended his way. A generous amount of amber liquid rocked alluringly within.

After the two men had sipped appreciatively, taken discreet stock of each other's appearance, and found nothing spectacular to warrant a comment, Etienne turned his thoughts to the thing, or rather person, who did greatly intrigue him. With his dark eyes levelled on Connor, he drew his booted feet across the Aubusson and sat forward, forearms on knees. 'If you want to talk of romance…well, you know I'm not here, risking pneumonia, on your account. Where's that beautiful, tricky wife of yours? It's about time I met her.'

At the mention of Rachel, Connor's hard handsome features softened into a smile. 'She's visiting friends in the village with her sister. And your mother is due any moment.'

'My mother?'

'Claudine's recently been a house guest of the Ormondes. Did you not know?'

Etienne shrugged. 'No. Ormonde is my father's cousin on the paternal side. I've long known my mother has a soft spot for him.'

'Do I detect an element of animosity?'

Etienne's brandy balloon was virtually emptied in one gulp before he replied. 'It makes no difference to me with whom she spends her time. We're not close; you know that. It's only ever been my grandparents cementing us together. And that's another place I must go before I return to Suffolk: to Cambridge to see how they fare. They're both in their eighty-second year, you know.'

Etienne avoided Connor's sympathetic gaze. Eyes the colour of bitter chocolate focused on leaping flames to one side of him as he drained his glass.

'How long can you stay, Etienne?'

Etienne speared him a look. What he read in his friend's face made him chuckle. 'I sense a man desperate for a little masculine company, even if he does have an urgent letter to be taken across the water to his attorney. Are you outnumbered by the ladies, Con?'

Connor looked a little abashed. 'Actually, the letter's not that important, but your company is. I thought, with apologies to Lady Avery, I might impose on you to stay at least a week and act as escort and charming man about town to your mother and my sister-in-law.'

Etienne collapsed into his chair and choked a laugh. 'For God's sake! How long have you been married? Too long for this! Three months—six at the most—is honeymoon time, you know. By my reckoning you've been leg-shackled more than a year and a half.'

'I like my sister-in-law very much, but sometimes a man has a desire to spend time alone with his wife during the day.'

'I do understand,' Etienne soothed him with a grin. 'And true friend that I am, I will be happy to oblige for a week. After that I have a desire to spend some time in London with Lady Avery…you understand?'

Connor grimaced a laughing response.

'Lady Devane must be enchanting,' Etienne said, admiration husky in his voice. 'I can't wait to meet her.'

Isabel Forrester stripped damp gloves from her long slender hands with a grimace. She vigorously shook them to dry them whilst answering a plea from her older sister. 'I will come along to the drawing room, I promise. First I must see how Marcus is. He said he felt poorly this morning before breakfast. I worried about sending him to school at all in this weather. But he has a way of exaggerating when it suits him.' She sighed expressively. 'I wonder if Noreen has brought back more complaints from Father Maguire?'

Rachel agitatedly swung her bonnet by its strings, too excited by her butler's news to pay much attention to her nephew's condition. 'Well, don't be too long. Gallagher says that Colonel Hauke is already arrived. I believe he is very rich and well connected. I've seen him from afar a few times. It was a long while ago, but he made a good impression on me then. In fact, I judged him quite a magnificent specimen of a man.'

'I'm sure, dear,' Isabel humoured her wryly, knowing only too well Rachel was an incurable and persistent matchmaker on her behalf; on the behalf of any unattached lady who found herself in the vicinity of a bachelor of reasonable status and character. 'But only think of the interim in which he has probably deteriorated quite remarkably. Bad teeth, thinning hair…'

'If he *is* balding, you must sell him a pot of your hair restorer. He will propose before the day is out.'

Isabel smiled at that. She had concocted a hair lotion from her physic garden for a new mother in the village. The woman was delighted when her hair loss decreased. Isabel thought it more likely to be due to her health strengthening now the child was being weaned than any miracle cure derived from rosemary and lavender.

Aware that her husband was even now awaiting her presence in the library to welcome to Wolverton Manor one of his oldest friends, Rachel Flinte, Countess of Devane, relinquished her cloak and hat to the waiting footman. With a toss of her golden hair, followed by a pat to subdue several buoyant curls, she was off in the direction of the library.

'Ma'am? It's dinnertime, ma'am. Are you awake?'

The harsh Irish brogue grazed Isabel's dreams, bringing her to bleary consciousness. She blinked herself awake to see Noreen Smith's freckled, frowning face close to hers. With a rub to her heavy eyes, she turned over on to her elbow and gazed at the wall clock. It was close to chiming the hour of eight. Isabel groaned.

Noreen's rusty red brows formed twin arches under which her eyes swivelled. A hiss of caution pushed through her pout. Isabel gleaned from these facial gymnastics that the maidservant deemed her reluctance to dine bad manners.

'Guests, ma'am…from England,' Noreen succinctly explained with a meaningful nod. Noreen was Rachel's servant. She had come overseas with the newly wed Countess of Devane and remained steadfastly loyal to her mistress. Isabel was virtually a stranger to her, although Noreen had served the Meredith family for more than a decade.

'It'll take but a moment to have you ready,' Noreen announced briskly. 'And no need to fret over the young master. He's tired out and in bed. He's been helping my Sam in the stables...' Noreen's lips pressed together. Her husband was too inclined to indulge the fatherless little mite. Busily she tipped warm water into a bowl.

Isabel's blue dimity gown received a shake to disperse the creases as she peered into her closet. Emerald silk was twitched this way and that.

'Your sister has on that new cerise satin,' Noreen volunteered helpfully. 'Sure an' it makes her look like a princess. And Mrs Hauke not long ago arrived with just one maid with her. All wet and windswept, wasn't they, but the lady full of smiles and thanks. Kind and gracious she is, that's what I'm thinking. She's dressed in lavender silk.'

Isabel splashed her complexion with warm water, then held a towel at her face before she looked at her reflection in the small glass on the washstand. Solemnly she inspected unusually pale skin and fragile-looking features. A spiralling curl of unruly beige hair was pushed back from her cheek. Cerise satin would never suit her colouring, and her looks were hardly princess-like. Her sister, Rachel fitted the bill on both counts. She watched the small mouth

in the mirror twist ruefully. So Mrs Hauke was newly
arrived but already dressed and ready to dine. The
woman must be famished! The towel was dropped to
the washstand. 'Rachel is wearing her new pink satin?
Then I'll wear the emerald gown, Noreen.'

'I'm so glad you braved the vile weather Colonel
Hauke, and are arrived in time for dinner. Connor
tells me you have agreed to stay a while. In fact,
Connor has told me much about you.'

'Has he, indeed? I hope most is good.'

'There was nothing bad, I swear,' Rachel laughingly insisted. 'But then I suppose my husband must
be diplomatic lest you retaliate with tales of his misdemeanours.' She slid a flirtatious look into
humorous, deep brown eyes. *Do hurry, Isabel, for
Heaven's sake—he is the most gorgeous man!* raced
through her bubbling mind. 'I suppose there were
some concerning Connor?' At her suave guest's quizzical look, she explained, 'Misdemeanours. No doubt
you and Connor weren't always angels whilst soldier-
ing far from home.'

'Nothing dreadful springs to mind, ma'am, I assure
you,' Etienne smoothly reassured whilst mentally
congratulating himself on telling the truth. Far from
being dreadful, indulging in sin far from home was
usually vastly pleasurable. Nevertheless, changing
the subject seemed expedient as he scanned the lovely

rosy face turned up to his. 'I'm disappointed I missed the wedding.'

'Oh, you weren't alone in that, sir,' Rachel informed him on a shy smile. 'The only people present were Connor and me and two witnesses. Even our parents missed the wedding. But it's a shame you were not able to attend our reception. We held that a few weeks later and it was a perfect occasion. Connor tried to contact you but, alas, you were again abroad.'

Etienne noticed the countess's hands nervously toying with her fan. She was afraid he might mention he recalled her juvenile antics that had rocked polite society. At nineteen she had callously jilted Connor, then six years later, when deemed by all to be on the shelf, she'd agreed to marry the newly ennobled Earl of Devane. Connor had never stopped loving her despite the torment she'd put him through. 'I'm glad…very glad that all turned out so right for you both. At one time it seemed it never would.'

'Yes, for a long, long time it seemed it never would.' Rachel tilted her head to meet his dark eyes watching her closely. Of course this man knew all her momentous romantic history: that she had hurt Connor, brought him to despair. He probably also knew that through those six barren years without Connor she had jilted other men. She couldn't be sure that beneath the colonel's charming exterior he wasn't disgusted and disapproving of his friend's choice of wife. Not that she expected him to like her on such short acquaintance. Yet she felt that after chatting to him for barely twenty minutes she was already on the way to liking him. The colour was beginning to burn in her cheeks, for no reason other than she didn't want Colonel Hauke to judge her on past follies too harshly or too soon. Her gaze focused on the broad muscular chest close by. She found a neutral topic of conversation. 'Why, Colonel Hauke, that waistcoat you have on looks uncommonly similar to one that Connor has. I believe you must have the same tailor. Connor swears Goldman and Stein of Draper's Lane are the finest outfitters in England.'

Etienne glanced down at the figured silk adorning his chest. Then he looked at the woman frowning at it simply because she was embarrassed. It had been arrogant of him eight years ago to think he had the right to meddle because he was Connor's closest friend. And it was sheer luck that Connor and his beloved had not discovered what he'd tried to do. Lady Devane seemed a charming woman; Etienne was beginning to like her. Thank God no harm had been done.

'You're very observant, ma'am. Actually, it is your husband's waistcoat. My packing case is stuck somewhere between here and the Fiddle and Flute. Connor kindly loaned me some clothes so I might appear at dinner dry and uncrumpled.' He opened the black jacket to fully exhibit the pearl-grey waistcoat and the rest of his sartorially splendid muscular frame. 'Everything I stand up in tonight is courtesy of your excellent husband.'

Rachel glanced modestly at the impressive torso on display. Her blush deepened with her involuntary husky laugh. 'And very well it fits and suits you, sir,' she murmured. 'You and Connor are of the same size.'

'What are you flaunting at my wife, Hauke?' Connor demanded teasingly as he crossed the room towards them.

'Just your superb taste in tailoring, Con… what else?'

'Take no notice of what he says, Rachel, he is a philanderer and not to be trusted with the ladies.'

'I think he seems very trustworthy.' Rachel declined her husband's advice with a cheeky smile.

Etienne acknowledged her championship with an inclination of his dark head, a glint of chestnut enriching a lock of hair that slunk on to his forehead. 'Many thanks, my lady.'

'Oh, enough of this *my lady*,' Rachel squeaked, feeling oddly more flirtatious now that her husband was here at her side. She looked about and her eyes settled on Mrs Hauke, comfortably ensconced in a chair by the fire, sipping a glass of sweet ratafia. 'I am going to have a chat with your mother, Colonel, to quiz her over any *on-dits* circulating among the *ton*.

If after a few more minutes my sister is not arrived, I shall go and fetch her down myself before we all expire from hunger.'

'I'm sorry to be late. I'm here now, Rachel,' soothed a melodic voice from behind.

Chapter Two

'How old is your son, Mrs Forrester?'

Isabel carefully put down her soup spoon. 'Just seven, Mrs Hauke.'

'And his name?'

'Marcus.'

'Ah, that's a fine name for a boy. Is Marcus named after his papa? Is he already abed or is he permitted to come downstairs later? I should like to meet him.'

'He is already in bed for he is up early for school in the mornings.' Even now, with many years and many miles separating her from prying eyes and malicious tongues in England, Isabel felt uncomfortable discussing her personal life.

A vague French intonation to Claudine Hauke's voice gave it a husky musical tone. They had chatted over trivialities whilst the first course of game soup was served and Isabel had cheerfully added her complaints to Claudine's concerning the appalling weather they were experiencing. Now the conversation was becoming disconcertingly intimate, although Isabel realised nothing sinister lurked in Claudine's dinner-table chatter. The woman seemed utterly charming and keen to be congenial.

A glance through scintillating candlesticks and spears of flame settled on Connor and Rachel, engrossed in conversation with their urbane guest. Peals of laughter were more frequent than the chime of busy cutlery from that side of the table.

An air of amity was pervading the atmosphere. Isabel anticipated Claudine asking more questions and ruining the harmony. As a diversionary tactic she asked one of her own. 'Are you well acquainted with the Ormondes? Rachel tells me you have been staying with the family. I met them once, about three months ago, just after I arrived in Ireland. I found them agreeable people.'

The Ormondes were the Devanes' neighbours. Lord Ormonde was a widower who lived with his aged mother and two teenage daughters in a vast and draughty fortress. Rachel and Isabel had received an invitation to partake of luncheon with them, but once within Ormonde Castle's perishing walls, had not stayed long enough to dine for fear of risking frostbite before they received one warming morsel.

'Lord Ormonde is a second cousin of my late husband's,' Claudine happily explained. 'When we were married he officiated as one of the ushers. After that we lost touch for a while…until my husband's death following an injury at Waterloo. Vincent attended his funeral. The following year Vincent lost his wife. We have since grown quite close.' Claudine folded elegant hands on the table, preparing to gossip. 'Vincent visits me in Chelsea and brings his daughters to enjoy the season. I think he hopes one—the eldest and comeliest—might eventually attract a husband. We have a nice time together. When one is widowed life can easily become empty and lonely. Of course, you must know that.' Sympathy resonated in her tone. '*C'est tragique* that you should be left with a small son to rear! A boy needs a papa. *Le pauvre petit!* Did your husband succumb to an illness? Was he still young?'

'He was a soldier. Quite young…' Isabel whispered unsteadily, wondering how on earth she had been slack-witted enough to allow the conversation to circle back to her own situation. She quickly, firmly banned any further mention of the subject. 'I'm sorry, I do not like to talk of it.'

'*Naturellement!* So sorry!' Claudine sibilantly whispered. She patted comfortingly on Isabel's slender hand resting on glossy yew. 'Sometimes people like to talk. Vincent likes to talk of his wife and the fine times they shared before her illness—'

'Ormonde likes the sound of his own voice. It seems to be a contagious affliction. I fear you've been spending far too much time with him, *cherie*.'

Startled by the harsh interruption, Claudine eventually choked out a squeak of embarrassed laughter, but her cheeks were rosily tinged beneath her powdery *maquillage*. For all her indignation there was real hurt in her dark, almond-shaped eyes. 'I assure you, *madame* that I intended no offence.' She shot an angry look at her son.

Isabel tilted her head to take a glance past candles at her unexpected champion. She felt shocked, not simply because Colonel Hauke had publicly rebuked his mother and come to her rescue, but because something about his voice seemed familiar.

The Colonel's eyes found Isabel's across the table, and held them with an intensity that kept her transfixed. Slowly his mouth moved; it was a private smile and evoked quite a mix of emotion to roil within Isabel.

Tonight, on being introduced, this man had behaved towards her with impeccable politeness… nothing more. Once seated, Colonel Hauke had glanced at her and smiled courteously, just the once, before resuming his conversation with Rachel. Isabel had felt oddly wounded by his indifference, for on meeting him a wistful feeling had involuntarily taken root in her breast. Rachel was right. He was magnificent; an impressive, imposing man, and a fine catch. He was not lordly, he was not conventionally good-looking, but he was vastly appealing and instinctively she knew women wanted him. And such eligible bachelors were not for her. They were for her sisters. Isabel Forrester, née Meredith, was a woman wreathed in secrets and shadows, as was her son. Such potent men were best ignored lest they caused her to become restless and dissatisfied with her lot. Still, she'd wished the Colonel had looked at her with more interest. Now he was; she had his undivided attention and a frisson of excitement came tempered with nervousness.

Earlier, when Connor had taken her and his wife into dinner, Isabel had watched the broad, elegantly clad back of Colonel Hauke leading his mother to dine. Suddenly she had felt the humiliating burden of her sister and brother-in-law's generosity. Not only were she and her son allowed to freely board and lodge beneath their roof but, on an occasion such as this, Rachel would also share her wonderful husband with her younger sister, so Isabel could briefly imagine how it felt to be cherished, protected and loved by a fine gentleman. Why it should rankle so this evening, when usually she allowed Connor's solicitude barely to unsettle her, she could not say.

Her eyes dropped away from that earth-dark gaze trained on her. 'Are you acquainted with the Fitzge-

ralds, Mrs Hauke?' Isabel pleasantly enquired, signalling gracious forgiveness. 'I have become quite
friendly with Clodagh Fitzgerald and her brother
Liam. They have a dairy farm to the north of here.'

After dinner Isabel stationed herself alone by the
French windows. She gazed into the blackness, and
was not at all surprised to hear footsteps cracking
closer over polished boards. Her heart beat uncomfortably fast, yet obliquely she realised she had separated from the others in the hope he might come
over and speak privately to her.

'I'm sorry about that.'

'I'm not sure why, sir. I don't recall you behaving
in a way that warrants an apology.' Isabel chewed at
her bottom lip, immediately regretting her petulance.
She had sought to be solitary, sensing it would lure
him. Now she was being silly in regretting her ploy's
effectiveness and churlish in abusing his good
manners. He wasn't obliged to apologise for his
mother's inquisitiveness when the woman herself had
already done so.

She remained staring through glass at spectral
shrubbery silhouetted by a full moon's silvery bloom.
The knot of tension lodged in her breast tightened
mercilessly.

The Colonel lounged back against the doorframe
to one side of her. She had but to shift her gaze a

fraction to look into his tough, hard-boned face or run a shy eye over that solid, athletic physique. She wanted to look at him. He had a face that was intriguing, kept one looking long after etiquette deemed it polite.

His features were rugged, savaged by the elements, not conventionally handsome by any means. He was not Adonis-like as was Connor, with his raven hair and beautifully proportioned and symmetrical face. But the Colonel had an equally commanding presence that had kept her mesmerised like a fool when they had been first introduced. It was the slight amusement skewing his sensual mouth as she stood entranced, her hand still in his, that had finally jolted her to her senses and speedily sent her, chagrined, to the opposite side of the dining table to claim a seat close to his mother.

'You looked, still look, as though my mother might have upset you. She has a tendency to be tactlessly prying.' The Colonel's tone was cool and crisp. He was acknowledging her chilly reception.

'I took no offence, I assure you.' Isabel managed a conciliatory smile. He must think her moodiness odd. It wasn't his fault that, after barely a few hours in his company, she found him…unsettling. She added lightly, 'I like your mother; even on such a short acquaintance. I believe she sincerely wants to show sympathy for others' misfortune.'

That comment elicited a sardonic laugh from him. 'She would far rather concentrate on a stranger's calamities than her own, it's true. Have we met before?'

Startled, Isabel looked properly at him. 'No…why do you say that?' With her heart suddenly racing, she wondered if he had sensed, as she had, an odd hint of something familiar. She knew it was ridiculous; if this man came into one's life, the memory of it ought be indelible.

He shrugged. 'I thought when your sister and Connor were engaged years ago we might have come into contact socially.'

Imperceptibly Isabel relaxed. 'I don't recall such an occasion.'

He smiled. 'Neither do I and I would, I'm sure.'

'You're too kind, sir,' Isabel shot back with just a trace of acid sharpening the honey of her tone. It still rankled that earlier he had virtually overlooked her. She shifted her gaze back to the window, hoping he would go now…no, hoping she could make him stay, just a while longer. A thirst for his calm, debonair person had parched her throat. Besides, a stubborn desire to keep him there so she could match his insouciance was bedevilling her. Talking about the food they had eaten seemed an obvious mundane topic. So she remarked on the diversity of the courses, informing him of the way that neighbours shared produce. He readily agreed that dinner had been exceedingly fine and a cooperative attitude amongst farmers was a most welcome and sensible situation.

Isabel liked listening to his drawling baritone voice; it had a slightly somnolent quality. But it was cultured English, very different from Claudine's intonation. She found another topic of conversation. 'Your mother has a very pleasant French accent, sir. Was your father French, too?'

The Colonel gave her a rueful smile, then a concise account of his lineage. 'No. He was an English captain in the Kings Own Dragoons. My mother was born into the French nobility…hard to believe, I know, when she displays such common inquisitiveness. Her father was a count and she was fortunate to find herself on the right side of the Channel when the French Revolution began. Naturally she accepted refuge with those English friends who had been her hosts. Her mother, father and brother, together with numerous aunts, uncles and cousins, were lost to the guillotine. I never knew any of them.'

Isabel was momentarily stunned into openly staring at him. Her eyes clung to his impassive profile in amazement and sympathy.

Etienne's eyes swooped to hers and were equally arrested. On first meeting her he'd been surprised by her sweet, ethereal looks. Connor had mentioned earlier that his wife's widowed sister and nephew were staying with them and, for some reason, he had imagined her to be a pleasant, matronly young woman. Isabel Forrester was anything but that. Despite some sense of recognition niggling at the back of his mind, what dominated his thoughts was that he could not possibly have met this woman before and not remembered the occasion. He would never forget such an exquisite face…those lovely eyes. He told himself that the most likely explanation was that he'd seen her likeness somewhere. The inner vision he couldn't dispel was of a solemn sylph with a garland of ivy calming her curls, reposing in a halcyon woodland glade with elves and fairies scattered about her tiny feet. It was probably a book illustration he'd appreciated. The graceful nymph he was now discreetly admiring had replaced the garland of greenery with a green ribbon that almost matched the colour of her entrancing eyes. Tresses that looked too luxuriant to be tamed with just one thin strip of emerald satin were confined at her nape in a coil as thick as his fist. The colour of her hair was unusual, a shade that merged brown and gold to give a fair shade of tan.

He had been impressed by her sister's looks. This woman was equally as beautiful, but very different. The Countess of Devane's china-blue eyes and golden hair would find immediate favour with most red-blooded males if they could draw their eyes from her lush figure. Isabel Forrester had a more subtle allure: petite, willowy…almost too slender. But her silk gown had a disturbing tendency to sway and cling in exactly the right places as she moved.

When Connor had informed him earlier in the day that his sister-in-law was rearing her son on her own, an unusual gravity to his friend's tone had conveyed that no further information would be forthcoming. Etienne had respectfully heeded that tacit warning and the subject was closed. Perhaps he should have taken it upon himself to caution his mother not to probe. In a purely selfish way he was glad she had, for now he knew a little more about Isabel Forrester. She had a son of seven years of age and her husband had been a soldier.

From her son's age he guessed she would have been married at least approaching eight years ago. Thus she must have married young, perhaps at about the time of Connor and Rachel's aborted nuptials. When had her husband died? Recently? No. She would still be in her widow's weeds. He wanted to know more, and a wry inner smile acknowledged the unseemly inquisitiveness he had condemned in his mother. Why did any of it matter to him? Soon he would be in Mayfair with other women to think about. He had a passionate mistress and a prospective wife awaiting his arrival.

Etienne's introspection was interrupted by a softly horrified voice. 'You have lost so many relatives to the Terror! That's awful.'

'I never knew them. They were quitting this life just as I arrived in it. My father's parents are still thriving. I have one set of grandparents.' There was a flash of rueful humour softening his eyes as he murmured, 'Sometimes I think they're more than enough kin to be getting along with.' After a pause he said, 'But I should have liked to know my French family.'

'Yes, of course!' Isabel agreed earnestly. 'It is not right that a child be deprived of his relatives.'

'At dinner your sister was saying that she misses England and her friends and family there.' Etienne angled a look at the Earl and Countess of Devane chatting with his mother on a settee drawn close to blazing logs. 'I imagine the Earl might be persuaded to go to London for the season. Will you go too?'

Isabel shrugged in a passably casual way. 'Ireland suits me very well. If my sister and her husband do go to England, I might stay here a while.' She was aware of dark eyes watching, of the silence indicating he was waiting for her to explain such an odd declaration. Why on earth would she stay at her brother-in-law's residence, far from home and family, once her sister was gone? She felt obliged to offer an explanation and then wished she had remained quiet. 'My son is at school in the village. I should not like to disrupt his studies. He has made friends…and some progress…' she added weakly.

'He attends a local village school?' Isabel was aware of the subdued surprise in his tone. Her status as sister-in-law to an earl would make most people assume her son enjoyed enough reflected privilege to be instructed by a good tutor at home until he was despatched to a reputable boarding school. That would be customary for the nephew of a wealthy gentleman.

Etienne watched her expression, watched her nervous hands smooth along her silk gown in a way that tautened emerald silk across her thighs. It was all the more erotic for being innocent and unconscious. She was agitated. Possibly that was due to the fact that it embarrassed her to admit she could not afford a proper education for her son. Perhaps her husband had died and left her in a parlous financial state. She didn't look shabby genteel: her clothes were superb. He knew of old that Connor could be altruistic. With his wife's sister he would be unstintingly, unconditionally generous. If she wanted her son educated, Flinte would pay without a qualm. And where was her father in all this? Edgar Meredith was surely comfortably off. Should he not be supporting his grandson? If the boy was being taught locally he was probably hobnobbing with the offspring of the lower middle-classes or tenant farmers; people with intelligence enough to desire for their children more than they had scratched from life, yet they were hardly his peers.

* * *

'It is an age since we sat down to dine together, then when we do you tell me off for a conversation. So, I shall try to stay quiet and please you. What have you been doing, *cheri?* And where are you next going? Am I invited to come and stay at Redgrave Park with you?'

Etienne acknowledged his mother's blunt interruption with a chill smile. 'You must try harder than that, *Maman,* if you sincerely wish to please me. No, you can't come to Redgrave Park. I'm not yet returning to Suffolk. I have business in the city. If you're at a loose end, perhaps Vincent might like you to stay a while in Ireland,' he suggested caustically.

A Gallic shrug contoured Claudine's elegant white shoulders. '*Peut-être;* but this Ireland is so cold and wet. Sleet…snow…rain…gales and all in the one day.' She slanted a crafty look at her son from beneath lowered lashes. 'Perhaps I know why you are going first to London. Is it business concerning a certain Miss Caroline Greenwood?' Claudine sent Isabel a conspiratorial look. 'Before I left Chelsea I heard a rumour. I hope you are not expecting your *maman* to scour the *gazettes* to find out for sure. Are you to publicly announce your engagement soon, *mon fils?* If so, I must tell your sister. Monique will be cross if she hears of it second-hand or reads it in *The Times.*'

Clearly annoyed that his private business was

being discussed, Etienne shoved back the thick chestnut hair that flopped close to his eyes. A flinty look encompassed Isabel. She automatically smiled at him in a dazed way.

'Should I decide to get married, you will be among the first to know, *cherie,* I promise.'

For a moment Isabel was sure he was about to immediately excuse himself. An impatient stride had already taken him away from her. He hesitated, then angled a look at her. 'Connor tells me I must stay a while to keep you company. Do you like to ride?'

Had Isabel not been stunned on learning this man was virtually betrothed, she would have felt very insulted by such blunt honesty. But she simply replied, 'Yes, I like to ride.'

'Good; tomorrow we should take the air together.' With that and a neat bow he walked away.

Chapter Three

'Sam says he didn't have no learnin', 'cos a groom don't need no learnin' 'cept about nourishing horses and doctoring their aches and pains. I want to work with Sam. So why do I need to be learnt?'

Isabel closed her eyes in exasperation at her young son's excruciating pronouncement. Marcus was spending too much time with Sam Smith, yet how could she deny him the happiness he gained from the groom's company? Her lonely son idolised any man who showed him a little time and affection.

The cockney groom's wife, fetching coats and hats, pursed her lips in vexation on hearing her spouse's rough wisdom repeated. Not that Marcus was fibbing; Noreen had been regaled with the same blunt theories on book-learning from her husband. With her cheeks flaming red enough to rival her hair, Noreen promised herself that, like it or not, Sam Smith would get a lesson himself later, when she had him alone.

'You will go to school, Marcus, and you will put on your coat and button it through. It's cold outside despite the sunshine.'

Marcus met his mother's instructions with a sulky glower, then glanced at Noreen, hoping for an ally. Noreen kept her face averted and her eyes concealed behind ginger lashes.

'And I have a headache.' Marcus pressed a small hand to his brow in a way his mother might solicitously do when he complained of feeling poorly.

'Put on your coat, Marcus,' Isabel ordered, trying to slide one of his evasive arms into a sleeve. 'Goodness! Do we have to have this very pantomime so often? If you refuse to attend Father Maguire's school, I shall have to get Mr O'Dare to come and teach you again at home.' The threat lacked conviction. The gaunt-faced nervous tutor she had employed shortly after their arrival in Ireland was unlikely to agree to come back. The man had seemed as intimidated by her boisterous, demanding son as he had seemed impressed at the prospect of tutoring the Earl of Devane's nephew. The only reason the man had persevered with the *unruly child* was because Connor paid him more than the going rate.

'I shall just run away again if you bring him back. I told you I don't like sums!' Marcus snarled.

'Hello, who is this young man who might run away rather than do his sums?' teased an amused, accented voice.

Isabel smiled distractedly at Claudine Hauke as the woman descended the gracious sweep of oaken stairs. Claudine was garbed in a bottle-green riding habit cut from fine velvet and edged in sable. Its excellent style neatly hugged her figure. For a woman possibly past fifty she had an enviably girlish shape, Isabel thought as she watched the French woman settle a matching hat atop her head and secure the strings. Mrs Hauke obviously had the wherewithal to purchase herself beautiful clothes.

Claudine approached Marcus with a curious smile. The boy looked back with a similarly inquisitive expression.

'Say hello to Mrs Hauke, Marcus,' Isabel instructed as she led him gently closer to their guest.

Claudine inclined towards the boy to scan his solemn fair face for a few moments. 'So! At last we meet. Where have you been hiding, young man? For days I have been looking forward to seeing you.' Claudine straightened and looked at Isabel. 'He is so beautiful and very like my grandchildren. My daughter, Monique, has twins: a boy and a girl just turned three years old. Sophie's hair is as blond…' one of Claudine's hands ruffled Marcus's fine flaxen mop '…and Phillipe's eyes are as round and bright but all brown, not tinged with green as are yours, young man. Neither do they yet spark with such mischief. But he can be a proper scamp, so his mama says. Are you off to school now, Marcus?'

Marcus kept his features mutinous a moment longer. A smile suddenly smoothed the pucker between his brows. 'Yes, ma'am,' he said politely.

'*C'est très bien.* A young chap must be good and learn his lessons, then one day he shall lead a useful life.'

'Grooms are useful. Horses think so.'

'Indeed,' his mother gently concurred. 'But first a groom must go to school in case…in case he changes his profession and wishes instead to study law or medicine. He might even decide to be a banker in the city like his grandpapa.'

'My grandpapa doesn't like me so I shan't be a banker. Perhaps I might be a sailor,' Marcus chirped up, shoving his arms helpfully into his coat and obediently buttoning the garment. 'Sam says he would have liked to be a Jack Tar who went to war on the *Victory* and killed lots of horrid Frenchies.'

'Your grandpapa does like you,' Isabel huskily corrected. She grimaced at Claudine in a way that conveyed her embarrassment and apologised for her son's gauche xenophobic remark.

Claudine merely shrugged off the insult to her countrymen. 'You are a good patriotic boy, Marcus.

I have little liking myself for a lot of those Frenchies.' The woman's voice was gruff with emotion and Isabel recalled what Colonel Hauke had told her about his mother's family being assassinated by insurgents. It didn't seem the right time to offer condolences.

'Come along now,' Noreen diplomatically broke into the silence and chivvied her young charge. 'If we're not soon away you'll be late for registration, so y'will, Master Marcus. The coach is waiting. You won't want to be late, at all. The Father will be cross, so he will.'

Isabel stooped, managed to skim a kiss against her son's fine fair hair as he whisked past. 'Be good!' A mother's anxious call followed his small figure as it hurtled down the steps. Samuel Smith helped Marcus to climb aboard his uncle's sumptuous coach.

'He's a lucky boy to arrive at school in such style,' Claudine remarked lightly, seeming recovered from her melancholy.

'Yes…most of the other pupils walk.'

'I am surprised…' Claudine tactfully curtailed her observation.

Isabel knew she meant to say she was surprised that her son attended such an establishment at all.

After a short pause Claudine concluded, 'Marcus could learn his lessons at home, *non?*'

'He did for a while. He…it didn't suit him. He is easily bored. It's best he is with his friends.'

'He looks like his papa,' Claudine stated softly.

Isabel swished about to dart a startled glance at Claudine. 'What makes you say that?' she demanded in a single breath.

'He doesn't look like you, although he is fair and handsome with green in his eyes,' Claudine reasoned. 'I suspect he has his father's face. Am I right? Does he resemble his papa?'

'I imagine he does,' Isabel admitted faintly.

Claudine Hauke gave a soft laugh. 'I have learnt my lesson and shall stop now. No more unseemly inquisitiveness or my son will again tell me off. He quite gave me the megrims the night we arrived with such a cruel set-down. I have the ache here still.' She rubbed a small hand across her brow. 'A brisk ride in the fresh air always blows out the cobwebs. He is to meet me at the stables before breakfast. It looks a glorious morning. Will you join us today?'

'No…thank you,' Isabel quickly refused the offer, as she had every other offer to ride. The Haukes had been guests now for several days but still a residue of indignation lingered that Colonel Hauke might feel obliged to spend time with her. Isabel more closely examined Claudine. The woman did look rather pale. 'I can prepare you a headache remedy, if you like.'

'Are you a herbalist, Isabel?' Claudine enquired with a final press to the crease between her eyes.

'I have always been interested in herbal cures and

my mother was grateful for my tending to the physic garden when I lived at home at Windrush. It is a useful plot when one has a family of four girls and a deal of female complaints as well as usual aches and pains.'

'In France, once upon a time, dispensing such cures brought one under suspicion of witchcraft.' Claudine clucked her tongue. 'That was a silly story to bring to your attention! Of course, we are all now more civilised about such things.'

'I know it's true. But for a century or so separating me from such ignorance, I might have been branded and burned at the stake.' Isabel delivered the comment with good humour.

'On that terrifying note I think I must leave you.' Claudine pulled on her leather gloves, smoothing them with long strokes. She glanced about the hallway. 'Have you seen my son this morning?' At Isabel's quick shake of the head, the French woman added, 'I suppose I should venture outside; he might already be waiting for me in the stables and get cross and ride off if he has to kick his heels too long on my account.'

Isabel hadn't seen Claudine's son this morning. But she had at dinner yesterday evening when he again asked her to join him on a morning constitutional. She had no intention of letting arrogant Colonel Hauke— the conceit of the man!—escort or entertain her during his week-long sojourn in Ireland with his friend.

Besides, today Isabel had a perfectly reasonable excuse to decline the Haukes' invitation to ride with them: she had already made arrangements to accompany Clodagh to Waterford should market day turn out dry. Against all odds, it had. She went to the large vestibule window to examine the landscape and scour the skies. It was while she was contemplating the vagaries of the Irish climate that the Colonel appeared.

Without once turning her head to look properly at him, Isabel was aware of him leisurely descending the stairs almost as soon as one mirror-bright boot hit the top tread. She knew that one of his hands was gliding along the banister while the other grasped a riding crop close to a buff-breeched leg. She knew that his dark brown hair was tinted auburn by slanting sunbeams entering through the high hall windows. She knew exactly the moment he became aware of her motionless presence half-screened by the deep window embrasure. She gazed sightlessly through glass, pondering whether to remain where she was, engrossed in the scenery, thus presenting him with an opportunity to discreetly take evasive action. She held her ground. Let him choose.

Within a moment he had joined her in the stone recess. A lean hand lounged, close to her head, against the window's sturdy frame. He greeted her with a polite, 'Good morning.'

Isabel felt her stomach flip at his closeness and hated herself for it. She was acting like an excited schoolgirl with a silly crush, not a woman in her mid-twenties with a seven-year old son and no desire to ever again be in thrall to a man. Especially one whose betrothal was soon to be announced, she wryly reminded herself. She politely returned his greeting; a congenial smile accompanied it for good measure. Then when the silence lengthened and they both appeared fascinated by clouds scudding at some speed across a washed winter sky, Isabel felt a betraying rush of colour to her cheeks. She felt annoyed with herself for again being far too conscious of his presence. A moment ago she had stolen a fleeting glance at him and held her breath in an instinctive response to his appearance. It was ridiculous!

'Your mother has just gone to the stables to meet you.' The comment was casually delivered. 'She was anxious not to keep you waiting, in case you got impatient and made off alone.'

'I see; she's made me sound like some sort of grumpy ogre.'

'No, not at all.' Isabel was keen not to exacerbate any tension that existed between mother and son. She had sensed on several occasions that all was not harmonious between them.

He said nothing, but another furtive glance at his profile showed her that a smile was tilting the edge of his lips. She guessed it was a reaction to her diplomacy, her instinctive desire to be nice. Perhaps immediate compliance was something he took for granted in people. But she wasn't one of his foot soldiers!

She turned to him fully, challengingly. 'Is your mother correct? Are you a grumpy ogre, Colonel Hauke?'

'Sometimes…' he agreed impenitently, with a thoughtful nod. Humour was apparent in his voice and made her bridle further.

Isabel glanced back through the window, no more than a lift of her finely drawn brows deigning to respond to that.

'Don't you want to know when that is or why?'

'When? Why?' Isabel obliged him, honeying her tone with irony.

'It's when I can't get my own way. And it's because I'm disappointed about something. As I am now.'

'Are you expecting me to want you to explain?'

'Of course.'

'Please explain,' she duly said, all sweetness.

'In a moment, if I ask you if you'll come riding with me, you'll decline again and leave me feeling that I haven't got my own way and that I'm disappointed. It's probably best that I don't ask.'

Isabel subdued a smile. 'Please don't take the Earl's instruction to spend time with me too seriously, sir. I'd hate your attempts at chivalry to become an ordeal...for us both.'

'I knew I shouldn't have said that. It was quite definitely a stupid utterance. It's true your brother-in-law asked me to keep you and my mother company this week but that's not why I'm asking. I'm asking for me, not for him. I'd like you to ride with me.'

'I'm sorry; I have other arrangements already made for this morning.'

'Which are?'

'You really are quite alarmingly unseemly in your persistence, Colonel Hauke. If you must know, I am meeting a friend. It is market day in Waterford and we are going shopping.'

'It's still early; there's plenty of time for shopping later.'

'Did your mother never teach you, sir, that you should accept rejection philosophically and gracefully?'

'Is that what you teach your son?'

Isabel's flirtatious smile faltered and she turned away from him. A silence laden with tension terminated with a whispered, 'Yes, that's what I tell him.'

'Where is he?'

'He's just left for school.'

'I'm sorry I missed him. I know you're not up and dressed at this ungodly hour to see me off on a morning gallop. Do you see him off to school every day?'

'Yes, of course.'

'Yes, of course…' the Colonel repeated softly.

'Is there something wrong with that?' Isabel demanded defensively.

'No, nothing at all is wrong with that. I should have liked it had my mother seen me off to school. Once or twice a year as I was packed off to board would have sufficed. You're a good mother, obviously.' It was a statement requiring no response and, with a curt bow of his dark head and a shove of a hand that propelled him sharply back from the window, he was gone.

Isabel was still standing there, feeling confused, when Connor and Rachel joined her. Her brother-in-law, as usual, looked darkly handsome in riding clothes and her sister epitomised elegance in her navy blue outfit with gold buttons and fancy braid frogging.

'Go ahead and saddle Willow for me, I want to have a chat with Bella. I've hardly seen her in days,' Rachel told her dashing husband.

Isabel could tell from Rachel's purposeful look what was coming next and pre-empted her with a casual, 'Yes, Colonel Hauke is attractive, yes, he is quite charming and, yes, I think he would make a good catch. Which is just as well for a certain Miss Caroline Greenwood. His mother let slip earlier in the week that he is on the verge of proposing to her.'

Rachel groaned. 'Not her! Heavens! I wonder if Connor knows? He's not said.'

'Connor might not have thought it worth mentioning,' Isabel suggested. 'Why do you say "her" like that?'

'Oh she's so…so insipid and her parents, especially her mother—who, by the by, looks like a horse, and not a thoroughbred at that—are quite awful social climbers. It is well known that Mrs Greenwood is title-digging for Caroline. I'll be surprised if he marries her. I think he has better taste.'

Isabel shrugged, but privately hoped Rachel was right. Why would such a man need to marry into a vulgar family? Unless… 'Perhaps he is in love,' she mentioned over her shoulder as she went to fetch her coat and hat from the hall chair.

Rachel gave a snort of laughter. 'Well, if he is, I must have misjudged his character. Her family have money…lots of it…from coal, I think. But Connor says Hauke has pots of the stuff himself and more to come when his uncle and his grandfather pass on. He is due to inherit from both.'

Isabel tied the strings of her bonnet beneath her chin. 'Title-digger? What title is Mrs Greenwood expecting to excavate? The Colonel's wife?'

'When he inherits from his grandfather he becomes an earl and the old chap is in his eighties.' After a pause Rachel said, 'I think Colonel Hauke seems particularly taken with you. Every evening you chat together or play chess. Has he been flirting with you?'

'No. We just find things to talk about.' At Rachel's arch look, Isabel laughingly elaborated. 'For instance, that first night we started talking because he wanted to apologise for his mother's inquisitiveness about Marcus and my husband.'

'That *was* a little indecorous. But I'm sure there was no malice in it. Had I imagined she might press you about…that I would not have asked her here.'

'No harm was done.'

'It always looks as though he is flirting with you,' Rachel persisted. 'When you are together he seems quite…intense.'

Isabel simply smiled neutrally. He hadn't flirted with her last night, or any night, but he had this morning…most definitely. And she had flirted back, even knowing he was a man with a fiancée in the wings and no proper interest in her. And that should worry her. But it didn't. For the first time since she had been with Marcus's father, she'd enjoyed and responded to a man's attention, however lightly given, however insincere.

But she'd been propositioned recently. Not that she expected Colonel Hauke to present her with anything so explicitly vulgar as his protection. He was the Earl of Devane's friend; Connor was married to her sister. A liaison between them would be in extreme bad taste. And, she thought on an inner smile to lift her spirits, she couldn't credit her own conceit.

She had not yet known the man for one whole week. All the Colonel had done was flirt with her for a little while and she was girding herself to rebuff his advances. But then, should they come...*would* she rebuff them?

Chapter Four

Isabel was softly humming, tipping her purchases out of her basket onto the bed when Noreen tapped at her door. At the instruction to enter the servant did so and handed Isabel a note.

'It's from Mrs Hauke, ma'am.' The explanation was rushed and the Irish woman seemed keen to absent herself.

'Noreen?'

A few reluctant steps brought the flush-faced servant once more over the threshold.

'Marcus is not in his room or in the nursery. Is he studying in the library?'

'Ah…I think he's…umm…he's most likely after being in the stables with Sam,' Noreen mumbled. 'I saw him heading that way.'

'Did Marcus say how he did at school today?'

Noreen's freckles were concealed by fierce florridity. 'No, ma'am. But the Father did say a sermon when I arrived to fetch him home. I was going to tell you in a while…after you'd had time to catch breath.' Noreen's pale blue eyes slanted at Isabel's bonnet still atop her thick fawn hair. 'That little devil Michael Murphy is a bad sort is what I'm thinking, begging your pardon for boldly saying so, ma'am. But after that day when he took your son away to town in that bad weather, and me nearly mad and tearing out me hair with wondering where he'd got to… The Father says the two of them were down by the wharf this afternoon, fishing. Young master 'ud be best off keeping his distance from that Murphy boy. Himself is sure to be coming over to see you about it all.'

Isabel looked at the note in her hand. 'Thank you, Noreen,' was all she said as she dismissed the servant. She closed her eyes and sank her small teeth painfully into her lower lip. Noreen had just let her know in no uncertain terms that she thought her son was lacking elementary discipline and she was lacking in parental duty.

Disciplining Marcus by sending him to his room was no use. When she had locked him in he had escaped via his bedroom window, risking serious injury in the process. She didn't ever seriously contemplate corporal punishment or banishing him to bed without his dinner. She couldn't bear the thought of him hurt or hungry.

She picked up the bag of candies she'd chosen for him, folded the top over, imprisoning the treats, and put the bag in a drawer. She had enjoyed her day. She had even forgotten about Colonel Hauke for a while, although she couldn't fathom why the wretched man should so dominate her thoughts on such short acquaintance.

With a sigh Isabel looked at the note still clasped in her hand and broke the wafer. Claudine's neatly scripted message politely requested a remedy for her headache, if it was not too much of an imposition, for the pain was still plaguing her.

Isabel had the necessary ingredients to hand. Going to a cupboard, she extracted some dark glass jars and took a little from each. Lavender, willow bark and vervain were each carefully measured. Folding the grainy powder into scraps of paper, Isabel thrust those into her skirt pocket. She was about to quit the room when she remembered her bonnet still tied beneath her chin. With a dispirited sigh she removed it, tossing it on to the bed before she closed the door and made for the East Wing.

Claudine answered her light tap within a moment, then went to flop back on her bed. Isabel looked at her with a worried frown. Quickly she dropped to her knees and chafed Claudine's cold hands. 'Has the pain worsened since this morning?'

Claudine nodded, keeping her eyes lowered, then

abruptly stood up. 'No. It is something else. I have a
pain, but I think it is squeezing my heart rather than
my head. This is so awkward for me. I do not know
where to begin. We barely know each other, yet I
must speak to you of a very personal thing and I know
now you do not like to talk of your bereavement.
Perhaps if I show you something… Oh, I don't know,'
she suddenly cried and her small hands cupped her
face. 'You will think me a fool if what I suspect is
wrong. *C'est incroyable!*' She again sank to the bed.

Isabel bent close to Claudine, shocked by the
woman's very real distress. Her elegant chignon had
loosened and strands of silvered hair were trailing her
wan cheeks. The hands concealing her face were all
a-tremble too. 'I think now you must explain what ails
you.' At Claudine's mournful look, glistening up
between tear-spiky lashes, Isabel smiled encouragingly.

Claudine pulled close an ornate walnut box and
lifted the lid. Within reposed a neat sewing set.
Coloured threads and small scissors and needles were
ranged neatly. Isabel saw, too, a gilt-framed miniature
nestling on the silks. Claudine gently, reverently lifted
out the painting and proffered it.

The portrait was of a solemn-faced child, blond
and beautiful; the likeness to Isabel's son was remarkable. She smiled at Claudine. 'You are right,
Mrs Hauke. One of your grandchildren is the image

of Marcus. This then must be…Phillipe. The grave expression he wears! So like Marcus in a mood.'

'That is not Phillipe…or Sophie. It is Etienne's portrait, painted over twenty-five years ago. He was about six years old.'

The information caused Isabel to freeze. It was a long, long time since she'd heard that name, but it never would quit that secret corner of her mind and still had the power to wound her.

'Etienne?' she queried in a whisper.

'Etienne…my son. He sometimes calls himself Steven, merely to annoy me, I think, for he knew I preferred the French version of his name. Even when he was little he would do all in his power to vex me.'

'Colonel Hauke? His name is Etienne?' Isabel forced out from a mouth so dry her tongue seemed welded to her palate. Stop being so dull! she told herself crossly. Etienne is a very common French name. Colonel Hauke has French blood. Why should that matter to me? Yet her mind clung to the news, absorbed it, refused to surrender it.

Struggling to display calm and reason, she said, 'There certainly is a likeness to Marcus. But fair children seem similar, don't you think? The features are so tiny it is hard to discern any important little differences—'

'I must tell you something,' Claudine cut into Isabel's calm reasoning. 'You can think I am being *stupide,* you can tell me to mind my own business, but I have been worrying so since I came back earlier. I had caught my gown on a bramble and was going to mend it,' she obliquely explained her seeking the sewing box. 'I found this picture beneath the green silks. Yesterday I could not even tell you where I had left this or when I last looked upon it.' A faint smile preceded, 'I am not one for doing the mending. Marie does such tasks. But today my maid is gone to market and not yet back so I decided to... Oh, it doesn't matter about that! It is fate that I should find it today of all days. The very same day I meet your Marcus.'

'I don't understand.' Isabel murmured, her heart hammering.

Claudine sat down, with a weary sigh, on the bed. 'First I must tell you a little of our history. My late husband, Etienne's father, and I...we did not have a happy marriage. It was simply a convenient arrangement: I was in England, visiting a school friend, when the Bastille was stormed. I was just eighteen, the daughter of a French count and I could not return home for fear of being incarcerated with the rest of my family. I needed proper protection and Benjamin, for his own reasons, needed a wife to please his father. So we married without any love, just a little respect and desperation.'

Claudine smiled sadly then said, 'Of course things rarely improve in such circumstances. It was wrong but inevitable that we would both soon seek comfort elsewhere. I was unfaithful first I'm ashamed to say. Benjamin also found someone to love. Mrs Smith was a young widow…or so she claimed. I think she was a professional courtesan who had never been near a church. She had a child by Benjamin, a boy, just a year after Etienne was born legitimately of our union. A mutual friend once told me that the bastard son and the legitimate son were so alike they might have been twins. By the time Etienne was thirteen he was my boy…dark-haired and quite French in looks. I heard that Mrs Smith's son stayed blond into adulthood. I have to know, please forgive me for asking, but I cannot get it from my mind that you might have married my husband's illegitimate son. Was your husband's name Christopher? You said he was a soldier. Christopher joined the army. When my husband refused to divorce me and marry her Mrs Smith moved far away, close to York, I learned, and married a man there. His name might have been Forrester.'

Isabel was numb with shock. She had listened intently, yet felt that she had missed vital information. Slowly she focused on Claudine and said, 'No, my son's father was not called Christopher. I hope that puts your mind at rest.'

Claudine visibly relaxed. 'I'm so sorry to have bothered you with it all.' A sheepish look accompanied the apology. 'But the portrait, the likeness, your sister told me you lived in York…it is all quite a rare and strange coincidence, is it not?'

Isabel forced a smile through stiff lips. 'Yes; quite an odd coincidence.' Her mind felt in turmoil, yet somehow she remembered the powder and extracted it from her pocket. 'I'll fetch some hot water to mix this and make you a brew.'

Claudine brightened. 'I think I might not need it after all. I feel better now I have got that off my chest.' A light sigh stressed her relief. 'Your sister tells me she has arranged an impromptu dinner party. Vincent and his daughters are to dine here tonight and some other people…the Fitzgeralds. They are the people you like, *non?*' Humming, she went to the closet and opened it, head tilted in consideration of the gowns within.

Isabel barely noticed the dresses pulled out for her to view; her eyes were once again with the small portrait. She picked it up and asked hoarsely, 'May I borrow this, Mrs Hauke? I think some people might like to see it. I will return it soon.'

'*Bien sûr!* And, please, no more Mrs Hauke. Now we have talked so intimately I think we are friends, *non?*' Claudine twirled about with a damson silk gown held against her slender body. Her pencilled eyebrows shot up questioningly.

'It's lovely.' The bright compliment flowed in her wake as Isabel quit the room.

* * *

Dusk was falling; what light remained was nebulous and deceiving, but adequate for her to know the likeness was true.

Isabel was standing by the window in her bedroom. Obsessively she once more turned the miniature to face the glass to absorb the twilight. She stared at each tiny feature in turn until not only were they imprinted on her agitated mind, but so too was every faint flake and fissure in the painted canvas. Her heart was thudding a slow tattoo beneath her ribs when finally she lay the portrait on her bed. Still she could not let go of it and as she circled back and forth between her clothes press, the chest of drawers and the washstand, her eyes were invariably locked with two brown dots that gleamed between black fringes. They seemed to follow her, mock her. She would never have guessed it to be Etienne Hauke's portrait. The man looked nothing like his child's self. Had she once met Christopher, his half-brother? Would he have masqueraded as Etienne? If so, why?

She washed automatically and was towelling her face when Noreen knocked at her door. The maid seemed in better spirits than when Isabel had spoken to her earlier. 'Faith! You're in the dark, ma'am.' Immediately Noreen went about, lighting tapers and lamps. The heavy curtains were closed against the residue of daylight.

On learning from the maid that Marcus was fed, bathed and in his nightclothes, Isabel felt a pang of guilt that since returning from Claudine's room she had barely given a thought to her own flesh and blood. Her whole attention was focused on the lifeless impostor on her bed. She sat at her mirror, allowed Noreen to dress her hair then help her step into her newest gown. It was cream muslin sprigged with apricot rosebuds. She knew it was stylish and suited her colouring, but how she looked seemed unimportant tonight. The appearance of the visage in the portrait dominated her thoughts.

Noreen chattered to her about this evening's little party, informing her in her broad Irish brogue that the Ormondes had already arrived an hour too early, sending Miss Rachel into a spin. Isabel was barely listening. As her hair was brushed in soothing strokes she relaxed. Perhaps she had been affected by Claudine's hysteria. Perhaps what was needed was a more objective opinion on the portrait. Abruptly she said, 'What do you think of the little picture on my bed, Noreen?'

Noreen looked a trifle surprised, poised as she was to defeat some rebellious curls. She put down the silver-backed brush and did as she was bid.

'Mother Mary! Now isn't that the look he wears?' Noreen grimaced in a fair approximation of the expression she was scrutinising. 'Sure an' I'm amazed you got Master Marcus to stay still long enough for it to be painted. He's a fine-looking lad, so he is. A rogue of a heart-breaker in the making, is what I'm thinking!' Reverently the picture was returned to the bed. 'Was it done in York?'

Isabel got up from her stool and retrieved the miniature from the quilt. 'No,' was all she said on a dismissing smile, as unconsciously she moved to a lighted candle and allowed its flame to illuminate the fair face she could again study it.

Rachel looked about at her assembled guests. 'The Misses Ormonde seem much taken with the Colonel,' she remarked to her sister. 'But then who can blame them? As you know I am quite partial to him myself. We all had a good ride towards the village this morning. Claudine has a fine seat: she again out-stripped me quite easily over the fences. You should have come along, if for no other reason than to uphold the Merediths' family pride.'

Isabel simply smiled at the compliment to her riding ability. But her eyes did settle on the Colonel…Etienne, she changed it to in her mind. The Ormonde girls had, indeed, cornered him and seemed to be enjoying an animated discussion with him. Isabel intended much the same for Etienne Hauke. She imagined he would prefer the dialogue with the young ladies presently entrapping him.

'You look pale. Are you cold or ailing?' Rachel asked her sombrely quiet sister.

Isabel treated Rachel to a smile. 'No, I'm just a little preoccupied. Marcus is again in trouble with his lessons. I see that Clodagh and Liam have just arrived.'

'Are you not hungry?'

The abrupt question startled Isabel from a dark reflection. 'Yes…no…not really.' She laid down the fork that had idly been pushing food about her plate.

'You seem…nervous. I hope it's not my presence ruining your appetite.'

'Not at all,' Isabel returned lightly. 'I'm afraid I overindulged in town today. We… Clodagh, Liam and I…enjoyed a very fine tea at the Fiddle and Flute.'

'That's a shame…I wish I'd known,' Etienne Hauke said.

Isabel slanted him a look. 'Are you rueing my poor appetite?'

'No, I'm regretting not knowing you would be stopping at the Fiddle and Flute. You could have brought back my trunk. Apparently it was there earlier today, having been returned by the innkeeper of the Black Swan who managed to repossess it from a couple of felons who had purloined it from the coach bringing it here. I am again kitted out courtesy of Connor's wardrobe.'

Isabel's eyes drifted to an immaculate cambric cuff adorning the negligent dark hand reposing on the table. It was difficult detaching her eyes from long fingers toying with silver.

An opportunity had presented itself to casually chat, and the other guests were all occupied. Just an innocent enquiry to start… 'When Connor and Rachel were engaged years ago, were you invited to the wedding, Colonel Hauke?'

His lips twitched ruefully. 'I was. Flinte couldn't be sure that his stepbrother, Jason Davenport, would survive his stag party. I was appointed stand-by groomsman. Jason is a serious imbiber, you see. In the event, of course, it was Connor who nearly didn't survive his stag night…'

Isabel was aware of a sombre note honing his tone and the way his eyes flickered low and oblique to target her sister.

'So you were in England at that time rather than abroad on military duties.'

'I was here for several weeks; longer than I intended to stay. It was a terrible time for Connor.'

'Yes, it was. But eventually it turned right for them.' Isabel grittily championed her sister.

'Who would have thought it?' he bluntly countered.

'You stayed with Connor in London, at that time?'

She was aware of a more probing look searing the side of her face. Her interrogation was losing subtlety.

'If my memory serves me, I stayed in London with Connor for a while and visited my grandparents in Cambridge. My grandfather has a habit of sending urgent and vital messages summoning me to his bedside because he is sure he is about to die. It is all just a ploy to make me visit. He thinks I am not quite the dutiful heir I ought to be. He keeps threatening to cut me off without a brass farthing of his.'

The humour in his voice made Isabel relax a little. So did the information that his time had been spent at those locations. 'It's fortunate you have ample brass farthings of your own, sir. An inheritance is not usually a matter for banter.'

Etienne laughed and looked at her. 'Have my bachelor prospects been under discussion?' he asked softly.

'I shouldn't have said that. I don't know why I did.'

'Don't concern yourself, Mrs Forrester. I'm enough of a realist to know that ladies discuss the financial status of bachelors. A decade ago, when my mother was hawking my sister, Monique, about in the marriage mart, there was talk of little else in our household than gentlemen's fortunes and prospects. I could tell you now how much Roddy Beauchamp or Tim Pendergast had in the bank ten years ago.'

Isabel blushed at the arrant cynicism in his tone. Hastily she picked up the threads of their previous conversation. 'So your grandfather sent a message to London threatening dire consequences if you didn't visit him?'

Etienne grunted a laugh. 'He did. And I remember feeling quite amazed that it ever reached me at all. It had been directed to Mayfair, then rerouted to the north. It was delivered just a day later to my lodgings in York.'

Chapter Five

'Y... York?'

The word was expelled on a strangled gasp. Etienne pushed back in his chair and took a scrutinising glance at her, guessing that embarrassment was causing her to stutter. Isabel Forrester had hitherto seemed coolly composed.

After many years, barely giving it a thought, tendrils of intelligence about Rachel's jilting of Connor seemed to be constantly infiltrating his mind. Of the four Meredith girls, one sister had accompanied the runaway bride to York to stay with an aunt. Logically it would be this sister. Isabel Forrester and Rachel Flinte seemed of a similar age. They were obviously close friends as well as kin to be living under the same roof. Again he pondered why Edgar Meredith wasn't providing a roof over the heads of his widowed daughter and his grandson. It seemed increasingly likely her husband had left her wanting.

'It was a long while ago, but I remember travelling to York and staying for a couple of days.' Mentally he grimaced at the memory. Quite an absurd task he had set himself too, haring, fired with moral outrage, after the fugitive Miss who had brought his friend so low he had nearly died. Connor's stepbrother, Jason, had found the heartbroken bridegroom in a drunken stupor on Clapham Common. Had he not, Connor would most certainly have died from exposure that freezing night.

Isabel couldn't trust herself to look at him. Her stomach was in knots, her heart drumming slowly, deafening her. She could no longer ignore what that seemingly inconsequential snippet of information might mean. Too many colliding coincidences were slotting snugly together. A kaleidoscope of images was jumbling in her mind, but she was frightened to demand he see it too. Yet she would not be able to live with her conscience if she did nothing, acted the coward, and allowed him to leave Ireland without talking to him further. She needed just one more answer, a final piece of proof to tip the balance. Persisting with her investigation here…now…in company, wasn't fitting. But she must persist. She owed that much to Marcus.

'Might I have a private word with you later? There

is something I think we ought talk about…concerning that time…' eventually was forced through her chill, stiff lips.

'Of course.' He smiled at a profile now obscured. Her head had dipped towards her plate and spirals of caramel-coloured hair curtained her cheek. Was she about to admit that she had been in York in the company of the renegade bride? She seemed loyal to Rachel, as a sister should be. If she had guessed his reason for travelling there had been to meddle in something that had been outside his role, perhaps she was not so much embarrassed as indignant on her sister's behalf and was about to reprimand him. He mused with masculine interest on a reprimand from Mrs Forrester and decided he would find it no hardship.

Although the dining room was humming with lively conversation, a still silence whispered between them. When Isabel gave no venue for their post-prandial tête à tète, Etienne eventually suggested lightly, 'Here? The drawing room? An assignation in the summer house?' A sideways glance indicated double doors that opened on to a vast stone terrace milk-bathed in moonlight.

His teasing tone made Isabel's head snap up. He was laughing at her, she realised furiously. He found her gravity amusing. A feral green glance raked his face and with an amount of triumph she noticed his mockery fade to a frown. 'The library is a private place to meet. It is situated by the foot of the stairs,' she informed him coolly. Soon he might be laughing on the other side of his face, she realised with some satisfaction.

'Yes...I know where it is.'

She ignored the wry comment. There was still a time to arrange. 'When we are finished dinner, I shall leave first; perhaps after ten minutes you would join me there.'

'I'd be delighted,' he drawled, but his nonchalance wasn't totally convincing. 'It sounds very clandestine. I'm intrigued. Am I to be told something shocking?'

Isabel couldn't prevent a breath of bitter laughter almost choking her. Her gaze flashed again to his, locked on to earthy dots glittering through sooty lashes. Their lifeless like had recently been tracking her from a portrait. 'Indeed, sir, I think you ought to prepare yourself to be shocked.' It was delivered so quietly he had to incline his dark head to catch the words.

'Wake up, dear...'

Marcus rolled over, irritably kicked his legs about in voluminous cotton, before burrowing his small skull comfortably into his feather pillow with a thumb parting his teeth.

'No, you must wake up, my love!' Isabel attempted

to quieten the agitation in her voice so as not to startle him. 'You may come downstairs for a little while,' she cajoled. 'Mrs Dooley has bilberry jam tarts cooling on a rack.' The enticement was augmented with a soft finger stroking at his cheek.

Sleepy as he was, nevertheless his intelligent little mind sought ulterior motives. 'I've done my sums… Noreen made me. Don't want to go back downstairs.' Marcus declined his mother's generosity and again nestled into his warm cocoon.

'No sums…or verbs…I promise. Come, you may take your soldiers and set them out in the kitchen. There is someone…one of the guests…I would like you to meet later. Have you seen Colonel Hauke who is staying here, Marcus?'

Marcus shook his drowsy head against the pillow as his legs emerged from his nightshirt and poked over the side of the bed. Jam tarts and soldiers were very tempting. He allowed his mother to help him into his dressing gown and slippers.

Mrs Dooley had been happy enough to give Marcus a plate of tarts and a draught-free corner by the cooking range for his army to mass in. Before quitting the kitchens, Isabel had given the senior scullion, a sweet girl of about fourteen, called Betty, an instruction on when to bring Marcus to the library. Isabel, her fists preventing sprigged muslin from

impeding her feet, then raced down the winding
corridor towards the library. Halfway to her destination, her silent flight over the runners faltered with her
courage. She stumbled into a window alcove, rested
her hot brow against cold glass. Her heart was battering so hard at her ribs they ached. She was wrong; it
was nonsense. Such scandals were fiction! They did
not really happen! But then scandalous nonsense had
been her whole life for eight years. She wanted to
know. There was just that one more discovery to
make. With a shivery restorative breath she sedately
walked on and entered the library with a composed
smile.

He was already there, lounging back at his ease in
a chair. He looked as though he didn't have a care in
the world. He immediately stood as she entered and
the hand cradling a book across its broad palm
snapped closed. The tome was placed on a table. 'I
was beginning to think I might have got the wrong
library. Is there another?'

'No. I'm sorry. I was delayed. I had to see to my
son.' The words were truthful and concise. Her smile
remained intact.

He smiled too; his eyes watched her.

She walked closer, her expression neutral. Limpid
green eyes scanned his face, searching, seeking a hint
of something solid. But in her mind all was
spectral…just shapes and shadows. Her memory for

noise was sharper and rustled up moaning wind and leaves sighing beneath driving rain. But there was only one sure way to know. Could she just reach out and touch…

He was watching her with narrowed eyes, faint amusement lifting a corner of his mouth. He was not displeased. She sensed his growing anticipation. With a flash of insight she understood what he read into the situation. He thought she had lured him here to solicit his protection. Over dinner she had stupidly hinted she knew he was wealthy. He had been cynically amused to know she had made it her business to find out. A hint of a sneer had coarsened his cultured voice when he admitted he knew women gossiped over gentlemen's wealth and prospects. After a few days of nothing more than civility between them, this morning they had flirted a little. She had refused his offer to ride out with him…but coyly. She cringed at a truth she couldn't deny. Soon he was due to leave for England. He thought she was done with playing hard to get and wanted to hook him before he left. The arrogance of the man! Just because she was a lone woman with a child, he expected… The scorn withered in her throat. It wasn't outlandish. She understood why he might think that. Her situation made her vulnerable prey to lechers. After Aunt Florence died and she and Marcus were living alone and frugally in York, a local businessman had sent her a detailed offer, delivered by a leering manservant. She had been shocked, not so much by his presumption, but by knowing he had noticed her that way. Previously he had barely acknowledged her existence other than to nod and mumble at her every Sunday morning at service.

'At dinner we were talking of York and how I came to be there all those years ago.' It was a gentle prompting.

Isabel's small white teeth were bared briefly in an approximation of a smile. 'Indeed we were. What did you think of York?'

'A plaguey place.'

The fierce look she sent him elicited a better explanation than that brusque complaint.

'I chose the wrong time to visit such a fine city. As I arrived York was suffering a scarletina epidemic. That was one reason I didn't linger there, but travelled on to Cambridge to see my grandparents before I returned overseas.'

'You had no reason to linger in York?' His words echoed back at him, sounding inconsequential. *He'd no reason to linger in York,* circled her mind woundingly.

'None whatsoever. To be truthful, I wish I'd never gone to the infernal place. I made a mistake. Hindsight can be a most humbling thing.'

'I see.'

After a brief pause heavy with tension Etienne stated, 'When Rachel jilted Connor and absconded she went to York accompanied by one of her sisters. It was you.'

'Yes, it was me.'

'You were safe from the infection?'

'From the scarletina… Yes.'

'Did you stay there long?'

'Yes. I was there a long time. Until quite recently.' She was aware of his intelligent gaze on her. Of course he sensed an undercurrent to the stilted phrases batting back and forth between them. With an inspiriting breath she walked closer, looked up into his face with eyes as arctic as the ocean.

'Have I offended you in some way, Mrs Forrester?' he asked quietly.

'Indeed, I believe you might have, sir, and if you would answer me one simple but, I regret, personal question I shall know for certain and can then opt to make either accusations or apologies.'

Etienne spread his hands in a gesture that parted his immaculate jacket, displaying an expanse of solid muscular torso adorned in slub silk. 'Ask away, madam, by all means.'

The words were polite and silky with mockery. Perhaps he deemed it all unnecessarily histrionic. The drama was real—so real that she itched to smack the self-assurance from his face. Her hands were gripped behind her back, fingers entwined. Be patient! she admonished herself. His smugness won't last a tongue-lashing. And so much more dignified than striking out. 'Do you have a long scar on the right side of your skull from a wound inflicted about eight years ago by a French sword?'

Her answer was clear, signalled by an instinctive suspicion narrowing his eyes. At the first glimpse of his guilt, she felt winded as though she had received a blow to the stomach. In a voice that trembled with her own astonishment and disbelief she exacted more final proof. 'And when you were in York, were you thin…much thinner than you are now, because you had been a prisoner of war for many months? And had your hair been cropped very short to enable the surgeon to attend that head wound you received whilst escaping? And, at the risk of sounding melodramatic, on one dark and stormy night did you meet a young woman in woodland and reveal that much of your history? Did you inform her your name was Etienne and you held the rank of Captain in the Hussars? And would you like me to tell you now how I could possibly know all of that?' By the time she finished her voice was vibrating with emotion.

'Please do.'

It was the sum of his response, but those two words were bitten out with such a menacing softness that they stopped her heart. For a moment Isabel could do no more than swallow convulsively and fret that her final proof—every bit of it—was not quite conclusive enough. But of course it was; she had seen each vital fact truthfully register with him. There was no going back. Courageously she began. 'I too, must admit to being put out by that epidemic of scarletina. Tonight I've learned that pestilence has a human form. You. You say you had no reason to linger in York so I doubt our…encounter…made much of an impression on you eight years ago. I suspect you would not be able to recall a lot of it now. Let me jog your memory. Yes, I accompanied Rachel when she jilted Connor and fled to York. Within a few days of our arrival the infection was running out of control. One evening when Rachel and Aunt Florence were abed I went to Elm Wood to gather ingredients for a concoction to strengthen our constitutions against the disease. Of necessity I ventured there at night because Aunt Florence would not let either Rachel or me out of the house during the day. She was terrified one of us would succumb to the infection and blame for it would fall on her. So when I should have been safe in my bedchamber, I was not. Had the night not turned unexpectedly stormy I might have heard and seen you coming, but with the moon lost and thunder crashing—'

'What are you saying?' he snapped in a voice more alarming for its icy restraint. 'That I raped you?'

Isabel's complexion drained of blood. 'No…' she whispered.

'No, indeed, madam.' His voice was low, silky with steel. 'I might have been guilty that night, but not of forcing myself on an unwilling woman. Now you have refreshed my memory, I can recall the incident, and pleasurable it was too, for us both. The most vivid impression I have of that coupling is a woman clinging to me, begging me not to leave her…to come again, if you will. And I'm amazed to learn I had the time or stamina to pass on so much information about myself. Conversation seemed to be the last thing on your mind.'

Isabel physically flinched as though slapped. 'None of those first sordid details matter now,' she whispered hoarsely.

'I beg to differ on that score. It's obvious you've brought me here to accuse me of abusing you. To me, those first sordid details matter very much. I'm not even sure I was the seducer.'

'I don't know how you dare say that! But then you're certainly no gentleman, are you, sir?' Isabel felt tears of utter mortification sting her eyes. She blinked them away, rallying every atom of courage she possessed not to flee. From being moments ago ignorant of her existence eight years ago, how easily he now could reminisce on what she would sooner they both forgot. 'This is all that matters now,' she blurted. Shaking hands extracted the miniature from her pocket and dropped it down on the table. 'Your mother first showed me this portrait this afternoon. She says it is your likeness, painted when you were about six years old.'

Etienne flicked a glance at it. His eyes were arrested, narrowing on a pale oval with a sense of foreboding. He remembered the portrait vaguely. He recalled thinking last time he saw it—God only knew when that had been—that it was hard to believe he once had been so fair. Recently he had seen a face like that. He had seen an Irish child and thought he looked familiar. Images tumbled into his brain: a handsome boy beneath his stallion's hooves, a wintry day sullen with sleet; an Irish woman swaddled against the elements glaring at him as, muttering and cursing in a broad brogue, she hauled the little scapegrace away to safety. Grave uneasiness was turning in the pit of his stomach. He recalled speaking to the lad and something about their brief exchange had jarred on his mind. Now he knew what it was. The child had spoken with an English accent.

That chilling reflection was being submerged by more sultry memories. Thoughts of warm, silken skin, sleek with rain, and a wanton maid who gave freely and spoke little rolled through his mind. This, then, was the earthy nymph he'd tumbled in a gamekeeper's hide! It was unbelievable! Damnation! Had he only known just how gently bred she was he would have put her on her feet and mounted his horse instead. He'd learned the hard way she was a virgin who spoke with the accent of a gentlewoman. God only knew he could have been forgiven for mistaking her for a practised harlot. He had recalled feeling sceptical that an ingenue would allow him to help her dress. Yet she had. He could picture them giggling together like children as he clumsily tied the bows on her chemise and fought with her petticoats. They had huddled close together beneath his caped coat until the worst of the downpour passed, whispering a few words in between kisses and cringes as thunder crashed and rain lashed the shelter. She had volunteered little about herself and had seemed as keen as he to go once their passion was sated. But before she'd raced off under dripping branches she had soothed his guilt with more kisses, murmured reassurances that she was well and happy, before begging him to meet her there again tomorrow. He'd agreed, from bogus chivalry, knowing full well that tomorrow he would be halfway to Ashcombe House in Cambridge to see if, this time, his grandfather really was about to expire. The same empty courtesy had made him offer more than once to escort her to her lodgings. Her adamant refusal had been a boon.

As he'd galloped through storm-soaked country-side he had obsessively thought of her and her frantic ardour. By the time he reached the Cambridge borders he had convinced himself he wasn't to blame. Only a *demi-vierge,* a woman versed in the arts of love if technically still intact, could have responded in the way she did. She spoke cultured English, but then so did plenty of courtesans schooled by rich old men who paid for companionship as well as sexual release. By the time he'd reached Ashcombe House he had persuaded himself it was best to forget her and was concentrating on someone he could trust: Lady Avery. At twenty-four it would not have occurred to him to have felt guilty over deceiving his mistress with a casual liaison, even though at the time he was besotted with the newly widowed baroness.

The rap at the door made Isabel jump. Swiftly she went to open it, silently praising young Betty for being a few minutes late, yet, so fortuitously, just on time. With a dismissing nod for the young scullion, Isabel drew her son into the room.

'Etienne!' Marcus exclaimed excitedly and, wriggling his fingers free of his mother's, he hurtled across the room, almost tripping as his dressing gown hampered his busy little legs.

'How does he know your name?' The demand was explosive.

'Would you mind explaining just what is going on now?' Etienne blasted at the same time, glaring back with tight-lipped ferocity. His thin mouth was bracketed by livid white grooves.

'Etienne nearly knocked me down,' Marcus happily added to the jumble of dialogue, making the two adults present unlock their combatant glares and stare at him instead.

Isabel felt maternal rage flare in her. She flashed a look of pure aggression at Etienne at her son's words. 'You nearly knocked him down?' Her voice hummed a low note of threat.

'It was when Murphy and me went to town and the Father found out and got Noreen to fetch me home. I ran away to warn Murphy that the Father was after us and Etienne nearly pulped me with Storm. He's high and black and shiny. He's better even than Uncle Connor's Pharaoh,' he proclaimed, naming the finest mount in the Earl of Devane's stable.

Etienne couldn't detach his eyes from Marcus. He was staring at the boy, ashen-faced, as though he was a harbinger of vile calamity. Isabel realised that was exactly how he would view her precious son. He would be a ghastly nuisance, and better left concealed in shadows. But she and Marcus had remained out of sight, unacknowledged for too long. She didn't want or need this man. For days past she had thought him attractive, had thought if only… Now she knew why he held such allure. Subconsciously she had recognised that once he had meant everything to her. On occasions too numerous to count she had slipped away to keep a vigil in Elm Wood. Now she finally knew just what a fool she had been. Here was her chivalrous hero, the man she was sure must have met disaster or death to prevent him returning to claim her. Here he stood in all his healthy arrogance. For weeks, months, a year she had dreamed of him; had trusted his promise to return. Now she knew he had forgotten her as soon as he had ridden out of the trees. Even with a babe in arms, it was a few months more before she had finally discarded her precious memories as ashes. She didn't want him, this callous philanderer. She had survived without him for eight hard years. But never once had she relinquished hope of respectability for Marcus. Unbelievably, through a pall of scandal and misery, she was watching her son's future emerge. Her instinct was to reach out and snatch and never cede, no matter what this man threatened.

Etienne glanced from Marcus to Isabel. The skin on his face was tight and white as parchment and huge-pupilled brown eyes gleamed like hellish embers. 'This is your son?'

'Did you nearly knock him down?' she countered.

'He ran in front of my horse to get his hat. He was unhurt.'

'I did run in front of his horse,' Marcus chirpily endorsed. 'Etienne told me off and said he could have easily pulped me. I asked him his name and he said I should remember my manners and say, what is your name, *sir.*'

Etienne spoke next, in a voice made husky and stilted with rage. 'I see your point. You've displayed the goods long enough, madam. I've no intention of bartering in his presence. Have the boy returned to his bed. There are obviously vital things we need to discuss.'

The cold disgust in his tone squeezed at Isabel's heart. He thought her capable of exploiting her beloved son for coinage! Her chin shot up at his autocratic tone. But the edict was sensible. Indeed, there were vital things for them to discuss and she didn't want her son witnessing more of the belligerence between them that was breeding fast as disease.

Before she could ring for a servant to take her son back upstairs, a knock came on the door. Noreen Smith nervously appeared and loitered on the threshold. Behind her tiny figure loomed a giant of a man garbed all in black. Isabel recognised the visitor at once and her heart plummeted to her toes. Father Maguire had, as Noreen prophesied, come over and was no doubt ready to repeat his sermon.

Noreen's pale blue eyes swivelled between the master's friend and the mistress's sister. The Colonel's expression looked dark as thunder. Mrs Forrester looked white as a shroud. 'Beg pardon, ma'am,' she blurted on a nervous frown. 'Father Maguire is here.'

A speaking look lingered on Isabel. She might just as well have said, 'Don't blame me! I told you he was coming.'

Isabel felt hysteria hacking at the back of her throat. There could hardly have been a less opportune time for the priest to arrive.

'Good evening to you, Mrs Forrester.' Father Maguire slipped past Noreen with surprising ease, considering his stature. His black trilby was not on his pewter hair, but stuck under an arm. A nod acknowledged Etienne Hauke. 'It's sorry I am to be interrupting, but it's important I speak to you about your son. Sure and something must be done!' Down the considerable length of a hooked nose, just one of the priest's eyes narrowed on Marcus. Silently, swiftly, the boy sidled to his mother's side.

'Have you been a good honest boy and told your mother what devilry you've been about today?' It was a voice laden with reprisal. 'Now don't look so surprised, Marcus Forrester, didn't I warn you what it is I must do?' A look slew to Isabel. 'He's in need of a thrashing, Mrs Forrester, if ever he is to learn and be a credit to you and himself. And what a sin if he's not mending his ways for he'll never be a credit to his father's memory either, God rest him.'

'I will be! My father was a brave soldier.'

'Hush, Marcus!' Isabel croaked, a hand stroking at his flushed cheek, silencing him. She closed her eyes,

imperceptibly. Then a composed voice she barely recognised as hers said, 'Father Maguire, I will speak to
you tomorrow. I am aware there has been a problem…
another problem…but I…it is not now convenient.'

'Another problem? Hah!' the priest spat out. 'Too
many problems, Mrs Forrester! If you will not let me
discipline this boy then he must be taken out of
school. He is a bad influence on the boys who either
do as they must or take their punishment. I know it is
hard for you being a widow as you are. Shall I be
speaking to his uncle? What the boy needs, to be sure,
is a firm hand. Shall I be speaking to the Earl of
Devane about it all?'

'No. You may speak to me.'

Chapter Six

'Who are you then, sir? A relative?'

'I'm Etienne Hauke, a friend and army colleague of the Earl of Devane. I'm pleased to meet you.' The two men shook hands.

Isabel felt her son's small fingers slip against hers. She squeezed loving reassurance against his plucking while discreetly observing the adult males present. Both seemed different. Father Maguire was wearing a look of deliverance that had ironed the pleats from his lofty brow. Isabel respected him as a good, hard-working man who would always strive to do his duty. If, in the process, he upset her, she knew it wouldn't bother him too much. But he was chary of alienating her brother-in-law, who was a most influential man in Ireland. He seemed confident a fitting comprom-ise would be reached now an intermediary, in the imposing form of a comrade of the Earl's, had stepped in to rescue the situation.

As for Etienne, the ogre and his anger were gone. Suave Colonel Hauke was back. If his charming smile was a little tight, Father Maguire didn't seem to notice. If a hard handshake was crushing the bones in the cleric's fingers, he piously suffered in silence. Neither did he seem to object to the affable hand on his shoulder deftly steering him away into the hall.

Isabel watched them talking together for a moment before she rallied her sense enough to instruct a gawping Noreen to take Marcus to his bed. 'Tomorrow we must talk about all this, Marcus. Father Maguire is right when he says that no more mischief will be tolerated,' she softly warned him.

He bowed his small head so his chin touched his chest. Chastened, he allowed Noreen to lead him away. As her downcast son was quitting the room, her radiant sister was entering, with small crab-like steps, so she could survey the people dotted about her hallway.

'We were wondering where on earth you had got to, Isabel!' Rachel declared without once looking at her sister. Her curious blue eyes were flitting between her nephew, climbing the stairs with Noreen in attendance, and the gentlemen deep in discussion.

'Father Maguire chose a rather inopportune moment to arrive on…a mission,' Isabel told her sister a trifle breathlessly. 'Colonel Hauke was...he was by chance in the vicinity and volunteered to have a word with him before showing him out.'

Rachel grimaced irritation. 'It's too bad of Father Maguire to come sermonising at this time of the evening when we are likely to have guests. Has Marcus been bad again?' At Isabel's immediate, defensive look Rachel added cheerily, 'Come back to the drawing room and join us in a game of cards. Everyone was just starting to miss you...both of you.' An arch look winged Rachel's vision skyward.

Inwardly, Isabel cringed. If only her sister knew what had really gone on between her and her husband's good friend, there would be uproar, not raised eyebrows!

'I think Claudine and Vincent Ormonde would like the carpet up in the music room. They keep telling anyone who will listen that there are enough of us to make a set for the Barley Mow. Claudine has offered to play piano if Vincent will turn the music for her.' Spying the Colonel approaching them, Rachel interrupted her social plans to sibilantly whisper, 'Do you think he has been regaled with all of Marcus's mischief? It's very good of him to despatch Father Maguire for you.'

'Yes, isn't it...'

Earthy eyes grazed past Isabel's, relentlessly grim, making her sure Etienne had detected the sarcasm honeying her few words.

'We were just saying you must come back to the drawing room and make up numbers for a country dance. Your mama has said she will provide the music. But not for an Irish jig, I promise you,' Rachel reassured on a laughing breath.

'You'll have to excuse me.' It was a courteous refusal accompanied by a flash of a smile. 'I was just on my way to the stables, to check on my horse, when the priest arrived and delayed me. Storm threw a shoe in Waterford earlier today. I want him fit for the morning. Mrs Forrester has graciously agreed to ride with me on my last day in Ireland.' He slanted a significant look at Isabel, challenging her to refuse to keep the appointment.

But she wouldn't; she couldn't. Too much had been left unsaid. More than anything she wanted to finish what she had started and secure Marcus's future. 'I certainly hope your horse is uninjured, Colonel Hauke,' she duly sympathised. 'If it will help at all, I can prepare a poultice to ease the inflammation. Rachel's mare, Willow, benefited when her fetlock was bruised.'

'Isabel is a wonder with her potions, you know,' Rachel enthused. 'She was always stirring and brewing things in a cupboard at home. Our mother would wonder where she'd got to.'

'Rachel! You make me sound like a witch,' Isabel muttered on an embarrassed twitch of a smile. 'Next you'll have me casting spells…' She fell quiet, fearing she might have dug a hole to fall into. But it was too late. Inwardly she flinched at the malicious gleam in Etienne's dark eyes.

'Ah, now that I can believe,' Etienne purred with just a hint of viciousness. 'I think it very likely your sister is an enchantress, tempting unsuspecting souls at dead of night. She has the look of a siren, don't you think?'

Rachel clucked and flapped an elegant hand at him. 'Stop it! Look, you've made poor Bella blush!' Her eyes skipped between her sister and her husband's friend.

She thinks he is joking, that he is being delightful and flirting with me. The realisation made Isabel swallow a hysterical laugh. If only Rachel knew of the resentment behind his pretty words! 'Do let me know if you need a dressing for your horse. I'd hate you to cry off and leave me in the lurch. I'm so looking forward to our ride.'

Rachel's eyes became watchful as she sensed the atmosphere. She diplomatically wandered away to speak to Gallagher.

'Don't be so eager, my dear,' Etienne sneered softly as soon as Rachel was out of earshot. 'A woman who is no challenge can be rather irksome for a man like me. But then you already know that, don't you?'

Isabel felt the blood flare beneath her complexion.

'Yes, I do know that. But, unfortunately for me, a man like you is all I have at present.'

'That's excessive unfortunate for me too, Mrs Forrester,' he drawled. 'I never knew the fellow, but I certainly regret your husband's passing. Did he know the boy was a by-blow? Perhaps you were able to pass the brat off as his. Is that it?'

Isabel felt ice cluster beneath her cheeks. The lump in her throat grew until she thought it might choke her. How dare he term her darling son so! 'No, I didn't manage anything quite so clever,' she eventually whispered. She walked past him at once and found Rachel, linked arms with her, and suggested it was time to return to the others.

Frost sprinkled like sugar was dissolving beneath weak February sun. Patches of verdant ground were emerging dewy and glistening. Isabel stood on the steps of Wolverton Manor and surveyed the still, quiet vista as air crisp and invigorating as champagne bubbled against her throat. She took a deep draught, smoothed her brown riding skirt and settled her hat at a jaunty angle atop her thick fawn hair. The brave gestures did little to bolster her confidence. A small riding crop tapped nervously against a leather-gloved palm. Well, she could either meet him or return to her chamber. Heaven knew she wanted to retreat into the comfort of her cowardice. But she would not.

Her valiant little son was conquering his demons. And so must she. She had left Marcus being dressed by Noreen. He had looked solemn, but had got out of bed as soon as he was bid this morning. The wobble at his lower lip had wrenched at her heart as she kissed his soft shiny hair, then left him in Noreen's care to be despatched in good time for school. Father Maguire was her son's nemesis. Now she must keep an appointment with hers!

Last night she had received a note from Etienne, delivered by a gimlet-eyed Noreen. It had been just a brief instruction to meet him at eight o'clock. She knew he'd chosen such an early hour to avoid them being awkwardly joined by anyone else out on their morning constitutionals. She knew what his first words would be when they were far enough from the house to be private: 'How much?' He would want to buy back his ignorance of her and their son's existence. Of course, her price was far more than he would countenance paying. She was ready for his scorn on that score. With firm resolve and tilted chin she set off towards the stables.

Isabel was aware that Sam Smith and his subordinates were curious as to why she was taking a ride with a man who seemed withdrawn and careless of her presence. Apart from a terse 'good morning', Etienne had virtually ignored her while he paced and waited for Storm to be saddled. She had chosen to ride

Fleur, half-sister to Rachel's mare, Willow. Fleur was a pretty bay with a flash of white on her nose and white socks. Despite her lack of hands she was a wiry little mare. Last time Isabel had ridden her she had been surprised that beneath a seemingly gentle temperament was quite a spirited, unpredictable creature.

Sam cupped his hands for her small boot, then hoisted her into the side-saddle. Once settled, she gave him a smile and thanks, then abruptly tapped the mare's flanks and set off towards the meadow.

As dainty Fleur leaped past the mighty black stallion it set the high-strung beast into a prance. She was vaguely conscious of Etienne cursing, taking the animal in a tight circle to calm and control it. After that was simple exhilaration and the wind combing icy fingers over her scalp, edging off her hat to droop on its ribbons down her back. Green grass, ice-spangled earth, brown denuded wood was a kaleidoscope of colour in her watery vision as she flashed past. It was so good to ride! If only she could fly on forever, beg the horizon to give her sanctuary, show her the rainbow she had long been chasing. She thundered on, heady excitement and apprehensiveness mingling, drumming an ache into her chest.

Fleur took the first fence that led to the brook in an easy soaring stride, then horse and rider came back to earth and were pounding away towards a sinuous snake of grey water fringed by skeletal poplars.

She knew he was close from the rumbling rhythm behind. She didn't turn. Her intrepid little horse was already slacking and Isabel felt guilty that she had urged the mare to such an early pace. Fleur was snorting gamely as she strove to outstrip the shadowy hunter, as though she also resented the preying males dogging them. With a rewarding pat to the little horse's neck Isabel urged her away to the left, let the supple stallion streak by, its hooves spitting turf back at them. She would have liked to veer off further towards the park and get completely away from him. But she didn't; she followed at a respectable pace and distance, as he knew she would.

By the time she caught sight of him again, by the stream bordered by sentinel poplars, the stallion was tethered and docile and so, it seemed, was its rider.

Etienne was seated on the gigantic bole of a fallen cedar that was precariously atilt, yet still anchored by fingerlike roots sunk determinedly into frosty soil. Isabel had seen the woody ruin before when riding. Again she felt sorrow that a magnificent specimen that had witnessed generations of hunters come and go was reduced to a fissured stump swaddled in ivy.

He seemed devoid of pity, relaxed and eyeing her over slanted silver at his mouth. He put the hip flask down by his side. A smouldering cigar was retrieved, replacing the bottle at his lips. She noted a pile of ash dusting dewy grass. He had been waiting some while for her. Well, she was here now, but he made no effort to rise and help her dismount. Isabel slipped easily from the mare's back and loosely tethered Fleur to a low branch.

Gentlemen, on the whole, politely refrained from smoking or drinking in a lady's presence. He was deliberately choosing to indulge in both. The inference was quite clear. He might not regard her as a lady, but then she certainly thought him no gentleman!

'May I?' An indolent gloved finger flicked at the metal bottle by his side. On impulse, begging a nip of brandy seemed suitably licentious behaviour for a hussy.

He looked at it, then at her. He held it out.

Slowly she approached, took it and had a minor struggle jerking loose the stopper. She had no need to look his way to know he was amused. She entertained him further by spluttering as the alcohol hit her novice throat. Isabel gave her head a wakening shake. She faced him again, composed, and neatly replaced the cork. 'Ah, that's better. Thank you.'

'You're welcome.' He drew again on the cheroot, watching her through curling blue smoke as she placed the flask down close to his hip on the cedar stump.

She distanced herself immediately, but the image of him was imprinted on her mind. He looked quite handsome, she supposed, sitting there with the sun weaving colours into his dark brown hair. It was as well she no longer found him in the least attractive. It was as well a man with such a fine physique was an arrogant heartless deceiver, deserving only of her contempt.

Time today was precious. She was sure he must be as keen as she was to get this meeting over. The rancour that had raged between them yesterday again animated her mind, firing her pale skin with a pink bloom. Quickly she opened negotiations with a polite preliminary, and a nervous gulp. 'This isn't going to be easy for either of us, Colonel Hauke…'

'You have a nice way with understatement, Mrs Forrester,' he mentioned.

She cleared her throat, tucked some wispy spirals up inside her hat and settled it primly back on hair glowing honey-gold beneath the cold sun. 'I would like to start by saying…by suggesting…that we endeavour to be as civil as possible. Further malice and insults will benefit nobody, least of all Marcus. We naturally feel a mutual antipathy. I believe it should be controlled the short while we endure each other's company.'

'I'm sure you're right. I stand suitably chastened for my rudeness.' The words were correct, yet at odds with his impenitent tone and the gleam in his eyes. He gained his feet to begin walking towards her with some purpose.

'First I must say thank you for dealing so efficiently with Father Maguire yesterday,' Isabel rattled off, feeling compelled to pace away from him in the opposite direction. 'Whatever you said to him seemed to do the trick. He left looking quite content.' She took a glance at his face. There was nothing in his impassive expression to satisfy her curiosity. She waited. He remained uncommunicative. Slightly impatiently she demanded, 'Well, what did you say? What did he tell you about Marcus?'

'He said the boy is undisciplined, wilful and lazy. He also said that you won't allow him to be caned for it.'

'He's not! He's not any of those things! He's easily bored. And I...I don't want the spirit beaten out of him!' She spun on a heel to conceal her spontaneous angry tears. 'He...he is not a stupid child by any means. And I have not neglected his education. But he needs friends as well as lessons. Sums and verbs cannot be everything to a seven-year-old who loves to run and ride and explore. He is an intelligent boy...and he shan't be beaten,' she vehemently concluded her defence of her son.

'Did your husband beat him?'

Isabel caught her breath, hesitating momentarily before quickly shaking her head. 'Father Maguire seemed pleased when he left. What did you say to him?'

'I told him what he wanted to hear: that the boy will no longer be attending his school. I told him steps were being taken to have him educated in England. It's no less than a truth that will be implemented shortly.'

A silence strained between them. Eventually Isabel blurted, 'I have a right to be consulted over my…our son's future.'

The words were hoarse with shock, yet held such grit that Etienne smiled. 'Indeed, you do, my dear, which is surely why we are loitering about here this freezing cold morning instead of enjoying an early breakfast at Wolverton Manor.' He made a conciliatory gesture. 'Come, you cannot have it both ways: you cannot accuse me of deserting the wretch then fuss over what help I offer. He is behind with his studies and running wild. He needs reining in before it is too late.'

She was frightened; things were changing too quickly, racing out of her control. Matters that needed careful thought, things that she would have mulled over in her mind for days, were indolently settled by him then swept aside. But there was truth in his assessment of her son if not a shred of affection or loyalty. Of course her attitude to things would be different: she loved Marcus. She was sure his father didn't even like him. No, that was wrong; he felt irritation, not dislike. No such strong emotion moved him where Marcus was concerned. For the most part he was indifferent to their son's existence. Could she hold him blameworthy? He didn't know Marcus, or her. They were all, farcically, intimate strangers. To gain a little thinking time she prevaricated, 'I thought you might deny he was your child despite the likeness to your portrait.'

'I'll admit it crossed my mind yesterday that a painting of a blond child that happens to be me yet looks like your son isn't conclusive proof that I've sired him. Neither is managing to recall the…*sordid encounter*…I think you like to term it. But I was intrigued by what the priest had to say about his mischief. If his looks and his character resemble mine, the two taken together seem pretty convincing proof that he is my flesh and blood.'

'Very magnanimous of you, sir.'

'It wouldn't be the first time a woman tried to pass off her dead husband's child as mine,' he snapped in response to her sarcasm. 'Another wastrel who had left his widow so poor she needed to go soliciting,' he muttered more for himself.

'You think my husband died penniless?'

'Didn't he?'

'It's none of your concern.'

'I'd say it is every bit my concern. I'd say your intention is to make your beggary a matter for my conscience.'

She strode swiftly close and a small palm cracked flat against a lean, tanned cheek with such a retort it seemed to echo away down the river valley.

'Well, that's a relief,' he drawled, briefly touching the livid brand on his jaw. 'I take it your righteous indignation means I'm mistaken. You don't want my money after all. What is it you do want? Are you out for revenge because you made no lasting impression on me eight years ago? If it still rankles, I apologise. If it helps at all, I'll admit I now can't get you out of my mind.'

'We were talking of Marcus, not us,' Isabel snapped in a low voice. She turned away from him to hide her humiliation. Yes, he'd easily forgotten her eight years ago. Now he wished he could. She knew from the irony in his tone that she and Marcus were a burr in his side, a distraction in his mind. 'There is more to this than simply Marcus's education.'

Etienne raised a lazy, quizzical eyebrow.

'There is much more to be learned in life than where Africa is to be found on the globe or why the Crusades came about or…or…'

'Or…that a basic knowledge of English and mathematics and other disciplines will be necessary for him make his way in life? The boy will one day be a man and must earn himself a living.'

'Yes, he will be a man, please God also a husband and a father. It's important he successfully undertakes those roles as well as being a breadwinner. He is a child who needs love to thrive.' She took a deep breath, simultaneously thankful and scared that their conversation had wended a path to a natural place for her to voice her demands. All she needed was the courage to brave his scorn and accept no less than was her due…for Marcus. 'He needs to feel he is part of a family…a proper family. He wants more than anything to be like his friends and have a mama and a papa. It is what he yearns for.'

Etienne's dark eyes narrowed on her pale, tense face. 'Before you say anything that might embarrass us both, let me remind you of a fact my mother inelegantly disclosed. I have a prospective fiancée. As soon as Miss Greenwood's father makes formal the financial inducement for me to take her off his hands, my betrothal will be announced. I shall be married shortly after and in due course shall be setting up my nursery…for my legitimate heirs. In theory it is all arranged.'

'Then I am sorry to be the one to foil your meticulous planning,' Isabel said icily, the tenor of disgust at his calculating quite audible in her tone.

'You shall not, Mrs Forrester, be very assured of that,' Etienne returned with steely confidence. 'I'll provide for the boy…and you too…but in my own way and on my terms.'

'Then we have resolved nothing here this morning,

Colonel Hauke. I fear your terms and your way will not reconcile with my terms and my way.'

He smiled in a way that chilled her heart. 'Be more specific about your terms, Mrs Forrester.'

She immediately complied. 'I want you…no, I expect you to marry me and to be a good father to our son.'

'Restrict your ambition to those first three words, my dear, and I'll see what I can do to oblige you.'

Chapter Seven

'You think you've shocked me, don't you? You haven't. You're probably also hoping to have humbled me. Again, I have to disappoint you, sir.' Ivory bone threatened to thrust through the translucent skin of her knuckles as her fingers clenched. 'I knew from the outset that a man as callous and selfish as you would expect something in return for any aid he offered. Aid, I might add, that he should feel obliged to tender quite unconditionally. But then I imagine acting morally ill behoves your cold-blooded schemes.' She managed a tight smile. 'What I am trying to impress on you, Colonel Hauke, is that you must be quite mad to think I would want you in that way or that I would ever consider a permanent liaison with such as you.'

'I have the gist of what you're trying to impress on me, Mrs Forrester.' A curt interruption and an offhand gesture supplicated for silence. 'My apologies in advance, for I risk being accused of indelicate talk to a lady. Nevertheless, to prevent further confusion, I think I ought to make something clear. In addition to an eager fiancée awaiting my arrival in London, I have also a dear friend. When I am married I shall continue to be very close to her. In short, there is no permanent role to be had in my informal life either. The only vacancy you might suit is in Suffolk. As you've already shown an aptitude for pleasing me, I would be prepared to oblige you with a residence there and a visit or two when I am in that part of the country. As to your son, I would be prepared to oblige him with a proper education followed by assistance in obtaining employment once he comes of age. I have contacts in the city and the army. Be assured that my supporting the boy is not dependent upon your agreement to become my sometime paramour. A refusal will not offend. All things considered, I think I am being more than fair and generous to you both.'

The effort of repressing her temper during his measured scorn had lividly blanched Isabel's complexion. 'I think you are the most repulsive man I have ever had the misfortune to meet,' she hissed. 'Why I ever let you touch me is a mystery, and will remain so, I expect, until the day I expire. Elm Wood must that awful night have been steeped in a noxious mist of henbane and liberty caps that rendered me witless.

I recall feeling odd…hot…not myself. An evil force must have got into me…'

He gave her a smile that transformed into a long low chuckle of real amusement. 'Mushrooms and henbane made you do it! God's teeth! I've heard it all now! And before you fantasise further, my dear, it wasn't a fairy king that penetrated you that night; it was me. I did it. As for feeling odd and hot and out of control, that's not alchemy, it's lust. Trust me. I have some knowledge of these things.'

It was more than Isabel could endure. Her fears… regrets…even the shame that had tortured her conscience for eight years were being held up to ridicule. He must have a good idea of what torment she'd endured when she discovered at seventeen that she was pregnant and alone, yet it didn't move him one iota. Yesterday she'd been a damnable nuisance, now she was risible entertainment. Within raged a huge fire she knew was out of control even before the small feral cry rasped her throat. She launched herself against him, thrashing at his face, his chest, any part of him she could reach. If she was aware of his angry reasoning giving way to fluent cursing as he backed away, she gave no sign of hearing any of it. Her fists continued to flail and when they were finally restrained in a powerful grip, she kicked out with her booted feet instead. Deaf and blind to his savage appeal she fought on, white hot rage blasting blood into her ears and blurring her vision with wrathful tears.

Suddenly she was off the ground and whipped around, her spine rammed hard against his torso, her feet running on air. 'Put me down, you bastard!' she seethed. 'Let me loose or I swear I'll kill you. How dare you! How dare you speak to me like that! As though I'm some Convent Garden drab!' In her incandescent ire she hadn't noticed that he was carrying her towards a spinney. He dropped her close to a wide-girthed oak, positioning himself at her back so she couldn't turn without forcing him away. She attempted it, but reversing just inches brought her up against a masculine body as unyielding as the ancient timber chafing her breasts. As though to complete her imprisonment, two immovable arms barred either side of her.

Isabel rested her smooth forehead against rough bark. She allowed a small corner of her mind to register that she had behaved appallingly. Outrageously; in the manner perhaps of an unpaid Convent Garden drab. A residue of rage churned her stomach, but she felt too exhausted to stoke the embers and flare at him once more. She gave her head a small shake to clear scraggly strands of tear-damp hair from her mouth. 'Get away from me! I swear I'll scream if you don't leave this instant!'

'Scream, then. There's nobody to hear you.

Besides, if anybody has a right to scream, it's me. I think you've broken my nose.'

Isabel's tensile quivering stilled. 'Truly?' she whispered. 'I have…I have hurt you badly?'

'Truly. That's quite a right hook you have. Where do you spar? I have a right to know so I can avoid the place.'

Even the wryness in his tone couldn't alleviate Isabel's self-disgust. Her shoulders slumped and her forehead again found wood. 'You shouldn't have spoken to me like that. I'm not what you think.'

'I'm not what you think, either. I'm not callous or selfish. I had plans in place for my future. In under one week you and the boy have turned my world upside down.' As though conscious he was explaining—justifying himself—he halted, cleared his throat. 'Nevertheless, I'm sorry I spoke to you like that.' A hoarse laugh stirred her hair. 'I came to Ireland to finally meet my friend's wife, not mine. Had I gone straight to London or Suffolk instead of diverting here to see them…'

'Eight years ago I had plans for my future, too, Colonel Hauke. Those plans didn't include living on charity courtesy of my eldest sister's feelings of guilt.' Isabel bit her lip. She hadn't expected him to dampen her ire so quickly with an apology. 'I don't mean to sound ungrateful; Connor and Rachel are very good and generous to us and take pains never to bring it to

my attention. I know our situation could be so much
worse.' She sniffed. 'Stumbling upon Marcus and me
must be the worst kind of bad luck for you. For me it
is the most fortunate thing to happen in a very long
while.' Isabel smeared her face clear of tears. Her
jumbled curls were tidied behind her small ears and
her returning composure put grit in her voice. 'I don't
want anything from you. But I'll do everything in my
power to ensure Marcus has a proper future. I made
a mistake a long while ago when I was just seventeen.
That's not his fault. I won't let him suffer any more.
Not now. Not when there's finally a way to put things
right. I hope you understand that.'

He made no response other than, 'If I let you loose,
will you promise to behave?'

His sombre plea sounded hysterically familiar; it
had been delivered in the manner in which she might
address Marcus when he was fractious. In her fraught
mind a despairing giggle racketed and rattled fit to
loosen her teeth; in reality she simply nodded. The
pressure of his body against hers eased. For a moment
she felt too weary from exertion, too humiliated by
her violent outburst, to turn and look upon the damage
she'd wreaked on him. She slowly pivoted about.

He had backed off some way and was regarding
her oddly. If she hadn't known him better, she might
have thought his expression quite gentle. She decided
pity had softened his features. He probably deemed

her a quaint freak. Certainly the disdain that had consistently curled his lip today had gone. Of course it was possible sneering might pain him. She must have caught him quite a blow on the mouth for one side was already purple. A trickle of blood ran from his nose. She stared at him, as much fascinated as appalled as she surveyed her handiwork. 'You shouldn't have spoken to me like that.'

'I'm sorry…'

If only he had berated her, called her a spiteful ill-bred bitch. To hear him utter words which were her due, words which still stuck in her throat, was too much. 'You shouldn't have…' she croaked, then hung her head.

'Don't cry, Isabel. Come, the situation is not so grim. We must try to find a way out of this mess. Hush! If you are sensible, we can make the best of a bad situation.' His calm, patient reasoning had the effect of making her flinch so forcefully she folded at the middle. Instead of delivering a desperate platitude, he might have landed a blow. Again, she wished those kind words had been foul curses.

Etienne placed a light hand on her shoulder. It carefully, comfortingly caressed over fragile shoulder bones. When that touch was permitted he drew her into his arms, but tentatively, as though at any moment he expected her to revert to a fire-spitting termagant.

Instinct, honed from more than a decade of

coddling temperamental females, made him drop his
face close to her tumbled, tear-damp locks. A
haunting scent drifted up. It was distinctive: a mixture
of herbs underlined with a warm womanly note of a
particular flower. A month ago the fragrance would
have held a pleasant unidentifiable redolence. Now
the blend was immediately suggestive of earthy,
urgent pleasure coupled with the rhapsodic beat of
wind and rain. The imagery was so complete that
more than his memory stirred. A groan denied his
reaction to being so close to her.

Isabel parted tear-spiky lashes to look at the
bruised face angled over hers. The fierce heat in his
sleepy eyes needed no explanation. It might have been
a long time since a tinder-box and sporadic misty
moonlight introduced that gleam, but she recognised
it. Her eyes were again drawn to his swollen sensual
mouth.

Etienne immediately focused on the same feature
on her tear-smudged face. Her soft lips looked unbelievably full and rosy against the pallor of her skin.
They parted, a small tongue touched and wetted the
lower, and his eyes were magnetised by the nervous
movement. His head was already inclining. Despite
the acrimony that had just smouldered between them,
it now seemed quite natural to want to explore what
they found, this instant, mutually fascinating. And
God knows he did want to kiss her...and more. The

fire in his mind had blazed a path to his loins. He
wanted her. He wanted a reason for the savage desire
she could incite with a flash of those cool jewel eyes.
But she wasn't so cold. Despite her frigid stance he
knew she could be hot as hell and he felt capable of
selling his soul to discover how quickly she would
burn.

He's going to kiss me! The absurdity of it confounded Isabel for a moment. Part of her would have
liked to feel his mouth again on hers, would have
liked to know if it felt the same as it did in memories
she'd nurtured until she knew by heart every breath
that had passed between them. But the longing was
crushed by the thought he might be simply testing that
aptitude she once had for pleasing him. Perhaps he
wanted to know whether she would be a worthwhile
baggage to haul to Suffolk. 'Don't do it, it might hurt
you,' she murmured with her eyes fixed on his ragged
skin.

He smiled, carefully, with one side of that damaged
full lip. It made him look roguish and vulnerable, far
too boyishly appealing.

'I'll be careful…and gentle…'

'But I won't, Colonel,' she whispered, tilting her
face to within a tempting hair's-breadth of his, so
close that as she brushed past him she felt the soft skin
of her cheek abraded by stubble on his chin. A light
laugh mocked him as she spun about to look him up

and down. 'I think you must be deranged to even try it. Perhaps I haven't made absolutely clear my dislike of you. Let me speak plainly. If ever you try to kiss me, I shall bite you. If ever you try to touch me in a familiar way, I shall hit you. Please don't make me again act in such an unladylike manner.' She straightened her skirts with an impatient twitch. 'But I'm very sorry I was…unnecessarily violent. I admit it was disgraceful behaviour. I should like to make amends and can mix you an arnica lotion for your bruising.' Her head slanted aside and she squinted professionally at his face. 'I don't think your nose is broken at all…just…' She trailed away into silence and approached him with a scrap of white she had extracted from the pocket of her riding skirt. She waved it up at him like a fluttering flag of truce. 'Here, take this to clean that there…' She indicated the place by touching her own face.

He took a larger cloth from his own pocket, rejecting her handkerchief with a bored, 'Put that away. Gore will ruin the lace.' He scrubbed unconcernedly with his plain linen at the caked blood, wincing momentarily before stuffing the dirtied handkerchief back in his pocket. 'It might not be broken, but it is throbbing like the devil.' The complaint was harsh and exasperated. That wasn't all that was pulsing fit to explode.

'Obviously you're referring to your nose.'

Etienne's eyes narrowed in masculine interest at her sly tone. 'Not necessarily,' he muttered, gravel-voiced.

'Well, it would hardly be your heart!' she sniped. 'I imagine even your so-close lady friend might have a task on her hands fracturing that. Either it's made of stone or you don't have one, just an abacus rattling beneath your ribs.'

Etienne stared at her, not knowing whether to burst out laughing or swear. 'We're at cross-purposes, Miss Purity. Let's leave alone the matter of what about my person ails me.'

Mistaking his raw frustration for an upsurge in anger, Isabel turned away. On trembling legs she hastened back to Fleur. She unhooked the mare's reins from a low branch and her eyes hunted about for a suitable mound for her to step upon to aid her re-mounting the horse. The ancient tree stump he had sat upon was too lofty and precarious to be used. As she paced back and forth searching, she informed him coolly, 'I'm afraid my terms remain the same, Colonel. You must accept that you now have the prospect of a violent harpy as a wife. I'm sure we might deal tolerably well together if we contrive to spend a minimum amount of time in each other's company. Needless to say, a nominal marriage is all I require. You may reassure your mistress that she has no rival in me. But I'm sorry that you must disappoint

Miss Greenwood. Perhaps in time your treasure might understand that, in fact, it is no disappointment at all; rather a fortunate escape.'

A sardonic inclination of his dark head acknowledged the finale to her scathing. 'I'm sorry too, you seem to be under the misapprehension that I can be easily defeated either with female tears or a few lucky slaps. Nothing has changed, my dear. Other than if you try that again, I'll hit you back.' Without a word, and so swiftly it made her gasp, his hands girdled her slender waist and he hoisted her on to Fleur, leaving her to scramble for balance and reins. He strode immediately away and swung himself up on to Storm and without a backward glance spurred the animal into action and was off towards Wolverton Manor.

Two hours later Fleur clattered over the cobbles of the empty stable-yard, her hooves echoing metallically. After a moment looking about, Isabel spied the bent heads of Sam Smith and an apprentice over the door of the farthest stall. Both stared at her as she brought Fleur to a sedate halt close by. Sam was soon out and helping her dismount with a look creeping from beneath bushy brows. Isabel knew he was wondering why the master's sister-in-law and his good friend had ridden out together and returned separately. If he had noticed the marks on the Colonel's face, he would have little trouble guessing the answer to the conundrum. Etienne had ridden off in a foul mood; she imagined that in the short while it would have taken him to storm back to the house, nothing would have improved his state of mind.

Sam looked increasingly speculative as, with a pat to the mare's neck, he led Fleur away into the stables. The jet-black stallion was already blanketed and munching at his feed. As she approached, the magnificent beast ceased foraging and his head emerged over the top of brickwork. He seemed to regard her with a mellow, critical eye. She hesitated, then succumbed to an urge to feel the handsome animal's sleek thoroughbred lines beneath her skin. Warm sable slipped beneath her palm as she passed.

It occurred to her now that perhaps she wouldn't see Etienne again. He was due to leave Ireland today. Yesterday evening, when he had returned nonchalantly to the drawing room and the house party, he had taken his leave of both Rachel and his mother just in case there was no further opportunity to do so. His mother had been persuaded by Vincent to return to Ormonde Castle to keep he and his daughters company a while longer and Rachel had social appointments that were due to keep her abroad most of the day.

Isabel doubted he had yet gone. He would never allow such a prized animal as Storm to be sent on after him. He would wait until the beast was fed and watered and fit to travel.

Isabel stripped off her gloves as she made for the house. She could either give up her hopes of Marcus being reunited with his father or she could fight on…perhaps resort to blackmail. The thought horrified her, but then so did settling for Etienne Hauke's remote assistance. He would not renege on meeting the cost of supporting Marcus through to manhood. He baulked at being Marcus's father, yet would settle bills presented for his son's tuition with less interest than he gave to those received for his paramour's dresses. Isabel felt her temper stir. She would rather feed the birds with those crumbs he intended throwing their way.

She wondered if Miss Greenwood would want to marry him if she knew he had no intention of honouring his wedding vows. Perhaps she wouldn't care that he kept a cherished mistress so long as he was discreet. Perhaps she was no more in love with him than he was with her. Isabel knew marriages were brokered simply to merge money and stock. Personally she had always found the design behind it distasteful and depressing.

Etienne Hauke was a fortune hunter and seemed unabashed to admit it. The only valuable objects she had were her Aunt Florence's pearls and her paternal grandfather's gold signet ring. Her papa had sent the ring to York. It was to mark Marcus's first year of good health in a city recovering from an awful epidemic. But Isabel understood its true significance: it was to ease Edgar Meredith's conscience because, since Marcus's birth, he had wished his only grand-child had succumbed to the disease. If she had lost her son, her father could have buried the scandal in the same coffin.

Isabel entered the house. The thought of eating breakfast made her stomach curdle. She was barely halfway up the stairs when the Colonel's valet, Reeves, and one of the footmen appeared, carrying a trunk between them. So, the missing packing case had arrived. It was leaving almost as soon. The men grunted politely, if breathlessly, as they passed her on the wide curve of stairway. Isabel watched their slow careful descent with the box banging and swaying between them. She took another step before a glimpse of muscular legs and shiny boots arrested her.

He was leaving. He was calling her bluff. She could proclaim to the world he was a ruthless seducer and thereby draw loathsome attention to herself too, or she could act with caution and dignity and perhaps live to fight another day. Something akin to fear gripped at her heart. She banished it. He would not cow her. 'I hope you have a safe trip to England, Colonel Hauke.'

'I doubt that you do. I think you hope that the ferry will sink, and I will drown.'

'I would be a fool to want anything of the sort!

Just yet, in any case, before matters are settled to my satisfaction.'

He positioned himself in front of her. An arm thwarted her attempt to sweep majestically past without deigning to comment further. With a simultaneous look over her head to ascertain if they were being witnessed he asked quietly, 'Have you calmed yourself enough to think sensibly about what I have offered?'

Isabel struck out with dagger-bright green eyes. But her answer was modulated to match his undertone. 'What you have offered is not acceptable. You have my terms. A great deal of sensible thought went into the preparation of them.'

A curse was expelled beneath his breath. 'You accuse me of being selfish, yet you would deny your son an education and good prospects because of your own wounded pride.'

'That's not true!' Isabel flared, with incautious volume. She whipped off her hat, the better to see him. Unruly curls were tossed back from her furious face. 'Marcus needs a home and affection as well as school and discipline. He needs a papa…and a family life. He is entitled to expect that from you! Please do not pretend you care about his welfare in any case. You would have quit Ireland without another word on the subject, would you not? In fact, you are no doubt greatly put out that I have turned up before you had an opportunity to creep away.' Her tongue-lashing was curtailed by a glimpse of an imposing figure she had noticed from the corner of a watchful eye.

Connor had wandered into the hallway, no doubt to investigate what was going on. She half turned to look properly at her handsome brother-in-law as he spoke to the men having a rest from heaving the burdensome chest. As Connor angled an enquiring look up the stairs, Isabel sent him a bright smile. 'I'm glad we have met, Colonel Hauke. I'm sure we shall again.' The hint of threat in her voice did nothing other than spark a lazy amusement in his eyes. One of his dark eyebrows curved quizzically. She understood the challenge: he might just as well have said, 'Do your worst; you'll never win.' With a bob she was soon past him and running up the winding staircase as though in the lightest of spirits. 'Have a safe trip…' flowed sweetly back at him. It wasn't until she turned the corner on to the landing that her fists raised and she spun about in despair as though looking for something on which to vent her furious frustration.

The Earl of Devane's carriage, as was to be expected of a rich and influential aristocrat's property, was jauntily sprung and its plump squabs were upholstered in supple hide. It was as sumptuous and comfortable as any fine travelling rig stored in the coach house at Redgrave Park. As the vehicle rocked over uneven ground the movement was rather soporific: Reeves was already dozing in the corner. Had his travelling companion been equally disposed to rest, he might have been sound asleep.

Etienne shifted irritably to the front of the seat, resting elbows on knees. He drew his feet in, examining the gloss on his boots as he tapped leather against wood in an irregular rhythm. The soles of his Hessians scraped impatiently away again over polished planking. His dark head fell back against the cushions. From beneath a fringe of conker-coloured hair his aimless gaze flitted over Ireland's lush pastures. A low sigh whistled out between set teeth.

Reeves opened a lazy eye; it settled on his unquiet master. One side of his lips lifted. A hand delved into an inside pocket and brought out a travelling flask. He tapped the Colonel's arm to gain his attention.

Etienne curtly shook his head, annoyed as much by the intrusion on private thoughts as the damnable thoughts themselves that refused to be quelled or regimented. Immediately he changed his mind, relieving the valet of the liquor just as it was about to disappear back whence it came. Etienne winced as alcohol stung his cut lip. Over the tilted flask he noticed Reeves watching him, one beady eye fully open, the other nearly closed.

Etienne scowled, skimming the flask back so it landed in his lap. He had the distinct impression that

Reeves knew what was vexing him. The fact that, early this morning, he had ridden out with a lady and returned alone looking the worse for wear would have spread like wildfire from the grooms to the other staff. It would be surmised that he had tried to take liberties with Mrs Forrester and she had defended her virtue a little too vigorously. Which was pretty much the truth, although her defence had come before his seduction was more than a glint in his eye. The intent had definitely been there. He shifted on the seat as his loins reminded him that, hours later, it still was.

He tried to sweep away time and a host of women and properly remember details that led to the most fruitful seduction of his life. What dominated his reminiscence was astonishment on discovering she had been a virgin. She had responded like a seasoned strumpet to whatever he suggested. He blocked any more thought of their feverish coupling and made himself concentrate on the outcome to it. They shared a history he had known nothing about. They shared a child. He had a son! His head dropped into his hands and long fingers grasped his scalp.

He was acting as stubbornly and stupidly as she was. Leaving without reaching an agreement was madness. He had had no intention of quitting the house without speaking to her again, of trying to reason with her again. Yet within a few minutes of them coming together the air between them had been thick with friction.

His meticulous plans for his future were disintegrating before his eyes. He felt resentful; in equal part he felt ashamed of his venality. Isabel Forrester was quite literally prepared to fight tooth and nail for her son's future. He was rueing the loss of wealth he would invest for heirs yet to be born to a woman he barely knew or liked. His eyes closed as he realised the gravity of the decisions Isabel Forrester was forcing on him. He barely knew or liked her either, but he admired her protectiveness, and God knows he desired her. She had shattered his orderly life in less time than it took to have a new suit of clothes made. And instinctively he knew that the pieces, once retrieved, would never fit back together the way they had once been. His life, whatever he decided, was irrevocably changed.

On impulse he sat forward, rapped out with his fist and bellowed for the driver to halt. Reeves watched him mildly, arms crossed over his chest as the carriage shuddered to a skidding stop. The shocked coachman probably thought the din heralded a disaster.

Etienne jumped down and strode to unhook Storm from the back of the coach. Reeves peered out, watching with a smile. He took a swig from the bottle. Well, who would have thought it? The disciplined Colonel, with his future carefully mapped out, looked like he'd lost his compass and didn't know which way to turn.

While they had been at Wolverton Manor Reeves had learned a little gossip about Mrs Forrester. He knew she was the widowed poor relation with a scamp of a son to contend with. For a man like the Colonel, with a shrewd eye to the prize in every deal, it wasn't good at all. But she was a fine-looking woman. Judging by the Colonel's bruises, she had a fiery nature beneath that demure exterior and wasn't settling for less than a ring on her finger. Any man would be tempted, even if it meant no cash and taking on a mischievous little wretch.

With a barked instruction at the coachman to turn about when he could find a suitable place, Etienne swung up in the saddle and gave a refreshed Storm his head. He travelled fast with a peaceful empty mind, and a driven primitive urge to locate the mother of his son.

He turned in at the avenue that climbed in a straight line to the house perched high above the coast. He reined Storm into a steady trot and wound a large rewarding hand into his mane, before caressing a warm graceful neck. It was as black silk skeins slipped through his fingers that he realised for days past he had barely given his mistress, Valerie Avery, a thought.

Chapter Eight

'When I said it would be good to see you again soon, I didn't think you'd take it quite so literally.' Connor rose from his chair with a grin on his face. 'What's the matter? Did you forget something vital?'

Connor's bantering tone failed to brighten Etienne's dour expression. 'In a manner of speaking,' he muttered.

Having ushered him in and poked the glowing coals of the fire with a toe of a boot, Connor settled once more into his desk chair, expecting to hear more. No explanation was forthcoming and his friend seemed intent on examining his dirty toecaps over a hand scrubbing across stubble. Powdery grime on his caped shoulders and silvering his dark hair suggested he had ridden back fast. The grim lines about his mouth were as much the result of weariness as the thoughts that were tormenting him. 'Drink?' Connor indicated the decanter. He grimaced, realising his letter to his attorney in London was now back with him.

A hand declined Connor's hospitality. Etienne wandered off to the window and stared out. His head and shoulders shifted, easing the strain in his muscles.

Connor's circumspect gentian gaze returned to him again and again as he removed the decanter's stopper. A sonorous chime was followed by a comforting lilt of flowing liquor. He sipped slowly, thoughtfully.

Connor already had an inkling of what might be distracting his friend and making it hard for him to leave Ireland. It was no fond farewell he had witnessed on the stairs earlier that day between his sister-in-law and this man. The attraction that existed between Isabel and Etienne had not gone unnoticed. He and Rachel had only last night discussed where it might lead. But lately a more disquieting atmosphere of conspiracy seemed to be drawing them together.

When Hauke had first arrived, Isabel had kept him at arm's length, although Connor had noticed that his friend made a subtle effort to slip under her guard. Now Isabel seemed equally keen for them to steal time alone. Rachel had been delighted that her sister seemed to be responding to their eligible male guest's interest in her. But Isabel was looking increasingly tense and contemplative. When he had disturbed the two of them earlier on the stairs he had again sensed something amiss.

Judging by the battle wounds his friend was sporting, their trysts were certainly full of passion but possibly not exclusively of a pleasurable kind. He was not sure how he'd kept a straight face when Hauke explained away the damage by saying he'd ridden into a low branch. The tale was decidedly implausible; the Colonel's horsemanship was renowned.

Contemplating a reason for their skirmishing put a crease between Connor's eyes. If Isabel had been approached in an unwelcome manner, then while she was living beneath his roof it was his duty—and not one he would shirk—to take his best friend to task over it. But Isabel had made no complaint and still seemed eager to slip away to meet him privately. She wasn't an untried maid, but a mother in her middle twenties. Connor's liberal views dictated it was not for him to interfere in her affairs until she hinted she wanted him to. Besides, he knew his friend; Etienne Hauke was judged by everyone to be a fair gentleman.

Oblivious to his friend's perceptive interpretation of his mood, Etienne paced the room. 'I want you to tell me about Isabel Forrester's husband. I know you hinted her past was not open to discussion, and I've respected that, but there are things I need to know. I don't even know the man's full name or what rank he held. All I know is he was a soldier. Which regiment? When did he die?'

It was an interrogation Connor had been half expecting. But the blunt manner in which it was executed took him aback. In a way he sympathised with this man's dilemma. If one were considering taking on a stepchild, it would be wise to at least know something of the sire's character and history. Unfortunately he couldn't help him at all. Nor would he if he could. Connor rose, went to the mantelpiece and carefully positioned his brandy balloon. 'I promised Rachel before we were married that what she told me in confidence about her sister's situation would never be repeated by me. I've no intention of ever betraying her trust, you must realise that.'

'I'm sorry to put you in an awkward position, it's just I need to know more about him than his name. Was he cruel to her or the boy? Why does nobody talk of him? Tell me, for God's sake! I have a right to know.' The words were blasted out in exasperation.

'Why do you? You tell me why you have a right to know anything about my sister-in-law. If I recall correctly, you intended dashing back to England not only to visit your mistress but to finalise a lucrative marriage contract.' After a tense moment Connor added gruffly, 'I can take a guess from what you told me that the business with Miss Greenwood is not indispensable. As for Valerie Avery, if your heart were in it, you would have made an honest woman of her years ago. It's no disgrace to overrule logic and let your heart lead, even if it takes you somewhere that seems unsuitable...somewhere you'd rather not be.' Connor cleared his throat and gave his friend a quirk of a smile, apologising for his unsolicited counsel.

Etienne stared at him as though startled by what he'd heard, then he strode to the desk and unceremoniously helped himself to a drink. The decanter clattered discordantly on a glass as he poured. 'You've missed your calling, Con. That sermon qualifies you for the pulpit alongside our friend Father Maguire.'

Connor grimaced at that; watched as his friend upended his tumbler and emptied it in a single gulp. 'I'm afraid I'm not done yet. I take it you are serious in this and your intentions are honourable. Have you and Isabel talked of marriage?'

Etienne propped an elbow against the window frame, five fingers scraped into his hair. 'Yes. We have spoken of marriage and God knows the situation is serious.'

'Have you asked her about her husband?'

'Yes.'

'And?'

'She told me to mind my own business.'

'You have your answer then. If Isabel wanted you to know about her past, she would tell you herself. Has she turned you down?'

'She turned down what I offered.' He knew from Connor's trenchant stare that he wouldn't be fobbed off with further ambiguity. He parried more questions by bluntly loosing some of his own. 'Did her father buy for her the first fortune hunter that happened by? Was Forrester willing to overlook the fact that his bride was pregnant with another man's child? I'd guess he simply took comfort in her dowry and ran through it as quick as possible. He's left her dependent on charity, hasn't he? And why is it you support Isabel and the boy? Did Edgar Meredith bankrupt himself burying the scandal?'

'That's enough!' Connor's voice was whiplash savage. The warning hand he struck out formed a fist. One finger slowly unfurled, pointed threateningly. 'We've been friends for a long time now. I hope you're not about to act in a way that makes it impossible for that to continue.'

'So do I,' Etienne said softly. 'But I want some answers and if getting them upsets you…so be it.' He spun on a heel, and gestured a terse apology. He was acting boorishly; he knew it, but couldn't seem to stop. An inner rage seemed to churn his mind and body, obliterating rational thought. He knew Connor had every right to demand to know exactly why he was interrogating him over a matter that, ostensibly, was none of his concern. He was confused himself why the dratted dead husband should interest him to the point of obsession. One thing he did know was that he would soon lose his oldest friend's respect and friendship. He would wither a little beneath Connor's disgust when it finally emerged that he had been the scoundrel who had propelled Isabel into scandal years ago.

'What exactly have you offered Isabel? When you answer, bear in mind that Isabel Forrester is my wife's sister. Bear in mind that I am extremely fond of her and her son. While they live with Rachel and me, they have the full force of my protection.'

'How very noble of you. Or is it simply guilt? Had Isabel not accompanied Rachel to York when she jilted you and fled, she would have been safe from that marauding bastard who ruined her.'

Connor's stance was outwardly aggressive; inwardly he felt some relief. His friend was furious and exasperated because he'd discovered that the woman he wanted had been seduced and abandoned. God! He didn't know the half of it. And that, of course, was the problem: Hauke wanted him to supply the missing pieces. But that was for Isabel to do. 'I think you had better explain just how…just what you are talking about.'

'I think you had better explain to me why Isabel and the child aren't given shelter by her parents.' Etienne watched for a reaction. The slight flicker and flinch in Connor's expression gave him his answer. 'They've exiled her, haven't they? Why? They got her respectable.'

'Until I hear you say you've asked my sister-in-law to marry you, and she has accepted, you have no right to expect me to divulge one blasted thing about any of my in-laws.' Connor's voice scythed through the atmosphere like fresh-forged steel.

'One final, simple question. Where is she? I've searched your damned house from top to bottom for her. Gallagher thinks she's out, visiting friends in the village. Do you know where she is?'

Friction between them had built to a dangerous level, yet the fact that Etienne felt so comfortable having the run of his house mellowed Connor. It reminded him of the days they had once been more like brothers than army comrades or business associates. Whether carousing or campaigning, incidentals such as standing on ceremony for etiquette would always have gone unheeded by them both. He was about to say that he believed his sister-in-law had visited Clodagh Fitzgerald, when it became unnecessary. With exact punctiliousness a peevish child's tone could be heard in the hallway, followed by a woman's patient voice.

With an amount of incredulity Connor realised his friend was now looking oddly apprehensive. He was likely to drop his guard while vulnerable. Connor slyly pressed home his advantage. 'Why are you so sure Marcus wasn't born legitimate?'

'Because I was the marauding bastard who ruined her.'

The study door burst open and a child hurtled in, still garbed in his outdoor clothes. As though the exertion had overheated him, he started to pull at his heavy coat.

'Marcus! Come here, please. You may speak to your uncle later if you— Marcus, come here, at once!'

Isabel hastened into the room after her fleet-footed son. She was unaware her brother-in-law was not alone but in conference with another gentleman screened by the wide open door. 'I'm sorry, Connor. Marcus hoped you might take him for a ride on Sky. The grooms will not suffice this afternoon, it seems. I hope he has not disturbed you. Perhaps later…if you have a little time to spare…' Her flustered attitude kept her from immediately noticing that her son had ceased plucking open the buttons on his coat and chaotically weaving between furniture legs. Now he was standing perfectly still, his hat and scarf trailing the floor from loose fingers.

Isabel quickly turned to see what absorbed her son's interest. She froze statue-still just for an instant before carefully removing her bonnet from her tousled honey locks. Unconsciously she smoothed hair into place as she took a proper glance at her brother-in-law. He too seemed dazed by his good friend's reappearance. Isabel wound the bonnet ribbons about a slender hand; the ensuing silence was only seconds long, but seemed to her to drag uncomfortably. 'Oh! You are still here, Colonel…' As soon as the phrase was blurted out she knew it sounded stupid. Obviously he wasn't *still* here; he had gone and returned. His travel-dusty dishevelled appearance was testament to that. She frowned, scoured her mind for something more intelligent to say.

'Are you going away?'

Etienne tore his gaze from the mother to the son. Lucid, wistful eyes climbed over him, pinned him down until the restless demons in him ceded and were still. 'What makes you think so?'

'I don't know.' Marcus shrugged his frail shoulders, his fair features contorted. With quiet confidence and a pursed mouth he nodded to himself. 'You'll go away.' His knowledge seemed to crush him momentarily. 'Sam let me sit on your horse.' Mischief sparked his tawny eyes alight again. Aimlessly, yet with a purpose that screwed up his sweet face, he whipped his scarf over the floor as though he would dust the parquet to death. 'He said I shouldn't tell you. Storm likes me. He didn't mind me sitting on him or stroking him. Do you mind?' The challenge was strong, hardening his glossy agate eyes and tilting his chin defiantly. The snaking scarf was tossed aside.

'Yes, I mind.'

Etienne saw the boy's bravado was fading. His

sharp Adam's apple bobbed behind a tracery of blue veins on white skin. Long lashes fluttered as a consequence of his behaviour troubled him.

'It wasn't Sam did it. I…it was me. I got on Storm by my own. I jumped on his back all by my own. It wasn't Sam.'

'That's clever of you. He's very big.'

'I am clever.'

'I'm sure you are.'

'You don't mind I got on him?'

'Yes, I do.'

'Why?'

'You didn't ask permission.'

'But you would say no if I did.'

'Hush, Marcus. Colonel Hauke is…he is busy talking with Uncle Connor as you can see. Come…' Instinctively Isabel's fingers threaded soothingly through her son's platinum hair as she led him towards the door. He pulled away.

'Will you take me for a ride on Storm before you go away?'

'Yes.'

Marcus still stared up at the man, his expression expectant. Suddenly his face lit to radiance. 'I didn't really sit on him yet. I made it up…Sam said I mustn't.'

'Why did you make it up?'

'I don't know.'

'Do you often tell lies?'

'No…' His baby-large amber eyes swivelled to his mother.

'It was a joke, then?'

Marcus nodded and peeped beneath fanning lashes at his interrogator.

Etienne raised his eyebrows. His expression needed no explanation. Marcus grabbed at his mother's hand at the silent rebuke. Remembering his scarf, he stooped to collect it.

'Colonel Hauke! I thought you would by now be on the ferry.' Rachel, smiling widely as though pleased by the assembled company, entered her husband's study. A maid close behind was carrying her shopping packages. 'Have you decided to yet stay a while?' Rachel's voice betrayed her delight at the idea and her wide blue gaze slipped sideways to subtly encompass Isabel.

As though he had only recently surfaced from the stupefaction of knowing his friend had seduced his sister-in-law and had just been conversing with his own offspring, Connor rattled off at a speed that made his wife frown, 'Come, my dear, now let's away and find something to eat and you must show me what you've bought.' He took her arm firmly and turned her about. Over a shoulder flowed back at his nephew, 'Shall we find your pony?' With a fierce look at Hauke, he added, 'Marcus, ask your mama if you may come with us for tea.'

Marcus did as he was bid. A hesitant smile and permission were bestowed on him. Before quitting the room with his aunt and uncle, Marcus solemnly looked at Etienne. 'You won't take me for a ride on Storm. You told a joke as well, didn't you?'

'No, I told the truth,' his father told him.

The door had been closed but a moment when Isabel sent Etienne a reproving glance. 'If you're leaving soon and won't find the time, I'd rather you didn't promise him things he can't have.'

'I've not promised him a single thing he can't have.'

Isabel looked at him again, warily. She laid down her bonnet upon the desk and with brisk fingers unbuttoned her pelisse. 'So, why are you back, Colonel? Did you forget something?'

Etienne smiled at his hand, noticing it was still clutching an empty tumbler. The glass was deposited with a thump on the mantelpiece. 'Connor asked me the same thing.'

'It seems a natural assumption to make. Why else would you come back?'

'Why indeed?' he mocked himself savagely. 'Are you hoping I'll say I've come back for you?'

'No,' Isabel shortly replied. 'I'm hoping you might say you have come back to do your duty. I would like to think that somewhere within my son's father is a conscience and a vestige of morality.'

'It seems there is, Mrs Forrester, and my surprise at the discovery is no less than yours, I assure you.'

Their eyes locked for a moment and then he said with an amount of gritty irony, 'I trust you're not expecting me to go down on bended knee?'

Isabel flushed. He would never let her forget for one moment that he was coerced into this. Not now or, she imagined, in ten years' time, if they survived those years together. When she spoke, she hated the unshed tears husking the words. 'You need not fear, sir, that I will gloat or appear victorious. I've no cause for celebration. Neither of us has won. If Marcus gains from our union that will be enough…no, it will be everything.'

'Not for me, it won't. I have every intention of also benefiting from our union, my dear.'

Isabel swallowed, her complexion stained deep rose. 'I have promised I will not interfere with your life. You and your…good friend need not fret on that score. I only ask you to be discreet. So long as you give Marcus and me a fair amount of the respect and family outings that we deserve we should get along reasonably well. In fact, in time we might even become friends and that would be nice…'

His sardonic grunt abbreviated her sweet attempt at conciliation. A nervous raise of green eyes noticed he was genuinely, savagely amused. Isabel felt her humiliation burn as hot as the blood suffusing her complexion. 'It was just a suggestion. It isn't necessary,' she said graciously.

'Indeed, it isn't. We got the wretch into the world being lovers, not friends. In return for giving him status as my son, possibly my heir, the least you owe me is to keep the status quo.'

'I think it best we talk about it once wed.' Isabel picked up her bonnet and headed, with graceful aplomb, for the door.

'I think it best we talk about it now, before vows are taken.'

Isabel hesitated, swished about and glowered at him. 'Very well…if you must have your pound of flesh, Colonel, take it. But you'll find it not to your taste. Never again will I be that.'

Isabel thought he might scoff at that, but he didn't even smile. He simply looked at her for a long moment before murmuring, 'Once we were remarkably compatible physically. I haven't changed that much.'

'But I have, sir,' Isabel bit out sweetly. 'Copious wining and dining and the finest feather bed wouldn't now tempt me.'

A glitter of amusement narrowed his eyes. 'I might be a little older, more sophisticated in my approach, but I could still oblige you with an al fresco rough-and-tumble if you prefer.'

Isabel swallowed the wedge of humiliation in her throat. 'You are a most hateful man.'

'But still you want to marry me. Why?'

'For Marcus's sake.'

'Is that really all there is to it? What's best for the boy?'

Isabel turned away from the biting insinuation in his voice. He might as well have said: if you don't want me, perhaps my money tempts you. She opened the door, her knuckles whitening on the handle. 'Yes. That's all there is to it. Oh, one other thing. The boy, the child, the wretch, has a name and it is Marcus.'

Chapter Nine

'Did Marcus know his father?'

Isabel shook her head, chewing laboriously on a mouthful of succulent chicken as though it were coarse black bread.

'Did Forrester die when the boy was very young?'

With difficulty Isabel gulped down the meat, then neatly laid down her cutlery. A frown accompanied, 'There is…something I must tell you about that…'

'I wondered if you would tell me before we stood before the minister. It doesn't do to masquerade behind an alias at such an important time.'

'I hadn't thought of that,' she said meekly.

'I had, Miss Meredith.'

'Yes; I'm sure you had,' Miss Isabel Meredith sniped. 'Such a discrepancy might lead to an annulment. In which case I'm surprised you have brought it to my notice.' She overlooked the way a corner of his mouth tugged into an appealing smile. 'I'm sure you want to hear me admit it, so I will. I have never had a husband. The only man I have been close to in that way is my son's father. Did Connor tell you?'

'The only man?'

When she glared tight-lipped at him, he added, 'Indirectly your sister let me know. But don't blame her. I simply asked her your mother's maiden name. She managed to change the subject, but the look on her face was answer enough.'

'As you seem eager to have it confirmed, I'll oblige you with a proper response. My mother's maiden name is Forrester.' Isabel picked up her knife and fork again and sliced ferociously into tender meat. 'I shall refrain from asking how you appear *au fait* with ruses used by ruined women.'

He ignored the jibe, rolling the slender stem of a wine-glass between deft fingers. A liquid chocolate gaze bathed her proud defiance. 'I imagined you might find it difficult to sever every link with your mother and father.'

'You seem very perceptive this evening, sir. For that exact reason I chose to call myself Forrester. Despite my parents wanting me out of their lives, and Marcus, too, I found I could cling on to them…in my own way.' Her head turned, glossy curls jaunty about her face, shielding a pensive expression. 'I am not surprised you have worked it out. It is hardly original for an unwed mother to purchase a cheap gold ring, then seek a new locality and identity as a respectable widow. The subterfuge has doubtless been used since time immemorial.'

'You stayed in York a long time. Why? It must have held no good memories for you.'

'On the contrary: it held our Aunt Florence. Even as children we would plead to travel there and visit her. She was always our favourite relative. When Rachel jilted Connor and fled there she knew, right or wrong, her welcome was assured. Aunt Florence's home became my sanctuary too. Although she had little experience of anything outside the village she lived in, she was a great practical help to me and never judged me. If anyone hurt or maligned any of us, Aunt Florence would do battle with them.'

'I imagine she would have liked to kill me for what I did to you.'

Isabel's eyes darted from logs crumbling into the grate to meet his smouldering gaze. 'No. I never lied to anyone about what happened between us. You need not fret that I told my family I had been assaulted.'

'That was very brave of you.'

'Unnecessarily so; you never returned to defend either of our reputations.' She huskily mocked her gullibility. 'I actually thought some harm had befallen you to prevent you returning.'

'I'm sorry. Had I known of your condition…'

'It doesn't matter,' Isabel interrupted. 'As I have said, none of those first sordid details matter.'

'It wasn't sordid, Isabel.'

Her cutlery was dropped, impatiently, with a clatter. 'Of course it's not sordid to you now. Not now we're to be man and wife and you would like to restore a certain…*unity*… between us.'

His silence and heady unwavering gaze sent her attention dropping to her plate.

'What have you told Marcus about his father?'

'No lies, I hope. I told him his papa was a brave soldier who fought in the war against the French… and didn't come back.'

Etienne smiled. 'I think I can claim the honour. What was this paragon's name? He surely wasn't known just as Mr Forrester.'

'I took my papa's middle name, Luke, and my mama's maiden name, Forrester. My bogus husband was known as Luke Forrester.'

'My French grandfather's name was Luc. My name in full is Etienne Luc Thomas Hauke. I was named for both my maternal and paternal grandfathers.'

Isabel's lips twitched wryly. 'That's quite convenient.'

'Every truth will be significant, however small, when we endeavour to sort out this mess.'

'I know.' Isabel's voice was huskily sombre.

'I would have preferred Luc. Etienne was my mother's choice. I sometimes use Steven.'

'Yes,' Isabel cleared her throat and managed a wavering smile. 'Claudine admitted as much.' White teeth clamped on her lower lip as she noticed his narrowed eyes. 'I like the name Etienne…and Luc too.'

'And what are we going to tell the boy… Marcus?' he corrected himself. 'How shall we explain that his papa is risen from the dead and is known by a different name?'

Isabel's hands fluttered in hopelessness. 'I've no idea. I would like to tell him as much of the truth as is possible…without him despising me as he grows and learns.'

'Would you like me to broach the subject tomorrow when I take him for a ride?'

Isabel stared at a point on the ceiling, her brow furrowed in alternating consideration and consternation. 'No…I think I should speak to him first. But then…perhaps if we both together tell him… Oh, I don't know!'

'I'll speak to him first alone.' The edict was polite but quite firm. 'I would like to introduce myself to him without the risk of any discord between us erupting while I do so.'

'You think I will be purposely disruptive at such a vital time for my…our son?' she ejected angrily.

'No. It's not *your* behaviour I'm concerned for. I am not always the most agreeable person when at bay.'

'Indeed. I would vouch for that.' Their eyes grappled over the rims of two raised wine goblets that sparked candlelight. Isabel replaced hers. 'What will you tell him?'

'As much of the truth as I can without him despising me as he grows and learns.'

The servants arrived to clear the plates and the next course was served. Steaming platters of beef and horseradish sent a piquant savoury aroma to warm the lofty room. As the servants filed out and all that moved were giant fiery shadows, Isabel said quite gravely. 'I fear we have driven the Earl and Countess of Devane from their own home.' She sighed as she recalled that her sister and brother-in-law had suddenly this evening thought of an important dinner engagement that would keep them abroad. 'It must be difficult for them to comprehend such astonishing news. Rachel is quite overwhelmed. And I believe Connor isn't at all sure how he should react: whether he ought congratulate you or punch you on the nose.'

Etienne choked a laugh as two fingers went to test the solidity of the bridge of his nose. 'Luckily so far he has opted for the former. I'm not sure my vanity could take another battering.'

Isabel dipped her head. The memory of her tempestuousness still wounded her. In response to that she clipped out, 'If you had not behaved in such a...a vile manner...'

'Pax!' He grinned. 'I deserved it, I know. As I learn more about you and what you've endured alone, caring for my son, I know just how much I deserved it...and more. Do you believe me when I say that had I known you were carrying my child I would have come back?'

'I don't know. Now you're aware I'm of your social class, and related through my sister to your good friend, there is no other proper way for you to respond and still seem human. Had I been what you believed me to be, I wonder would you have worried that I or your child starved?'

'What is it you think I believed you to be?'

Answering that particular question was beyond her courage. Instead she demanded, 'Do you have other offspring? Perhaps you've no idea how many fair children that resemble your portrait are dotted about the countryside.'

'There are none.' The words were curt and he drained his glass as soon as they had been uttered.

'You said there was a woman who tried to pass off her dead husband's child as yours.'

He abruptly stood, shoving his chair back noisily against parquet. He strode to the fire, and hands that looked foreign gripped against ghostly white marble.

In the darkling room his face looked devilishly bronzed by leaping flames in the hearth. 'I wish to God I'd never mentioned the incident.'

The controlled anger vibrating in his voice made Isabel flinch. 'I'm sorry. I've been unforgivably rude. I have no right to question you over such aspects of your life.'

'Yes, you have, dammit! In a day or so you will be my wife. You have every right to know that and more about me. Question me about anything you like but know this: Marcus is my only child.'

He was quite sure that was the truth. Whilst in England he was faithful to his mistress. He had no reason not to be satisfied. Valerie Avery was an attentive and energetic lover who made it her business to keep him thoroughly entertained. In the army he had kept a pretty young camp follower in exorbitant style, which meant she had stayed clean and eager lest she lost her envied status to a rival. Not wanting the distraction or responsibility of a host of bastards, he had done his part to protect his women against pregnancy and let the sheets catch his seed. Which made it all the more curious as to why, eight years ago, he had abandoned sense and caution to such a disastrous degree with a sensual sylph who had ambushed him body and soul. Yet he had. He could recall quite clearly lying with her, their bodies entwined, in congress, as they recovered from a frenetic passion.

He looked at her now, cool, solemn, poignantly sad because of that very coupling…

To chase the rising desire from his mind and body he demanded, 'Did my mother give you that miniature because she recognised I was Marcus's father?' His voice sounded rough and angry.

'No,' Isabel reassured quickly. 'It wasn't that at all. Claudine thought that I might have married your half-brother.'

'My half-brother?'

The outrage in his voice kept Isabel silent for a moment. She wondered whether to divulge any more of what Claudine had told her about her unhappy marriage. 'Your mother meant no harm. She simply recognised a family likeness between the portrait and Marcus. Naturally she would not think you were his father. She had seen us conversing quite normally together. We would both have needed to be consummate actors and thoroughly shameless to have done so, knowing our illegitimate son was asleep in the nursery of Wolverton Manor.'

'What did she tell you about Christopher?'

'That he was very like you; that you were of similar age and when young you could have been taken for twins. She said that when older, you grew darker and he stayed fair. I imagine that was why she imagined he might have fathered Marcus. The fact that he and his mother moved to York, where I was living, compounded her suspicions. Claudine knew I had lived there until recently and that my sham husband was a soldier. Your half-brother joined the army too, she said. These were odd coincidences so it was a logical assumption to make.'

Etienne stared into glowing logs. 'I imagine she has made my father sound like an adulterous brute while she was the wronged, dutiful spouse.'

Isabel was aware of bitterness in his profile. 'She admitted that they both sought comfort elsewhere.'

'How magnanimous of her to take some blame. It must be the first time ever. My mother always came first in his life. He would never divorce her so he lost the woman who loved him. He financially supported Christopher after his mistress married a wastrel. Christopher married and moved to the New World some years ago. I rather miss him, for we'd kept in touch until then.'

Not sure how to respond to that Isabel murmured, 'I'm sorry your parents were unhappy.'

'So am I,' he drawled on a breath of a laugh. 'For it could be hell on earth for us all.' After a very brief pause he added, 'He isn't able to defend himself so I will do it for him. My father was an honest, honourable man.'

'I'm sure he was.'

'Why are you sure? You didn't know him. Are you convinced of his goodness because he has such an honest, honourable son?' The self-disgust was apparent in his tone. 'Had my father been alive and discovered what I'd done to you, he would have been out for my blood sooner than your own papa.'

Carefully she said, 'I'm sure of his goodness because he has a fine grandson. I wish Marcus could have known him. He's never known the love of grand-parents.'

'Well, he now has Claudine, for what that's worth.'

'It's worth a lot to Marcus. He knows so few rela-tives.'

'When he's older and more discerning, perhaps he might think that particular kinship not worth a jot.' He paused, gestured regret. 'My apologies. It's not the time or the place to trawl though family feuds. I know you've had enough rifts with your own family. I'm pleased that Connor and Rachel stayed loyal to you. Guilt or no over that damnable jilting that started it all, they could have abandoned you like the others.' He strolled to the window and stared out over sombre lawns. 'Have I your permission to take Marcus out for a ride tomorrow and introduce myself to him as his father?'

'Yes.'

He inclined his dark head in acknowledgement. 'If you'll excuse me, I have rather a lot to do if we are to be married before the end of the week.'

'Yes,' Isabel again said with cool dignity. *That*

damnable jilting was the cause of all his ills. With sudden clarity she knew why he had been in York. 'Did you go to York eight years ago to look for Rachel? Did Connor ask you to bring her home?'

'Connor didn't know a thing about my pathetic meddling.' A soundless laugh rasped his throat. 'He was comatose through drink and fighting a fever when I left to bring Rachel back. The irony is they both escaped the consequences of my stupidity…you didn't. You were the innocent…in all of it, Isabel. And that's hard for *me* to bear. God knows how you've borne it.' He had gained the door and Isabel was sure he was about to quit the room, but he hesitated and looked at her.

'I'm not going to lie and pretend sentiment I don't feel. But I will care for you and Marcus and I do want you…so much that it gives you quite an advantage. My desire to restore a certain *unity* between us, as you put it, would be a powerful tool of retribution should you use it against me.'

Isabel felt her heart pumping slowly at the raw throb of need in his voice. He desired her, but he didn't love her. Years ago desire in her had withered and died, stifled by guilt and relentless shame, but the yearning to be loved had flickered and endured. She stood, placing her hands flat on glossy wood. 'I'm sorry you feel that way. I think once you return to England and your…good friend…you will find the matter resolves itself.'

* * *

Horse and rider streamed against the azure skyline like a jet banner.

The panting steed was skilfully reined in until it trotted into the poplar trees then out again, winding a serpentine path through skeletal wood. Finally it clopped to a steamy-breathed halt. The horseman lifted the child from beneath his cloak to stand in front of him on the moulded sinews of the stallion's broad back.

'Turn around.'

The boy did as he was bid, balancing carefully, a wondrous smile animating his small face.

'Did he go fast enough for you?'

The boy simply nodded, for a delightful exhilaration had wedged words in his throat.

Etienne lifted his son, positioning spindly legs to straddle the horse so they sat face to face. With something akin to parental pride he scoured the boy's fair features. He was handsome, no doubt about it.

Marcus looked right back, quietly, without fidgeting.

Etienne let the reins drop and Storm ambled to the water's edge to forage.

'Do you recall that yesterday you asked me if I am going away?'

Marcus nodded, his eyes, his whole demeanour, gravely expectant.

'I am going away and so are you and your mama. You are both coming with me to England.'

'Does Mama mind?'

'No, she's glad.'

Marcus's solemn expression brightened. 'I'm glad too. My grandparents live in England. They don't like me.'

'Yes, they do like you,' his father told him huskily. 'It's me they don't like.'

'Why don't they like you?'

'Because I went away. I left you and your mama alone for a long time and that was wrong. I was away so long that people thought I had died and would never come back. But I wasn't dead, I was on the continent fighting in the war. Now I've come back.'

'Are you my papa?'

'Yes.'

'Were you brave? I told everyone you were brave.'

'Yes. I was a brave soldier.'

'The war was over a long time ago when Napoleon was defeated at Waterloo. Did you get lost?'

Inwardly Etienne smiled. For a child who paid no attention to his lessons, he knew a hell of a lot it would have been convenient that he didn't.

'Yes. It took me a long while to find my way home.'

'Did you fall out of a tree?'

Etienne barked a laugh. 'What?'

'Murphy's brother fell out of a tree and knocked his head. He forgot where he lived. His ma sent his da to find him. Then he got thrashed.'

'I didn't fall out of a tree, but I did get hit on the head.'

He lifted small white fingers and dipped his dark visage. He felt his son's steady touch press across the proud cicatrice beneath his hair.

'Frenchies did that?' Marcus asked, wide-eyed.

His father nodded. 'I did some equal damage to them. I was escaping and they tried to stop me, but I got away.'

'So you could come home to me and my mama?'

'Yes.'

Marcus looked fascinated and proud and ready to burst with happiness. 'My mama said my papa's name was Luke.'

There was barely a hesitation before his father explained, 'My full name is Etienne Luc Thomas Hauke. I didn't like the name Etienne for a long while so didn't much use that name. Now I quite like it.'

'*I* like it,' his son kindly endorsed. 'If your name is Hauke, why is my name not Hauke too?'

'It is. Your name is Marcus Forrester Hauke. Your mama called you just Marcus Forrester because… because Forrester reminded her of her parents and because she wasn't sure if I was still alive.'

'My grandparents aren't Forresters, they are Merediths.'

'Your grandmother was named Forrester before she married your grandfather.' This was no dunce he was dealing with. Etienne felt a surge of paternal pride. But before any further questions occurred to his sharp little son he quickly lifted him up and spun him about so his spine was back against his torso. 'It's time to get back. Your mama will be waiting.'

'Shall I say we went very fast?' Marcus's head tilted up over a shoulder as he sought his father's advice.

Etienne smiled and an instinctive hand cupped a soft rosy cheek. His immediate answer would have been: 'Let's keep it a secret.' Instead he said, 'If your mama asks then you must tell her the truth. But she might not ask…'

He kicked the horse into action and as the biting wind whipped against his face and the boy snuggled against him, warming his cold heart, he wondered how many years it would take before his son wanted to know why, when his father was escaping from the French, he had not yet been born.

Chapter Ten

'Am I vulgar and mercenary to have coerced a wealthy man to provide for Marcus and me?'

'No!'

'No? Even though he despises me for toppling his ambitions? I'm sure he thinks me a schemer with vengeance on my mind.'

'Who would blame you for that!' Rachel exploded. 'It is right a child's father should care for his own flesh and blood.'

'He would have more willingly done so outside wedlock.'

'He returned of his own volition to propose marriage. He's not past redemption. And he's obviously attracted to you still. Are you out for revenge? Had I been abandoned so long I expect I might have been out for blood!'

That morning's emotional parting from her sister was rudely dislodged from her drowsing mind as the coach swerved around a pothole. Isabel's eyes flew wide, focused, after rapid blinking, on the other two occupants of the vehicle. Neither was bothered by the bumpy ride.

Her son had coiled, cat-like, as close to his father as he could without actually reposing on his lap. Etienne seemed to neither welcome nor shun the small limbs imprisoning him. Even asleep her son managed to keep in contact with his father.

Before being taken off to bed in the evenings, Marcus searched for Etienne with a dogged determination that was heartrending to observe. No explanation that he was out riding or attending business in town would suffice. He needed to see him before he would settle. For his part, Etienne had so far been unfailingly patient with Marcus's foibles. She imagined he would display similar tolerance of an acquaintance's child.

At the start of their journey, Marcus had interrogated his father about his new home in Suffolk. Each lively question had been concisely answered. Just once on the journey Etienne had taken sufficient notice of Marcus when he continued to vault from seat to seat, despite his mother's instruction to sit still, to speak to him in more than a single sentence. 'Either you calm yourself or one or other of us must travel outside. As I'm not willing to incur your mama's wrath by forcing you to sit with Reeves up top, or hitch a ride with the gypsies, I shall need to get out and ride on horseback.'

Etienne had not once raised his voice; indeed, his tone disclosed his tedium at needing to issue an ultimatum at all. It produced the desired effect. Marcus had looked sulky, but settled back quietly into the creaky leather with his hands folded primly and his short legs sticking out at right angles to the seat. Within a mile or two his flaxen head was drooping against his father's caped chest.

Now Etienne was frowning out through the coach window as though a riddle of some complexity was concealed in the looming rain clouds leadening the horizon. Motionless fingers were curled close to his slanted mouth.

Isabel felt a surge of poignant frustration tighten her insides. Marcus was excited by the adventure, and overjoyed with his new papa. Etienne's lack of reciprocation hadn't yet dampened his delight. She and her son were travelling to a new life of comfort and respectability. She had got everything she wanted yet there was an emptiness where gladness and relief should have been. The man who had acquiesced to her demands looked as though he would extricate himself from the trap she had sprung as soon as he had fathomed a merciful way to do it.

She guessed he would, at this precise moment, much prefer to be flying ahead on Storm than to be wedged in a corner of a lumbering coach with Marcus's sleeping form draped over him. There was a latent energy…a restlessness about him that made his stillness seem unnatural.

As though aware of her observation, her husband turned his dark head and caught her gazing forlornly at him.

Isabel was glad of the fading light as she drew her cloak about her and turned her flushing face away.

'Are you in need of a stop before we reach the Red Lion?'

'No.' she said huskily. 'Thank you.' A nod indicated her drowsing son. 'Is he…do you want me to hold him?'

'He's no trouble…'

In response to his neutral acceptance of the burden that was her beloved son, Isabel managed a small faltering smile. It adequately concealed her inclination to quietly weep.

They were communicating at last and she would rather make small talk with him than sit in oppressive silence until they reached their night's lodgings. She settled on the first topic of conversation that entered her head. And indeed it had worried her when he had previously brushed the matter aside. 'You ought to have sent word of our marriage to your mother at Ormonde Castle.'

'Why? She'll find out from gossip soon enough.'

'As a courtesy, don't you think you should have been the one to tell her? After all, you promised she wouldn't hear of your betrothal second-hand.'

'Well, dutiful son that I am, I've kept my word on that score.'

The irony in his tone made Isabel chew her lip and regret her attempt at cordiality.

He raised a dusty boot, jamming it against the seat opposite as he eased his position on the seat. 'The news won't trouble her. At this precise moment she's likely to be more concerned with plotting a wedding of her own. I'd say she's successfully hooked him this time.' A sardonic smile acknowledged the puzzlement on his wife's face. 'Surely you realised she is Ormonde's mistress? She's long had an ambition to improve her status.'

'Why…why…no,' Isabel stuttered. 'I thought Vincent Ormonde was a relative of yours on your father's side.'

'He is. To give my mother her due, they weren't lovers while my father was alive. Ormonde was the richest man at the wake, and he'd left his ailing wife at home. He was persuaded to stay on as a house guest for a few weeks, to succour the grieving widow.'

'I'm sure Claudine needed a friend at such a time.'

'Indeed,' he drawled, his long lashes drooping as

he sensed her championing his mother. 'She needed
a very good friend. Someone generous enough to
keep her in the Paris fashions she likes so much. My
father's last will and testament settled everything on
me with little more than a living allowance for her.
She was rather irritated by that...until she spied
Vincent Ormonde. Or perhaps it was the ruby on his
finger she noticed first. I've seen smaller pigeon's
eggs. Vincent has always been untroubled by good
taste. Which no doubt accounts for his lengthy liaison
with my dear mama.' He turned his head to gaze into
darkness. 'It can be entertaining watching her homing
in on some unsuspecting fool who looks likely to pay
for the privilege of being seduced. I believe she
managed that without too much trouble the night of
the funeral.'

'Oh...I see,' Isabel ejected in a strangled mutter
that brought his head around.

'Knowing you as I do, I find your prudishness
quite unexpected.'

'You don't know me at all. And I'm sorry it offends
you,' Isabel replied with quiet dignity.

'I've known you in the biblical sense, which is
pertinent. Prudishness doesn't offend me; I could find
it charming. Is it false modesty or are you really as
innocent as you seem?'

'I haven't been innocent since I was seventeen, as
you well know and are at pains to remind me.'

A flash of a smile mocked her prim indignation. 'Not all women lose their innocence when they lose their virginity.'

'I must bow to your superior knowledge on that,' she answered with sweet acerbity and turned completely from him, gathering her cloak about her and resting her head against the side of the coach. Her studied reluctance to converse further was ignored.

'There's something intriguing me even more than your naïveté, Isabel. Do you know what it is?'

'No,' she sighed. 'But I fear you might tell me even though I've no interest in your musings.'

'You're right to be worried about some of my thoughts,' he admitted through laughter in his tone. 'But I think you ought to oblige me with an answer on this. What puzzles me is what the hell you ever found attractive about an emaciated, shaven-headed young army officer who came close to trampling you with his horse and whose first words to you were thus less than complimentary.'

'I can't help you. I've yet to solve such an absurd riddle myself,' she murmured icily.

'I don't believe that. You know. Tell me what about me appealed so much that it made a beautiful, well-bred virgin allow herself to be such easy prey.'

The silence lengthened and Isabel kept her eyes trained on the shadowy woods. She shifted beneath his burning gaze. His bantering tone had been belied by a relentless demand that thickened the space between them.

'Come, tell me,' he cajoled throatily. 'How can I reproduce it if I don't know what it is?'

'You can't ever do that, so don't bother trying.' A whimsical mood momentarily transcended her embarrassment. 'It was of that time…that place…a fantasy…your white horse…'

'My what?' His mocking amusement was choked by astonishment.

'Nothing!' She was back to earth and turned to glare through the dusk at him. 'I don't want to speak of it,' she hissed with such vehemence that she saw Marcus start. An appealing look begged her husband to stop teasing her. 'Is it far to the Red Lion?' she whispered, as her son burrowed back to sleep.

'No. We'll be there soon,' he said softly, his eyes entrapping hers before they slowly closed and he settled his head back against the squabs.

Isabel watched him, studied his features of rough beauty, brutal still in repose. Breath wedged in her throat as she wondered what accommodation he had bespoken for them at the inn.

She had been married four days…and nights. Her husband had yet to properly kiss her, let alone consummate their union. After a brief marriage ceremony he had touched her on the cheek with cool, fleeting lips before his fiery eyes melded to hers. That look could have been stoked from desire or threat of retribution for forcing his hand. But he had so far left her alone and she was glad. Coercing a man to marry one was degrading; tolerating his loveless lust was much worse. Yet once she had, she reminded herself, barely wincing. But she had stupidly mistaken it for something else entirely—then she had thought she had found her soulmate.

The hero she knew by heart had incarnated from the wraith inhabiting her girlish imagination. Her love had come to claim her on his white charger, as she'd long dreamed he would. He was no stranger. Laughing together beneath his cloak as they sheltered from the storm, it seemed she had known him a lifetime. His charm and kindness promised an intimacy that appealed so much she felt, even now, the excitement twinge her insides. His touch had been as she expected…gentle yet strong; his voice one she recognised, cultured yet seductive. The first magical kiss was all it should be and presaged bliss and a lifetime of sharing. Why should she not have given him all of her? The magnitude of her pathetic romanticism still had the power to take her breath away.

Now she had shackled her gallant to her. A flickering glance took in his powerful strength as he feigned relaxation. Penned, perhaps, but he was not tamed…now or ever.

A quiet ceremony held in Wolverton Manor's small

chapel had marked her victory. An Anglican clergyman had officiated. Connor and Rachel had attended but, apart from a small wedding breakfast shared by the four of them at the Manor, there was no celebration. And it was soon over. There was now a sense of embarrassment between them all. Connor and Rachel had wished them both well, and Isabel didn't doubt their sincerity, but because they were cooler with her husband than with her, she withdrew a little too. Oddly, when he had done nothing to demand it or deserve it, she yet behaved loyally to her spouse.

She had felt quite sure that her debonair bridegroom would claim his reward for giving her and her son his name and protection. But despite his frequent intense glances as the hour grew late, he had not, as she feared, attempted to beat a path through their dressing room into her bolted chamber on their wedding night. Perhaps he had not wanted to outrage their hosts with any uproar as he exerted his conjugal rights. Perhaps he simply had not wanted her as much as he had said.

The following few days spent at Wolverton Manor had been busy with preparation for departure. They easily avoided each other until they dined in the evening and four people blithely strove to maintain an adequate amount of conviviality during six courses.

After dinner the bride would visit the nursery to see her sleeping son before she retired. From the lack of noise in her husband's adjoining chamber, Isabel knew he came late to bed. On one occasion it appeared he did not retire at all, but instead went into town carousing. On her way down to breakfast Etienne had been on his way up the stairs. He had looked quite outrageously dissolute with his long dark hair tangled and his concave cheeks appearing yet more hollow, shaded with stubble. His jacket, hooked on a finger, had hung neglected over a shoulder in a condition likely to give his valet a fit. They had barely exchanged a greeting as they passed, like the strangers they were. It was only as she sat watching her tea rock in her cup at the breakfast table that Isabel realised her sleepy-eyed bridegroom might have spent the night with a local woman.

They were man and wife, yet no bond of affection existed between them—just a simmering sexual awareness that coloured each word and glance. With a woman's instinct Isabel knew that the restraint he was imposing on himself was responsible for his detachment. If she punished him with coldness, he would retaliate in his own way.

Her eyes closed wearily. She was prepared for difficulties, she told herself, attempting to empty her chaotic mind and feel peaceful enough to catnap a while. It was no proper marriage, but she had got her son his father and his future, and that was all that mattered.

* * *

It was the icy draught that woke her. Isabel came
to with a start, her drowsy mind still haunted by men
with creased brown visages who steered a vehicle
daubed with many colours. Nervous and barely conscious, she slid along the seat to grab at the carriage
door, slightly ajar and whining on its hinges in a bitter
breeze. She peered out of the window, blinking at the
whitewashed building with low serpentine roofline
and four fiery square panes promising a warm
welcome.

Spying Reeves by the horses' heads, she called to
him softly so as not to wake Marcus still asleep on the
seat. Her husband was nowhere to be seen.

'Have we reached the Red Lion?'

'Yes, we have, Mrs Hauke.' The valet parted from
the ostler, to whom he'd been chatting, and hurried
towards her.

'Are the gypsies still close?' Isabel demanded. The
residue of her nightmarish dream about the band of
travellers they had passed on the road earlier that day
still disturbed her. Three patterned wagons had
followed them at a distance for some miles along the
isolated track before they were lost to view.

At one point a caravan had got close enough for
Isabel to see the leathery faces of the men who sat on
the driver's seat. She'd also observed the fierce-
featured woman who sat between them, gold hoop

earrings protruding from beneath a red shawl that was also protecting her hair from the elements. Something about their intent black eyes had alarmed Isabel. But Marcus had been delighted by the spectacle and had poked his blond head out of the window to wave at them before she had time to restrain him. She had instinctively sought to shield him from view and suddenly she knew why: gypsies were rumoured to abduct young children.

Etienne had seemed unperturbed and faintly amused by their fascination as though, for him, the sight of such tribes on the highways and byways was fairly commonplace.

'You don't want to be getting worried about those sort of folk, Mrs Hauke,' Reeves reassured her. 'They scavenge about the farms and hedgerows but won't come bothering gentry unless they have bits and bobs to sell.' Briskly he rubbed together his gloved palms. 'A chilly night it is, to be sure. Ah, here comes the Colonel now.' The valet nodded at a tall shadowy figure striding from the inn towards the coach.

Etienne reached in and scooped Marcus into his arms. 'They have a clean chamber ready and decent food. I've ordered a meal to be served in the annexe and hot water to be prepared.' He stood aside for Isabel to alight. With Marcus cradled against his chest, he followed her into the inn.

* * *

'Where is Etienne?'

'I expect he is settling with the innkeeper for the food we have eaten. It was tasty, was it not? Are you full?'

Marcus nodded, simultaneously ducking his face away from the washing cloth. Isabel put a controlling hand on his flaxen head. 'Keep still, please! You have gravy on your chin.' Finished with wiping his face, she turned her attention to his grubby hands. Steam rose from the warm water the landlady had provided. 'Rinse your hands,' she instructed her son and he did so, purposefully splashing some water into her lap and soaking her gown. With an exasperated little huff, Isabel caught at his wriggling fingers and towelled them. With an inner grimace she realised her son was probably too lively to settle down to sleep now he had enjoyed an hour or more of repose in the coach.

'Into bed with you!' She clapped her hands playfully to hurry him, then blew out the candle by the cot positioned to one side of a high four-poster bed.

Isabel eyed the bed apprehensively. It was layered in white linen with a good thick quilt spread on top. As her son slid beneath his pristine bed sheets, Isabel pulled back the covers on the four-poster, testing the firmness of the mattress. There was nothing to complain about at all. The food they had eaten had been ample and delicious, the chamber was spacious and spotless, the landlady, Mrs Broome, had been friendly and cooperative. Mr Broome had vowed, with a discoloured grin, that he had given the lady the best room to be had anywhere in the county.

It was also the only room he had to bestow. A party of raucous dandies enjoying a local shoot had taken the other chambers. One of the gentlemen had recognised Etienne and had struck up conversation with him just as Mrs Broome led her and Marcus away along the corridor to the quiet annexe she kept for Quality.

Isabel imagined her husband's lengthy stay below stairs in the taproom was not simply a courtesy to allow her time to suitably attire for the night. Possibly he was content to enjoy better company than he would find with her. She didn't want him to join her upstairs. Yet for no reason she could understand, being abandoned pricked her bride's vanity.

Isabel opened her travelling bag and pulled out an embroidered white night rail. He might like his foppish friends better than her, but she doubted he would stay with them the night through. He needed a good night's rest as much as she did. But it would need to be a wicked man who would expect more than sleep tonight when their child lay barely a yard away. Etienne was not that.

Slipping out of her dusty travelling clothes, she folded them neatly, then washed in the herbal washing water.

'Where is Etienne?'

'Hush, go to sleep, Marcus,' Isabel purred as she tied the ribbons of the cotton nightgown.

'Where *is* he?' Marcus demanded querulously, sitting upright in bed and looking at his mother through the guttering tallow.

'He is taking a drink with the hunters. And he must pay the innkeeper, too, for our dinners.'

'You said he has already paid that fat man. Will he go away and leave us? I don't like it here.'

Isabel sat on her son's narrow bed and soothed him with a cool lavender-scented hand. 'Lay down, dear. Your papa won't leave you, I promise. He is taking us to our new home. Can't you hear the gentlemen laughing in the bar? Listen! They are chatting and clinking their glasses of beer.'

'Don't blow out that candle,' her son entreated in a thin voice. His head dipped at the one solitary flame still burning.

'I won't, I promise. Now go to sleep,' she crooned.

Marcus descended into his sheets, a thumb at his pouting mouth.

Isabel watched him from a chair until his small ribs were rising and falling rhythmically. She turned the key in the lock then placed it on a hook by the door. Etienne had in his possession a similar key to the room. Obliquely she realised the noise in the bar had quietened. She gratefully sank into soft down and stared up at the brocade canopy overhead. It was damson coloured with heavy tassels and looked familiar. Just before exhaustion claimed her, she realised the canopy resembled the shawl the gypsy woman had used to cover her raven hair.

Isabel awoke with a start and instinctively turned towards where Marcus slept. Icy fear was squeezing her heart even before she properly focused on her son's empty bed.

Her sheets and blankets were tossed back and in an instant she was simultaneously searching for her slippers and thrusting her arms into her wrap. The key had gone from its hook and without thought for propriety she was, flimsily attired, risking observation on the landing. The flickering stump of candle grasped in her hand was in danger of extinguishing, so hastily did she dash back and forth along the creaky boards while repeatedly hissing a whispering call to her son.

'Gawd! Do leave off! He ain't in 'ere. This one's name's Jack be all accounts,' shrieked a coarse female voice. A vulgar giggle was joined by a rumbling male chuckle, then other sounds that made Isabel's cheeks flame and hastened her flight to the head of the stairs.

Isabel sped below, frightened to call Marcus again lest she attracted further unwanted attention to herself. She raced along a beam-blackened corridor and yanked at a door. The squat snug contained just the smell of stale ale and cheap tobacco. She quit the room quickly to continue her hunt. The next room was silent but for the shifting of a few embers in the grate. Eerie shadows leapt upon the walls and a fitful flame illuminated a couple of abandoned tankards. The last room she dashed within, she disturbed a trio of grizzled men silently playing cards. In unison they turned to stare grimly and aim their clay pipes at her. She backed away, tears coagulating in her throat, as irrational fear squeezed her heart.

Her son was gone, and so too, it seemed, was her husband. Not properly awake, reason was impaired and her imaginings became feverishly hysterical. It would suit him to dispose of the inconvenience that was their son, and abandon her. He wanted rid of them both. And gypsies were close by. Had he not said, but for her presence, he would have put Marcus out on the road to hitch a ride with those heathens? Suddenly she felt petrified and certain of her sweet son's fate. Her husband had stolen Marcus while she slept and taken him off to be sold to gypsies. And she was alone, in England, with little money and no friends. How would she find him? Or buy him back? She yanked open the door at the end of the corridor and a blast of icy air whipped her thin night rail back against her legs. 'Marcus!' she shrilled in desperation and stood shivering as she surveyed a bleak landscape of moon and frost silvered soil. She had barely put a slippered foot outside when a gripping hand arrested her and spun her about.

'What the hell are you doing?'

Chapter Eleven

'What are *you* doing?'

Her uncontrollable quivering, part shock on being startled, part fury at his imagined wickedness, sent a riot of fawn ringlets dancing about her slender white shoulders. 'What have you done with my son?'

The door was rammed shut and a draught of icy air swirled about her ankles, billowing her nightclothes away from her unsteady legs. She was trapped against the wall by his aggressive stance, her narrow fleshless back, little protected by cambric, adhering to clammy distemper. 'And where have you been all this time?' she stormed, biting back tears.

From between close black lashes his eyes glittered at her, pinned her down. 'Where have I been? I've been keeping my undesirable person out of your bed, my dear, which is what I imagined you wanted.'

Etienne's gaze was involuntarily drawn from her wan face to the allure of a pert bosom heaving a mere shiver from his chest. 'As for our unattended son, he found me some hours ago playing dice with an acquaintance in the annexe. I would have returned him to you, but I anticipated my arrival in your bedroom might have earned me a slap for my pains. Besides, Marcus was reluctant to go and said you were asleep. I decided to leave well enough alone as he soon settled down on a chair.'

Isabel felt relief and shame clog her throat. She should have known her son wouldn't properly settle until he located his father. His child's intelligence had led him back to where he had last been with Etienne—Mrs Broome's best parlour in the annexe. In a frenzy of prejudice she had convinced herself the taprooms would be where her grudging reprobate of a husband was to be found. A shuddering indrawn breath preceded, 'Good. I'm glad he is safe and sound.' She attempted to sweep past, a hand swiping wet from her lashes before it became obvious. Two palms slammed against the wall either side of her, imprisoning her.

'You asked me what I'd done with your son. What did you imagine I'd done? Abducted him? Murdered him?' Arrant scorn coloured his glare, then faded from his eyes to be replaced by fury. 'My God! You did! You believe I'd harm him.'

'No!' Isabel blurted, but found she couldn't compound the lie. Instead her fingers gripped at his sleeves, shook at the material in her desperation to make him understand. Never had she seen him look so savage. Even when she had lashed out at him, cornered him into a marriage he didn't want, he had not been so obviously enraged. 'I was so frightened when I found him gone. I remembered the gypsies. They take children. I couldn't find you either. I needed you, but you were nowhere to be seen.'

His eyes lowered insolently to the slender body trembling beneath *broderie anglaise*. As a nasty laugh scratched his throat, Isabel caught the sweet scent of alcohol breezing past.

'Well, I'm here now, Isabel, do you still need me?'

A barely perceptible shake of her head denied him. Her fingers, finished with spoiling the fine material of his sleeves, sprang over solid forearms in a vain attempt to move them.

'Well, it's a pity you do not,' he murmured hoarsely. 'Because, God knows I need you. You make my blood boil and not simply because you deem me capable of disposing of my own child. In truth you're the one I'm likely to throttle, my dear. If I resist that urge I might instead trade *you* to the Romanies, if I can persuade them to take such a shrew. But that's for later. We made a bargain. I've kept my side of the deal, now it's your turn.' He removed the candle from her grip and placed it on a table close by.

Isabel instinctively ducked to escape and retrieve it. She was entrapped and immediately put back against the wall. 'Be sweet to me,' he mocked, velvet-voiced. 'I have a very bitter taste in my mouth.'

'That's because you've drunk too much,' Isabel snapped, yanking at his wrists. The muscles beneath her fingers flexed, but he remained unmoved.

'I'm sober enough to consummate my marriage. It's time we had our honeymoon. Not the choicest venue for a romantic wedding night, but needs must when the devil drives. And I am the devil, sweet, aren't I?'

Isabel felt the fight go out of her. The small fingers, clamped on his brawny forearms, relaxed. He was incensed and with good reason. She had treated him awfully…again. 'No, you're not the devil,' she whispered. 'So far, you've treated us both well. Please don't spoil it. I awoke with a start after dreaming again of those travellers. I panicked when I couldn't find Marcus and imagined harm had befallen him.' She attempted a smile. 'I know it's stupid, but I've never before seen such grim-faced people and I cannot put them from my mind.'

Etienne's head lowered, an abrasive cheek grazed the soft skin of one of hers, nudging so her mouth closed with his. 'Forget them. You've cast *me* in the role of villain tonight and I'm ready to oblige you. Play the part of a sweet innocent. That would definitely oblige me…' His mouth slyly lunged, but she quickly averted her face, presenting him with a screen of softly coiled ringlets.

'Let me pass. Marcus needs me more than you do.'

'He's fast asleep.'

'He'll get cold and catch a chill.'

'He's covered with blankets.'

'He hates being alone in the dark.'

'He's got a brace of candles and my friend Thadeus Staines snoring in a chair to keep him company.'

Isabel ceded. She turned her head just a notch until the warm brandy breath on her cheek warned her to be still. She'd hurt him badly by thinking him capable of such dastardly behaviour. Far from harming Marcus, it seemed he had cared well for him. So far he had cared well for her too. Was that about to change? She rallied her courage; she was no more intimidated by him now than when she had confronted him over their son's future, she told herself. Whipping her head about, she glared up into eyes like embers. 'You know I have already told you what will transpire if you try to kiss or touch me.'

'You wouldn't fight me for long, Isabel, we both know that.' The smile he gave her was breathtakingly confident.

'I'm sorry you're inebriated enough to think that.' Barely a tremor betrayed the worth of the warning.

'And I'm sorry that I've acted the perfect gentleman since our marriage in the risible hope you might appreciate my noble restraint. You've always believed me a heartless degenerate. Now I've a mind to act like one.'

A dark hand moved up, a single firm finger outlined her sharp chin. The touch was teasingly light; she could have easily slapped it away. Yet she felt enchanted by the lulling sensation and her breath caught in her throat. Her lowered eyes followed that single digit out of sight. At the same moment it traversed to skim a breast she sought to escape. Dark hands clasped about her nape and two thumbs flicked her face up to his.

His mouth was hot and hard, his tongue silken, teasing at the clamped line of her lips. A solid thigh insinuated between her legs, tipping her craftily, almost imperceptibly, so her groin chafed on its rocky sinews. A tussle ended in her being overwhelmed while the onslaught on her mouth continued, veering between selfish demand and slick seductive skill. Dew was dilating her lips and pelvis, draining her of resistance, chilling then heating blood that throbbed with urgent decadence about her pliant body. She felt herself lifted, her limbs guided, moulded to fit about his. A hand smoothed along the feverish satin of her inner thigh, drawing cambric in its wake. And then it was over. She was on the ground, back against the wall, her feeble palms cupping plaster to keep her upright.

Isabel blinked into darkness, her lungs heaving as she fought to calm her racing heart. She bit her lip to stop herself calling him to come back. His dark clothes made it difficult for her to locate his silhouette at all in the corridor, then what was left of her candle stump illuminated his lean profile at a distance.

'I'm hungry. Will it be soon time for breakfast?'

'Yes…not long. Your mama has been looking for you.'

The disembodied words haunted the hallway. Etienne turned, beckoned, and the candle stump's weak flame revealed the boy now in his arms.

She obeyed him automatically, gliding forward at the signal, a ghostly figure in the gloomy corridor.

Etienne drew her close, an arm about her shoulders. It tightened on her at once, perhaps to warm her, perhaps to prevent her pulling away. Despite the battle between them just moments before, rejecting him now had not occurred to her.

'There's yet time for us all to get some sleep before we journey on,' Etienne said quietly. 'Tomorrow will be a long day of travelling.'

'I'm hungry…'

'We have some biscuits in the chamber and an

apple. That must suffice, Marcus, until it is light.'
Isabel finally found her tongue. She cleared her throat,
hoping the quaver in her voice was banished too. 'You
should not have left the room. I'm very angry with
you. Where is the key? Give it to me.'

Marcus pointed back towards the annexe, from
whence he had come.

'I have a key,' Etienne interjected peaceably.
'Come, apologise to your mama for worrying her.'

Marcus did so, albeit with his bottom lip thrust
petulantly. Isabel stole a quick look at her husband.
Just his eyes were in light; she would have needed to
shift the taper to gauge the rest of his expression. At
the back of his steady regard was a hint of apology,
but as their eyes entwined, he allowed desire bold
precedence. The candle wavered and she saw the slow
smile that was intensely self-deprecating. He took
her elbow and steered her towards the stairs.

In what was left of the night, Isabel woke just once.
She blinked herself to awareness when the covers
resisted being pulled up to her chin to ward off the
fierce fireless chill.

Etienne's fully clothed weight was firmly anchor-
ing the quilt. Isabel wriggled down carefully into
warmth, blinking at the dusky male head on the pillow
next to hers. By the light of the candle she studied him
from beneath heavy lids with a rapt fascination.

Now, at last, she could yearn for the boy she'd once known. In repose he looked much younger…sweeter. Elemental grooves that bracketed his mouth and radiated from the sun's attack seemed less noticeably etched in his skin. Five long fingers curled against his temple looked anything but brutal. His face was angled slightly away from her; long mahogany hair rippled back in skeins from his skull as though a hand had recently raked though it. Isabel squinted, but it was too luxuriant to betray pale skin in the half-light. A nervous finger tiptoed to slink within, slip feather-light over his scalp.

She shrank back with a gasp, but those innocent-looking digits had already imprisoned her wrist. With imperceptible speed he had rolled on to his front and was rearing on an elbow over her. Her impertinent hand was thrust down on the pillow above her head. 'It's a bit late to be seeking proof.' A significant glance incorporated the child slumbering in the cot next to the bed. The fingers straining in his for release were brought to his mouth, mockingly saluted. Just one was shoved across the jagged scar on his scalp, then flung from him immediately as though it were a burning brand.

'Satisfied?' He flopped on to his back with a grunt of stark sarcastic laughter.

Isabel hadn't the temerity to ask what amused him.

'Don't touch me, Isabel. Not in anger or curiosity.

And never while lying beside me in bed unless…' The sibilance died away, incomplete, and in a move that was isolating, his hand rose again to his temple and his face averted. A leg drew along the quilt, bent at the knee. The barrier between them complete, he closed his eyes.

It was a moment or two before Isabel felt able to withdraw her fingers from where he'd discarded them. She felt awkward…chastised. Yet an apology clung to her throat. She knew he didn't want to hear it any more than he wanted her prying fingers on him. If they touched physically it would be on his terms only—to satisfy his lust. Other than that he had no need of her ministrations. He wanted no comfort or companionship. He had told her, had he not, that he had no desire to be her friend. He already had a lady friend of whom he was very fond. For the first time she felt a stab of jealousy for the woman who had her husband's love and respect.

She lay still and wondered if he had been cold while he slept, for the fingers that had captured her wrist had felt icy. He had retired fully clothed and it had not occurred to her to offer to share the quilt. Once Marcus was finished with the biscuits and off to sleep, they had sought their own rest with barely a word passing between them.

With a heavy heart she glanced towards the small window and noticed an impenetrable darkness behind the thin drapery. She guessed dawn to be fast approaching. With a sigh she burrowed without a perceptible movement into a warmer spot. As exhaustion again claimed her, her body instinctively curved towards the man beside her.

'How long will it be before we reach Suffolk?'

'About three weeks.'

Isabel's gaze darted from an uninspiring vista of undulating muddy brown fields. 'Three weeks?' Green eyes widened on her husband's face. 'Is that a joke? Why on earth will it take that long? We are travelling to Redgrave Park, surely?'

'I don't recall saying that we were heading there. We're going to London.' He sounded quite puzzled.

'You…you spoke of our home in Suffolk,' she argued excitedly. 'Yesterday you were telling Marcus about Redgrave Park.'

'Yes, I was. And we will go to Suffolk, but not just yet. I have important business to attend to in town. You must have known that my hasty marriage would result in problems. I have vital matters to attend to in the city before I can go home.'

'Yes, but…'

'I have a very comfortable house in Eaton Square. I keep it staffed and well equipped. You will have everything you need.'

'It is not that. I'm sure your house is more than

adequate. I do understand that you have business to attend to, but first you must take Marcus and me to Suffolk. No, there is no need for you to accompany us. We can journey on alone, but you must provide us with transport. You may stay in Mayfair.'

'Thank you.' Her bold, breathless arrangements were met with an exceedingly dry response. 'Unfortunately I have no intention of allowing you to travel without me. We are all going to London and will remain there until I have dealt with every matter to my satisfaction.'

'I am not staying in London.'

'Don't be ridiculous.'

'I am *not* being ridiculous,' Isabel cried desperately.

'You are my wife and you will go where I do.' A fierce hooded look levelled at her. 'I believe you recently vowed to love, honour and obey. I accept the first two are unenforceable…' He didn't bother concluding the threat. Their eyes held combatively for a few seconds. At the same instant they became aware of their child's unusual stillness. Marcus was no longer regimenting his soldiers on the coach seat, but listening to their low-toned altercation with a grave solemnity.

Isabel's eyes swerved accusingly to her husband.

'I think we need to talk privately,' Etienne muttered bleakly. A clenched fist banged for the driver to halt.

As the coach skidded to a shocked stop he flung open the door and was out before the wheels ceased turning. 'Stay there. We will only be a moment,' he told his son with quiet authority. Marcus slid himself back on the seat and neatly entwined his fingers, his hazel eyes poignantly watchful.

Etienne offered Isabel a hand and urged her immediately down, then was pacing at speed away from the coach, forcing his wife, her fingers imprisoned under his on his arm, to skip to keep up with him. The small spinney at the side of the road gave the seclusion necessary to evade the sidelong glances from Reeves and the coachman. A few yards into the shrubbery he came to an abrupt halt, making Isabel tilt back to avoid bumping into him.

'What in damnation is this all about?' The words were gritted and vibrant. Through a screen of denuded wood, he immediately peered at the coach as though to satisfy himself his son was not also being insubordinate and following them.

Isabel took a deep breath. She had hoped that this particular secret would not be necessarily revealed fast on the heels of the confession that her widowhood was a sham. She had hoped, in time, to bring a little dignity to the disclosure of her supposed demise. The idea that there might be a proper way to break such outrageous news almost wrung from her a hysterical laugh. As usual, when put on the defensive, she launched an attack. 'You will not bully me! Nor will you make me feel guilty about my wedding vows. How dare you be so hypocritical as to take *me* to task when you also blasphemed before the minister.'

'As I recall, that particular blasphemy was rather forced upon me.'

Isabel visibly winced. He would never let her forget that he was a reluctant partner in this marriage. 'No doubt your wedding to Miss Greenwood would have seen you uttering absolute truths about love and fidelity,' she snapped.

Etienne stared at her, then grimaced defeat. *'Touché,'* he muttered sardonically and stalked off a yard or so. 'Is this fit of temper prompted by what occurred between us last night?'

'I…it has nothing to do with what occurred last night. I have already forgotten about that.'

Etienne spun on a heel, raked her flushing face with piercing eyes. 'Have you indeed?' he said softly. 'I wish I could say the same.' He plunged his hands into his coat pockets. With his shoulders hunched he stared at bleak columns of bark. 'I apologise for acting like a drunken lout. I was angry with you, but the threats were empty. You had nothing to fear. I'm no more likely to violate you now than I was eight years ago. I'm sorry if I frightened you. I would have told you so earlier this morning, but an opportunity to be private didn't arise.'

The awkwardness and regret she read in his tense profile were emotions that were still bedevilling her. Being honest seemed only fair. 'I'm sorry too. I know I acted irrationally. What a stupid thing, believing you might have taken Marcus to the gypsies!' The hollow laugh withered in her throat. 'Let's not dwell on it, please.' She looked appealingly at him and he returned her a slanted smile.

'Nothing about this marriage is going to be easy, Isabel,' he told her quietly, reflectively. 'Every single day will be hard for I fear duty will never be quite enough for either of us.'

'I know.' Her agreement was little more than a sob.

'Why are you so set against going to London?'

'I…I cannot face the gossips. It is a long time since Rachel jilted Connor and I disappeared from society, but some people might enjoy resurrecting a mysterious scandal. I do not want Marcus exposed to the nastiness I know awaits us once our identities are discovered.' It was the truth, she thought, if not the whole truth.

'You are my wife and Marcus is my son. Do you think me so weak and ineffectual that I could not protect you from such malice? I know we have a mess to sort out and gossip to face. I will help you deal with it, I promise.'

'You don't understand,' Isabel said in a strangled voice. She looked off into trees, trying to find the words to explain. 'It is not just that people will be unkind. My family…my parents and my sisters…I have them to consider too. It is awkward…'

'You don't want to see them?'

'I want to see them very much, but I fear it is impossible.'

Etienne's eyes fixed on his wife's beautiful anxious face. Tears sparkled on her lashes in the weak early morning sunlight. Something stirred within him, something new that transcended masculine egotism in his vow to protect this courageous woman and their child. An urge to reach out and move her close, kiss and caress her was prompted by a desire to comfort rather than to assuage his lust. His hand involuntarily started to move towards her, was instead made into a fist and withdrawn. Any touch from him was likely to be met with suspicion. And after last night he couldn't blame her for that. He carefully thought over their predicament. 'Is there a secret you are holding back? Something I ought to know, but you are reluctant to tell me?'

Isabel gulped in a breath and nodded, thankful of his sharp perception.

'Well, we're halfway there, Isabel,' Etienne encouraged quietly. 'I know there is a problem, now all you must do is name it. Thereafter we can solve it.' He came close again, tilted up her downcast face with a single finger. 'Do you not trust me to put it right?'

'I trust you to try…but it is an insurmountable problem.'

'Let me be the judge of that,' he soothed, honey-voiced.

'Can you bring me back to life, Etienne? For in polite society I'm believed to be dead.'

Chapter Twelve

'Believed to be dead?' he echoed with a phantom smile in the words as though he thought her joking.

Isabel put a slender hand to her brow. A massaging thumb and forefinger bridged skin like alabaster. 'Let us return to the coach,' she breathed. 'Marcus will be fretting.'

'*I* am fretting,' he returned exceedingly quietly, a hand on her arm arresting her. 'Tell me a little more about your passing. Not so very long ago dismissing you as a figment of my imagination would have been most welcome. Now I'm not so sure. Lately I've appreciated having you around in the flesh.'

'It is not a matter for jest,' Isabel stormed. 'I am deadly serious. My parents did not anticipate my long absence would give rise to such rumours. It was no secret that I had accompanied Rachel when she jilted

Connor and fled to York, or that a scarletina epidemic occurred whilst we were there. Rachel returned home to Hertfordshire, I did not. Sensitive people drew their own conclusions to my family's distress. Believing them bereaved, they let matters lie. Those who probed had their impertinence met with silence. My parents did not confirm or deny a single thing.'

'How very good of them. So the ruse of you being a widowed mother never circulated in the *ton?*'

Isabel shook her head 'There was no point in compounding the deceit unnecessarily. I knew I could never move back to Hertfordshire and blight my sisters' marriage prospects with a hint of scandal. But in York I needed to protect Aunt Florence's reputation for she would have been tainted with my shame. I assumed a respectable history and became Mrs Forrester. And there was Marcus... I couldn't bear the thought of him being branded a fatherless bast...' Completing the slur was impossible. 'I'm not sure the pretence was believed by all, but we were generally known as genteel, if shabby.'

'Did your father not properly support you during the time you lived with your aunt?'

High spots of colour rose on Isabel's cheeks at the blame in his tone. 'My papa has done enough for me...more than most would in the circumstances. I might have been welcomed home had I agreed to certain conditions. Papa sends bank drafts every so often.'

'When did you receive the last? How much was it for?' Etienne demanded.

Isabel bristled with filial loyalty. 'My parents have three other daughters, you know! At the time of Marcus's birth none were married. Rachel was thought to be on the shelf after jilting Connor. June was fifteen and soon due to make her come out, and Sylvie was just a child with her education *and* her début in front of her.' She listed her father's costly duties with a degree of proud indignation. 'There was much to be borne before he even began to think of weddings he must pay for and dowries he must settle on his three daughters.'

'He has four daughters,' Etienne reminded her. 'Did he consider buying *you* a husband somewhere out in the sticks? An indigent curate or the like?'

'Yes, he offered to do that.' She tipped up her chin revealing the fierce flush staining her throat. 'He also promised it was still possible I could return home to the bosom of my family, supposedly recovered at last from scarletina.'

'But you would not abandon Marcus.'

'No,' she replied simply, without emphasis or sanctimony. In a quick evading movement she was past him and striding out of the trees. It was not until she was sliding across the hide seat to instinctively, reassuringly gather her precious child to her that his warmth, seeping through her clothes, made her aware how chilled she was.

* * *

They had covered a few quiet miles before Isabel plucked up the courage to boldly ask, 'Will we arrive in Suffolk before nightfall?'

Before looking up, Etienne positioned his French general at the head of his army. Marcus commenced assassinating him with a battalion of English artillery, scattering tin figures over hide in the process. 'I cannot indulge you in this, Isabel.' His tone was mild, but his adamant refusal easily traversed Marcus's guttural gunfire. 'It is vital things are sorted out. The other business I have in town can wait. But I have a hankering to be introduced to your father as soon as possible.'

'What do you think on it all?'

'Mrs Drake don't let us gossip. Master don't like it. I don't think. I just do.'

'I reckon the nipper has a look of the Colonel about him. Give him a mop of dark hair and lovely brown eyes and he'd be a chip off the old block.'

'Shh…' Miriam Clarke put a work-rough finger against her lips. She flicked a duster at Felicity, the pretty young scullion who today had escaped the unpleasant heat of the kitchen due to a colleague's sickness and was promoted to assist above stairs. The two women were polishing fine yew furniture in the elegant drawing room of Number Forty-Nine Eaton

Square. Miriam's eyes swivelled. Satisfied they were private, she easily relented to the urge to tattle. 'Little Master Marcus is a handsome lad. A heartbreaker in the making if ever I saw one.'

Felicity shot a sly look at her superior while tickling the top of a vase with feather tips. She had no wish to hurry through these duties and be relegated to the steamy bowels of the house. Rose-petal air spiced with beeswax polish was the sweetest perfume compared to the odour of cabbage water. 'The big master is a looker too and the one I'm better interested in. I'd say he's definitely a heartbreaker and lusty with it or I don't know me onions.'

'You don't want to let Mrs Drake hear you talk like that,' Miriam warned the newly recruited Felicity of the housekeeper's strict adherence to decorum and duty at this distinguished address. 'If she catches on you're getting above yourself, and you not here yet two whole weeks, you'll be back on the pavement sharpish. Best not let Mrs Hauke hear of it, neither. I know she looks a bit too refined to be bothered with the likes of saucy scullions; then again she might just smack your face for you. She's a bride, after all.'

Felicity clucked her indifference to the threats. 'I know what I'm doing and 'tain't scouring pots much longer, that's for sure.'

'You got more chance of warming Prinny's sheets!' Miriam scoffed. 'The Colonel's got a right swell ladybird to visit if his wife's indisposed. A proper beauty she is. Me and Jenkins saw her once in a grand carriage the master bought for her. A cabree-lay, Jenkins says it is; he should know, 'cos he used to work in the coach house before he got his bad back. It's all shiny black paint with a silver crest and done out inside with silver cushions.' Miriam folded her arms across her chest, conscientiousness abandoned. 'She were dressed in silver-grey too, with her hair all done up and sleek as the black carriage horses. So dignified…'

'Grey cushions!' Felicity derided with her wrinkled nose joining up her freckles. The feather duster was let drop to the table. 'I'd want crimson; and gold wheels and white horses so everyone could see me coming.'

'That's 'cos you're common!' Miriam snorted. 'Lady Avery is a widow so she favours grey out of respect. She's a lady. She's refined.'

'Not *too* refined, though, is she?' Felicity sniped pointedly. 'Anyhow, when he's home she ain't available.' A suggestive wink accompanied that.

Miriam dismissed it with a hand flick. 'Mrs Hauke might not be a raving beauty, but she's got a look about her that's very nice. Anyhow, I reckon it's a love match.'

'Never! She's thin and pale with too much curly mousy hair. She must be a rich widow to get a man like him.'

Miriam pointed a warning finger. 'You'd best sheathe those claws, you cat. Colonel Hauke don't need another man's money. He's flush, he is. You're just jealous 'cos the Colonel's fallen for her.'

'Have you no work to do?'

Miriam and Felicity froze into twin statues: each with one hand on one jutting hip and chins aggressively jousting.

Isabel hadn't wanted to eavesdrop. Unfortunately, once she had gone into the anteroom to sit and quietly read while enjoying the last fading light to be had through the west window there was only one way out: past these two. She had hovered as dusk descended, hoping they would leave the room first and spare everyone's blushes. Finally, when their arguing began grating on her nerves, she had become annoyed enough at them, and at herself for feeling intimidated, to make her presence known. She now gave the petrified housemaids a cool assessing gaze. 'What are your names?'

'Miriam Clarke, ma'am,' the older woman gulped.

Isabel turned her attention to the younger servant. A raise of her finely shaped eyebrows elicited, 'Felicity Wright, ma'am.' It was ejected so feebly that Isabel barely caught the name. She felt her pique fading. The eager seductress looked little more than seventeen. She also appeared so ashen and terrified that Isabel feared she might swoon.

These two faces were vaguely familiar from when
the staff had assembled to welcome her when she had
arrived almost a week ago. Since then the only servants
with whom she ever had regular dealings were Mrs
Drake, the housekeeper, and the butler, Roland Forbes.
The others she occasionally saw in passing. They had
all treated her with due respect and deference…to her
face.

Felicity Wright, then, was an ambitious scullion;
had Isabel not heard it from her own lips she would
have gleaned it from her appearance. She was the
underling of the two women, yet her demeanour was
superior. Her uniform was spruce and well fitting,
her starched cap set at a jaunty angle on golden hair
that was curled stylishly beneath it. 'How old are you,
Felicity?' she asked quietly.

The maid's nervous tongue tip flicked at her lips.
'Sixteen, ma'am,' she croaked.

A sixteen-year-old temptress who had designs on
her husband. As Isabel discreetly studied the comely
young woman, she wondered how Etienne would
react should Felicity succeed in letting him know.

'You both seem to be finished here.' Isabel delib-
erated on the idle dusting cloths and polish. 'I noticed
a spillage has occurred on the floor close to the fire
in the morning room. Perhaps my son's cordial was
overset.'

'I'll see to it now,' Miriam garbled.

'I will too,' Felicity gasped and snatched up her duster so hastily rose petals were dislodged from overblown blooms and floated down to spatter shiny wood.

The ensuing stampede brought a twitch of a smile to Isabel's lips. 'Felicity, please stay a moment.'

The girl turned at the door, shocked. She cast one despondent look at Miriam. Her colleague refused to meet her eyes and slipped quickly away.

'Come here, please.' Isabel crooked a finger and reluctantly the scullion obeyed.

'How long have you been working here?'

'Two weeks, ma'am.'

'Speak up please, Felicity. Where did you work previously?'

'Lady Osborne's, ma'am, in Cavendish Square.'

'Were you a scullion in Cavendish Square?'

'No, ma'am. I was undermaid to Lady Osborne's maid.'

'Are you better suited to those duties?'

Felicity peeped warily through her lashes as though she believed it must be a trick question.

'Are you able to stitch neatly and dress a head of hair?' Isabel shortly persevered.

'Yes, ma'am, when I worked for Lady Osborne I did embroidery and hair styling. Lady Osborne's maid was training me up to work for Lady Catherine, Lady Osborne's daughter. I liked it.'

'Why did you leave? Were you unhappy there?'

Felicity looked confused and remained silent.

'Did Lady Osborne give you a character?'

The girl looked uneasy. 'No, ma'am,' she croaked.

'Why not?'

Felicity blushed and her lips wobbled. "Cos…'cos I was put off when her son took particular notice of me.'

'I see. And that is why you have been taken on scouring pans here? Because you had no character to give Mrs Drake?'

The girl nodded miserably.

'Well, I have need of a lady's maid and I would rather train someone to do things my way. I always use my own herbal preparations. Would you be interested in helping to prepare lotions and so on?'

'I would…yes…' Felicity resonantly stressed.

'I shall speak to Mrs Drake then about your change in duties. That is all. You may go.'

'Thank you, ma'am,' Felicity garbled. She hovered close by the door and Isabel knew the girl was trying to find a way to apologise for her audacious personal attack. They both knew her comments had been overheard. 'You may go, Felicity,' Isabel directed firmly for she had no wish to be reminded of them.

Isabel dredged the scattered petals into a fist. She wandered to the half-open window and let them fall to the terrace flags. Despite her desire to forget the gossips, her imagination would not allow her peace. It was surprising how servants' opinions veered between the mundane and the fascinating. Odd, too, that one could feel flattered or humiliated by the observations of people deemed to be of little consequence. Isabel took a silky spiralling curl and brought it into her line of vision. It was definitely *not* mousy. She'd always liked her hair's unusual shade of fair.

The maidservants' gossip was not all news to her. She already knew her husband kept a mistress; he'd freely disclosed that information himself. But Miriam and Felicity had coloured the sketchy image she had in her mind of a woman Etienne might love. She now knew his good friend was a titled lady and that he had provided her with a luxurious cabriolet carriage upholstered in silver to compliment her shiny black hair and penchant for grey gowns. Lady Avery was deemed refined. Little wonder her husband was besotted with such a paragon, Isabel thought with a wry smile.

As for Felicity wanting to improve her status, there was nothing novel in a maidservant's aspiration to climb out of the kitchens and into the master's bed. Similar shenanigans occurred in households throughout the land. What *was* peculiar was the master's wife providing the interloper with an opportunity to get a foot on the stairs. Why had she just promoted Felicity to a position where she was likely to frequently encounter the object of her desire?

A poignant ache within provided her answer and it was an insight she would rather ignore. Malice had prodded her into action, she realised. Felicity Wright, pretty as she was, would always be less important to Etienne than his love. But Lady Avery might have her power diluted by an eager rival. With a stab of anguish Isabel realised she resented the woman's grip on Etienne. And that was a terrifying thing. She didn't want to care. She didn't want to want him…ever again. She had married him to provide a decent future for their son, not to try and wrest his affection from the woman he loved.

Since their arrival in town Isabel had realised just how strong was his bond with his mistress. He was rarely at home. Sometimes he did not even return for dinner in the evening and she dined alone with Marcus. At night his chamber, connected to hers by a dressing room, was invariably quiet enough to be unoccupied.

She had nothing of which to accuse him. Their every comfort was met. He had made it clear she could purchase what she liked: furniture for the house, clothes for herself or their son. A substantial allowance was available to her should she wish to make visits or outings. She had thanked him politely for his generosity and refrained from reminding him that she had no friends here and no need of new gowns in which to socialise at home…alone.

She had never visited Suffolk, but yearned to move to that unknown county as soon as possible. She therefore did not have the heart or interest to replace furniture in his Mayfair townhouse that, in any case, was of the finest quality and taste.

The sound of the front door closing shattered her poignant introspection. Her stomach clenched in something akin to excitement and that made her tremble. She didn't want her husband's arrival home to affect her in such a way. She didn't want to find herself listening for the key in the lock. Nevertheless, she could not prevent her hands going to automatically check her dress and hair as she emerged into the corridor of his gracious house. She ran an appreciative eye over the fine paintings, the carved plasterwork and sombre oak doors as she walked towards the vestibule. She was lonely without Rachel and her friends in Ireland, she told herself as her pace quickened. It was the reason for her eagerness to have a little adult company every so often. It wasn't specifically *him* she wanted to see. Yet she had found that, when he bestowed his time, she could enjoy their conversations.

'Is Colonel Hauke home?' she needlessly asked Roland Forbes. She could tell from the greatcoat and cane he was carrying to the cloaks cupboard that he indeed had returned.

'He is, madam. I believe he went off toward his study,' Roland told her with a kind smile.

Isabel hesitated with a hand raised to knock. She let it drop to her side and with a deep breath walked in, unannounced.

Etienne was standing with his back to her, close to the smouldering coals in the grate. His dark head was bent towards the mantel; so lost in thought did he appear to be that he did not even turn at the sound of her arrival.

'Am I disturbing you?' She hated sounding so timid. To make amends she said more firmly, 'I just wondered if you would be home for dinner this evening. I wondered whether to wait…or dine earlier with Marcus.'

'Are you asking me to stay home for dinner this evening?' He turned slowly to look at her.

Isabel returned his stare, taken aback. She had not anticipated he might say that. She searched his handsome face with eyes that were soulful. *Yes…* whispered in her mind. Aloud she said briskly, 'No. But there are important things we ought to talk over and as you are rarely home during the day…or night…'

That waspish observation elicited a half-smile. 'You sound as though you've missed me, Isabel,' he said with soft mockery. 'Have you?'

Isabel felt her face getting hot. She wondered whether he had spent this afternoon with Lady Avery; shopping with her, perhaps, or driving with her in her smart carriage with silver cushions. 'I imagine I've missed you as much as you've missed me,' she countered with an admirably insouciant smile.

'And that sounds as though you'd like to know whether I have missed you. Would you?'

'No,' Isabel lied quickly. 'But I would like to know whether you have missed your son, for he is always looking for you.'

'Well, I'm certainly aware when he's not around,' Etienne returned ironically, but his tone was not unkind.

'He can be rather…boisterous,' Isabel admitted on a twist of a smile.

'So could I at that age. Thank you for the invitation to dine with you. I accept.'

Isabel opened her mouth to retort that it was not an invitation, but the humorous look in his eyes kept her silent. He had anticipated a rebuff. 'We ought to talk about our move to Suffolk and how Marcus is dealing with his new tutor. Mr Barton seems efficient but rather…rather blunt in his manner.'

'I understand, Isabel,' he said quietly. 'You want me for the problems and practicalities only. I understand that…'

Isabel dropped her eyes. After a pause she ventured, 'I'm sorry if that seems selfish to you…'

A hoarse laugh erupted and he turned and stabbed a toe at the fender. 'Selfish? No. Vengeful? Yes. But as we're civilised now you'll keep your vengeance gentle, I know. I don't anticipate any more obvious battle wounds.' He abruptly pulled a decanter close and tipped a shot into a glass. 'Dinner is at eight, I believe?'

She was being dismissed, Isabel realised. She backed away a few paces, her chin high. 'Yes, it is. Please don't be late. Marcus will be hungry,' was all she said as she closed the door.

Chapter Thirteen

'I have appointed a lady's maid from amongst your servants.'

'Good.'

'Her name is Felicity Wright,' Isabel informed him casually.

Knowing the identity of the young woman altered her husband's expression not one jot.

'She is young but quite bright and ambitious…and pretty.'

Etienne lifted his glass to his lips. 'She sounds deserving of promotion,' he remarked conversationally, but without any indication he recognised the person under discussion. 'What were her duties previously?'

'Scouring pots and pans.'

Etienne replaced his wine untasted. A frowning smile flickered over the candelabra gleaming midway between them on the dining table. He obviously understood enough of the female servants' hierarchy to know such an elevation was extraordinary.

'She arrived here without a character. Lady Osborne put her off,' Isabel quickly explained.

Etienne's bemusement increased. 'Are we taking on waifs and strays now?' He paused to lounge back in his chair. 'Earlier in the week Marcus had a son of one of the grooms in his bedchamber, sorting through soldiers. Today he had two more scruffy young scamps I've never before seen playing chase in the garden.'

'Yes, I know,' Isabel said. 'I told them all they were very welcome to play. They are polite children. It is good Marcus has friends.'

Etienne picked up his wine goblet, twirled it in his fingers while looking reflectively into ruby ripples. 'I agree. But do you not think he ought be socialising with children of his own class?'

'What class is that, pray?' Isabel asked quietly.

Beneath lowered brows Etienne's dark eyes slanted to hers. 'It is a class that befits his new station in life as my son and intended heir. He is my natural, first-born son. I have every intention of securing the succession for him. If he succeeds to an earldom he will probably also take a viscountcy, if my Uncle Archibald dies without issue. As he is now sixty-one and has never shown the remotest interest in women or marriage, I imagine that will be the case.'

Seizing a change of subject, Isabel asked on a nervous laugh, 'Does your uncle not like women?'

'He prefers men.'

At this blunt statement Isabel frowned in consideration, then blushed. 'Oh, I see.'

'My uncle's predilection for lifelong bachelorhood spurred my father to marry too young and too soon: he wanted to reassure his father that he was not of the same persuasion. My grandfather was also keen for the ultimate *mésalliance*,' he remarked with dark irony. 'He wanted his younger son to provide him with grandchildren, as the heir apparent was unlikely to continue the line. My grandfather successfully fought to secure the earldom for my father and his descendants on his death. He had no intention of expiring and allowing Archie to inherit. He is convinced his detested heir will see out his century. My grandfather and uncle haven't spoken for more than forty years.'

To spare her further blushes at this highly improper information, Isabel reverted to discussing their son. 'Marcus would also like his friend Michael Murphy, from Waterford, to come and visit him once we are settled in Suffolk. Would you object to me writing and asking his parents' permission?'

'When he gets to school, Marcus shall make friends amongst his peers,' Etienne returned evenly.

At the oblique refusal Isabel picked up her wine-glass. 'Of course… I had forgotten how very high and mighty you are.'

'How foolish of you,' her husband said, impenitent. 'Now, tell me why it appears I am taking in Lady Osborne's castoffs. The maid you mentioned earlier is acceptable here, but not there? Why?'

'It's true she was taken on without a character and put scouring pans,' Isabel confirmed slowly while her mind quickly sought a justification for that peculiarity. 'I expect Mrs Drake noticed her worth. Beneath that stern exterior I think your housekeeper is fair and wise and she has recognised that Felicity is sharp and smart.'

'Sharp and smart enough to be caught pilfering from Lady Osborne?'

'No. It wasn't that.' Isabel leapt to her new maid's defence. Felicity was showing great promise and very real humility for having spoken with such saucy impudence of her master and mistress. 'She isn't a thief. Lady Osborne's son took a particular interest in her, that's all.' The realisation that she was unwittingly digging a deeper hole for poor Felicity to tip into left her busily attending to her dinner.

'*That's all?* For Heaven's sake!' Etienne's groan was followed by a bark of laughter prompted by sheer disbelief. His wine goblet found the table with a thump. 'And no doubt her bastard will be coddled in my household or I'll again be accused of being high and mighty.'

Isabel stared at her plate and sighed softly. 'No, I don't think we need worry over…that.'

Etienne's sardonic amusement softened; his eyes became warm and intense. He inclined towards her, resting his elbows on the table. 'It hadn't occurred to you that perhaps we should, had it? And that surprises me,' he added, velvet-voiced. 'Considering our circumstances and your history, I imagined you were already feeling empathetic and destined to help the poor ruined maid. You really are an innocent, aren't you?'

'She isn't ruined and you don't need to mock me so.'

'I'm not mocking you, Isabel,' her husband said with husky sincerity. 'Truth be known, I'm humbled by the way you've coped alone for so long. I admire you…in lots of ways…'

'I've not coped alone. I have had help from my relations.' Isabel championed the Merediths while challengingly holding his gaze. 'Are you drunk?' She eyed his empty wine glass with suspicion.

'No, I'm not drunk. Do I need to be drunk to pay my wife a compliment?' He pushed back his chair and stood up, sleepy-eyed and purposeful.

Isabel stood too. He looked groomed to perfection and heartbreakingly handsome, resplendent in close-fitting fawn breeches and black tailcoat. In his snow-white neckcloth winked a sizeable emerald. He looked ready for an evening abroad. He looked like a gentleman with an important assignation. 'Are you going out?' Isabel demanded in a tone that couldn't quite conceal her disappointment at the likelihood.

'No, I'm not going out.' Etienne ceased stalking her. 'Are you?' The irony in his tone told her he had noticed the way she was instinctively retreating towards the door.

'Me? Going out? Where would I go? *I* don't have a special friend to visit.' The thoughts dogging her mind were involuntarily voiced and she turned away from him, mortified. 'I'm sorry, I shouldn't have said that. Forget I said that, please.'

'I don't want to forget you said it. I'm pleased you're jealous. But there is no need to be.'

'I am *not* jealous,' Isabel stormed, furious that he had sensed the emotion tormenting her. She didn't want to acknowledge its existence; she certainly didn't want *him* to know Lady Avery bothered her.

'Do you want to know why I've been absent from home so often since we arrived in London?'

'I've no interest in what you do socially,' she lied. 'When we struck our bargain I expected no more than your discretion in a token marriage, I told you that.'

'And now?'

'And now I have no complaints,' Isabel stated in a proud, husky voice.

'Well, I have,' Etienne told her quietly. 'We're

dining together, talking together about children and servants. We're doing natural things married people do. You welcome me now because you need me. I need you too, Isabel. There are other natural things married people do…' His words tailed off and his eyes slid past and narrowed on the door.

Isabel watched his lips form a soundless curse and five fingers wreak havoc on his neatly combed long hair. He strode to the mantel and braced a weathered hand against it. His focus was now the highly polished boot he'd jammed on the fender.

As the draught from the door whispered into her silken skirts Isabel whipped about with an inkling of the reason for her husband's barely concealed irritation. 'You should be abed, Marcus!' she softly chided her son loitering on the threshold.

Marcus wrinkled his nose, gathered his dressing gown away from his feet and padded closer. Brightly he declared, 'I'm not tired. I'm still hungry.'

'How can you be hungry?' Etienne demanded in a blast of frustration. 'When you left the table you were full. That was barely an hour ago. Now off to bed with you this instant! Your mama and I have things we must talk about in private.'

Marcus stared, shocked and unblinking, at his father. His lower lip began to wobble before it was thrust defiantly.

Isabel raised appealing eyes to Etienne. 'Don't shout at him please, it never helps. He…he…'

'He is spoiled; he is in need of heeding some rules,' Etienne supplied with soft steel.

'He is not spoiled.' Isabel moistened her lips, then allowed softly, 'He is…wilful, I know, but that is not entirely his fault.'

'No, it's mostly my fault,' Etienne accepted quietly. 'And I'll rectify it. Go back to bed now,' he directed his son with absolute calm authority. 'If you do not, your friends will not be allowed to come here and play and your friend in Ireland will not be allowed to visit Redgrave Park.'

'I don't care!' Marcus burst out belligerently. His large eyes skipped warily from his father's harsh forbidding countenance to seek reassurance from his gentle mama.

Isabel quickly blinked away the heat in her eyes and held out a hand to her beloved burden. 'Come, I'll take you back to bed.'

'Marcus found his way here on his own. He can similarly find the way back,' Etienne stated in a perilously mild voice. 'He is, after all, a boy of seven years old, not a baby in leading strings. He is not infirm and has no need to be taken about by the hand.'

'I'm not a baby, Mama,' Marcus bravely echoed his father's words. 'I can go on my own back to bed.' After a few moments standing there poignantly uncertain, he retreated a step, then another until he was again in the hall.

'How dare you!' Isabel choked when the door was closed. 'How dare you criticise *me* over the way I have reared him…cared for him.'

'When did I do that?' her husband asked, his anger tightly controlled.

'*When?* All the time! Not blatantly, perhaps, but there is a hint of disapproval in every look, every word you direct his way. I'm sure you enjoy finding fault with him,' she cried.

'That is not true, Isabel, and you know it.'

'It is true!' she insisted. 'You may despise me if you like, but you ought have the decency to fairly treat an innocent child. But why should you care for his feelings?' she choked through a coagulation of tears in her throat. 'You don't love him; you don't even like him. You resent giving him your name and I don't believe you will endeavour to make him your legitimate heir. To you he will always be the brat who was foisted on to you by that scheming harlot you once—'

Through a misty blur Isabel saw he was getting closer. The heel of a palm smeared the wet from her eyes. She had again said too much and made herself appear hysterical and foolish. Swiftly she shook back her rebellious curls from her smudged face, then swished about and made for the door. Before she had opened it an inch a hand slammed across her shoulder, shutting it again.

'You might be finished, my dear, but I am not. Don't run off just as things are getting interesting. Refresh my memory over this scheming harlot, for I'm damned if I can recall much about her…yet I'd like to.'

Isabel whipped about and flattened against the door. Her glistening green eyes raked his hard face. Despite his anger sultry desire was radiating from between long black lashes, bathing her in feverish heat. 'That's all you're interested in, isn't it? Getting your reward for marrying me and providing for my son. I agreed to the bargain; you need not fear I will renege and beg you not to,' she breathed contemptuously up at him. 'You want your pound of flesh so much. Have it! Now!' She ripped at the buttons on her dress with trembling fingers. The bodice gaped, her small, lush bosom visible over a froth of lace on her chemise. She went on to tiptoe, furiously slammed her mouth onto his, and ground her soft salty lips against the cool inflexibility of his while fresh tears slid between them.

A hand delved into her honey hair, winding a silky hank about a broad palm. Slowly, as though the denial was an ordeal, her mouth was moved back from his. 'If I was desperate, perhaps I would. But you know I'm not. I've been seduced with more finesse, Isabel, lots of times. Even by scheming harlots.' The words were flippant, taunting but he couldn't quite discipline his yearning eyes from ravening her delectable swollen flesh, pure and fine as alabaster. A hand hovered by her throat before just one long finger, slightly unsteady, lowered to trace the valley between her silken breasts.

Isabel gasped an involuntarily shuddering breath at the exquisite sensation, and dusky pink crescents peeped over a snowy filigree to tease him.

Within an instant he had swung her away from the door and deposited her on the nearest armchair with a speed that indicated a vehement need to be distanced from her. Isabel grasped at the arms to prevent sliding to the floor.

The dishevelled picture of wanton womanhood she presented, with her clothing awry and her mermaid hair trailing her naked pearly shoulders, brought dull slashes of heat to highlight Etienne's cheekbones. With a savage curse, that he this time made no attempt to modulate in volume, he turned his back on her. A hand went to the inside pocket of his jacket and a letter was extracted in a savage rip. 'Here; the reason why I've been away from home so often.' He pivoted on a heel and the letter was skimmed at her, landing on the rug by her feet. 'I've been tracking your father between Hertfordshire and Mayfair. He quit London just before we arrived. When I reached Hertfordshire

I was informed by the staff at Windrush that your parents had set out for Berkshire to visit your sister, Sylvie. She's a pupil at an academy there. I left a message with your father's steward at Windrush. This is his reply. Your parents are due to arrive in London tomorrow and are coming to visit us at three in the afternoon. I'll endeavour to be home by then.'

'Is Etienne coming back?'

'I expect so, Marcus. Come here; let me straighten your waistcoat. You will not want to meet your grandpapa and grandmama looking untidy.'

'I wish Etienne was here. I don't want to see these relations people. They don't like me. Is Etienne cross with me? Does *he* like me?' Marcus asked his mother anxiously as he succumbed to her ministrations. He stood obligingly still while she tucked in his shirt and fastened small pearl buttons on his blue waistcoat.

'Yes, of course.' She gave her son a reassuring smile and went to the window for what seemed like the hundredth time. It was almost two o'clock in the afternoon and she had not seen her husband since he had departed yesterday. The dining-room door and the front door had been slammed in quick succession and with such force that the noise had reverberated around the marble vestibule, bringing Roland Forbes to investigate the din. She was thankful she had had the sense to straighten her clothing before the butler appeared. Kindly he had insisted on fetching her a warm drink to take to bed before he tactfully withdrew, sorrowfully shaking his head to himself.

So now the servants also knew they were at loggerheads. They had parted on awful terms, but would Etienne still be so angry that he would punish her by letting her face her family alone? Was he capable of such incivility? She pushed the curtain back into place, increasingly agitated. The prospect of an audience with her parents was so nerve-racking that she hoped Etienne would reappear just so she could castigate him for having arranged it. Yet she knew it to be a vital meeting and less daunting than other confrontations that were sure to ambush her on the rocky road of her return to society.

On impulse she approached a writing desk. Her frantic fingers scrabbled the recesses for a pen and parchment while she fretted over the wisdom of despatching a note to Beaulieu Gardens, her parents' London residence, postponing their visit.

'If Etienne comes back I'll be good…I will. I won't get out of bed again. I won't be bad…'

'Well, that's good news.' A hint of gruff irony was in the praise.

'Etienne!' Marcus rushed to embrace his father about the knees.

Etienne looked down at a rapt upturned face. Abruptly he lifted his son and imperceptibly skimmed his fair hair with his lips. 'What did we agree you must call me now?' he asked softly.

Marcus raised his laughing eyes. 'Papa.'

'Yes. Papa. Have you been good this morning for your mama?'

Marcus looked thoughtful, then nodded quickly.

Putting him back on the carpet, Etienne walked over to where his wife sat. Her nervous fingers dropped the pen she still had poised over parchment.

Isabel suddenly got to her feet. 'I don't want to see them. I was about to write and tell them so.'

'Yes, you do want to see them.' Etienne corrected softly, a hand light on her arm, arresting her flight.

Isabel raised her eyes to his, losing herself in the velvet depths of his regret until she realised it was very probable his tardiness was due to the fact he had only lately torn himself away from his mistress.

As though reading her thoughts exactly, Etienne said, 'I made the acquaintance of an agreeable gentleman at my club. William Pemberton is by all accounts married to your sister June. I stayed there last night.'

'With June and her husband at Richmond?' Isabel's astonishment was plain in her voice.

'No. At White's.'

'Well, I'm sure *William* did not. He and June are *happily* married.'

Etienne allowed a sardonic quirk to tilt his lips at

the inference in that. 'Yes, he told me so...many times. He seems a contented man. I envy him. But he did stay at White's. I'm not sure why.'

This information rather took the gale out of her sails. She had always got on well with her sister June. 'I haven't seen June since their marriage,' she said nostalgically. 'I was not invited to attend, of course. But shortly after their honeymoon they came to secretly visit us at Aunt Florence's. They kindly brought Marcus a present: the soldiers he plays with all the time. I don't expect he would remember his aunt and uncle. It was almost two years ago that they were married.'

'Well, they are eager to see Marcus again; you too. I had to dissuade your brother-in-law from dashing home to fetch his wife and calling on us immediately. They are visiting us tomorrow.'

'I'm not sure I want to see any of them. It's been so long...'

'You need to be reconciled with your parents and your sisters. It is the first step back into the land of the living, Isabel.' Her husband smiled wryly. 'I've no intention of letting you hide away. Rumours might start that I have shut my bride away in the attic, never to see the light of day,' he gently teased. 'I'm not ashamed of you and I won't have people think that I am. In fact, I'm proud of you both.'

He sounded sincere and Isabel yearned to believe

him. But so much bitterness and betrayal lay between them. Niggling doubts persisted about his motives. Was it self-interest? She didn't think Etienne Hauke was a man who would take kindly to being mocked or pitied. He would want his wife and his son to be a credit to him and accepted by the *ton*. Perhaps he was determined to mould Marcus and her into characters worthy of the privileges soon to be bestowed by an earldom.

Etienne watched her face, and knew from her quiet introspection that the truths he had humbly tendered were met with cynicism. He could hardly blame her for being sceptical considering the turmoil they had been through. 'We must have in place a plausible story to outwit the scandalmongers.' A rueful smile preceded, 'I'm afraid we must do more than simply explain ourselves to friends and relatives. There are those people who are neither, who will relish shredding your reputation…mine too. So, we must socialise for a short while just to confound the gossips with our shameless unconcern.'

At the look of apprehension on her face, he smoothed his hand soothingly against her cheek. 'You can do it. It is the only way to win, Isabel: to broadcast our own version of events in the hope of stealing a march and deflating the windbags. There need not be a major scandal if we provide them with a minor one of our own choosing.'

Chapter Fourteen

'What sort of scandal?'

Etienne slanted a significant glance at their son. 'Why do you not fetch your soldiers, Marcus? I'm sure your grandpapa might like to see them. He will be here soon with your grandmama.'

Once the boy was from the room he continued without preamble. 'You have been in exile for many years. During that time you could have been anywhere. The last that was commonly known of your whereabouts was that you travelled to York with Rachel when she jilted Connor. It was no secret that a day or so later I went there too, although my purpose was kept private. That much of our history is real. Thereafter we must romanticise a bit.'

Etienne found himself drowning in the twin green

pools of a serene gaze. How trusting she looked when she needed him.

'In York, we met by chance and fell in love at first sight,' he continued calmly and then expended a moment wondering where was the sarcastic laugh he had intended should accompany the myth. He forged on, 'Although we were virtual strangers we eloped, intending to be married as soon as possible, but there was no time for a wedding in England as I was called back to my regiment to give evidence at a court-martial.' The spinning of the yarn was broken for him to interject, 'It is the truth. After I arrived at my grand-father's house in Cambridge, I received a message almost immediately ordering my return overseas.'

'It is as well there are some actual facts,' Isabel remarked, intrigued by the weaving of the fabrication. She nodded at him to continue.

'You accompanied me to Belgium, prepared to follow the drum for my sake and it was there I seduced you. In the chaos preceding Waterloo we were separated and you scraped by, helped by fellow soldiers' consorts. Some months later you heard I had been taken prisoner behind enemy lines and executed by the French. You managed to get a passage home where you lodged with your Aunt Florence in York and gave birth to our son a short time later.'

'But you were a prisoner of war before we met, not after.' Isabel interrupted to point out the discrepancy.

Etienne chuckled softly. 'I know that and you know that, but we must hope that people don't bother referencing dates. So long as a thread of truth runs through it all I'm hoping our audience will be dumbfounded by the quixotic nature of it all. Besides, it is all in the past. Now you are a perfectly respectable married lady you will probably be fêted for your magnificent courage in risking all for love.' He concluded the tale with an optimistic smile. 'Meanwhile I escaped my French gaoler and was distraught to hear a tale that the vessel you had been aboard, en route to England, had foundered in a storm. Thus we both believed the other perished.' Noting Isabel's dubious frown, he reassured her, 'It is only comparatively recently that a chance meeting between us has been likely. Although my friend and your sister have been wed almost two years, it is the first opportunity I have had to visit them at Wolverton Manor. From that point we can revert to the truth. It was at their home in Ireland that we renewed our acquaintance, falling in love all over again, and immediately getting wed. A fitting ending to the epic.'

Isabel gave a sour laugh. 'I applaud your vivid imagination. The finale is a great work of fiction, apart from the fact that we did meet again and get married.'

'As I said before,' he murmured, 'the calendar is slightly out; nevertheless, there's truth in it, Isabel.'

'Mr and Mrs Meredith are arrived, sir,' Roland Forbes announced into a still silence.

Etienne took his wife's small, unsteady fingers, pressed them to his warm lips before drawing them through his arm. He turned her about to face the door. 'Please show them in, Forbes.'

Isabel felt stunned; her parents' arrival was almost incidental as her mind dwelled on what her husband had just implied. Was he saying he loved her? Or was he simply boosting her courage with flattery? She took a quick glance up at his impassive profile. Perhaps he arrogantly believed that she was still yearning for him. A poignant feeling stirred. As he'd confidently declared, there was truth in it…

Any further private talk was impossible. Marcus was trotting back in to the room with an overflowing armful of tin. Edgar Meredith was behind him, stooping creakily at intervals to retrieve those clattering soldiers scattering in his grandson's wake.

Of a sudden four voices were disjointedly mingling without any proper preliminaries having taken place.

'Here, you dropped these, young man.'

'Are you my grandpapa?'

'Bella…oh, Bella! How well you look! How beautiful…' Gloria Meredith gushed, her voice so overflowing with tears that her daughter's frozen heart melted.

'Mama…' Swiftly Isabel slipped her hand from

beneath her husband's possession and glided across
the carpet to her mother. After an infinitesimal hesitation in which dear features were devoured, they
clung, dipped heads concealing dewy eyes.

'This one is my favourite,' Marcus announced to
his grandfather, thrusting a figure towards a grizzled
face. 'He looks like my papa. Isn't he fierce? So is his
horse. That's Storm, you know.'

'Hmm, I see, yes,' Edgar Meredith mumbled with
a squint at a featureless cavalry officer brandishing a
lance and mounted on a sinewy destrier. He took a
peer at the flesh-and-blood model detachedly
watching the proceedings.

Etienne squarely met that appraising glance. He
strolled forward and offered a hand. 'I must thank you
for responding quickly to my letter. I'm pleased to
meet you, sir. There is much we have to say to one
another.'

Edgar Meredith straightened to his full height,
bringing him just short of Etienne's shoulders. The
older man looked up coolly at his host before extending a hand and gamely challenging his grip. 'Indeed,
there is much needs to be said,' he agreed, but with
an air of pious condescension. 'Nevertheless, I'm
pleased to meet *you* at last and overjoyed to find my
daughter and grandson are finally respectable.' A
sentimental look slanted at his wife and daughter conversing in low intimate tones.

Isabel led her mother towards a chair then went to the bell pull, announcing, in her first role as hostess, that they must all have tea. Gloria Meredith was soon up out of the comfy seat and bending down close to her grandson. One of her plump, elegantly bejewelled hands went to cup his fair face. She studied him with adoring eyes as he held up more soldiers for her to inspect.

'Etie…my papa,' Marcus corrected himself with a shy smile for his vigilant father. 'My papa said you might like to play soldiers.'

'I would indeed,' his grandmother agreed and, settling herself on a settee, she ranged her infantry alongside her satin skirts.

Edgar glanced at his besotted wife and his eyes became misty. 'It is a tragedy to have been deprived of our daughter and grandson for so long. But I like to think I don't bear grudges,' he ended briskly. 'I know it was not *all* your fault. Isabel admitted as much. And now things are come right at last, you need not fear we will be cold to you.'

'I think it best we leave our wives to get to know each other again while we talk in private. Would you care to accompany me to my study so that we might be properly introduced?' Etienne barely waited for his father-in-law's nod before he excused them both and headed for the door.

Once buffered within his darkly carved and

panelled den, Etienne gestured his hospitality at his guest with a crystal glass and decanter.

Edgar accepted and was soon in possession of a fine goblet holding a generous measure of Madeira. After a silent few minutes, in which he began to shift uneasily beneath his new son-in-law's ruthless regard, Edgar rumbled, 'Hmm, well, it's not too late for you to make amends to all concerned. I've heard from my eldest daughter, Rachel, that the boy can be a mite mischievous. But he is young enough to be corrected. I'm sure you are sorry to have abandoned and neglected your own flesh and blood.'

'Indeed. But then I was ignorant of Marcus's existence. What is your excuse?' Etienne enquired with deadly quiet.

Startled, Edgar dropped his glass away from his desiccated lips. 'What?'

'You heard me. I asked, what is your excuse for neglecting your own flesh and blood?'

'How dare you, sir, accuse *me!*'

'Very easily do I accuse you,' Etienne bit out silkily. 'How generous has been your financial help to Isabel over those years? Why have you not taken it upon yourself to arrange a proper education at a decent school for your grandson?'

Edgar thumped down his drink on a table, slopping wine over a polished surface. 'My Jezebel daughter is fortunate she has parents who still acknowledge her!' he roared so violently that the whole of his small frame quivered. 'Were we not so devoted we might have cast her off with not two halfpennies to rub together to keep warm her and her bastard. For more years than I cared to countenance I met the cost of a modest keep for them with my wife's widowed sister, Florence.' A mottled hand swiped irate foam away from his mouth before he resumed his tirade. 'Would you have had me keep the hussy in equal style to her virtuous sisters at home? When the disaster occurred I did everything in my power to try and persuade the little fool to see sense and give up the boy. I found a couple willing to shelter him in amongst their brood. Money changed hands—an inducement for them to take him—and was lost to their avarice when Isabel refused to let him go.'

'But you deemed these people suitable foster-parents for your grandson,' Etienne mentioned with such icy calm that Edgar blanched.

'Don't dare moralise to me, sir! Where were *you* in all this? *I* wanted to help give Isabel a decent future after you ruined her. It would have been simple enough to blame the epidemic in York for her lengthy absence. I would have welcomed her home with open arms had she seemed remorseful and unlikely to corrupt her sisters. But try as I might to persuade her, she wouldn't give up her child, or show proper penitence for disgracing us. None of our daughters were then married, nor ever would have been had the extent of the scandal leaked out.' Edgar's complexion became ruddy with blotches and blood vessels as vainly he attempted to govern his swingeing ire. 'Now you dare to find *me* wanting in this disaster of *your* making?' he exploded. 'You want to bring *me* to book for not paying for *your* son's education?'

With the exasperation of a man who knows history will not be reformed, no matter what money or curses he throws at it, Etienne bawled, 'Why in hell did you never try to find me?'

'*Find you?*' Edgar scoffed in an equal bellow. 'How was *I* to find you? *She* knew little enough about you, so she insisted. I think she knew more than she let on, but was afraid I might just have you tracked and horsewhipped. The little fool was under the impression you would soon return of your own volition to claim her. And I could not disabuse her of that innocent opinion, no matter how often I lectured on the ways of men and the wicked world. I had found a tempting dowry and a husband who would get her to the altar before the child was born. He was an inoffensive bookkeeper in his middle years, living with his widowed mother in a village north of Windrush. It was close enough for us all to keep in touch. She refused him. I think even when the babe was mewling in her arms, she still fantasised of happy endings. She believed that you would come back.'

Edgar barely paused for breath before rattling on in a seething tone, '*And* you need not think that we are yet free from the taint of it all. We must yet brave the gossips. What fun they will have.' Edgar took a stomp about the room, returning to stand and march with his back to the warm grate.

'Harry Greenwood is a vexed man. The dragon he is married to is breathing fire. By all accounts you led them to believe you would offer for *their* chit, Caroline. I've not had the nerve to let on that it's *my* chit you've married.'

'Nothing was formally agreed. I have already made my apologies to the Greenwoods. I have to say Miss Greenwood was less concerned than her mother that I would not be paying further addresses to her. Harry is resigned to it all. We have some other business of mutual benefit arranged.'

'Ha! That won't quieten his lady. You'll need St George for that! *And* she is friendly with my sister and my daughter June's mother-in-law, Pamela Pemberton. It don't bear thinking about. What I want to know is, what are we to *say* about it all?'

Etienne smiled with trenchant irony. 'If I can slide a few words in, I shall be happy to oblige you with that information.'

Once Etienne had recounted the mitigating circumstances concocted from truth and falsehood, Edgar seemed a mite mollified. It wasn't just the charming ruse that explained away his daughter's scandalously overdue marriage to the father of her child that pleased him. He recognised, beneath his son-in-law's bellicose exterior, a man who was fundamentally decent.

Etienne Hauke had had no need to marry Isabel or formally take on his illegitimate son. He could have made discreet provision for them before again burying them in his past. It was the usual way affluent gentlemen disposed of such unforeseen aberrations from their youth.

When Edgar had received the fellow's confessional letter his first reaction had been astonishment that, after so many years elapsed between the passion and the present, the knave even owned up to the deed. To volunteer to accept such a weight of responsibility with good grace was little short of bizarre. The bridegroom seemed genuinely protective of his family and concerned that Isabel and Marcus should not have wanted during his absence. He acted like a man doing more than his duty. Suddenly Edgar felt his chest swelling in satisfaction and pride. Like the rest of the *ton*, Edgar knew this man kept a lady of rare beauty as his mistress. Yet for two pins he would wager his new son-in-law was enamoured of his Isabel. He couldn't have selected a finer husband for her from amongst the best Almack's had to offer at a Wednesday assembly. He might be somewhat tardy, but

Isabel's prodigal beau had returned to claim her…as she had always said he would.

Edgar mumbled deep in his throat, 'I suppose there's no point in being at loggerheads. I expect I might have done things better for Isabel and the child. He seems a nice little chap…and fair and handsome with it. The boy favours our side.'

'Marcus.'

'Eh?'

'My son's name is Marcus.'

'Yes…Marcus. That's it. You're a lucky man to get a son. I've daughters and three of the four have put me through the mill, I can tell you. Even the youngest, Sylvie, is promising to top the lot for wilful insubordination.' He took a fortifying gulp of wine. 'We have just returned from visiting her at her finishing school. We were summoned by the Principal.' He shook his sparsely covered head and moaned. 'Sylvie has it in her head to quit her education and become a missionary in Africa! Before that Rachel was no end of trouble to me until Connor, bless him, took her off my hands. Thank heavens June was biddable and sweet. She would be welcomed back home at any time, but she has been married for two years to a good chap and no problems there.'

Etienne dwelled on William Pemberton's overnight stay at White's. In his humble opinion all might not be right there but, with the reticence of a man who knows it wise to get his own house in order before he comments on others, he kept quiet. His sympathy for his father-in-law's ordeals in rearing girls was thus limited to a neutral grunt.

His mind lingered with great tenderness on one of those wayward daughters. His brave noble wife had fought like a tigress to safeguard his baby. She had shunned her family's advice and refused to give up Marcus or revile her seducer for abandoning her. With sweet trust and innocence she'd believed he also cherished the memory of their loving. Etienne felt the breathtaking tightening in his chest and, for the first time since he was a boy watching his parents' bitter fights, felt he might weep with the inalterable anguish of it all.

'Anyway, I'm not that much of a wealthy man.'

From a long way off Etienne heard the sly grumble and focused on it. It helped him force a quirk of a smile. 'You must let me know what I owe you for providing for my wife and son in my absence.'

Edgar waved a dismissing hand. 'No…no… wouldn't dream of it…' he muttered beneath his breath.

'But I insist.'

'I'll send over the account.' Edgar picked up his glass and drained it.

The following day at the appointed hour June and William Pemberton came to visit. While the gentlemen repaired to Etienne's study to talk and supervise from a window three young scamps scaling the apple trees, the ladies opted to take a drive for it was a mild day in early spring.

'It is so good to see you, Isabel. I can't believe that this day is finally come.' With a burst of sisterly affection, June leaned forward and spontaneously embraced her sister before resettling on the seat of her smart barouche. 'I would have written more often. And visited more often but for Papa being so very worried that regular contact might lead to the secret being uncovered and set malicious tongues wagging. Now I think he and Mama are more concerned that Sylvie will blight her own chance of marriage. She has some rather odd ideas, I must say. She insists she will travel the globe before settling down. It is not a good idea: she is far too pretty to safely undertake such shenanigans.'

Isabel smiled. 'Papa told Etienne that Sylvie is keen to become a missionary in Africa.'

June's face was a picture of appalled distaste. 'Heavens!' was all she said.

'Etienne met William in White's. He says that William is a very happy man.'

'Is he, indeed? I wish he would tell that to me once in a while,' June declared roundly.

Isabel frowned. Despite being away from June for years, they had slipped easily into sisterly intimacy. 'You are very happy too, June, aren't you?'

June looked a little ill at ease. She sighed, 'Yes, of course; most of the time. It's nothing.' A languid hand was used to dispel Isabel's concerned frown. 'We had a little tiff because of his mother. She knows exactly how to stir things up between us. I don't know why I let the old besom bother me.' June shrugged and sighed. 'Have you met Etienne's relations?'

'Only his mother: Claudine seems pleasant enough. She is French. His father is dead and he has a sister, Monique, who is married with twin children. Oh, and he has grandparents in Cambridge on whom he seems to dote, although he would have one believe otherwise.'

June's sweet face animated archly. 'You two get on well together, don't you? It's amazing he found you so far from York and not knowing you were connected in any way to Connor.'

The smile that sprang unbidden to Isabel's lips was exceedingly wry. 'It is good Marcus has his father at last but…things have not been easy between us. I can't pretend that Etienne was overjoyed to discover he had a son and responsibilities. He was virtually spoken for elsewhere, you know.'

Isabel shrugged. '*Virtually* is nothing. Half the *ton* is on the point of becoming betrothed, if one believes the tattle. Anyway, Caroline Greenwood has been making sheep's eyes at Lord Fairbright for ages. He must have been…surprised…'

'Who…Lord Fairbright?'

'No! Etienne must have been surprised to discover he was a father.'

'I think flabbergasted is a better description.'

'Well, for all that, you seem so…right together.' June took her sister's hand and squeezed it encouragingly. 'I imagine no couple has a perfect marriage. But sometimes I suppose it might be wise to turn a blind eye to men's weaknesses and peccadilloes.'

Isabel smiled at the passing street scene. 'I take it from that piece of advice that you are aware Etienne is in love with Lady Avery.'

'I know she is his mistress. Was his mistress,' June quickly corrected. 'I'm sure it is all in the past, Isabel. You seem to deal so…so naturally together. And his eyes are on you all the time with a certain look.'

'He's probably checking I don't disgrace him in company.' Feeling ashamed of the petulant remark and knowing it to be untrue, Isabel sighed. 'It is having Marcus between us that has made us endeavour to be compatible. There is much to arrange for our son's future.' Isabel paused before reflecting sadly, 'It will never be a marriage as happy as yours. Etienne does love Lady Avery. He honestly told me straight away that he would always be close to her even after he married. But it doesn't matter. He has done his duty and been good to us.'

Chapter Fifteen

'You look beautiful.'

'Thank you.'

Felicity Wright suppressed a pleased little smile on overhearing the master's compliment and her mistress's shy response. The erstwhile man of her dreams had greeted her by name and barely given her a glance on passing moments earlier. Undismayed, the maid tactfully withdrew into the dressing room through which Colonel Hauke had recently gained entry to his wife's sleeping quarters.

Peeking out at them, while gathering up combs and brushes from the dressing stand, Felicity's female eye appreciated a lofty masculine frame in profile. Charcoal tailcoat and breeches, a starched white cuff, a stylish shoe that looked like Reeves had sweated over shining it… Indeed, he was a looker, she chuckled to herself. And her mistress *was* a beauty. She wondered now how she'd ever thought her plain. Mrs Hauke's hair might not be flaxen, but it slipped like silk skeins across her hand when she brushed it. And no tongs needed to curl it! Her complexion wasn't roses, but it was fine and unblemished and needed no powder or patch. *And* she was a lady with a good heart. Felicity more than any knew that. She slanted another squint at the handsome couple. In Felicity's estimation a woman who wore grey and whose hair looked like a nag's mane just couldn't compete with *her* heroine, no matter how refined she might be. Silver cushions! She scoffed as she quietly closed the door and went about her business.

Eyes as glossy as summer grass briefly merged with an earthy gaze reflected in the mirror. Isabel fiddled with the neat pearls at her throat with nervous fingers. More than a month married and this was the first time her husband had invaded her unlocked citadel. A tight curl was coaxed to unravel on to a fragile collarbone. Her plucking was unnecessary; Felicity had made a competent job of styling her hair. 'Are you waiting for me? Am I late?' It was an abrupt query, aimed to stir him from simply studying her with low-lidded eyes concealing his expression.

'No, we've plenty of time…'

Isabel jumped up from her stool in front of the

dressing table. 'I'm not sure I can go through with this folly.' She spun away from him in a rustle of leafy silk, ashamed of her cowardice.

'Yes, you can. I'll be close at all times if you need me.' His voice was honey sweet and suddenly he was behind her. His breath stirred her hair and muscular arms drew her back inexorably against him. Warm lips grazed her nape, making her shiver, then instinctively melt against his hard body. Gladly she accepted his comfort…before she stiffened. Intruding into her languor was one of the reasons she wanted to cry off their first social engagement as man and wife. The thought of being brought face to face with Lady Avery was daunting.

Sensing her frigidity, Etienne moved away. 'I have brought you something to wear.' He withdrew an elegant rectangular case from his pocket and snapped it open. 'It occurs to me I've been tardy in presenting you with a wedding gift.'

Isabel blinked at the dazzling flower bursts of emeralds and diamonds planted in platinum. Never before had she seen such an exquisite suite of jewellery. Her stony eyes tore away from the awesome sight. 'You gave me a wedding ring. That was all I ever wanted,' she rebuffed proudly as unsteady fingers rotated the plain band.

'I know that's all you wanted,' he soothed. 'But I contest meanness joining other crimes you may hold against me. You're my bride and I should like you to accept my wedding gift.'

Her eyes stole back to glorious gems. Her Aunt Florence's pearls were the only jewellery of worth she possessed. Take it! a stubborn inner voice scolded her diffidence. Why should you not enjoy his bounty? A smart carriage and matching horses cost a pretty penny. If he sees fit to lavish gifts on his mistress, why should his wife not enjoy a little luxury too?

'I thank you for your generosity. I have no wedding gift for you, I'm afraid.'

'Nothing at all to bestow?' he asked with ironical inflection and a glint of sultry humour in his eyes. 'Are you sure?' After a tense pause he added wryly, 'There's no need to look quite so alarmed, Isabel. I'd settle for a kiss.'

Isabel felt the sting of blood warm her cheeks, but returned composedly, 'I believe I might have something to give you actually. It's of little monetary value. Nevertheless, I'm sure Marcus would like you to have it until he is old enough to make use of it himself.' She had swept to the chest of drawers in the corner whilst speaking and withdrew a small battered casket.

In solemn silence gifts were exchanged.

Isabel looked on anxiously as he opened the ring box. 'It belonged to my grandfather: my papa's father. When Marcus had his first birthday my papa sent it

to him as a gift. I know it is rather worn…' She
noticed then the solid square signet ring that already
adorned a long patrician finger and wished she had
kept her precious paltry heirloom to herself. The dis-
parity in their gifts seemed ridiculous. 'Its charm lies
in its sentimental value. I wouldn't expect you to wear
it. It's just a token.'

Etienne removed the ring from its threadbare bed.
He smiled as the pitted gold slid snugly over an olive
knuckle. 'Perfect fit,' he said and held up his left hand
for her to inspect his wedding ring.

'How odd,' she remarked on a little laugh. 'He was
not at all your size. He was quite short and tubby. He
was my favourite grandparent—a lovely kind gentleman.'

'Then I'll always wear it. Perhaps it will transfer
some virtue to me.' Etienne pulled her slowly towards
him and his lips brushed on hers. 'Thank you.'

Taking the jewellery case from her hand, he placed
it down then turned her gently about. He removed the
delicate warm pearls and replaced them with weighty
gems that stroked with icy sensuousness against her
throat. Her fingers went up immediately to touch the
hard lustrous stones as he urged her to inspect her reflection in the pier glass.

'Do you like it?'

'It's beautiful.' She glanced down at the other
pieces in the parure: eardrops and a dainty tiara, a

bracelet, and the *pièce de résistance,* a cabochon emerald and diamond ring. 'It's all so very beautiful.'

'I'm pleased it finds favour. I hoped you would like emeralds. I wasn't sure what to choose. But as they match your eyes and you like to wear green…'

'Yes, I do. It's one of the few colours that suits me.'

Etienne raised a hand, skimmed his dark knuckles along the side of a pale satiny jaw. 'Anything would suit you, you're almost perfect.'

'Almost? A comment like that is certain to raise female hackles…and curiosity. In which way must I improve?' It was lightly said; in fact she felt gayer than she had all day.

'Be more demonstrative in your gratitude.'

Isabel felt herself submerging in his rakish charm, in the lambent amber lights bathing her. She tore her eyes away from his. 'Don't!'

'Don't what?'

'Don't treat me like a fool. Don't flirt. Don't pretend that this marriage is anything more than a sham,' was fired at him in a rapid burst. 'If you now want us to be friends…good! I am glad! There is no need for you to—'

'For me to—?'

'All this…this wooing,' exploded from her tightly, her frustration manifesting in a whirling hand. 'Don't do it. Please! It is all so…so unnecessary, in any case. We both know it is false. If you must flirt, do so with your good friend. Save all your seduction for Lady Avery.'

For a moment he simply looked at her while a silence roared between them. A withering laugh grazed his throat, a barely audible oath followed. Within a moment he was by the door. 'In case you are interested, Isabel, since we were married the only good friend I have had is you.' With that he left her alone.

'You didn't really imagine I'd let you face all the malicious battleaxes on your own, did you? After I received Mama's note bringing me up to date, and I realised you were not in Suffolk but still in London, I knew the old tabbies would have their claws out for you. I would have swum the Irish Sea if necessary to get here in time. Thankfully Connor's yacht cracks along at quite a speed.'

Isabel smiled. 'I'm so glad you are here, Rachel. Although I did have dear June for moral support, you know.' She squeezed at her younger sister's arm.

Rachel chuckled. 'The more Merediths present the better. It is a shame Sylvie is not also here. It would be that imp's idea of a great prank to arrive at Lord Fairbright's ball before she has attained her sixteenth birthday or made her come out. That infamy would really make them snort at their salts.'

Isabel's eyes skipped nervously over groups of

people. Some guests seemed unabashed to openly glare their disgust; others were secreting their despising behind quivering fans or sly eyelids. Quite a few gentlemen appeared to be using unemployed drinking vessels as shields over which to ogle them.

Rachel announced cheerfully, 'I imagine we shall be under siege on all sides. The petticoat brigade must be grinding away tooth enamel now that Colonel Hauke is no longer available, and the old besoms are bound to be eager to rummage in our cupboard now the skeleton has evacuated.'

'We should use military tactics,' June chipped in. 'If we become separated and surrounded, we must divulge only name and rank, then retreat and regroup, by this pillar, to launch a counter-attack.'

A mutual giggle mingled as the three young women came close together in an affectionate embrace that proclaimed loyalty and solidarity to their audience.

'What *would* I do without you two?' Isabel murmured with a catch to her voice. She knew her two dear sisters were doing their utmost to boost her courage with their support. She was exceedingly grateful. Yet people were entitled to deplore her outrageous past, even that heroic version her husband had concocted. She didn't allow her mind to dwell on the *ton*'s private reaction should it ever discover the base truth.

Here and there about the vast ballroom were stationed groups of young débutantes, eyeing her with sulky disdain. They would not deviate from fastidious observation of rules and etiquette before marriage. To them her wantonness must fly beyond the pale.

From the corner of an eye Isabel could just glimpse the man who had made her again acceptable, if not welcome. His physical presence wasn't strictly necessary. Now she could mingle in society with her sisters or her parents and not risk a demand she be ejected from decent company. She was a married woman, protected by her husband's name. And she was envied. Bright bitter eyes that raked her person made that clear.

Isabel sniffed and tipped her head to a haughty angle. Humiliation could wait for another day. 'Let battle commence,' she announced with a defiant glint animating eyes that rivalled the lustrous emeralds she wore. Linking arms with her allies, she urged them in perfect time and satin slippers to gracefully march towards the ballroom.

Behind the trio of blond beauties, close enough to be escorts, yet at a distance that respected their independence, strolled three urbane men.

Connor slanted a look at his friend's tense jaw. 'Relax,' he advised. 'Rachel won't let anyone succeed in insulting her.'

'Neither will I,' Etienne responded quietly without removing his eyes from the subject of his vigilance.

'Women can be vicious cats,' William Pemberton remarked as his gaze skipped about and found the reason he was well acquainted with that particular aspect of the female character. His mother, resplendent in violet satin, acknowledged his attention with a gracious smile.

Receiving a minimal response, Pamela Pemberton's eyes shifted from her son to her daughter-in-law. She still found it hard to understand why her dear boy had chosen to marry beneath him, and to such a mouse. Her eyes narrowed as they encompassed the two other Meredith girls. Hardly timid, they! Rachel had always been an incorrigible little madam and now the world knew that Isabel had long been an incorrigible little minx. Both had, nevertheless, netted husbands that would make a duke's daughter bilious with envy. In fact, Pamela was hard pressed to know if she felt more in awe than in judgement of Isabel's infamous conduct. She was certainly casting a covetous eye over the magnificent gems the hussy had about her person. Naturally she was scandalised, as were most people, to discover that Isabel Meredith had not been lost years ago to disease but to disgrace. But what a resurrection! She was back in circulation with a distinguished husband close by her side. The Colonel had been one of the most sought-after bachelors during the previous season. Little wonder the Merediths had the gall to look so preposterously pleased with themselves.

Edgar squeezed his wife's hand. 'Chin up, my dear, and smile. It is our Bella's big day. We might have missed her nuptials, but we are here to witness her reception back into society.'

'Can she emerge from the embers without getting a serious scald?' Gloria whispered via a smile that was making her jaw ache.

'Indeed she can!' Edgar hissed back encouragingly. 'And what feathers has our phoenix! Look at those sparklers. My goodness, he *has* done her proud. She couldn't want for anything more.'

Gloria managed to quell his jubilance with a severe stare. From a corner of her mouth emerged, 'Isabel has need of affection, too, you know. Does he *love* her, do you think?'

Edgar's chuckle transformed to a grimace as words spat through his teeth. 'You think a man spends that sort of cash on someone he *likes?*'

Gloria looked a mite mollified.

'I fear it is not a mutual regard, Gloria,' Edgar sighed out below his breath. 'She seems a little… reserved with him. She ought to be overjoyed he has made her respectable.'

'I'm sure she loves him still,' Gloria muttered.

'She ought soon make it plain, if she does. He has

another attachment, you know. A man in demand don't wear his heart on his sleeve for long.'

'She'll let him know when the time is right, Edgar.' Slipping her hand through her husband's arm Gloria urged him forward. 'Come...let us greet our beautiful girls.'

'Well! The brass-faced cheek of it!'

Pamela Pemberton felt her companion's fingers nip her arm then shake it in emphasis.

'Look! The shameless little trollop is actually parading like she hasn't a care in the world. I'm surprised she didn't bring along her bastard to flaunt. I've heard tell the boy's blond and nothing like the Colonel!'

'Hush, Mama! Someone will hear you.' Caroline Greenwood was grouped with her mother and her mother's friend. She frowned her disapproval, then took a quick, circumspect look this way and that.

'I hope they all *do* hear. I'm not afraid to declare I'm disgusted. I'm only saying what others think.' Noting a few sympathetic eyes on her, she responded with a satisfied twitch of the lips. 'In my opinion the Colonel's been tricked by those crafty Merediths. If the baggage ever *was* a camp follower, I dare say she couldn't identify which redcoat sired the wretch. In my opinion there is a less glamorous explanation for such a scandal than seduction and shipwrecks.'

'He must idolise her to have given her such wonderful jewellery,' Caroline said stubbornly.

'It makes one wonder what she did to get them.' Insinuation coarsened Pamela Pemberton's voice and lifted one thin eyebrow.

'I imagine it was the same thing as got her the brat,' Mrs Greenwood sneered.

Caroline blanched, then blushed. Her large eyes swivelled about to detect eavesdroppers. *'Mama!'* she protested. 'Please don't make your…your *disappointment* so vulgar. I truly don't mind that Colonel Hauke has married someone else. He never actually proposed to me.'

'I doubt he ever actually *proposed* to *her* either. But she's got him down the aisle. And so could you have done with a little more effort. One day you would have been a countess. Now we are a laughing stock.'

'We would not have been, Mama, had you not started wedding preparations prematurely.'

Pamela Pemberton was quite entertained by the unhappy dialogue between mother and daughter. The tale circulating about the Colonel and his lady *did* beggar belief. It was because of that most people accepted it as true. Etienne Hauke had forgone an alliance with the Greenwoods, which would have earned him a small fortune, to make an honest woman of the mother of his son.

Along with her cronies, with whom she had

savoured the tale's juicy details long into the previous night, Pamela had felt a delightful frisson over the romantic and raffish appeal of it all. All the ladies in her coterie had been impatient to scrutinise Isabel's appearance to see whether in their opinions she was a beauty worthy to star in such a drama. Pamela had to admit that, whilst not as strikingly lovely as Rachel, the heroine was decidedly pretty in a rather winsome way.

'Colonel Hauke has spread the news about their relationship. I don't see why he would lie about any of it, Mama.' Caroline challenged her boiling-countenanced mother.

'I don't see why he would lie either,' Pamela concurred, simply to stir the pot.

'And neither do I,' said a dulcet, cultured voice at their shoulders. 'In fact, I own that I know it all to be true.'

Pamela gave Lady Valerie Avery a nervous smile whilst wondering how on earth they had merited such a notable's attention. Lady Avery moved in quite exalted circles and, but for an acknowledgement now and again, ignored her little clique. 'We were just saying, Lady Avery, we recognise the ring of truth to it all. Why would the Colonel fabricate a story?'

'Why indeed? He is one of the most honest men I know.'

'Of course, you *know* him well, Lady Avery,' Mrs Greenwood fawned venomously.

'That is also true.' Valerie Avery allowed a smile. 'I've known him very well indeed for a long time. We were good friends at the time of the...incident, and I can thus vouch for its veracity. I can remember quite clearly how distraught the Colonel was when he returned from overseas having been a prisoner of war.'

'You *knew* that Colonel Hauke thought he had lost his beloved in tragic circumstances? He *told* you that?' Mrs Greenwood lost subtlety as her inquisitiveness escalated.

'I was his confidante. We discussed everything: happy and sad. More than that I cannot say for fear of betraying trust...you understand.'

With twin expressions of sage sympathy both Mrs Greenwood and Mrs Pemberton nodded at Lady Avery.

Caroline stirred herself from her embarrassed daze. It was an open secret that Lady Avery was the Colonel's mistress and had kept that coveted place in his life for many years.

At one time, when her mother was fretting the Colonel wasn't keen enough in his courtship, she had directed her to copy this woman's look and style. But though her hair was dark, it had a stubborn curl to it and resisted being sleek. Her skin with its tendency to high colour would not whiten no matter what amount of powder her mother pressed on to it.

Caroline had been mortified when she ended up looking like a marionette with scraped-down hair and red spots of colour breaking through her *maquillage*.

Lady Avery smiled at Caroline with an amount of encouraging empathy. It helped Caroline find her voice. 'I think the Colonel must be very proud of his wife. In my opinion, Isabel Meredith has been extremely brave.'

'I think so too,' Lady Avery agreed. 'In fact, I desire to tell her so. Do you?' Valerie's eyes held a glint of challenge.

Caroline took a glance at her mother's dropping jaw. *Her* chin went up. 'I do, Lady Avery. Yes…I *do*.'

Chapter Sixteen

'Three of the finest catches the *ton* has ever had on offer are *our* sons-in-law.'

'I know, my dear,' Edgar said. 'And I think that fact irks some of these females more than the beauty of our daughters.' He turned about with the intention of casting a contented eye on those distinguished gentlemen. His desultory gaze snagged on a sight that made him groan then splutter. 'Oh, my heavens! Look who is almost upon us, Gloria!'

'Mr and Mrs Meredith! How nice it is to see you again. It has been some while, has it not? I think we last met at Rosemary Clairborne's *musicale*.' Valerie Avery graciously inclined her head at Gloria's jerky bob and Edgar's equally ungainly bow. 'I am acquainted with June, of course. Will you not introduce me to your other two daughters?'

Edgar manfully expanded a pigeon-chest, opened his mouth to utterly defend his brood. Alas, no sound issued. He turned an appealing look on his wife.

'Indeed...of course, Lady Avery, let me introduce you to Rachel...Isabel, too,' Gloria weakly babbled.

At the mention of Lady Avery's name, Isabel had frozen, ceased hearing Rachel talk to her friend, Lucinda, and pivoted about.

Calm grey eyes featured first in Isabel's observation. Then she saw sleek jet hair. The woman's other attributes merged into a painful awareness of exquisite beauty and a pearl-grey gown shimmering over a shapely figure. Quite remotely she realised she would have recognised her from her servants' description. Refinement seemed to bathe the atmosphere in which she beatifically breathed. It was little consolation to know she was possibly Etienne's age, if not a year or two older.

'Lady Avery, this is my daughter Isabel. *Mrs* Isabel *Hauke,*' Gloria robustly emphasised as maternal instinct asserted itself.

The immediate vicinity was quietening as conversations withered and people strained to overhear what was being said. The unanticipated meeting between the wife, the mistress and the fiancée was a fascinating and welcome spectacle.

If Lady Avery was aware her civility had engendered such gawping, she chose to ignore it. With true aplomb she extended a hand of welcome to Isabel.

Where are you, Etienne? Why are you not equally suffering this excruciating situation? The pressing thought was drumming an ache in Isabel's head. It had not occurred to her that her husband's mistress would boldly solicit an introduction to her lover's wife the moment the reprobate disappeared.

Yet there was no malice in Lady Avery's mild demeanour. In fact, a gentle pleading seemed to radiate from her eyes as though begging her pardon, begging her understanding. Slowly Isabel extended her emerald-weighted fingers.

Valerie Avery gratefully received those fingers, squeezed them in welcome. With Isabel's hand still in hers, she drew forward Caroline who she then introduced.

'We felt we must come and tell you we are pleased to meet you. And also convey our felicitations on your marriage, Mrs Hauke.' Valerie's speech was accompanied by a reassuring smile for every vigilant Meredith. Rachel had now stopped chatting to her friends and had joined her parents and June, protectively close to Isabel. 'You have been away from London for a long while. It is not always an easy environment to return to. You have braved it and we admire your courage.' Valerie continued undisturbed by the hushed auditorium. 'We sincerely welcome you back and wish you much happiness.'

'I…yes…thank you,' Isabel said and looked quickly at Rachel, who was listening intently as though prepared to intervene at the first hint of offence.

'My eldest daughter, Rachel Flinte, Countess of Devane.' Gloria realised she had been remiss in that introduction.

Valerie Avery extended a hand to Rachel, too. 'You are to be congratulated, Mrs Meredith. Three beautiful blond daughters and another I believe at home. How very lucky you are.'

'We were only just saying the very same thing,' Edgar burst out, all *bonhomie* now his guard had been lowered by the lady's disarming charm. 'Sylvie is at school and already as handsome as her sisters.'

'Blond hair is divine. I hear your son is blond, Mrs Hauke.' Caroline had sincerely intended to be amenable. But her complexion became ruddy on recalling her mother's spiteful remark that the boy was nothing like his swarthy father. 'I expect he is like you.'

'He is a little like me,' Isabel kindly agreed.

'Perhaps in the future we might take a drive in the park together, Mrs Hauke. My nephew Robert is eight and likes the menagerie. Perhaps we could go there with your son…or…or somewhere else?'

Isabel understood, in such a unique situation as they found themselves, it was difficult to weigh the constraints of etiquette with a desire to be friendly. Caroline was endeavouring to capture just that balance and Isabel's heart went out to her. Suddenly she felt an inner spring of tension uncoil. This was not some malicious ploy by two females with ulterior motives. With simple insight she realised her husband's mistress and his rejected fiancée had, against all odds, chosen to join her as allies. She smiled with shy, sweet gratitude. 'I would be delighted…Marcus would be delighted…to go with you to the zoo.'

'We must not take up all your time,' Valerie said. 'I see there are other people waiting to speak to you.'

Isabel's eyes darted about. Incredibly there were now quite a few people jostling for position, trying to catch her eye with a smile, as though keen for an introduction.

As they walked away, Valerie patted at Caroline's hand, revealing her relief that a tricky situation had been successfully overcome. 'I see Lord Fairbright is looking a little bereft now the ladies are all keen to be introduced to Mrs Hauke and her entourage. I expect our host might like an attractive young lady to talk to.' Her dismissal was mitigated by a smile. She walked on gracefully alone.

'So tell me…how many times were you a prisoner of war?'

Etienne spun on a heel and squinted into the

darkness. A white grin split his dark face as he recognised the identity of the man silhouetted in the gloom. Leaving Connor and William leaning on the terrace railing, smoking, he strolled over. 'As many times as I need to be.'

The fellow laughed, flicking away the smouldering stub of a cigar into the night. 'I've always loved a romantic tale…and a misbehaved woman.'

'Yes, I remember.' Etienne said wryly. 'I was just thinking the other day that I hoped I'd run into you. Have you still got that temperamental white stallion? I forget his name.'

'White stallion?'

'I borrowed him to take to York…eight years ago.'

'Ah! I remember; *that* temperamental white stallion. Star. He's out to graze at Stratton Manor.'

'I'll buy him from you.'

'I'll have him sent over. No charge. Wedding present.'

Etienne gave a nod in appreciation of the man's generosity. 'How is Elizabeth?'

'She's very well. She was talking to your wife a little while ago. She wanted to approach her immediately you arrived, but I advised her to wait. Then, just as Elizabeth was about to make her move, Lady Avery and Miss Greenwood beat her to it. Thereafter a queue formed.'

Etienne's dark eyes narrowed on his companion. A curse hissed out through his teeth.

'It wasn't a problem. It was a very astute move, actually. I have to say I admire your taste in women…all of them. The righteous are now falling over themselves to be nice to your wife.'

Etienne peered over a shoulder at the French doors and then set out towards them at quite a pace. He turned, walked backwards as he called to his erstwhile army comrade, 'Thanks for the wedding present, Trelawney. You and Elizabeth must visit us…'

'Don't run away…please.'

When he was a step away from a globe of golden light spilling from the ballroom, that throaty plea lured Etienne back into the shadow of a mulberry tree.

'Don't be angry with me. I can see from your face that you are.'

'I'm not angry, Valerie. I hear I should be thanking you.'

Valerie Avery's mouth twisted ruefully. 'But you won't. You're more concerned with knowing whether I have upset your wife. I haven't, Etienne, I promise.' A careless touch on his arm contrasted with vivid melancholy in her eyes. 'I too must say thank you. Thank you for letting me show the world that it is I who bring our friendship to a dignified close. And I have done so at the first opportunity. You wanted to allow me that one small scrap of comfort…didn't you? That is why I have seen nothing of you, heard nothing from you, isn't it, Etienne?'

Etienne gave a small wry smile. 'Yes.' In truth, he had hoped that his mistress would allow her pride to dictate her future. He would have hated it to be obvious that he was putting off a woman who pined for him. Valerie had shown him nothing but loyalty and devotion for many years; the last thing he wanted was her humiliation. 'You're far too young for a pension, Valerie,' he said softly. 'I knew you wouldn't want that.'

'No. I wanted you to marry Miss Greenwood. Then nothing would have changed between us,' she said with a raw throb to her voice.

Etienne bowed his head, examined the toes of his shoes. 'I'm sorry…very sorry…'

'Don't be! We all deserve to fall in love. If one is lucky enough to fall in love with one's spouse, how wonderful that must be. I understand. She seems sweet…'

Etienne missed the hint of cattishness as he choked on a laugh. *'Sweet?'* He tested the epithet. The single word bonded longing and exasperation and an affection that made Valerie's last hope that he might succumb to seduction shrivel and die.

'I see you are restless to be off. Just one last thing,

Etienne…' She quickly went on to tiptoe and pressed her soft lips hard against his, as though she would weld them together forever by that touching patch of skin. His response was minimal, no more than polite. Valerie forced a light laugh. 'That was just a little parting gift…for old times' sake. Almost eleven years and yet I can recall as though it were yesterday the time we met.'

It was the impatient glance over her shoulder that helped her to step away. 'I wish you happiness, my love.' In a moment she had disappeared into the throng in the ballroom in a rustle of silver satin.

Etienne closed his eyes and a curse sighed beneath his breath. Having acknowledged he was a bastard, he turned towards the French doors with relief swamping him that the deed was done. He glimpsed a flash of green on the periphery of his vision but was so intent on finding Isabel he unwisely gave it little thought.

In the weeks that followed Isabel found she could have socialised every evening had she so desired. Invitations to balls, soirées, and all manner of functions arrived daily. Some were addressed to her and Etienne as a couple; others were for her as lady of the house. On the rare occasions in the evening that her husband appeared to dine, Isabel civilly consulted him as to which they might attend.

Neither of them had ever mentioned that first outing as newlyweds when Lady Avery had set the seal on her approval by polite society. Isabel had kept to herself the anguish she had felt on witnessing such a tender scene between Etienne and his mistress. She knew he had immediately sensed her coolness after he joined her in Lord Fairbright's ballroom. Soon after they had left and returned home in frosty silence. The awful irony was that she had been happily searching for him on the terrace to tell him that she was beginning to relax and enjoy herself when she caught him kissing Lady Avery.

When making a fleet-footed retreat that night, the motive for Lady Avery's largesse had become woundingly apparent. It had been a finely timed charade. Etienne had no doubt persuaded his mistress to patronise his wife and her family whilst he loitered outside. And Lady Avery had done so, to great effect, and had been rewarded with a kiss. The lovers had obviously believed the gauche wife to be out of sight. But then perhaps they believed they were too, tucked beneath the spreading branches of the mulberry tree. It was simply a shimmer of silver as the moon fled a cloud that had betrayed them.

Isabel's faraway gaze focused on her coffee cup. She picked it up and sipped, grimacing as the lukewarm liquid filmed her lips. She pushed the beverage away and with it her uneaten toast.

She stared out over an expanse of polished wood to the place it would be usual to see one's spouse in the morning at breakfast. But of course he was not there. He was rarely there and when she did see him she had too much pride to demand to know where he spent his nights, or with whom.

Besides, she knew the answer to that. She had no need or inclination to embarrass either of them by becoming emotional or clingy. And what right had she to condemn him? She had told him to use his flirtatious seduction on Lady Avery. He had no need to know that she frequently wished she could retract such stupid words and conquer her pride enough to say she loved him, that she had never stopped loving him, and could they please try to be happy. Instead, they came together from time to time and conversed in the language of spare formal politeness as if they were strangers.

She thought of her plans for the day. Caroline Greenwood would arrive later. They were going to Madame Tussaud's Waxworks with Robert Wilson, Caroline's nephew, and Marcus. The boys had played together before and had got along famously.

Caroline had been sipping tea with Isabel in the sitting room after their expedition to the menagerie when Etienne had unexpectedly arrived home. Considering that once they had been on the point of becoming betrothed, neither Etienne nor Caroline seemed particularly uneasy in the other's presence. As Caroline had reassuringly told Isabel on their first outing to Hyde Park, it had been an arrangement of convenience, not courtship.

The banging front door brought Isabel to her senses. Automatically she reached for her cup and took a fortifying gulp of unpleasantly scummy coffee. She was replacing the cup with a grimace on her face when her husband entered the dining room.

Dark eyes slanted at her from a gaunt, unshaven face. 'Is that scowl anything to do with my arrival?'

The sardonic tone he used made her colour heighten. 'No. The coffee is cold.' She noted he was pouring himself a cup from the silver pot on the sideboard. 'Shall I get some fresh brought in for you?'

Etienne took a cautious sip. 'This is fine.'

'The pot must have kept it hot. Mine was cold in the cup.' Isabel fell silent. Why on earth was she justifying her expression of distaste for cold coffee? 'Would you like something to eat?'

'No. I'll breakfast with Connor. I'm only home to clean up.' Another look arrowed her way as though he expected her spirits might lighten at that comment. 'We have some business to attend to.'

'More business?' Isabel shrilled gaily. 'How very enterprising of you! Every day you have so many deals to keep you busy…and abroad. Meetings with Connor and William and Mr Greenwood…'

'It's how I afford to keep us all in the style to which we've become accustomed.'

Isabel flushed and her eyes flinched from his, prompting an oath beneath his breath and a hand to swipe the bluish bristle on his face. 'I'm sorry, Isabel. That was a stupid, churlish thing to say. All I meant was that I have a few unforeseen expenses, and money that isn't readily accessible to meet them at present. Besides, I thought my absence would please you.'

'You don't need to explain to me,' Isabel rebuffed as she gained her feet. 'A wife and a child foisted on to one must be financially burdensome, I'm sure.'

'It's not you or Marcus that's a problem. Do you want me to be home more?'

'Not if you would rather be somewhere else.'

'What is that supposed to mean?' he demanded. On seeing her whitening face, he banged down his cup. 'God's teeth! Why do we always end in arguing?'

'Possibly it is because we spend so little time together that misunderstandings arise.'

'I need to stay away, Isabel. I need to keep busy. It helps stop me being…'

'Being *what*? Being at home?'

'Being frustrated,' he gritted through barely moving teeth.

'I'm sorry I have ruined your life and your prospects.'

A look at her indignant face had him choking a

laugh. 'It is *not* that sort of frustrated, Isabel. You've not thwarted any ambition I had that was worth a moment's pause.'

She looked curiously at him before blushing.

'Yes, *that* frustrated,' he muttered with a mix of amusement and apology. 'Where is Marcus?' he asked, turning away.

'His tutor is with him. Later we are going to see the waxworks. It is a shame you never accompany us on such trips.'

'I know. I would today but I have promised your brothers-in-law to meet them at the Palm House. We have documents to sign.'

'Yes. I understand.'

'I don't think you do, Isabel. I don't think you want to understand what's wrong in this marriage. But you're not so naïve. We made a baby after all, didn't we?'

Isabel flinched, expecting the door to slam as he went out, but it closed quietly and she stood motionless, crying, listening to his footsteps die away.

Both Rachel and June joined Isabel and Caroline on the outing to the waxworks. Later the boys wanted to sail boats in Hyde Park's lake before returning home.

June linked arms with Isabel and sighed as they paraded the perimeter of the park. 'It is a shame our poor husbands are stuck in a dingy office with a dusty old lawyer instead of taking the air with us.'

Isabel smiled neutrally.

'Of course, they will enjoy this afternoon's entertainment.'

'Will they?' Isabel enquired lightly.

'Did Etienne not say? There is a boxing bout arranged between an English and a French fighter at Gentleman Jackson's.'

'Oh.'

Marcus rushed up to his mother and thrust a dripping wooden yacht into her hands. 'May Robert come back with us for tea?'

'Of course,' his mother told him.

At five of the clock Connor and William arrived to join them for tea and to take their respective wives home.

'Is Etienne not with you?' Rachel asked Connor conversationally about their host's absence.

Isabel barely faltered in encouraging Robert to have more cake.

'I haven't seen Etienne since we left Bank Street. He didn't watch the match. He received a note and went off in a hurry…'

Conversation died, the room quietened, and Isabel knew without looking up to see expressions that embarrassment had settled on the company. Most men, she realised with a quiver of despair, would be grateful for such devoted attention from Valerie Avery.

With a smile fixed on her face, Isabel stood up with the cake plate and insisted everyone must have more.

Chapter Seventeen

It was in the unendurably long hour between darkness and dawn that Isabel decided things must change.

Once the die was cast she was unable to sleep further and climbed from her warm bed. A moon scudded out from beneath a quilt of cloud to stripe mercurial light through the wide chink in the curtains. She lit tapers quickly, then took a few moments dislodging her travelling trunk from the top of the clothes press. By candlelight she calmly started opening drawers in the chests and packing her clothes.

An irrepressible urge drew her eyes to the dressing-room door. She let the chemise in her hand drop into the case and glided trance-like through no-man's land. Without hesitating for a moment she turned a handle and trespassed for the first time.

She approached her husband's bed on noiseless feet, mounted the small dais on which the four-poster grandly reposed, and gazed forlornly down at undisturbed pillows and eiderdowns.

'I don't want to go!'

Isabel stared at her son, stunned by his vehemence. An anxious lump had formed in her throat. She swallowed and reasoned calmly, 'When your papa told you about Redgrave Park, you seemed eager to go there and invite your friends to stay.'

Marcus looked mutinous still. 'Is Papa going there with us?'

'No. But I expect he will visit us when he is able. You know he has at present some business to attend to with your uncles here in London. He cannot be with us all the time.'

Marcus's face suddenly brightened. 'I shall stay here in London with Papa when you go to the big house in Suffolk.'

'Don't be silly, Marcus!' Isabel chided with a dazed little laugh. 'Of course you must come with me.'

'Robert is staying with his papa while his mama is away. And his Aunt Caroline looks after him and takes him on outings.'

'That is only because his Scottish grandfather is very ill. I'm sure Robert's mother will soon be home to look after him.'

'Aunt June might take me out and look after me.'

'It is not that simple!' Isabel's burst of exasperation was sharpened by hurt. The notion that she might be dispensable to the child who had altered the course of her life had never occurred to her and the shock registered in her wan face. Had she found Marcus his father only to lose him herself?

'I'm afraid you must do as you are told, Marcus. *We* are going to Suffolk.'

When he remained sullen-faced, she attempted cajolery. 'Do you not want to go fishing and riding the fields with Michael Murphy?'

The lure didn't work. He shook his blond head. 'I might later on, I suppose. But now I want to stay here with Papa.'

'I cannot just *leave* you here,' Isabel cried distressfully. 'Your father will be home soon. I have sent him a note at his club. We shall see what *he* has to say.'

When Etienne received his wife's brief summons to immediately return home it brought a slow thoughtful smile to his lips. A confrontation between them had been imminent for some time. He had been patiently awaiting it. He had sensed that Isabel was ready to explode the vacuum between them. His dread had been that she might opt to settle for that suffocating civility that was their marriage. Yet, despite her aloofness, he'd noticed she couldn't always conceal her pleasure on discovering he'd slept at home on a particular night. God knows he hated playing at a gaming table into the small hours as an excuse not to go back to be tormented by an unlocked door...that was nevertheless impregnable.

At times over the past months, the maxim that absence makes the heart grow fonder had seemed to him to be profound wisdom. On other occasions leaving her alone to brood on their problems seemed to be rank stupidity. His desire to simply storm in and demand she tell him outright whether she loved or hated him was not easily quashed.

Etienne thus arrived home in the spirit of a man taking heed of the fact that what transpired in the next hour would be critical to his future happiness. When he noticed the packing case in the hall, philosophy was abandoned. A demand to know where was his wife was barked at his butler. He was taking the stairs two at a time before he had properly heard Forbes' reply.

Marcus charged to the door at his father's abrupt appearance and, as usual, imprisoned his muscular thighs in an embrace. A dark hand instinctively cupped his blond head, but Etienne's eyes were on the open trunk digging an indent into the quilt on his wife's bed.

As fierce brown eyes met hers, Isabel's chin went

up and she smoothed the skirts of her sturdy twill travelling skirts.

'Are you leaving me?'

'I'm leaving London...yes.' As if to reinforce that statement she picked up her bonnet and smoothed her amber curls in readiness to don it.

'Why?'

'Because...I made a mistake in ever coming here. Because I have had enough of this charade that is our marriage,' she informed him with a quiet dignity that was at odds with the flinging of the bonnet back on to the nightstand.

Simultaneously Etienne and Isabel flicked glances at their watchful son.

Etienne held the door wide and gently propelled Marcus outside.

Before Marcus dashed off, he appealed to his father. 'Might I stay with you, Papa? I don't want to go with Mama to the big house in Suffolk.'

'I'll talk to you later.'

The sound of childish feet pounding the landing boards died away.

Etienne strolled closer to the bed. A casual hand violently rammed the case shut. In an instant it was heaved to the floor, and a foot sent it skidding to the wainscot.

'What have I done wrong? My behaviour has been impeccable. I've stayed out of your bed, paid the bills, arranged for our son's schooling. What else do you want me to do, Isabel? Tell me!'

Isabel faced him across an expanse of pure white sheets that might have been the murkiest territory both were afraid to invade.

The savage pain in his eyes made her heart leap to her throat. 'It is not all your fault,' she offered huskily. 'It was wrong of me to force you to marry me. You knew from the outset that it would not work. You said duty would never be quite enough for either of us, and you were right.' She briefly paused. 'But it might have been tolerable a while longer. I asked…expected you to be discreet. I said that I wanted nothing from you but some of your time and your discretion. You have given me…us…very little of either.' Her eyes flinched from his, for she could feel the betraying hotness in them as she succumbed to the lure of his presence. Even crumpled clothes and a dangerous air of louche virility couldn't detract from the appeal he held for her. Her stomach was brimful of butterflies. It would have been so easy to fall into his arms and beg him to love her.

'When have I not been discreet? When have I refused my company when you asked for it?' he demanded.

Isabel glanced at him and snapped, 'I think you know the answer to that.'

'Are you referring to when I said I was too busy to accompany you and Marcus to the waxworks?'

'Yes, I am. You were too busy to take your son out, yet you found time enough to rush to your mistress's side when she summoned you with a note in the middle of the afternoon.'

Etienne looked at her and frowned.

'Don't deny it,' she cried. 'And don't blame Connor or William for letting it slip out that you didn't go to the boxing match with them.'

'Ah...*that* note.' A sudden glint of amusement fired his eyes.

'Yes, *that* note,' Isabel fumed. 'Which leads me to ask whether you think *that* is discreet behaviour. Or that it is discreet to kiss your paramour when your wife is close by. Or that it is respectful to arrange for that...that woman to patronise your wife in company.' The tears that slipped over her lashes were furiously dashed away. '*That* is why I am leaving. Marcus tells me he wants to stay with you. I have said he must come with me. I hope you will not even think of indulging him in this.'

'For a while, Isabel, I thought there might be some hope for us. I thought if I let you be you might forgive me, remember what it was that first drew us together. Not the lust,' he said softly, then for the first time felt churlish to have made her blush. 'Something else; that inner sense you had that we were special to each other. But you continue to distrust me, and I can't blame you for that. I need a lifetime to make it up to you, not a few months.

'Yes, I did receive a note from a woman that day. It was from my mother. Claudine is returned from Ireland and distraught because Vincent resisted her demands that he marry her. In the role of scorned woman she's upset him to a degree that he is refusing to pay her bills. I have been settling them and have sent her off to visit my sister in Bath before she bankrupts me. Besides, if she stays in London, she might meddle in our domestic troubles, whilst we are regaled with her woes. I don't want my marriage to be as grim as was my parents,' he told her, his tone heartbreakingly hoarse.

'As for Valerie Avery, I have seen her once since I married you. It was the evening she welcomed you back to London. I knew nothing of her plan to do that. But I admit I was grateful to her for it. Yes, she kissed me—in farewell. We both knew our relationship was finished. But I won't say she wasn't a good friend to me or that I wasn't fond of her. I don't love her. In a way, I wish I could.'

'I don't know whether you're telling the truth.' Isabel's turmoil was plain in her strained face.

Etienne grunted a mirthless laugh. 'I know. That's why I despair of there being any hope for us. That's why I wish I could love Valerie. She said to me at Fairbright's ball that it must be wonderful to love one's spouse. It isn't; it's hell. Loving you, Isabel, and knowing you despise me is torture. A fitting punishment, I suppose, for the way you have suffered because of me. I watched my father die a little each day because my mother wouldn't love him, yet he couldn't crush his feelings for her. I promised myself that I would never allow that to happen to me…'

Isabel stared at him with unblinking green eyes. 'How could you possibly think I despise you?' she whispered. 'If I have made it appear so, then I'm sorry. All I ever wanted was to know you cared.' Then, because her son was inextricably part of her, she blurted, 'Do you love Marcus, too?'

'Yes. But not yet with the strength of feeling I have for you. You're the source. Loving him springs from loving you.' He smiled ruefully. 'It's not a ploy to make you stay with me. It's not blackmail. It's just the way it is.'

Isabel started to speak, moistened her lips. A hand fluttered to her face, covered the beginnings of her joyful tears.

'Don't cry. It doesn't matter. Just stay with me… please. I swear I'll treat you well, and Marcus.'

Isabel's head bowed into two hands.

'Don't make me beg, Isabel.' It was a raw request, no more than a murmur. 'I will if you want. I know you deserve to see me humbled.'

Isabel nodded, snuffled into her palms.

'You want to see me beg? Or is that an agreement

to stay with me?' The hint of humour in his tone was belied by the tremor in his voice.

Isabel quickly turned her back, hiding her watery face from him until she could bring some order to her appearance. 'It is both,' eventually emerged in a tear-choked voice. 'You ought to beg—as I did. So many nights I sold my soul to the darkness, hoping to bring you back. I'd look at the stars, know you saw the same ones, and will you to think of me. I wept at the thought you might again be a prisoner and prevented from returning, then fantasised you would bravely deem all physical hurt nothing when compared to the agony of our separation. When daylight and reason came, I raged at you, made excuses for you…but I never stopped loving you, Etienne. No one could slander you well enough to make me do that.'

It was Etienne's turn to shield his distress. His head tipped up and he gazed at a splintering ceiling. 'I'm sorry.' It was simply said, but the two words were entreating her not to have him grovelling on his knees. 'Do you love me now, Isabel?' It was a faltering, almost diffident, pleading.

Fair curls were shaken away from damp cheeks. Tear-spiky clumps of lashes parted, showing him glowing green eyes that promised him his dignity.

He looked at her, then blinked away the moisture filming his vision. 'You do,' he muttered with some astonishment.

'Yes, I do,' she told him in a voice husky with re-assurance. 'Of course I do. I knew you'd come back for Marcus and me… someday.'

He coughed, sniffed, took stock. 'Will you come to bed with me?' he gauchely blurted out.

She nodded.

Etienne swiped a hand over his mouth, his eyes devouring her over the top of it. 'Are you sure?'

'Yes.'

She noticed his dark fingers jump, then hesitate before fumbling at his neckcloth. In a moment it was off and the front of his shirt was gaping to reveal a column of strong brown throat.

'Etienne! You can't mean now,' Isabel gasped out. 'It is…it is after noon. Marcus might come back…or the servants arrive to clean.'

In a moment he had locked the door and his jacket was flung towards a chair. Then he was walking slowly towards her. The large hands framing her radiant, grubby face were trembling. 'Don't say no. Not now. Forbes will keep them all away. I swear to be quiet, and you must try to be too…not like last time…'

The serious desperation in his voice made her giggle and bury her face against his shoulder. 'There are some things about that time I see you have not forgotten.'

'I've lived them over and over in my mind a

thousand times since you reminded me of them,' he said huskily and soothed her blushing with a stroking hand.

'You didn't really forget me at all…did you?'

'No,' he vowed softly and felt quietly astonished as a treasury in his mind finally surrendered its soulful secret. Isabel accepted the truth, and, for the first time in eight years, her arms wound about his neck. A seductive peep up at him from beneath long lashes preceded, 'I hope you have not forgot what it was we did…for I liked it very much.'

He smiled against her soft, parted mouth and a voice of gravelly velvet reassured her. 'I haven't, sweet, don't worry about that.'

'Good, for we've no time for a rehearsal,' was all she cheekily said, then was kissing him with such innocent ardour, such sweet longing, that she wasn't even aware when they found the bed.

'Marcus wants a brother. He told me so.'

Isabel dreamily, caressingly, shifted her face on her husband's warm chest. 'And what did you say to that?'

'I said I would see what I could do.'

Isabel raised herself on an elbow. Sated and blissful, she traced his jaw with a languid finger. 'I've told you not to promise him things he might not have.'

Etienne drew her head down to his, kissed her with

wooing tenderness. 'I've never promised him a single thing he can't have, Isabel,' he said softly. 'But you'll have to help me in this…for Marcus's sake…'

Epilogue

'Sit by me.' The boy patted the stair by his hip. Automatically one of his arms fell fondly about the infant who curved trustingly against him.

'Mama might be cross if she catches me. But if you are hungry, I'll get you something,' he bravely promised.

The child nodded its curly flaxen head against his arm. A thumb found a dewy mouth and large green eyes looked up through the dusk, glossy and alert.

'Do you want just biscuits or some of Cook's cinnamon bread, too?'

'Drink.'

'And a drink,' the boy echoed with a nod. 'We shall have a midnight feast,' he decided, smiling into the adoring eyes fixed on his face.

Suddenly a door below opened and a gentleman

and lady came out followed by the children's parents. The boy watched them walk, quietly conversing, from the dining room to the drawing room. On the threshold of the drawing room his mother and father hesitated, drew back, then kissed before following their guests into the room.

'Wait here.'

Within a moment the boy was back with a cinnamon-fragrant cloth made into a sack and a cup that held milk.

'Come on.' He held out a hand. The girl immediately extracted a wet thumb from her mouth and placed damp fingers in her brother's.

With a sigh of utter contentment Marcus Forrester Hauke led his sister back to bed.

* * * * *

The *Regency*

LORDS & LADIES
COLLECTION

More Glittering Regency Love Affairs

VOLUME TWENTY-NINE

Miss Verey's Proposal by Nicola Cornick

After a disastrous marriage, Alex, the Duke of
Delahaye, is determined his younger brother Philip
be safely married to provide the heir. The chosen
bride, Miss Jane Verey, wants a husband, but it's
Alex who makes her pulse leap…

The Rebellious Débutante by Meg Alexander

The Earl of Rushmore had secretly been impressed
with Perdita's feisty spirit. But the biggest surprise
of all for the Earl was that *he* now had marriage
on *his* mind!

On sale 2nd January 2009

www.millsandboon.co.uk

The Regency

LORDS & LADIES
COLLECTION

More Glittering Regency Love Affairs

Volume 17 – 4th January 2008
One Night with a Rake by Louise Allen
The Dutiful Rake by Elizabeth Rolls

Volume 18 – 1st February 2008
A Matter of Honour by Anne Herries
The Chivalrous Rake by Elizabeth Rolls

Volume 19 – 7th March 2008
Tavern Wench by Anne Ashley
The Incomparable Countess by Mary Nichols

Volume 20 – 4th April 2008
Prudence by Elizabeth Bailey
Lady Lavinia's Match by Mary Nichols

Volume 21 – 2nd May 2008
The Rebellious Bride by Francesca Shaw
The Duke's Mistress by Ann Elizabeth Cree

Volume 22 – 6th June 2008
Carnival of Love by Helen Dickson
The Viscount's Bride by Ann Elizabeth Cree

Volume 23 – 4th July 2008
One Night of Scandal & The Rake's Mistress
by Nicola Cornick

M&B

The Regency

LORDS & LADIES
COLLECTION

More Glittering Regency Love Affairs

Volume 24 – 1st August 2008
The Reluctant Marchioness by Anne Ashley
Nell by Elizabeth Bailey

Volume 25 – 5th September 2008
Kitty by Elizabeth Bailey
Major Chancellor's Mission by Paula Marshall

Volume 26 – 3rd October 2008
Lord Hadleigh's Rebellion by Paula Marshall
The Sweet Cheat by Meg Alexander

Volume 27 – 7th November 2008
Lady Sarah's Son by Gayle Wilson
Wedding Night Revenge by Mary Brendan

Volume 28 – 5th December 2008
Rake's Reward by Joanna Maitland
The Unknown Wife by Mary Brendan

Volume 29 – 2nd January 2009
Miss Verey's Proposal by Nicola Cornick
The Rebellious Débutante by Meg Alexander

Volume 30 – 6th February 2009
Dear Deceiver by Mary Nichols
The Matchmaker's Marriage by Meg Alexander

www.millsandboon.co.uk

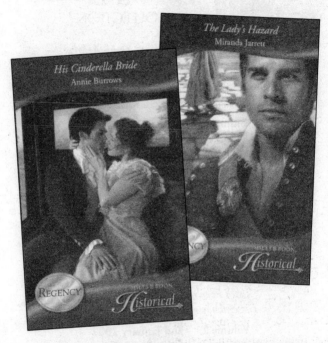